And then he was kissing her.

Dizziness assaulted her and she knew he must have noticed. He lowered his hands to her arms and held her closer. The sweet contact with his lips never wavered.

Angel didn't know why he was suddenly doing this—didn't care. All that mattered now was that he did not stop.

She noticed movement from the corner of her eye. It hit her then. Tavov had stepped onto the balcony; he was watching them. RJ was putting on a show. He was only kissing her for Tavov's benefit.

Hurt opened fire on her heart. All of a sudden it was too much: their arguments, his demands, the tension. And the taste of him... his heat up against her.

Something snapped. She pulled her arms out of his grasp and lifted them around his neck. His sharp intake of breath didn't even make her hesitate. She stepped closer to him, feeling the rock of muscle that lined his frame.

She spoke low into his ear. "Oh, we need to be *so* much more convincing than that..."

THE MARRIAGE OF INCONVENIENCE

BY

NINA SINGH

First Published in Great Britain 2017
By Mills & Boon, an imprint of HarperCollins*Publishers*
1 London Bridge Street, London, SE1 9GF

ISBN: 978-0-263-92314-8

23-0717

Our policy is to use papers that are natural, renewable and recyclable products and made from wood grown in sustainable forests. The logging and manufacturing processes conform to the legal environmental regulations of the country of origin.

Printed and bound in Spain
by CPI, Barcelona

Nina Singh lives just outside of Boston, USA, with her husband, children, and a very rambunctious Yorkie. After several years in the corporate world she finally followed the advice of family and friends to 'give the writing a go, already'. She's oh-so-happy she did. When not at her keyboard she likes to spend time on the tennis court or golf course. Or immersed in a good read.

For my generous, kind-hearted,
and encouraging husband. And for my amazing,
wonderful children, who make me proud every day.

Also Barb, Dee and Deb. You've been there
every step of the way and I am thankful beyond words.

CHAPTER ONE

So now she needed his help.

R. J. Davet shifted in his chair and looked down for the third time at the email message waiting for him on his laptop. Even if she hadn't signed the message, he would have known whom it was from. Brief and to the point, apologetic yet demanding at the same time. All the characteristics of the woman he had known better than anyone else on earth. He almost laughed at the thought. He had known her intimately once. And it had cost him.

Outside his hotel window, the crowded street in London's East End bustled with activity. Delivery trucks skirted around the road. Morning commuters rushed to work, and cafés were filling with caffeine-hungry customers.

A silver tea tray with steaming scones sat untouched on the antique table next to him. He was oblivious to all of it. His appointment with the investors in a few minutes, the importance of this trip, the weeks of preparation. He couldn't bring himself to think of any of that now. After all this time, and all the pretenses, she was asking for his help.

A fleeting impulse to ignore the request entered his mind. After all, she hadn't indicated it was urgent. Every self-preserving instinct told him to pretend he'd never received it.

But that thought was gone in a second. He would go to her. Of course he would. Even with the little information the message provided, he couldn't ignore a plea from her. Besides, the past was behind them now. There was no reason he couldn't assist her professionally. He was the best. Arrogance or immodesty had nothing to do with it. He knew his strengths and he knew his shortcomings. He knew his reputation within the field had compelled celebrity and politician alike to seek out his expertise, even this early in his business. He'd worked his butt off since leaving college.

Now his skills were being sought by the one woman who could have had that and a lot more at her disposal. The bitter tang of memory formed an unpleasant taste in his mouth before he swallowed it.

Rubbing his eyes, he stood and read the email once more.

R.J.
It's been a while. I find myself in the unexpected position of requiring your assistance. Only you have the background. Let's discuss at your earliest convenience.

She'd included a small icon of a dancing couple at the end: *What do you say, Princess? Shall we dance?*

He leaned forward to reply to her and stopped himself. There was no reason they couldn't interact like the true professionals they were, but there was also no reason to be hasty either. He wasn't going to jump the instant she snapped her fingers. No doubt that's what she expected. Surprise for her, he'd changed.

He powered off the laptop and packed it into his briefcase, making sure hard copies of the financial spreadsheets were there. He had a lot to do in the few short hours before his flight back to the States. He didn't need a distraction like her just now.

His estranged wife would get his answer soon enough.

"He's here, you know."

Angeline Scott jumped at the announcement, then tried to calm herself before turning away from the window. She leveled a gaze at her assistant, who was also her dearest friend.

"He's here," Shanna repeated. "R.J. just signed in downstairs. He's on his way up."

Angeline managed a nod in acknowledgement. She couldn't go through with this.

"Shan, I think we should just forget this whole thing. I'm not even going to tell him why I asked him here. I've changed my mind."

"Are you going to ask your father, then? For the money?"

Angeline gave her friend the side eye for that question. "You know that's out of the question. I refuse."

Shanna rewarded her with a look of pride. "That would only be a temporary fix anyway."

"But to ask R.J. to do this…" Angeline let herself trail off.

"We really have no choice, do we?"

"I guess not. But I know him. He's going to look at me like I have two heads, pop a hand on his hip—" she fisted her hand and set it on her hip in demonstration. "And then he's going to laugh. Then he'll become angry because he'll think it's a joke. At his expense. That's exactly what will happen." She blew a stray strand of hair off her forehead, then added, "Not necessarily in that order."

"Then why did you ask him in the first place?"

"Because he's the only one who really qualifies, isn't he?"

"True. Technically he's still your husband."

Angel sighed. Yes, R.J. was still her husband. In name only. The only reason being that they had never gotten around to finalizing their divorce. And now, after close to three years apart, she had to demean herself by asking him to pretend they'd never split up at all.

Shanna smiled at her. "Go straighten yourself out, Angel. Your cheeks are flushed. It's just not becoming on someone with your olive skin tone. And those curls." She held a hand up in frustration to the mass of unruly hair Angeline knew was spilling out of her loose bun. "We can do this. Just pull yourself together. It's the only way."

Angeline plunked herself into the wide leather chair behind her. Shanna was right, of course. They had gone through every other feasible option.

"Fine," she said, then looked up in defiance. "But I refuse to straighten myself out."

Shanna stole a quick glance into the outer room. "Looks like you don't have time for it anyway. Our fella just walked in."

Angeline gripped the armrests on the chair and tried to assume a perfect poker face. Her heart was in her throat, and adrenaline coursed through her veins like a river during a storm. But she was certain none of it showed. R. J. Davet might turn her insides to lava, but she knew how to mask emotion well.

Shanna gave her a reassuring wink and went to show him in.

Angeline took advantage of the time to try to calm her nerves. She was a mature businesswoman now. Not a foolish young college student. She'd graduated top of her class, even with the distraction that was R. J. Davet.

He wouldn't affect her the way he used to. She was much wiser with a good head on her shoulders. She was over her once all-consuming attraction to him. She was over *him*.

Angeline stood up to greet him, feeling much more certain of herself. It was ridiculous to think he could still hurt her.

But then he walked in. And it hurt just to look at him.

She managed to curve her lips into a smile. "Hello, R.J. Long time, no see." She cringed as soon as she said it. Nothing like dazzling him with witty conversation.

He didn't say anything for a long moment, merely looked at her. Just for an instant, the hurt fell away and she was staring into hypnotic, deep chocolate eyes that were so familiar. There was nothing between them, there was nothing around them. As if sensing her thoughts, his expression suddenly became aloof and guarded.

"Hello, Angel." He smiled when he said it, but his eyes remained distant.

He made his way toward her with the same confident gait she remembered. Except now there was so much more polish. In a dark Italian-cut suit, he had the elusive manner that only self-made successful people have. He looked like the powerhouse he'd always wanted to be, had always talked about becoming. He looked like the man he had left her to become.

She checked the impulse to step back as he approached, afraid of her reaction. His wavy black hair reflected almost navy where the light hit it. The strong set of his jaw lent a hardened austerity to his face.

Her dreams had not done him justice.

She cleared her throat. "So, I hear your business is doing well. You're trying to expand Davet Corporate Security into Europe, aren't you?"

"That's the intent, yes." His voice rang clear with impatience.

"I can't believe all you've accomplished in the short time since college."

He gave a slight nod in her direction. "Likewise."

Angeline felt herself shiver. R.J. wasn't interested in small talk. "It must have been a surprise to hear from me after all this time," she said in a lower voice.

"Getting your message was a few notches higher than surprise. Closer to shock, actually."

She tried not to bristle at the hostility in his voice.

R.J. shoved his hands into his pants pockets. "Let's cut to the chase here, shall we? We're both busy people. You didn't call me to play catch-up. What can I do for the reigning tea queen of the Western Hemisphere? I imagine you have some type of corporate security concern. Were your systems hacked or something? Is that it?"

Regret washed through her. He was obviously not thrilled about being here. While he couldn't wait to leave, she was aching inside at seeing him again. Yep, she was a fool one hundred times over. "Not exactly. Please, have a seat." She motioned him to the red brocade chair across from her desk and waited for him to sit down.

Swallowing past the lump of apprehension in her throat, she began, "I'd like to discuss a business proposition with you. An alliance, so to speak."

She saw the curiosity flash in his eyes before he managed to suppress it. "What type of an alliance would the head of a thriving tea retail and distribution business form with the CEO of a corporate security firm?"

"I need your help. But not in the way you think."

He lifted a brow in question. "I'm listening."

Angeline walked over to the large window overlooking metro Boston. Past the traffic, the Charles River gleamed like liquid gemstone as the sun reflected off the water. Her back to him, she could feel the intensity of his gaze and imagined his eyes roaming over her. The way his hands had not so long ago. She squeezed her eyes shut.

Somehow she managed to find her voice again. "I'm in some trouble and it could affect other people. A lot of other people."

He was up and behind her in an instant. She recognized the poignantly familiar scent. That same distinctive cologne coupled with the aroma that was purely male and purely his. She tried to still the shaking in her hands and clasped them together in front of her. Heavens, this meeting was playing havoc on her senses. Pure attraction. Attraction that in the end hadn't been enough to keep them together. But the flames of desire apparently still burned strong.

For her anyway.

"Angeline," she heard him say. "Are you in some kind of danger?"

She took a moment to answer. Technically she wasn't. But in every other sense she was. Without warning, a firm set of hands gripped her by the shoulders and turned her around.

"Answer me."

"N-no, I'm not in any danger," she managed to stutter while fighting the urge to lean into the strong, masculine chest that was so close.

He dropped his hands. Disappointment pummeled her. He clearly wasn't as interested in touching her as he had been once.

Better to get this over with. "It's the business, R.J. The TeaLC chain. I'm worried that if I don't expand soon, we may not survive."

He quirked an eyebrow. "But I thought your business was flaring."

"It's also very costly. The distribution end brings in a good amount, but the retail chains aren't terribly profitable. Plus, I have some very expensive overhead. I need a sales spurt, soon." She took a deep breath. "And I think I just may have come up with a way to achieve some growth."

"But?"

"But it won't be easy."

He narrowed his eyes. "Go on."

Here it was, the tough part. She braced herself for the certain embarrassment and decided to just blurt it out. "We never signed the papers to finalize our divorce."

A dark shadow flashed in his eyes. "Is that what all this is about? You want to take care of the divorce finally?"

"No! No, that's not it at all." This was even harder than she would have imagined. "Actually, it's kind of the exact opposite."

Silence. He searched her face for clarification.

"I need to act like I'm happily married. Just for one night. I need you to pretend we're still a fully married couple who never separated." Oh, man, she was making a complete and utter mess of this whole proposal. But there was no way to back out now.

She lifted her palms in appeal. "It wouldn't be for long. I realize what I'm asking and—"

He cut her off with a quick raise of his hand. "Let me get this straight. You have to act like you're still happily married to grow your business."

Before she could answer, he turned around and walked toward the center of the large room.

She stepped toward him, afraid he was going to leave without hearing her out. She'd gone too far to back out now. As difficult as this was, she had to see it through.

"R.J., wait. Can I just explain?"

He didn't answer. Angeline rubbed her arms to calm herself. He was so angry he couldn't even speak!

And then he turned around, looked into her eyes and broke into laughter.

She really was too much.

R.J. didn't know if he was laughing more from amusement or the unsettling experience of seeing her again. This had to be some kind of joke.

He didn't feel much like laughing, though, when she lifted those deep brown eyes up to his. She looked like a wounded doe.

His breath caught in his throat. "Wait a minute. You're serious."

"I wouldn't have asked you to come all the way out here if I wasn't serious."

"I think I'm missing something here."

"This isn't some attempt at a reconciliation. I know things are over between us."

"You're right about that."

She flinched. "I just need you to do some convincing acting for a day or so."

"You want me to pretend we're still completely together? That I'm still your husband in every way." He'd done everything he could for the past three years to try to forget what that was like. "What kind of game are you playing?"

"It's not a game, it's a business proposition," she said in a firm, official voice.

A what? He had to try to calm down. No one else could ever get him so riled up. Taking a deep breath, he concentrated his gaze on her face.

He wouldn't have believed she could have become more attractive. The girlish, soft qualities had been replaced with the maturity of a beautiful woman. Breeding and class were etched in every inch of her. It had thrown him off so many years ago, the passion that lay beneath her proper demeanor. Just thinking about it now was throwing him off again. Three years hadn't made enough of a difference, apparently.

"Maybe we better start from the beginning."

"It shouldn't take more than a day or so of your time," she began, becoming animated.

He lifted his hand to stop her. "Before we get too far with this scheme, suppose you fill me in on the details. What happened? Last I heard, you'd grown the business tremendously since you started it." She'd done an impressive job, too. Angeline had moved quickly on the sudden popularity of tea and had become a leading distributor in no time. She was one of the youngest successful CEOs in the United States. Like him.

"It all stemmed from such a terrific idea."

Her tongue darted to lick her lips, and he lost his concentration for a moment. Her dark features were drawn tight. Slight dark circles shadowed her eyes. Even so, her regal grace never left her. It was that quality that had knocked him senseless when they'd met freshman year at university. He'd fallen hard for the contradictory mix of private school breeding and wanton boldness. Not to mention the drop-dead body that had turned his gut to fire every time he'd laid eyes on her.

"What idea?" he asked, turning back to the conversation.

"I thought there would be some opportunity for growth given the big wave in the herbal tea market. Lots of people swear by the healing benefits of some of the herbs and plants found in tisanes. I thought we'd stress that to set us apart from the competition."

"What has that got to do with being married?"

"Well, I started doing some research. It led me to a variety of plants. It's mainly grown along the Black Sea, on a small island nation called Mondolavia."

"I've heard of it."

"I traveled there with Shanna to check it out, and true enough, the stuff is invigorating. They've been drinking it in that part of the world for years. Anyone who's tried it insists it's like a magical potion. And it tastes great. Like nothing we can compare to in this hemisphere. If TeaLC was the first chain to bring it here, it would put us in a whole other category. This could be the start of a whole new product assimilation. And we'd be the one to start it all."

"So far, so good."

She nodded with excitement, clearly taken with the idea. "We were all ready to arrange for the supplier to start shipping. Even drew up a contract for exclusive distribution rights for the next several years."

"That's fantastic. I still don't see why you'd have to be married."

She shut her eyes tightly and let out a deep breath. "That area is a completely different part of the world. The plants are all grown and processed by a very traditional Mondol family. Mila and Tavov Bay have been married for decades.

They're very particular about how their product is being sold and positioned. And they don't believe it's good to do business with a single woman. They'd much rather deal with a so-called stable, family operation."

Now he understood. "And you figured you had a way to accommodate them." He didn't care that his voice was thick with sarcasm. All this time had gone by without a word from her. But suddenly she was reaching out. And for what? A business deal.

She cleared her throat. "We didn't start that way. Shanna and I initially tried to protest. But it didn't look like they were willing to hear any arguments. Then things just seemed to spiral." She leaned back on the edge of the desk. "Next thing we knew, I was talking about my 'silent partner' husband."

"I see."

"Except for the silent partner part, it's not technically a lie."

"Is that how you see it?"

"We didn't mean to be deceptive or anything. You have to believe that. I just mentioned that I had gotten married young and was about to explain that it hadn't made me a better businesswoman. But they just latched on to the married part and asked why I hadn't said so before. I just found myself not denying it."

He was having trouble coming up with an adequate response. This was the last thing he'd been expecting when he finally heard from her again.

"It started as a language issue," she continued, near to pleading. "Though they're fluent, their English is a bit broken. Then we just had to go with it." She stepped toward him and touched his arm, her eyes imploring him to understand. "It's just that we'd gotten so far. And then it just seemed to steamroll. I found myself telling them all about your accomplishments, that you've built your own computer security services company."

Her gaze dropped to where she'd touched him, and R.J. expected to see sparks from the contact. She removed her hand and stepped back.

"And it almost worked," she added. "They said they would be glad to do business with us. But not before they came to the States to check out the operation. And to meet the husband they'd heard so much about."

He'd heard enough. For such a smart, savvy businesswoman, Angeline had somehow put herself in an utterly ridiculous position. And had managed to take him along with her. "What in heaven's name were you thinking?" Perhaps he was being a bit too forceful, but what she'd just told him was so profoundly absurd. "I've heard of adapting to the global marketplace, but what you did is borderline slapstick."

"Listen, I'm not proud of it, but I did what I thought I had to do." A hard glint appeared in her eyes.

"Why doesn't that surprise me?"

She crossed her arms in front of her chest. "That sounds like condemnation."

"More like characterization."

Her eyes narrowed on him. "I don't know what that's supposed to mean. I do know that I've done a darn good job with this company. Don't you think I should fight for it if that's what I have to do?"

He rubbed a palm over his face. She *was* a fighter. They both were. That part he understood. He'd fought hard for everything he'd wanted. Except once. But then he'd had no choice.

He took a deep breath and tried to calm down. This was getting them nowhere. "Angel, you don't need to convince me on that score. Ever since I started hearing about your success I've known this was the perfect outlet for your abilities. I just don't understand how you plan to pull this off."

"Well, it's quite simple. You just have to pose as my husband for the day or so that they're up here." She flashed him a smile that nearly crumpled his knees.

"You're the only one who's ever had any kind of practice in the role."

And practice they had. Long, steamy nights had often turned into languid, satisfying mornings. He cursed himself as his body started to respond to the memories.

She went on. "A few weeks after they leave, I'm scheduled to go back to their orchards to sign the deal. Right before the harvest. By then they'll have realized how mutually beneficial the partnership is. And in return for your assistance, I help you expand Davet Computer Security Services to Europe. I read somewhere you were trying to find overseas clients. I present you as our security firm and help convince all our European partners to consider hiring you. And you have your expansion."

He was about to tell her his latest trip had done just that. That he'd left London just last week with a deal to become the leading provider for a major British jewelry chain. Something stopped the words from forming on his tongue. It would be the simplest way to end this nonsense idea of hers. So why didn't he just tell her she couldn't help him?

Because he couldn't deny the fact that a lot of this was indirectly his fault. Angeline's current state of financial shortage and her lack of resources were in large part due to him and their marriage.

But he just couldn't do what she was proposing. His soul would not be able to take such a pretense. He would help her, but he'd find another way.

Angel continued to smile. Man, it was hard to deny her anything when she looked at him like that. But this was too much, he just couldn't go through with something like this.

"Angel. I'm sorry. I just can't. What you're suggesting, it's just too far-fetched. Too much of a charade. Too much could go wrong."

She lifted her palms in appeal. "But—"

"Angel, no. I'm sorry."

She looked down at the floor. All the light seemed to have gone out of her. "Then I'm sorry to have wasted your time. I see now what a mistake it was to try to involve you."

R.J. cursed silently. Nothing like a good dose of guilt to start out the day. He found himself selfishly replacing it with anger. "How could you even consider it, Angel? The two of us acting like a real couple?"

She looked up, a wealth of emotion in her eyes. Anger? "R.J. This isn't about you and me."

"It isn't?"

"It's a business deal. Nothing more."

He tried not to flinch at that. "A deal where we have to pretend we're still devoted to each other and together in every sense."

"Just for one lousy night. I'm not asking for eternity."

He rubbed a hand down his face in an effort to calm down.

"Listen, I'm sorry. But it's just too ridiculous. The idea of us acting married again."

Her gaze dropped to the floor once again. "Yes, I suppose it is."

"How about we set aside some time? You, me and Shanna. We'll put our heads together and come up with a plan." Without thinking, he reached out and took her hand in his. Her skin was soft, silky. Experience reminded him she felt that way all over. He quickly let go.

Angeline sighed. "I'm afraid there's no more time for that. It took you a bit longer to get back to me than I thought."

She wasn't looking at him. He had to strain to hear her.

"The supplier will be here in less than a day. If you won't do it, I'll have to come up with something else. And fast."

Like another man to play the part maybe? That thought had his gut tightening. Of course there had to be other men in her life. She was probably just too embarrassed to approach someone she cared about with something like this. Maybe she would even rush the divorce now so that she could go to someone else with her plea.

He knew what her response to his next question was going to be before he even asked it. "Let me put some money in the company, then. Consider it an investment. Or even a loan if you'd prefer."

As he'd guessed, she started to shake her head before all the words even left his mouth. "I can't let you do that. I know you're trying to grow as well and need those funds for your own firm."

He was about to protest when she stopped him. "And anyway, that would only be a temporary fix. This deal would actually make TeaLC profitable for years to come. We'd become sole retailer in the United States for a revolutionary beverage."

She was right. No amount of money he could extend would make up for the loss of that kind of opportunity. "Angel, I'll come up with something."

Her eyes softened, but she didn't reply. Instead, she opened the door and leaned into the outside foyer. "Shanna, would you mind seeing R.J. out, please?"

Turning back to face him, she gave him a tight smile. "Thanks for coming, R.J. It was nice seeing you again. Sorry to have wasted your time." She stepped aside to let him out of her office. And out of her life once more.

CHAPTER TWO

SHANNA SEEMED TO be taking her time summoning the elevator. And R.J. wanted nothing more than to get out of the building fast. Away from the memories, away from his ex. Only she wasn't really his ex. Not yet.

"Did you grab a cup of tea on your way up?" Shanna asked while they waited.

"Uh, no." He tried to sound polite. "That looks like quite an operation you have on the first floor, though."

Shanna nodded. "It's one of our biggest cafés."

He didn't respond. His mind was still reeling. The shock of seeing Angel again after all this time—he had to get out of here and find a punching bag or a weight bench. Anything to help him vent the frustration of not being able to touch her. Or help her. He had to think, to try to come up with a different solution. One that didn't involve the disaster she was floating.

"You should stop in." Shanna interrupted his thoughts. "The pastries are to die for. And the tea of the day is an Indian Spicy Chai that will curl your toes." She lifted a pencil to her chin and looked him over. "Then again, you might want to order something decaffeinated."

He had to laugh at her reference to his agitation. "Angel's lucky to have an assistant with such a flair for advertising. I think I will stop down for a cup."

"Great. Make sure to tip the server well. She's in a bit of dire straits."

"Yeah?" R.J. asked with mild curiosity as the elevator doors opened. He stepped aside as Shanna stepped in and then followed.

"Yes, a single mother with a toddler to support. We're one of the highest payers. But toddlers can be expensive."

"I'll tip handsomely, then."

"Good."

Shanna continued. "Our store manager has a lot on her mind, too. A young child with severe asthma. The medical insurance she gets through her job at TeaLC is absolutely crucial. Then there's Suzan. She's a college student who has to save every penny."

R.J. stilled as understanding dawned. He refused to be manipulated. "Why are you telling me all this?" he demanded, knowing it was wrong to take his agitation out on her.

Shanna whirled on him. "Because those are the kind of people who are going to be affected if this business doesn't stay profitable."

R.J. blinked at her suddenness. This was getting ridiculous. "Shanna, you know me well enough to realize I'd do anything I can to prevent that, but… But this isn't a plan, it's a fiasco. I'll find a way to help. Just not this."

Shanna actually snorted. "Shame. This deal would have been the perfect way to grow our company and secure our employees' futures. She sank her whole trust fund into this place. There's not a penny of it left. And she won't even consider going to her father."

R.J. clamped down on the anger that surged through his chest at the mention of the man who'd sired Angeline. Water under the bridge now, but it still stung. As for Shanna, he wasn't sure what to say to her.

Shanna blew out a breath. "Unlike the rest of her wealthy family, Angeline cares about giving back to the community. It's one of the major reasons she's fighting so hard to keep this place going."

He had no reason to, but he felt a sense of pride nevertheless. "How?"

"We work with the local women's shelters, try to place those ladies when an opening comes up. Single mothers, ladies trying to figure out how to stand on their own two feet. Sometimes the money we can offer isn't great, but it's better than nothing. And it gives them a chance to be productive and useful. But it's an expensive business strategy. We spend the time and money to train regardless of past experience. And turnover's higher than standard for the industry. It's the primary reason we're not as profitable as we could be. But it's worth it. Just to be able to give those women a chance to move on."

A chance to move on. Would his own childhood have turned out differently if his own family had had such a chance? If his mother had found a way to get them away from his abusive, alcoholic mess of a father?

He shook off the memories, focusing on what Shanna had just said. He'd stopped reading about Angeline and TeaLC in the business journals because it had just become too painful. Seeing her beautiful smiling face in print. So confident, so content. Content to be without him.

"I didn't know. How many TeaLC employees fall into this category?"

"About twenty to thirty percent. A few in every store in the States."

"It does sound like a costly program." Another unsettling thought occurred to him. "Have there been threats? Ex-husbands or past boyfriends?" A lot of women in shelters had to be running from abusive partners. Something he had firsthand knowledge of.

Shanna smiled. She looked pretty proud, too. "Sure there have. Angeline won't let that stop her. There's a security presence in every store, and each one is alarmed to the hilt. The public knows we won't take any chances with our employees, so nobody's tried anything."

"She's not one to back down, is she?"

"No, she's not. And you have no idea how much it took for her to ask you this."

R.J. bit out another oath. He looked up at the ceiling and exhaled slowly, wearily. So much for not being manipulated. He fished his phone out of his pocket.

"What are you doing?" Shanna asked as the elevator jolted to a stop.

He started dialing. "I have to call my secretary and tell her my schedule has changed for the next couple of days. Where's the nearest jewelry store?"

Shanna's dark brows lifted over her piercing blue eyes. "Why?"

"Married people wear rings."

"That feels good doesn't it, sweetie? I know it feels good." Angeline stroked a loving hand over the warm, eager body nestling closer to her.

"You've missed me haven't you?" Moist, soft eyes looked back at her with enthusiasm. Here was total acceptance, unconditional love. Right now it was exactly what she needed.

"I saw him again today, you know," she continued.

A knowing grunt responded.

"He came back, Max. He came back and he's going to do it." She stopped and took a deep sigh. "I didn't want him to know about the women. He wasn't supposed to want to do it because of them. But he knows now, and he's going to help."

The brown eyes staring at her started to droop with sleepiness. "Anyway, he did that thing he always does, where he just sort of takes command and handles all the details with efficiency and haste. He studied all the sales projections and started doing some research on Mondolavia. The whole office was eating out of his hand." She frowned. "Especially my female crew. They couldn't do enough for him.

"Still, I didn't realize how much I'd missed that. To

be able to rely on someone else without worrying about appearing weak or out of control. I've always loved the take-charge quality about him. And, of course, he's still as handsome as I remember."

She stopped for a long sigh. "Oh, Max, I think I might be making a huge mistake here.

"Anyway." Angeline shifted. "He's on his way over."

Max lifted his head at the announcement.

"That's right." She looked around the plush, Eastern decor of her condo. Would he like it? She was surprised to realize that it mattered to her. A burgundy-and-black patterned Oriental rug adorned the hardwood floor. It matched the draperies that hung from the bay windows on each wall. The full-floor condominium had a large kitchen and two bedrooms positioned on opposite sides. A far cry from the one-bedroom apartment they'd shared off campus for their brief union as man and wife.

"He's bringing over some of his stuff," she continued to her captive audience of one. "We have to look like a genuine married couple."

The chime of the doorbell interrupted them. Max moved himself off the sofa and made a mad dash to the door.

"Traitor," Angeline mumbled.

On shaky legs, she went to let R.J. in. As soon as she opened the door, Max barreled into him.

R.J. laughed in surprise. Bracing himself, he looked across the threshold at her. "I can't believe he remembers me."

She smiled. Max had been the poor soul to hear all about her foolish pining since R.J. had left. She hadn't given him a chance to forget R.J.'s name.

"Is he still chewing the rugs?" R.J. asked as he picked up the dog.

Angeline nodded. "Yeah, the vet says it's just something some breeds do."

She stepped aside to let him in. He was dressed casual, black tailored pants with a V-neck beige sweater that showed just a triangle of dark chest hair. Even with the lanky dog still in his arms, he looked like the phenomenal success that he was.

"I didn't know he had a breed," R.J. said and carried the dog in. "I thought he was just a small furry black mutt."

"He is," she replied. "But somewhere in that confusion is a breed that feasts on fabric fibers."

Angeline watched as he playfully wrestled Max to the floor. His tan skin reminded her of the bronze statues she'd studied while in Europe. His large shoulders shook with laughter as Max nipped at his face. A hint of sorrow hit her as she realized he'd missed their hound but resented having to see her again.

He straightened after several moments of playful tussling. A slight sheen of perspiration dampened his brow.

The amusement faded from his face as he looked at her. It was replaced by something foreign, something she couldn't name. But it had her quaking.

She cleared her throat. "So, I see you found the place okay?"

He nodded.

"It's pretty humid out there, isn't it?" Lord, she hated small talk.

"Yeah, I guess there's a huge storm on its way east."

"I hope the Bays' flight doesn't get canceled." She forced a smile. "Logan still shuts down at the hint of a raindrop."

He nodded, his stare intense.

She closed the door and turned to face him.

"Here." He held out his hand to her. A large stone glittered in his palm. "Your ring."

She reached for it. "I—I didn't realize you were going to get a ring. It's lovely."

"I tried to find a large one," he said. "In case Tavov and

Mila are wondering why you don't always wear it, they'll just assume it's because of its large size."

"Well, it is a big stone." She picked it up, a part of her wishing he'd slip it on her finger himself.

"We have to look authentic. I rented it, along with a band for myself."

A lump formed in her throat. "I still have my original wedding ring," she admitted, unsure why.

"Oh." He cleared his throat. "Well, I needed to get one. Besides, a large diamond is far more suited to you. Always has been."

She wasn't sure how to respond to that. An uncomfortable silence settled between them. He hadn't even held on to that small symbol of their marriage. It shouldn't have disappointed her, but it did.

"Anyway," R.J. continued, "I brought over a few things so it looks like I live here when your guests arrive tomorrow." He lifted the leather carrying case in his hand. "The rest will be delivered in the morning. Just show me where I can put it and I'll have to be on my way." He was brusque, to the point. R.J. clearly didn't want to spend any more time alone with her than he had to.

"I emptied part of the closet. It's through those doors," she directed him.

She wanted him to stay. It had been so long since they had talked to each other.

"Can I get you something to drink? Some tea? Or wine? I happen to have some of the red I know you like." She happened to have it because she'd searched all of the North End's Italian district for it.

"Used to like," he corrected her. "I don't drink that anymore."

"Oh." A dull ache nestled in her chest. She didn't even know what he liked anymore.

So much for having him stay awhile.

An idea began to form. "Well. That might be a problem," she said with more enthusiasm than she should have.

"What? That I don't drink the same wine I used to?"

"No, that we're supposed to be happily married still and we don't know anything about each other now. I think we need to discuss this. Get our stories straight for the dinner conversation tomorrow night."

She started pacing along the long coffee table in the middle of the room. Max walked with her a few steps before settling himself near the fireplace.

"There are all sorts of things I need to know about you, all kinds of questions I should ask, and vice versa."

R.J. looked uncomfortable for a moment. Letting out a deep breath, he rubbed his palm over his face. "I suppose you're right." He sat down on the sofa. "Looks like I'll need some of that wine after all," he added with a dry tone.

An almost giddy relief washed over her. He would stay. "I'll be right back," she said and ran into the kitchen.

When she returned, Max was snoring and R.J. had settled himself comfortably on the sofa.

"All right, let's start easy. How hard was it to start your firm?" she asked as she poured the glasses.

He lifted his head to look at her. "That's easy?"

"No? Okay, we'll get back to that one. What's your favorite dish now?"

"Franks and beans."

She felt her stomach turn over. "I've always hated franks and beans."

"I know."

She waved her hand. "Okay, what do you like to drink? I know it's not this anymore." She indicated the glass she was handing him.

"Ouzo. I like ouzo."

"Ouzo? Isn't that a bit hard-core?" Although it made

sense, because so was he. He'd always been a firm man, but now he seemed harsher somehow, colder and more distant.

"I just got back from the Mediterranean and found I'd acquired an appreciation for it. It tastes like liquid licorice with a punch."

She tried not to turn up her nose. "I've always hated licorice."

He waited a beat. "I know."

"All right, let's move on. What music are you listening to these days?"

"A little bit of everything, really. Except Armstrong. I don't like Louis Armstrong at all. Much too lax and easy for me."

This wasn't going well. "I love Louis Armstrong."

"I know."

It dawned on her suddenly. "You're teasing me."

The corner of his mouth lifted.

She leaned a knee next to him on the couch and gave him a useless shove on the shoulder. "Robert James Davet, you've been teasing me all this time with contradictory pretend answers."

He reached up and tapped a playful finger on her nose. "I guess I must know more about you than you think."

Electricity crackled between them. She had the sudden urge to ask him the questions that were running through her mind. The same ones she'd been seeking the answers to every day for the past three years.

Is there someone special in your life now?

Has someone been lucky enough to snare your interest and attention the way I used to?

She cleared her throat. "What's the last book you've read?"

He told her, but it didn't register.

She nodded. "What do you do in your spare time?"

Do you still like to linger in bed Saturday mornings?

"Work," he answered.

That much she should have guessed. "What's been your proudest achievement?"

"The phenomenal growth of Davet Security Services."

Ditto.

"And your greatest failure?"

He hesitated, staring at her, almost looking right through her. His eyes were full of meaning. A gust of wind rattled the windows outside. Understanding dawned on her, and she felt a wrenching ache start around the area of her heart.

He was thinking about the two of them. She knew it. He was thinking their marriage was his biggest mistake.

She tried to pretend the world hadn't crashed in around her. Slowly seating herself on the ottoman in front of him, she tried to change the direction of the conversation. She would somehow get past the burning pain. "I bet you haven't changed the way you drink your coffee. Or the predawn workouts you never skipped."

He nodded.

She decided to go on. "And I'm guessing you can still ride a motorcycle like a daredevil. I bet your pool game is as smooth as it used to be. And something tells me your poker hand has lightened casino coffers all over the world these past couple of years." She looked up to see a muscle twitch in the hard set of his jaw.

He leaned toward her, a scant inches from her face. "That's right, Angel. I still have all the characteristics that made me an unfit son-in-law for the Scott dynasty."

She bit her lip. "That's not what I was getting at." Looking away, she added, "I'm so sorry for everything you were put through. My father can be a ruthless man."

R.J. sniffed an ironic laugh. "A ruthless man who had definite ideas about whom you should marry. And it wasn't anyone like me."

She should have been prepared for this, should have seen

it coming. Damn her father and his ideals for her future. He'd done everything he could to make sure R.J. knew he thought he wasn't good enough. "Maybe this isn't the time to get into all this."

"Why not? Don't talk about my background? Don't talk about who I am? Who I've always been."

"That's not what I mean." He was putting words in her mouth.

"What do you mean, then?" he asked. "You know me well enough, Angel. You know I'm South End litter, from the part of Boston people like you avoid."

"That's not true. I've always been impressed with what you've managed to accomplish despite everything. You know that."

He let out a sarcastic laugh. "Is that why you came on to me that night at the campus party? Was it some type of debutante bet? To see who could win a token from the wrong side of the city?"

She lifted her chin. "I came on to you because I wanted to. Because of the way you were looking at me."

"But we both should have known better. It was against all the rules, you were out of my league." He let out a weary sigh. "I should have stayed away from you. As your father made crystal clear."

Like it could have been so easy. "What about what we were starting to feel?"

His sharp features seemed to take on an even more angular set. She felt compelled to continue, perhaps foolishly. "I know it wasn't my imagination, R.J. I know I saw attraction in your face those first few times we ran into each other." Her voice came out in a whisper. An imaginary fist had wrapped itself around her throat, its fingers strong and relentless.

He leaned back into the cushions, putting some distance

between them. "I remember you've never had a problem being bold."

She cleared her throat. "Then we have changed after all. Because I certainly don't feel that way now."

"Perhaps I'd better go."

"Are you walking out on me? Just because the conversation has gotten a little serious? Again?"

His laugh was sharp. "Now, that's an interesting question. If I recall, I asked you to come with me. As long as we're remembering, we may as well be accurate."

She sighed, trying to find a way to explain how difficult such a move would have been for her back then. "There was no easy way for me to do that. You don't understand. And you didn't then either." She noticed his fingers tighten around the glass and worried it might snap in his hand.

"So it would appear."

"Besides," she continued, "things had gotten bad for us way before you took the physical steps out the door. We had my father set against our union from the very beginning. And we were both much too focused on our professional careers. I regret that." She decided to take a chance and move forward with her next question. "Why didn't we try harder, R.J.? Why did we let outside forces drive such a wedge between us?"

He stiffened ever so slightly and set the glass down hard on the coffee table. "What does it matter now? We have to take care of this one scenario, and then the past will be dead and buried." He paused, then added, "Once again."

Angeline felt the mask of neutrality she'd put up begin to crumble, and she tried to hold on to some semblance of control. Why did his nonchalance hurt so much? It didn't take a genius to realize he wanted out as things had gotten difficult. Granted, her father's behavior toward him had been reprehensible, down to promising to cut her off entirely if they did get married. A threat her father had followed through on. Well, she'd prove to Richard Scott that she didn't need his money to be successful. He didn't have a right to meddle in her life the way he had with R.J. She couldn't let him get away with what he'd done to alienate her husband from the very beginning.

In the end, her father had won. Her marriage had crumbled. R.J. had walked away.

Angel hadn't seen or spoken to her only parent since. Unable to forgive and forget, she refused to contact her father. Not that he'd bothered to make any contact either. Apparently they were stuck in a stubborn standoff to see who would blink first. She vowed that it wouldn't be her.

In a daze, she nodded. "You're right, R.J. I agree," she lied. Her voice sounded strained even to her own ears, and she glanced at him to see if he'd noticed.

A wave of sorrow struck her for what she'd lost. Her eyes moved over his face of their own volition. Nostalgia for days gone by engulfed her, and she found herself moving closer toward him into the sofa.

His low voice reached her through a dense fog. "It was nice while it lasted. But it's ancient history now. It doesn't make sense to dwell on the past. We got married way too young. Neither one of us was ready for such a commitment."

The words barely registered. "Mmm, it was nice, though, wasn't it?" Just for a moment she allowed herself to remember the sweet, not the bitter.

Nice was a drastic understatement for the way things had been between them. They'd had everything a young couple could want. Almost.

"We were good together, weren't we?" She wanted him to say it, needed to hear him agree.

She saw something flare in his eyes and instantly recognized the familiarity of old longings.

So much time had passed, and she'd missed him. Her

mind may have ignored it, but her heart had ached all the while he'd been gone. But he was here now, and he was so close. She could smell the sweet woodsy scent of the imported wine on his breath. His familiar cologne triggered long-forgotten memories in the back recesses of her brain.

Her gaze settled on his lips. Firm and full, the way she'd remembered. Would they taste the same? Would his skin hold the same texture and warmth it had years ago?

The pounding of her heart grew painful. She watched as he lifted his hands up to reach for her. What would it be like to feel his touch again? She knew the reality would blow away even the dreams she'd had every night since she'd last seen him.

The heat of his hands burned through her silk blouse as they settled around her shoulders, his touch gentle, yet strong. She moistened her lips and moved into him. All she'd have to do was reach for his mouth with hers. She inclined her head, mindless now, and ready to take what she so desperately wanted.

He started to speak, and anticipation assaulted her. He had to acknowledge the magic their marriage had once held. Despite the bitter and swift ending, despite the searing pain of loss, he had to agree that they had been happy together as man and wife once.

She wanted to taste him again, wanted his mouth on hers like they'd never been apart. She reached for him.

His lips moved. "Don't."

He said it in a strained, barely audible whisper, but the single word struck her with the force of a physical blow.

His command echoed through her desire-fogged mind, and she froze. Yanking herself out of his grasp, she turned away from the tightness in his face.

Shaking with embarrassment, she kept her back to him. Dear heavens, she'd just tried to kiss her estranged husband.

And he'd literally pushed her away. "Perhaps you had better leave after all."

There was rustling behind her as he stood.

"Angel, you don't—"

She didn't let him continue. "I'll see you tomorrow, R.J. Thanks for taking time to come out tonight. By this time tomorrow, it will all be over and we can both pretend this never happened. None of it." Was she trying to reassure R.J. or herself?

She heard him let out a deep breath and moved her head sideways but couldn't bring herself to face him. He patted the sleeping dog, then made his way to the door.

"I'll see you tomorrow, then," he said.

For one final time, she thought, and a sharp hurt sliced her heart.

CHAPTER THREE

TIME ZERO. AND it was going to be a very trying night. R.J. braced himself in the hallway and tried to prepare for the upcoming evening. Stalling, he was definitely stalling.

He squeezed his eyes shut. It was one night. How hard could it be? After all, it hadn't been that long ago since he'd lived the part he was being required to play. Surely, he could act out a role he'd already experienced. So why was his head pounding?

Because he had no business even being in the same room with Angeline Scott. This was insanity, an affront to any sense of equilibrium. Hell, she'd tried to kiss him last night. How could she taunt him like that? Did she think he could be immune to her twice in one lifetime? For her own good, he swore he'd try to stay unmoved throughout this whole charade. He couldn't toy with rekindling their affections. He'd tried too hard to stay away. Angel deserved better. Because of him, her father had severed all contact with her and cut her off financially.

And any hope that the man may have changed had been shattered last year when they'd run into each other at an international business symposium. Richard Scott had made it very clear that, CEO or not, R.J. would never be in the same league as his daughter.

R.J. knew Angel had no hope of reconciling with her father unless R.J. remained out of the picture. Then maybe she'd have a chance to regain all Richard was keeping from her.

She was the sole Scott heir. How could R.J. allow himself to be the reason she lost that? In fact, if it wasn't for him, Angel would have access to all the financial resources she needed right now to ensure her company survived. But she'd lost it all. For him.

He had to make that right.

He also had to purge all of that from his thoughts at the moment. It only served to agitate him further, and he couldn't afford that right now. Tonight, it was all for show.

He used the key she'd given him to enter the apartment. The aroma of home cooking and a bristling fire hit him as he stepped in. Sudden, almost painful nostalgia overwhelmed his senses. He had entered their studio apartment countless times like this. Back then the various scents from the kitchen had been more mundane. Usually plain pasta or some meat roasting in the oven. Angel's culinary skills weren't quite enviable at that point, but she'd tried and he'd loved the attempts. He'd loved her for trying.

Without warning, she breezed into the living room through the swing door of the kitchen. As she spotted him, the silver tray in her hand slightly tilted off balance.

"You're here," she stated.

"Just walked in."

She set her load down on the cocktail table. "The Bays are set to arrive in a few minutes."

He took in the snug fit of her feminine tuxedo-cut black suit. The form-fitting jacket accented her waist. The lace camisole she had underneath peaked at the V below her neck and practically screamed *temptation*. His hand tightened around the wine bottle he was holding.

"You can set that in the kitchen," she ordered, and then moved with catlike grace to the mantel and lifted the silver candle set.

Without responding, R.J. made his way into the kitchen. This night was not going to be over soon enough. She'd always been stunning, but he realized that now she was in her element. He set the wine bottle down and braced his palms on the counter in front of him. Dark, thick clouds moved through the window above the sink.

The storm was moving closer. He would have to make sure to still the one brewing inside him.

This was why he couldn't be around her. This burning need to touch her, to claim her as his. It was the same insanity that had nearly destroyed both of them in the past, when they'd let physical desire rule their better judgment. By the time he found out how mismatched they were, the damage had been done. The memory of that pain should have been enough to guarantee he'd keep his distance tonight.

He walked back out into the living room just as the doorbell rang. Angel froze in the act of lighting a candle. The fiery glow of the forgotten match threw shadows over her face. Her eyes sparkled before the flame.

He took her palm and blew the match out. "We better let them in, don't you think?"

"I—I guess so."

"You guess so? It's kind of late to back out now, Angel." He was still trying to ascertain just how far they had come and how he would manage to recover.

"Why would I want to back out? I just need to tell them this little white lie until I can prove to them what good hands their tea plants are in. By then they won't care anymore."

"And if they do care?"

She gave a quick shake of her head. "I can't worry about that now. I'll need to think about it later." She threw a slight Southern accent in imitation of the famous *Gone with the Wind* line.

He smiled. "In that case, Scarlett, I'll go let the Yankees in."

She nodded and swallowed. It was surprising to see her so nervous. She'd been the most self-assured woman he'd ever known. Granted, the circumstances were a little unusual, but something was throwing Angel off like he'd never witnessed before.

He had to wonder- could it have anything to do with him?

Of course not. She was worried about her business. She was worried about failing to continue the jobs program for all the women who worked for her.

He took a deep breath as he went to answer the door then yanked it open. A smiling, middle-aged couple stared up at him. Both of them had dark hair, hers a shade less brown. They both smiled wide, warmth exuding their features.

"Good evening," R.J. said as he stepped aside to let them in. "I'm Angeline's husband." He nearly choked on the last word.

Angel strode toward them, beaming a warm, welcoming smile. She seemed to have recovered from her earlier nervousness. "Tavov. Mila. So nice to see you again. Please come in."

R.J. felt her hand on his arm and flinched. He tried not to look affected. There was nothing unusual about a wife taking her husband by the arm as they greeted guests.

Man, it was going to be the longest night of his life.

"Nice to see you, too, dear. And very nice to finally meet you." The older man flashed a wide, friendly grin as he turned to R.J. He stretched out his free hand, giving R.J. a welcome excuse to free his own arm. "We weren't sure we'd ever catch up to you," he continued.

"Tavov, Mila. Very nice to meet you both," R.J. spoke over Angel's head as Mrs. Bay had her in an affectionate hug. "I'm R.J."

"Did you have any trouble getting here?" Angel inquired, still locked in the embrace.

"None at all. The driver was waiting for us right at the gate where we landed," Tavov replied.

Before R.J. knew what was happening, Mila moved toward him and he found himself in the same bear hug he'd just witnessed. A stab of guilt hit him at the way he was deceiving such warm, genuine people.

One look at Angel's pale face told him she was thinking the same thing. For one insane moment he wished with all his heart that it could have been different. That the charade had not been necessary.

Where had that thought come from? He didn't have time to speculate. An awkward silence had settled around the foursome. Angel appeared to be frozen in her spot. So far, they weren't doing a very good job of personifying the perfect American couple.

"Why don't we move inside?" He guided the older couple in front of him. Waiting a beat for Angel to catch up, he cupped her elbow and pulled her to his side.

She was shaking. A sheen of perspiration had formed above her lip. He remembered that to be a bad sign. At this rate she wasn't going to be able to go through with it. He gave her hand what he hoped was a reassuring squeeze. She leaned into him, and without thinking, he moved his arm around her waist.

He just held her, close to him, as if his closeness could absorb her anxiety somehow. In a moment, her breathing seemed to even, and he started to lead her toward the living room, where the other couple had seated themselves.

"It's all right," he whispered in her ear. "It will all be over soon."

"I know, it's just—I'd almost forgotten what nice people they were." She wrung her hands. "I wish it hadn't come to this."

He dropped his arm. A sudden sense of loss hit him as soon as he did so. She felt so right near him, up against him. She always had.

"You'll tell them the truth soon enough. For now, let's

go take care of business, all right?" He gave her a small nudge forward and followed her in.

Angel composed herself enough to start serving the hors d'oeuvres.

"Tavov, Mila," she began. "It's so lovely to have you here finally. How was your trip?" she asked over her shoulder as she held the tray out to R.J. He shook his head to decline. Somehow he couldn't quite summon up an appetite.

"Oh, it was pretty uneventful," Mila answered. "But it's always so exciting when we come to the States. So much changes, yet it's always the same. The energy level you Americans have, it's just harrowing."

"We should all slow down a little bit. It can get a little tiring to be on the go all the time."

"Yes, my goodness, dear. I can imagine it can be exhausting," Mila agreed.

"What we could use is that soothing herbal tea in this part of the world," Angel said as she set the tray down and sat. He had to hand it to her. She knew how to segue.

"I can't argue with you there, young lady," Tavov stated. "That's why we're here."

"Well, I'm anxious to start talking about it myself. How is the latest crop of Mila's Bloom faring?"

"She hasn't stopped talking about it since she got back," R.J. added. He was pretty certain it was true enough.

She looked up and sent him a smile. A jolt of pleasure shot through clear to his toes. How adolescent of him, he thought.

"Well, it is turning into a pretty impressive crop." Tavov nodded.

Angel jumped up in her seat. "Excellent. So we'll be ready to start shipping when I come down for the harvest?"

Mila squinted her eyes and smiled. "That's what I love about you, Angeline. Always assuming the sale."

Angel had the decency to look sheepish. Then she lifted

her head and gave R.J. a pointed look full of meaning. "I've managed to acquire some invaluable things that way."

For an instant, silence took over the small room as the two of them just stared at each other. R.J. couldn't seem to pull his eyes away. When he finally did, he watched as Mila's smile turned into a wide grin.

"How romantic." Mila laughed. "And to think, you gave us the impression originally that you were a staunch businesswoman with no mind for family or roots. And it's so confusing that your last names aren't the same."

"That's not uncommon in the States, Mila," R.J. responded. "A lot of women prefer to keep their birth names for professional reasons."

Tavov swallowed the last bit of his shrimp cocktail. "Well, we make it a point to deal only with family-run operations. We've found things are much more stable that way. Remember the last fiasco with that European businessman?" he asked his wife as he patted her knee.

Mila nodded. "Oh, it was awful. That man was much more concerned with turning a fast profit than nurturing a business. All the more resources to buy his bachelor toys. We swore we wouldn't make that mistake again."

"That's why we're so glad to see how happy the two of you are together," Tavov said. R.J. noticed Angel's slight cringe.

"You know, dear, they remind me of another young couple," Mila spoke to her husband.

"They do." Tavov beamed as he turned back to her and R.J. "We happen to have a major event to look forward to. Our groundskeeper's son is marrying our cropper's daughter. Two of the sweetest kids. So in love. We're holding the ceremony right on our estate."

"That's quite generous of you," Angel said.

"Nonsense," Tavov retorted. "We're almost more excited than they are about it. The ceremony will fall right on the week that you're visiting us, Angel. I'm sure they'd love it if you could join us. Practically the whole town will be there."

Angel's expression became wistful, but it disappeared an instant later. "I would be honored. And I wish them every happiness together," she said.

Mila nodded. "They seem very happy to have found each other. Those two are very committed, as if they just know they were meant for each other."

Then they'd be rare exceptions, R.J. thought. A sudden flash of lightning tore through the sky in the window behind the Bays. The storm was going to be a furious one.

Mila leaned closer to him. "So tell me, R.J., what's your secret?"

"Uh, secret?"

She smiled. "Yes, how did you know that Angeline was the one for you?"

Angel prayed for a strong gust of wind to tear the roof off and suck her right out of the apartment. This was excruciating. Mila Bay was actually asking R.J. about their relationship. R.J., the same man who hadn't even held on to his wedding band.

She stood up quickly, sparing him the discomfort of having to answer.

"What's wrong with me? You two must be starving after such a long journey. Let's get started with dinner. R.J., would you show our guests to the table?"

He moved toward the dining table and pulled out Mila's chair. Then he motioned for Tavov to sit down. Just as if he was the true man of the house.

"Excuse me while I start to serve."

R.J. cleared his throat behind her. "I'll help you."

They both moved into the kitchen. Angeline couldn't get to the sink fast enough. Splashing water on her face, she turned to catch R.J. watching her, his arms crossed in front of his chest.

"What?"

"Why are you getting so nervous? It's going great."

"Great? You think this is going great? Our guest just asked you to tell her what makes us such a great couple."

He grinned. "I could have come up with something."

She walked over to him, entranced by the way his smile transformed his face. "Oh? And what would you have said?"

"I would have said that you fell madly in love with me on sight and I couldn't get rid of you for anything."

Angel opened her mouth wide in shock, then saw his mischievous grin. She poked his chest with her index finger. "You wouldn't have dared."

He grabbed her wrist playfully and pulled her toward him. "Wouldn't I?"

"R.J., if you had said something ridiculous like that, I'd, I'd—"

He pulled her closer, an amused glint dancing in his eyes. "You'd what?"

"I'd have laughed in your face."

He gave an exaggerated shudder. "Ooh, violent."

His sarcasm was not lost on her. "Then, I would have pretended to accidentally spill hot soup into your lap."

The grin faded. "You wouldn't."

She shrugged. "You sure about that?"

"That would hurt."

"That's the point."

He seemed to contemplate that for a moment, then let go of her hand. "All right, I'll try not to make any snide comments."

She laughed when he gave her a painfully put-upon look. "Why, thank you."

He returned the smile, and it was so easy to remember all the reasons she'd fallen so hard for him. Nothing she'd experienced before or since had even come close to what they'd shared.

"Just be careful with that soup." R.J.'s mock reprimand pulled her back into the present. "Actually," he said as he moved toward the stove, "I think I'll serve it."

Angel watched him walk back out to the dining area carrying the serving dish. Still giggling, she was only vaguely aware that their little exchange had lessened her anxiety.

Minutes later they were all seated around the table, the aroma of cream of asparagus wafting up from the plates.

"Angel mentioned that you own a corporate security firm," Mila directed to R.J., then blew on her spoonful of hot soup.

"Yes, that's my primary focus right now. Angel heads most of the operations for TeaLC."

He had managed to answer the question without one lie.

"Such a dynamic field, network security," Tavov said. "I imagine something as trivial as tea distribution isn't very exciting to you."

Uh-oh. Angel swallowed. "More soup for anyone? R.J., I see you're done already." She started to stand.

"No, Angel. I'll hold off until the main course." He braced his elbows on the table and leaned toward the other man. "On the contrary, Tavov. I find my wife's side of the business fascinating. But I would never presume to understand as much about it as she does. She's the brains behind TeaLC. She always has been. I can only be impressed by her tremendous success."

Angel blinked at R.J.'s answer. He was impressed with her as a businesswoman? She gave a mental shake of her head and spread her napkin back on her lap.

R.J. was playing his part as the doting husband. And he was doing it quite well. It was no more than that. He might sound convincing, but she couldn't forget how fictional all this was.

Tavov seemed mollified.

Angel let out the breath she was holding and pushed back her chair. "Excuse me, I'm just going to go get the entrée. We're having grilled salmon with a parsley glaze. And pasta. I hope that's okay with everyone."

"That sounds delicious, dear," Mila answered.

"Just be careful serving the glaze." R.J. winked.

She gave him what she hoped was an admonishing glare, then turned toward the kitchen. The smile she was trying to keep from forming on her face broke free as soon as she turned her back.

Forty-five minutes later, Angel rolled the serving tray with all the dishes into the kitchen. They could be rinsed in the morning.

Rejoining her guests in the living room, she walked over to the stereo. "I think we could use some music." She pressed the selection on her entertainment center. Moments later the mellowing notes of classic Armstrong filled the room.

"Why, that's a lovely tune you have playing, Angeline," Mila commented.

"I'm glad you like it. It's one of my favorites."

"Just beautiful." Mila smiled at Angeline. "I remember you telling us how much you and R.J. enjoy dancing together. Tavov and I don't do much of it anymore."

"Was that a shameless way to get me to ask you to dance, my dear?" Tavov asked with humor, then stood up. He extended his hand to his wife. "Well, I'll do it only if Angeline and R.J. join us."

Angel tried not to wince. R.J. was probably cursing the forces that had ever brought them together. Here he was being urged into dancing with an estranged wife he thought he'd been rid of years ago.

"I—I'm not in a dancing mood tonight," Angel hedged, trying to make things easy for him.

"Please," Mila insisted. "You don't know what it takes to get this man to dance."

"I really don't think it's—"

R.J. stood before she could finish. In disbelief, she watched him extend his hand to her.

"What do you say, Princess? Shall we dance?"

She looked up at him, at a loss for words. The first time he'd ever touched her, he had uttered those very same words. The double meaning in his invitation had been clear, then.

Lost in memories, she stepped into his embrace. The older couple started to dance next to them.

It felt so right. He felt so good. The way it had every time he'd touched her. Their bodies molded perfectly, their rhythms completely in tune. Apparently they still moved well together.

Her feelings must have shown on her face, because he pulled her closer. Her chest molded tightly on his.

She instinctively rested her cheek on his chest, his heartbeat rhythmically pounding up against her ear. She'd always loved dancing with him, swaying in his arms. Every weekend while in school, they would move together to the sounds of cool, slow jazz at one of the clubs around campus. She longed for those days when she'd really been his partner, on the dance floor and everywhere else.

Their first dance had been nothing less than thrilling for her. After weeks of her trying futilely to get his attention, he'd finally talked to her. She'd kidded him about it that night.

Oh, you had my attention, all right. Let's just say I have this silly quirk about self-preservation.

She shut her eyes against the memories. How could she have lost a man like this? How could she have been lucky enough to find him and foolish enough not to hold on to him? She sighed into his chest and felt his arms tighten around her.

"We'd better be careful," he whispered into her ear, his breath thick and hot against her skin. "We get in trouble when we dance together."

"If I recall," she started in a low voice, "it wasn't the dancing that got us into trouble."

He laughed softly. "Maybe not, but it didn't help. Logic seemed to fly out the window whenever I had you in my arms."

"Like now?"

He pulled his head back to look at her. She wet her lips when his gaze fell to them. She saw his expression harden, the arms around her suddenly becoming much more lax.

"We're different people now."

They certainly were. Now, rather than seeing desire in R.J.'s face, all she could see was self-condemnation. For what? For having to touch her? For allowing himself into such a position that he'd had to dance with her three years after separating?

"People can't change so much so quickly, can they?"

"Maybe not. Maybe they just face tests that bring out their true priorities."

There was no bitterness in the statement. Just what sounded like pure acceptance. It made her realize how much distance there truly was between them. As far as R.J. was concerned, they had made their decisions years ago. Even though he really hadn't given her much of a choice.

The song came to an end. R.J.'s hands drifted slowly down her arms and rested gently on her waist. She moved her hands lower on his shoulders, and for a moment they both just stood still. Finally, R.J. stepped back, and she could have sworn her feet hadn't touched the floor until then.

"Well, little lady," Tavov said to his wife, "we've had a

long day. What do you say we make our way to our hotel and retire?"

Mila sighed. "Yes, I suppose it's getting late."

"That it is, dear."

Angeline forced herself to step away from R.J. and turned to her guests. "Then I guess I'll see the two of you at our lunch meeting tomorrow."

The digital audio player behind them switched to the next track, "Fantastic, That's You." Angeline guided the other couple toward the door. She could only hope that they didn't notice the moisture gleaming in her eyes.

CHAPTER FOUR

IT WAS OVER.

Angeline moved to join R.J. where he stood in front of the window watching the fall of the rain.

"I guess that went as well as we could have hoped," she said, doing her best to sound casual.

R.J. merely nodded.

The jazzy melody sounding from the stereo momentarily succumbed to the thunder outside. The evening had gone off without any glitches. But Angeline didn't feel much like celebrating.

"Looks like a nasty storm."

As if on cue, the lights flickered, then resumed their full brightness.

"Did you park far?" she asked.

"Yeah. I did." He moved to the bar and set his glass down. "I better start making my way back, come to think of it."

She could only wait silently as he grabbed his bag from the closet.

He wasn't looking at her when he came back into the room. "I think that's everything," he said. "I guess I'll see you around."

Before the words were out of his mouth, another round of lightning pulsated through the dimly lit room. The lights gave one more flicker, then went out completely. Heavy rain pelted the glass windows.

"It looks like you may be too late."

She heard a sigh of pure weariness. He didn't say anything.

"You don't want to be walking out in that mess," she spoke into the dark.

"I don't have a choice. It doesn't look like it's going to let up anytime soon."

Angeline knew he was close enough to touch. "You could wait it out."

He was quiet for a moment. She couldn't decide whether she was fortunate or not in not being able to see him. "Here? I don't think so," he finally answered.

"R.J., there really is no reason why you shouldn't. We're both adults. It's silly to risk storm and cold when there's plenty of room here. I might even be able to dig out one of your old pajamas."

"You held on to my pajamas?"

A nervous laugh escaped her before she could stop it. "You know what a pack rat I can be."

"No, that's okay. I have to leave, Angel. I should go right now." But she knew he hadn't moved. "Listen, it was great seeing you again. I hope this all works out for you."

"Wait! We're not finished yet. I mean, I still have my part of the bargain."

"The bargain?"

"I'm going to help you expand into Europe. Remember? Our deal."

He cleared his throat. "We can talk about that later. I'll have my assistant call you or something."

She felt her legs start to weaken. He was going to walk out of her life again. And there wasn't a thing she could do about it. He didn't want to deal with her directly about the expansion. Hell, he wanted nothing more to do with her.

While she still felt the burn on her skin from his touch.

"At least let me walk you down. Just let me find a flashlight."

Just give me a few more moments.

Distracted by his closeness and stumbling in the dark,

she turned to make her way into the kitchen. A loud thump followed by a sharp pain told her she'd walked right into her coffee table.

"Ow!"

"What is it?"

"My shin."

"Your shin?"

"Yeah, it's what I use to find things in the dark."

She heard his small laugh. "Are you all right?"

"Yes," she lied. "This is just all so awkward."

"Yeah, I know. Who would have thought that we'd ever be in such a strange predicament when we saw each other again?"

She remembered a time when awkwardness hadn't existed between them. They'd watched numerous storms together, holding each other.

"Funny how things turned out in the end," he added.

The end. "Yes, well, let me go find that flashlight."

An agonizingly short time later, they were out in the front lobby of her building. A few emergency lamps and the streetlights outside afforded the only light.

"Well, goodbye, Angel," R.J. said suddenly. The next moment, she was watching him exit out the revolving door.

Her heart took over before she could rationalize. She wrapped her suit jacket tighter around her and ran out after him. Thick pelts of cold rain shocked her the instant she stepped outside.

"R.J., wait."

He stopped and slowly turned around. She moved closer, the cold starting to make her shiver. Now that she'd stopped him she didn't know what she wanted to say.

He spoke first. "Angel, get back inside. You're getting soaked."

"It's okay," she insisted, though her chattering teeth

said otherwise. "It just occurred to me that I never really thanked you, I mean tonight."

His eyes searched her face. What in the world must he be thinking? What exactly did she want him to say? You're welcome?

"Really," she went on, feeling completely foolish. "You went above and beyond the norm."

Then she did the only thing she could think of—she extended her hand and waited for him to shake it.

Somehow she'd ended up shivering in a cold, powerful storm, shaking hands with R. J. Davet. And chances were very good she'd never see him again.

He was gone. Angeline stepped inside her dark apartment and closed the door behind her. Her ceiling lights flickered, then came back on, once again illuminating the normally cheery decor. Except now the place looked empty, in a way it never had before.

She should be elated that they were finally done with this insanity, that the Bays hadn't suspected the truth. Instead she wanted to huddle in a dark corner. Forever. She couldn't help but feel low for deceiving such warm people. Yes, technically she wasn't lying, but she certainly wasn't exactly telling them the whole truth.

But none of this was really for her own benefit. She was doing it for all her employees. For all those deserving women who had no one else and nowhere else to turn to. When would she ever get another opportunity like this to secure her employees' futures in such a long-term way?

The reminder did little to lessen her misery. She felt downright unsettled. As if she'd forgotten something crucial after leaving for a trip but couldn't remember what it might be. If only R.J. had stayed longer. It would be so helpful to be able to talk to him right now. To explain why she'd had to go through with tonight.

She could call him. Just to talk. Explain her motivation, make things clearer.

She had her phone in her hands before she stopped herself. With disgust, she threw it against the back cushion of her couch. What in the world was she doing? Her pride was all she had left. For heaven's sake. She'd already run after the man in the middle of a lightning storm.

She had to accept that it was over. Her business was all that mattered now, and it allowed her to help those less fortunate. There was absolutely no reason to doubt her life. It was exactly the way she wanted it. She'd worked very hard to get here and had no reason to feel guilty. Sometimes the end did justify the means.

She forced herself to step away from the door and walked back toward her bedroom. Max lay snoring at the foot of her bed, and Angeline quietly tiptoed around him. At least R.J. had not fought for custody. How much loss could one girl take?

She undressed quickly, too tired to do anything but throw her wet clothes on the floor. Pulling her thick flannel nightgown over her head, she crawled into bed.

She wasn't going to cry. Damn it, she wouldn't. No matter what it took. Her marriage was over. She'd been through crying over it years ago. And she was going to stop tossing and turning this minute and get some sleep.

A knock on the door stopped her midtoss.

R.J. It had to be. She sucked in a gasp of air. He wasn't going to leave after all! Possibilities started running through her head as she flung the covers away. She'd known it all along. He didn't want to leave things this unsettled between them either.

Struggling to maintain both a steady breath and her composure, she ran back into the other room. Every sense she possessed told her it was him knocking.

She pulled the door open. "R.J., it's you."

His eyes traveled over her, and he lifted an eyebrow. "I see you've changed your sleeping attire over the years."

"You decided to come back."

He ran a hand through the soaking-wet hair now curling with dampness. "I had to, Angel. I couldn't leave."

"You couldn't?" Her breath caught, her chest hurt. He hadn't been able to walk away after all. He was back to see things through this time.

"Yeah, the damn roads are starting to flood already," he said as he stepped inside. "They've blocked all traffic onto Storrow." He shrugged out of his suit jacket and threw it onto the sofa with clear frustration.

He was here only because the roads were blocked.

"I see." This time she really did see. She saw clearly her foolishness in pining for something she'd already lost. His reason for coming back had nothing to do with her.

His next words only drove it home. "Listen, the whole street is dark. I'm not going to try to drive through the city tonight. I'll call around to see which hotels have power. Where are the Bays staying? I'll be sure to steer clear of that one."

She steeled herself as all last traces of hope fled. "Now you're being silly. A hotel is hardly necessary." Turning, she spoke with her back to him. "I have a guest room you're welcome to use. You can leave in the morning."

"Don't go out of your way, Angel. This isn't a sleepover. As soon as the roads clear, I'll be on my way."

She walked over to the hall closet and grabbed a large terry towel. "I expected nothing more, R.J. And believe me. I'm not going out of my way." Not anymore, she thought and flung the towel toward him. He caught it with one hand.

"The guest room's down the hall," she continued. "There's a bathroom off of it. My bedroom is across the hall if you need anything. Have a good night. And if I don't see you in the morning, thanks once again for your help."

By the time her head hit her pillow, the trail of tears on her face was completely dry. Closing her eyes, she waited for the painful, poignant memories to revisit her like spirits in the night.

Dreams born of memories were the most restless kind.

What in the world was that incessant pounding?

Angeline pulled the covers over herself and prayed for the noise to go away. She couldn't have been asleep more than a few minutes. And now someone was trying to torture her with loud knocking.

The door. Someone was at the door, and apparently whoever it was had no plans to go away.

Grabbing her silk robe around her, she ran to answer it. The hum of the running guest shower told her R.J. hadn't left yet. A month ago she would have sooner dropped dead than bet that Robert James Davet would be showering again in her apartment. A twinge of sadness hit her at the less than intimate reason for his stay.

"Hang on. Hang on." The scolding she intended for the offensive knocker died on her lips as she yanked the door open. The woman on the other side was not someone she expected to see.

"May I come in?"

Angeline quickly recovered and stepped aside. "Mila. By all means."

"I'm sorry," Mila began as she walked past her. "I know it's early. I wanted to get here before Tavov awoke."

"Is everything all right?" Angeline asked and shut the door. Was Mila suspicious? If so, did she have it in her to bluff?

"Actually that's what I wanted to ask you, dear." She sat down on the sofa.

Angeline knew she should offer her tea or something,

but curiosity overrode her manners. "I beg your pardon? I'm not sure what you mean."

"Well, for starters, do you need to talk to someone?" Genuine compassion shone in her eyes.

"I'm sorry, I don't understand." Her mouth had gone dry. Mila appeared truly concerned about her, though she had no idea why. Angeline felt even guiltier than she had last night.

Mila cleared her throat. "Let me explain. My husband and I were having so much fun here last night. We didn't want the evening to end. So we stopped for a drink and to watch the storm before heading to our hotel." She paused before adding, "At the tavern across the street."

Across the street.

Mila continued. "Right before all the lights went out, we noticed your husband leaving. He was carrying what appeared to be a small suitcase."

"I see." Angel sat down on automatic pilot.

"Then we saw you chase after him, and—this is the part that confuses me—the two of you shook hands. Even in the dark it was easy to tell you were upset. So I wanted to come see if you were all right."

"I—uh—don't know what to say." At least that was the absolute truth.

"Now this morning," Mila continued. "I can't help but notice that you've been crying. Tavov will just say I'm a nosy old woman, but I couldn't help but be concerned. We feel we've gotten to know you a little bit, and the two of you just looked so happy last night." She leaned forward. "Is everything all right between you and R.J.?"

Don't panic. Stay cool. Angel took a deep breath to try to calm herself. It was almost humorous. Everything had almost gone off so perfectly. How coincidental that something as happenstance as a storm would wreck the whole effort. This was it, she had to confess everything. And fond of her or not, Mila and Tavov would never go through with the business deal after she told them.

She cleared her throat and prepared herself for what was to follow.

R.J. picked that moment to walk into the room. Only a towel covered him, hung low around his hips. Even in the state she was in, she couldn't help but notice the complete magnificence he exuded. Droplets of silver water glimmered on his chest. His dark hair was dripping.

"Mila." The one word sounded more like a question than a greeting. "What are you doing here so early? Everything okay?" If R.J. had noted Mila's shocked expression, he wasn't showing it.

"R.J., you're here," she said, confusion still etched in her voice.

R.J. shrugged. "Of course I'm here," he said, then blandly added, "Why are you here?"

Angel cleared her throat. "Mila and Tavov saw you leave last night," she explained. She tried to implore him across the room for forgiveness. He was going to hate her for what was about to happen.

"I do have a confession to make," she began.

R.J. snapped his head up. He lifted his eyebrows as if to ask her if she was certain. Angel took a deep breath, ready to proceed. This charade had gone far enough.

"Are you sure you want to admit it, Angel? Surely they won't be able to tell the difference. After all, they had no idea last night."

Angeline nearly moaned aloud. Dear God, he didn't have to blurt it out without giving her a chance to explain. She opened her mouth to spill out the awful truth. R.J.'s voice stopped her.

"All right, then," he continued. "I suppose we had better tell you." He moved toward the center of the room, crossing his arms in front of his wide, bare chest. "The fact of the matter is, the meal last night was catered."

Mila squinted her eyes. "That's it? That's the confession?"

R.J. walked behind Angeline and settled his hands tenderly on her shoulders. "It's part of it. The truth is, normally we would have prepared a meal together, but it's been hard to find time for such things lately. As a result—" he gave her shoulders a gentle squeeze and sighed "—our relationship has been a little strained."

Shock at the strange turn of the conversation along with the intimacy of his gesture prevented any words from forming on Angeline's lips.

"We had a bit of a spat last night," he continued. "I'm embarrassed to admit I stormed out afterward, somewhat childishly."

That was rich. Angeline couldn't imagine him ever acting in a childish way. Not even when he was an actual child. But Mila appeared to be buying it.

"That's what you witnessed last night. But I regretted it almost instantly and came back. We vowed to work on our marriage." His tone still held just the right amount of politeness to maintain a cord of amicability, but there was no mistaking the determination underneath. No one would question such a tone of voice.

How did the man manage to exude such authority wearing nothing but a large bath towel? Even standing there half-naked, there was no mistaking the man who had gone from the barest of beginnings to owning his own corporation.

"I said some things I shouldn't have said," he went on. "But I've promised to make it up to her. As soon as we decide where to go, I'm taking her away for a nice vacation. So we can get away together."

Oh, dear. Now he was outright lying for her.

Mila put a hand to her chest. "Oh, I'm so glad to hear

it. Aside from our desire to form a partnership with a family operation, we've grown quite fond of Angeline over the past few months. I know I sound foolish, but I had to come make sure you were okay, Angeline." She stood up and grabbed her bag. "I'll just leave you two to go about your morning, then."

Angeline's shoulders nearly sagged with relief. Finally, she found her tongue. "No, it doesn't sound foolish at all. I really appreciate how concerned you were for me, Mila."

The older woman smiled affectionately. "Well, you've come to mean more to us than a mere business associate, you know." R.J. dropped his hands from her, and the two women started walking to the door.

"Besides," she continued, "we couldn't have had you depressed on your visit to sign the papers." She suddenly stopped midstride and turned around.

"Wait, I have a terrific idea." She glanced first to R.J. then to Angeline. "Why doesn't R.J. join you when you come?"

Oh, no. Angeline swallowed the lump of apprehension that shot through her at Mila's words. She had to stop this drastic turn at the curve. "Well, um, he has a very demanding schedule. I don't know how we'd ever be able to swing it."

Mila's expression turned crestfallen. "But I thought you said you were planning a trip and that you just had to decide where. Perhaps I'm biased, but there isn't a more peaceful or relaxing spot on earth as far as I'm concerned."

"Yes, but who knows when he'll actually be able to clear the time."

Mila gave a dismissive shake of her hand. "Nonsense, we're very flexible. There're weeks still before the harvest. You can postpone your trip and come down when it's convenient for both of you."

"We just can't," Angeline insisted, unable to come up with any more excuses.

Mila looked utterly confused. "Well, why not?" She turned to R.J. for an answer, apparently giving up on Angeline.

Dear God, what must he be thinking now? She wouldn't be surprised if the firm hands resting gently on her neck a moment ago were itching to strangle it.

She laid a hand on Mila's arm, praying she would understand. "Fine, I need to level with you—"

R.J.'s baritone cut through her admission. It was about time he said something and aided her in averting this disaster. "I'll have my secretary clear my schedule next week. That way, Angel, you won't have to bother postponing."

She whirled around. "What?"

"I said, I'd love to accompany you. We can't turn down such a lovely gesture, now, can we?" His eyes seemed to dare her to deny it.

"What about your business? What about your expansion into Europe?"

What about the fact that we're not really even together?

"I'm ahead of plan on almost everything. This actually would be a perfect time to focus some attention to your side of the holdings."

"That's more like it. I think you're making a very wise decision," Mila said behind her.

Wise was the last word for what R.J. had just done. There would be no way out of this one. One look at Mila's expression made it clear—any attempt to back out of this commitment would be fatal for the pretense.

It was impossible to tear her eyes off R.J.'s face. She couldn't quite interpret the look he was giving her. If she didn't know better, she could have sworn it was one of reassurance.

"Mila's right, Angel. Besides, it's about time I became

more than a silent partner." He looked back to the other woman. "Please include my office in the travel arrangements. My wife will give you the requisite information and a name to contact. Now, if you'll excuse me, I have some appointments this morning."

Not sparing either of them another glance, he walked back toward the hall, leaving Mila smiling.

And leaving Angeline gaping in shocked confusion.

R.J. squeezed out a dollop of shaving cream and stared at his face in the mirror. He had to focus solely on the task at hand. In due time he would think about what he had just committed himself to. But not right now.

Oh, he'd wanted to help her. He'd pretty much decided that the day in her office when she'd first asked him. Even before Shanna had cornered him, he knew he would be returning to present Angel with other options.

After all, he was one of the reasons she was in this mess. But it never occurred to him he'd actually take the masquerade to such new heights himself.

But he owed her this. Angeline would have access to all the wealth and resources of the Scott dynasty if she hadn't been cut off by her father.

He shook his head. What a mess.

Furthermore, these days that area of the world wasn't exactly the safest. With all the global turmoil, he'd be worried sick about her going alone. She might not be his wife anymore, but he still felt an obligation to make sure she was safe. They'd shared a lot during their brief union as man and wife.

See, all very sound and logical reasons.

He forced his mind back to his shaving and applied the razor to his face. Up, down. Up, down.

He heard Angel's footsteps approaching. Damn, he should have shut the door. He didn't have any explanations for her yet. Hell, he couldn't fully explain to himself what he'd just done. How would he begin to tell her that he felt as if he owed her something? Felt as if he had to make it up to her for choosing him? At first anyway.

And Richard Scott wasn't one to forgive and forget. That had been made very clear when they'd run into each other. CEO or not, R. J. Davet would never be a fit son-in-law for the Scott dynasty. He'd never fit in at the yacht club or the exclusive charity auctions. Even if he could now afford it. Nor should he have ever had the gall to think he could.

Richard Scott was certain R.J. would never be worth anything when it came to what counted: breeding and class.

Pretty much echoing everything his own old man had been saying to him his entire life. Only in more educated terms. Plus, his father had liked to make his point with physical blows for emphasis.

Angel knocked with hesitation before entering. "We need to talk, R.J."

He offered her a glance before returning his concentration to his remaining stubble. "You think?"

She brought long fingers to her mouth. Angeline Scott at a loss for words, twice already. Another subtle difference since she'd been his wife. How many other changes had he missed?

"I never meant for your involvement to get so complicated."

"We didn't appear to have much choice, though, did we?"

She started chewing her lip. "We do have a choice. I'll tell her the truth. I can't expect you to drop everything you're doing and travel to the ends of the earth with me."

"And what happens to your deal if we don't?"

"I'm guessing it will be dead in the water."

He shrugged. "All right, then, it looks like we'll be taking a trip."

She touched his shoulder, and he tried to ignore the resulting electricity. "But you don't have to do this. I'll figure out another way."

He shrugged. "It was my doing. I should have never mentioned taking a trip together. That comment gave her the idea in the first place."

"None of this is your fault," she argued. But she was oh so wrong about that.

"Well, we started this sham, we have to finish it. Besides, you said so yourself, Angel. There is no other way to get your expansion."

"I know that," she said. "But I realize now what a mistake all this was. There's no need to push it any further."

"Yeah? How are you going to explain it all to the Bays?" He waited, knowing she had no answer. "The only option is to go through with this trip and act like the committed, devoted couple."

"We both know it's not that simple. We would need Academy Award–level talent to pull something like that off. I don't know about you, but I'm not that comfortable with my thespian skills."

"You'll have to brush up on those skills quickly."

"This whole thing was a foolish, thoughtless endeavor." She pulled her hair back off her forehead, agitated. "I don't know what I was thinking. I just, I mean, all I thought about was the people who depended on TeaLC for their living. All I could see as the deal was falling through were the faces of those women when they first come in for placement. And the transformation that happens afterward, once they realize someone is willing to invest in them."

She maneuvered herself closer to the bathtub behind him and sat down on its edge. "R.J., some of these women have no work experience. They can't even get a low-paying waitressing job. And in no time, with the dedication and hard work they usually display, they're managing whole centers, or working out of corporate. All they needed was that push."

He turned to face her. "I know, Angel. And I should tell you I'm really impressed that you went out on a limb for what you felt was important."

She blinked. "Do you really mean that?"

"I know the work and effort it takes to keep a business running. Setting up a whole work placement program on top of all that showed real dedication."

"And that surprised you?"

He shook his head slowly. "Not really. I know you're the kind of person who makes even business decisions with her heart." That knowledge only added to the guilt he felt now. How much would she be capable of if she still had the backing of her father?

She seemed surprised by his words. Silence descended on the small bathroom as his eyes locked on hers.

He wanted to touch her, burned to. She was completely disheveled. The white robe around her looked about three sizes too big. Her hair was a mess of curls, her lips red from the way she'd been chewing them. He wanted to soothe those lips with his own. He wanted to taste her skin as he trailed kisses down her neck.

She took a small breath and he reflexively moved toward her.

A small clanging noise behind him startled him back to his senses. The razor had fallen to the floor.

Steady there. Angeline Scott was off-limits. She always had been. He was old enough and wise enough now not to ignore that crucial fact. Angeline had no hope of a reconciliation with her father if R.J. reentered her life. He couldn't do that to her twice.

"So now what?" she asked, her head tilted back.

He stole a look at his watch. "Well, now I don't have time

to run to my office before my first meeting anyway. So we may as well eat. I'm starved. Can I buy you breakfast?"

She clapped her hands to her legs and rose off the tub. "The least I could do is whip you up some breakfast."

R.J. couldn't clamp down on a grimace. In response, her face twisted into an expression of comical hurt.

"I appreciate the offer, Princess, but if I remember correctly, your culinary skills, particularly when it came to breakfasts, weren't exactly polished."

"But that's just not so anymore. I can prepare a lot of stuff. In fact, I managed to acquire a recipe for some mouth-watering apricot scones. It's one of the recipes printed on my packages. I made some the other day, and there're a few left. And I've got some ginger cake left over that goes great with jasmine tea. It'll take no time to throw it together."

He turned to fully face her again and leaned his hip on the sink behind him. "I don't know how to tell you this, sweetheart, but I was thinking more along the lines of home fries, scrambled eggs with bacon, and thick country toast soaked in butter."

She wrinkled her nose. "Those hardly work well with even the briskest of teas."

"And a strong cup of steamy, dark-as-coal coffee."

Angel let out an exaggerated gasp and clapped a palm to her chest. "I can't believe you said the *C* word."

He grinned. "Real bastard, aren't I?"

"I suppose I should go see if I even have a stash of that contraband on the premises."

"Hey, you offered breakfast. If that means you take a walk to Java Jay's, then I'll see you when you get back."

"More forbidden words." She performed an exaggerated shudder. "I can't be around you any longer."

"Sorry, sweetheart. I was never much of a tea drinker."

"Well, you needn't goad me with the competition."

"Would you rather I lied to you?"

"Only if you do it with sincerity." She brushed by him with an exaggerated huff. He snapped her playfully with a towel as she walked out.

Minutes later, the delicious aroma of coffee reached his nostrils, followed by the scent of clearly greasy breakfast home fries. His stomach grumbled. Oh, yeah, it appeared his wife had undergone quite a few changes.

The scene that greeted him in the country-style contemporary kitchen caused an ache deep within his chest. Angel stood over the granite counter, still wrapped in the thick terry robe, fixing breakfast for the two of them. Her collar had fallen off her shoulder. For a moment, he imagined it slipping farther down, lower and lower, exposing the creamy skin of her smooth back. He took a deep breath and made his way to the round wood table in the center of the room.

She turned and acknowledged him with a smile that didn't look very convincing. The events of the morning hadn't been forgotten.

"Voila." She bowed and lifted the cover off a large serving plate to display a heaping serving of eggs, toast and potatoes.

"You did this?"

She glared at him. "I am in the business, sir. You needn't look so surprised."

He figured it would be safer to dig in than risk further reply. He sank his fork into a mound of eggs and barely allowed himself a chew before he swallowed. Early-morning deception tended to give a guy an appetite.

"Mmm, that's great, Angel."

"Glad you like it." She leaned over the table to serve herself. His gaze shifted automatically to her exposed shoulder. She looked up in time to catch his stare and shifted uncomfortably. Slightly embarrassed, he looked away.

He gulped down some of the coffee. It wasn't terribly fresh, but the caffeine jolt was more than welcome.

Angel lifted her hand, and he handed her the salt shaker before she had a chance to ask for it. She took it without looking up.

"R.J., what in the world do we do now?"

"First of all, I guess we need to set up our trip," he said, stalling. "I understand it's a very pretty area."

"Um..." Angel replied, still chewing. "Especially closer to the Black Sea coast where the Bays' property is." She smiled. "You should see how beautiful these rows and rows of plants are. Mila's Bloom is a gorgeous shrub. It grows so lush and full. There are some black tea orchards right around that area, too. And the beaches are beautiful."

"Well, I'll be able to see it firsthand soon."

She set her fork down. "So, we're really going to go through with this. I guess that European expansion is a lot more important to your bottom line than I had thought." She put her fork down and waited for him to answer.

He ignored it. "Then we can see about the flight arrangements."

"What about your responsibilities? Are you going to be able to get away for so long?"

"I have a right-hand man. I can trust him with my life." He stopped and added, "And with my business."

"Sounds like quite a guy. Can't wait to meet him."

There was no need to tell her Tom already knew about her. No need to talk about the reckless, drunken rant he'd gone on one night when he'd been particularly missing her. He cleared his throat.

"What about you—who'll take over for you here?"

She swallowed. "Shanna's more than capable of handling things while I'm away. And she loves having Max stay with her, so she'll do that, too."

"You two make quite a team."

"We do seem to complement each other." She smiled and picked further at her plate. "Well, our backup in the States seems settled."

He stopped eating. "That's it, then. Looks like we'll be going undercover."

As true man and wife, no less.

CHAPTER FIVE

WHEN IT CAME to late-night wallowing, Shanna Martin always came prepared. Evidence of the fact sat scattered all over the coffee table in the form of candy, ice cream and various other sugar products.

Shifting her legs under her, Angeline tore open the chocolate-covered almonds and popped three of them into her mouth at once. A nearly empty pizza box sat precariously on the arm of the sofa next to her.

"So, you and R.J. will be playing house for a while, huh?"

She started to deny Shanna's depiction but then sighed. "Pretty much." It took an amazingly short time to suck right through the chocolate candy straight to the nut at the center.

"How are you going to make sure the Bays don't become suspicious?" Shanna asked as she stirred her root beer float.

"Shan, I don't know anything anymore. How did this get so convoluted? It was supposed to be one night of playacting until we could get the Bays to listen to reason."

"Instead, you're traveling in a few days to one of the most romantic spots on the planet with your estranged husband."

"Exactly! How did all this happen?"

Shanna looked like she was on the verge of a giggle, then had the sense to squelch it.

"My life seems to turn completely upside down every time that man is in it." Angeline stopped to wash down two chocolates with cola.

"So now what?"

"So now it's happening all over again. So much for our

well-thought-out foolproof plan. We should have been over with this whole thing by now."

"Is that what bothers you? The fact that we're way off plan?"

Angel swallowed and gave her a quizzical look.

"Or is it something else?" Shanna asked while taking great effort in squeezing just the right amount of chocolate syrup onto a pint of French vanilla ice cream. Then she handed the sundae to Angel.

"Isn't that enough?"

"There seems to be more to it. You look almost angry. Surely not at R.J. He's being very generous. What's going on?"

"Oh, he's generous to a fault. Doesn't seemed bothered at all that we'll be spending so much time together."

"Mmm-hmm."

Her blood sugar having reached full tilt, Angel wasn't cautious enough not to take the bait. "What do you mean, *mmm-hmm*?"

"I mean, there's something else bugging you about this whole thing."

"What are you talking about? We're misleading two wonderful people to help grow a business that employs numerous hardworking, deserving women. Not to mention the whole fiasco of a sham marriage. All of that is bugging me."

"Right." Shanna put her drink down and turned to face her friend. Uncomfortable with the scrutiny, Angel studied the smeared fudge on her spoon. "But, you're definitely not the objective, savvy businesswoman you usually are, Angel. Tell me what's up."

She blurted it out without really wanting to. "It just hurts, Shan. To see how unaffected he can be about the whole thing. He acts like it's not going to bother him at all, pretending we never broke up."

"Like you're wondering how much the marriage meant to him in the first place."

Feeling the tears pool beneath her lids, she could only nod.

Shanna moved closer and gave her a reassuring hug. "Baby, you know he cares for you, he loved you."

"I don't know anything of the sort. Maybe he only loved the fact that I was willing to risk everything for him."

"You don't believe that. Anyone who saw the two of you together could see the intensity whenever you even looked at each other."

"Yeah, the intensity of foolish youth thrown together with a healthy helping of ordinary, basic lust."

"I know you don't want to minimize it that way. Everyone could tell back then that no one else existed for the two of you when you were together."

Angel hmphed a laugh. "That didn't stop several people from trying to come between us. They ultimately succeeded, didn't they?"

"Did they?"

"You need to ask? We split up, remember?"

"Angeline, the only people who can split a couple up are the two people in it."

Angeline paused as the force of each word hammered home. It was true. Somehow she had failed miserably with the one man she'd ever felt anything for.

"You never talked about it, you know," Shanna continued. "You never talked about the specifics of your breakup, I mean." She paused. "And I didn't want to push."

It was true. Shanna was one of those friends who would never prod, just always be there to listen if you needed. It was one of the many reasons they'd stayed such steadfast girlfriends since childhood. Angeline gave a small shrug. "We just grew apart."

"But why?"

"I don't know, we just argued about everything. And the last straw broke when he wanted to move to the West Coast, to be closer to the tech industry. I couldn't drop everything I was doing and follow him to another city." She felt her lip quiver and hated herself for it.

"You were his wife. Couldn't you two work out some sort of compromise?"

"How? I had an idea and a business plan. I'd already put in a large investment."

"And R.J. had a problem with this?"

"He wanted me to look into setting up my business out there. But that was just too risky. Besides, this is my home. R.J., on the other hand, wanted to completely break free from all our Boston connections."

"Doesn't sound like either of you was willing to budge."

Angeline sighed. "It was a very difficult situation, Shanna. I was trying to start my own business."

"Angeline, lots of couples go through what you described. Not all of them end up in splitting. So why did you two break up?"

Angeline snapped her head up to look at her. Random thoughts skittered around her brain like insects. There seemed to have been so many things that went wrong before all that, so many disagreements that escalated. Eventually, even the fire of passion hadn't been enough to keep them together. And there was always the looming specter of her father and his disapproval. She'd initially thought they'd be able to survive it all. Toward the end, she'd realized she didn't even know if she was fighting for her marriage or fighting against her dad. Eye-opening moment, indeed.

"It certainly didn't help that my father was against us from the beginning. Threatened to cut me off if I married R.J. Then held true to his word. As always."

"You married him anyway."

"I'd fallen in love," Angeline said, grabbing another

candy, then slamming it back down on the counter. Suddenly, she didn't feel like eating anymore. "And it's not like my father and I had much of a relationship in the first place. Hence, all the hours I spent at your house as a kid."

Shanna smiled. "We were happy to have you."

"I'm glad someone was. My father treated me as barely more than a nuisance. Something changed in him after my mother left us. He grew cold, distant. I was little, but I still noticed."

"You look a lot like your mom."

She had considered that, of course. "A reminder of her he didn't want." She shook her head in dismissal. "This is all old news. Nothing to do with what's happening between R.J. and me now."

"Maybe. Maybe not. Did it ever occur to you that R.J. may have felt guilty? For coming between you and your father? The only family you had?"

Her pulse hitched. The truth was, she hadn't really examined R.J.'s motivation. She'd been too hurt. But that theory made no sense. "So his response was to give me an ultimatum about moving away with him to the West Coast?"

Shanna leaned closer, her head practically on Angeline's shoulder. "Maybe he knew you well enough to know you'd turn it down. Leaving the ultimate decision in your hands."

Shanna's words felt like a jolt through her chest. Could that have actually been R.J.'s intent? All this time, she hadn't once considered he might have made his West Coast ultimatum in order to give her a way out.

Shanna gave her a look of sympathetic understanding at her silent answer. "That's what I thought," she finally said. "Neither of you stopped to consider what you were really throwing away. Pride and youth kept getting in the way, I imagine."

She watched as Shanna started clearing the mass of junk food in front of them. Had she been uncompromising? She thought back to the woman she was three years ago. Starting and expanding TeaLC had been the ultimate goal. It had been thrilling to investigate the growing tea market, to research the best distribution channels. She'd worked so hard. Sacrificed so much. While her friends were traveling the world after graduating or immersing themselves in social functions, she was poring over project charts and earnings projections. She'd given up so much, her youth, her friends. Her husband. Had it all been worth it in the end? These days, the only thing exciting about TeaLC appeared to be the Works program.

Had she really not stopped long enough to see what her husband was dealing with because he'd married her?

She pulled herself short. Why was she doubting herself all of a sudden? For doing nothing more than pursuing a dream. He'd been at fault, too. If Shanna was right about R.J.'s intentions three years ago, he should have been honest with her from the beginning.

Shanna made a studious effort of studying her scarlet-red fingernail. "Apparently nothing was resolved by the two of you breaking up. You're going to have to address that, even if this is only a short-term 'marriage of convenience.'"

Angel had to stop herself from jumping up and pacing around the living room like a nervous cat.

Shanna continued. "Who knows, maybe that's the reason all this is happening. Maybe the universe is finally answering your need to face some of this stuff head-on. Before you finally move ahead and sign those divorce papers."

Angeline began clearing the table, as well. "Don't you go into one of your New Age, karma-based, transcendental philosophical lectures on me. All this is happening because I'm trying to buy tea from the two sweetest but most stubborn people on the face of the earth."

Shanna threw a chocolate drop at her. "If you say so. But something tells me there's much more to it."

Angel spread her arms wide in a frustrated gesture. "Oh, like what? Perhaps fate has chosen this way to bring us together again? Come on, Shan. Even you can't believe that, romantic that you are."

Shanna shook a spoon in the air. "Don't be so sure. We romantics believe in love above all."

"Despite all the horrors we see at the TeaLC Works program? All those women who commit to the man of their dreams and end up with a nightmare instead?"

"Those women are moving on with their lives. They'll find real love, too. Eventually."

Angeline gave a weary sigh. "And us?"

"Darling, there's only one of us who hasn't had it happen to her yet. And my turn is right around the corner. I can feel it."

Angel ignored the first part and grinned. "Whoever he is, he's a lucky man."

Shanna winked. "Well, I'll be sure and tell him that when he shows up. Now, I should get going and you should go to bed. We have a pretty full day tomorrow. Don't forget you have that formal dinner in the evening with the Women in International Business."

Angel tried to rub some tension out of her brow. "That's right. I'm not so sure how social I'm going to be. I can just see the conversations now—'Angeline, why don't you tell us about your current overseas projects?' How would I reply?" She placed her hands on her hips and looked up at the ceiling as she thought of a mock answer. "Well, I'm in phase three of 'Operation Marriage Scam.'"

Shanna laughed. "Don't go giving away all our trade secrets."

"And I suppose, before the day is out, I should call R.J. about our trip."

"Looks like you've got a pretty interesting day ahead of you."

Angeline dropped herself back down on the sofa. "That's the problem. Things have just gotten way too interesting since my ex returned."

Angel stepped out of the double doors of the World Trade Center. Cool harbor wind licked her face and offered some refreshing air. The business dinner had been a chore. She hadn't been able to concentrate. All she could think of was the trip.

She still hadn't called R.J. to talk, had put if off all day. She looked down at her watch. Seven thirty. A walk would soothe her tension. She could grab a cab right afterward and then call him. The wind was crisp and she was wearing heels, but the air would do her good.

Pulling her wrap tighter around her exposed shoulders, she moved down the steps. In the distance to her right, the flickering lights of the city twinkled against the skyline. From the harbor behind her came the unmistakable aroma of low tide.

She turned and started walking toward the city. The building that housed her TeaLC's headquarters stood west of center. It loomed before her like a symbol of her life. She thought about what she was ready to do for the business that building housed, the trip she was about to take and the underlying deception behind it. But she had to. She couldn't let any of her employees lose their jobs.

R.J. was willing to do so much to help her. But that was just his nature. She couldn't take it to mean he still cared for her. That would be a mistake, one too costly for her heart to handle. By all logical conclusions, he had moved on. For all she knew, there was probably even a woman in his life right now.

And what about all the things Shanna had brought up last night? Had R.J. indeed left because he'd made the misplaced assumption that she'd be better off?

Did she dare confront him about it?

She hadn't been able to admit it to her best friend, but the simple fact was that Angel had fully expected R.J. to come back. Maybe in a few months. Perhaps even up to a year. She'd told herself it was just a matter of time before he returned to her.

But he hadn't.

The sudden blare of a car horn sounded as a motorist cut off a van in traffic. The noise brought her attention to her surroundings. She hadn't realized she'd gotten so far. She'd passed the aquarium and all the construction around it without even realizing. Her watch told her she'd been inadvertently walking for almost fifteen minutes.

The hustle of downtown Boston buzzed around her. She tilted her head back to stare at the building before her. Somehow she'd ended up at the last place she wanted to be.

Only one thing left to do now.

R.J. glanced at his watch, then looked back up at her. "What are you doing here, Angel? Did your chauffeur take a wrong turn?"

"I was hoping we could talk."

He lifted an eyebrow. Angeline stood still, braced on the doorway of his hotel suite, afraid to move. The pain in her calf from the long walk in high heels had her lifting her leg to rub it gently. She looked up to see heat swimming in his eyes. He turned away quickly, leaving her to wonder if she'd imagined it.

She straightened. "Can I come in?"

He let out a breath before stepping aside and motioning her inside.

She moved into the room and took a breath for courage. R.J. had the lights dimmed. A large picture window overlooked the city. Rich mahogany furniture adorned the room along with a plush sofa and love seat. It was quite a leap from the one-bedroom studio they had shared as man and wife. That place had only the bare essentials. But R.J. had refused any assistance, including the use of her trust fund. And this was worlds different from the dingy studio over the North End bar where he'd lived during college. She knew it took a rare person to go from a place like that to surroundings like this. Not to mention, this was just one of the properties that R.J. owned. He had real estate holdings all along both coasts.

"I wanted to give you one more chance to change your mind," she began. "I mean, about coming with me."

"I made my decision that morning, Angel. You don't have to worry about me pulling out at the last minute."

She felt some of the tension leave her shoulders. Deep down, she'd known he wasn't going to change his mind. But she had to offer him the out.

"I'd say you're the one who might be having doubts."

She shook her head. "No, I haven't changed my mind."

"You're certain?"

How could she be certain of anything when he looked at her like that? The warm glow of the dimmed lights threw shadows over his face. His eyes were piercing, intense. His undone collar exposed a triangle of bronze skin and dark chest hair she longed to run fingers over. A small shudder escaped through her, and she hoped he didn't notice.

"I'm certain we've both gone mad." She tried to laugh. "But I know what I have to do. And I appreciate your willingness to help."

"No sweat." He shrugged and walked over to the bar in the corner of the room. "Can I get you anything? Something to drink?"

The last thing she needed in his presence was a drink. Any drop in her inhibitions and she'd be likely to go to him, to touch him the way she'd done the other night when he'd pushed her away.

"No, thank you. I—I just wanted to see you, you know, to be certain."

He nodded and thoroughly looked her over. She tried not to shift uncomfortably under his stare. Suddenly, the low-cut style of her dress, though tasteful, left her feeling exposed. She fought the urge to shift the velvet wrap higher to cover herself. Everywhere his eyes touched felt like steamy water running over her skin.

She cleared her throat. "Perhaps you can answer a question for me, though."

He took another large gulp of his drink and seemed to be in a hurry to swallow it down. "Shoot."

"Why are you willing to do all this? To drop everything and travel across the world with me?"

He only shrugged in answer.

"I know it took a lot of hard work and dedication to get where you are," she continued. "Something tells me that if you want an overseas expansion, you'll find a way to get it yourself."

He looked surprised at her comment. "Thank you for that," he said quietly.

"Which leads me back to my question. Why?"

He shrugged again. "You asked for my help."

She wanted to press it, but there was a warning in his eyes that stopped her. She couldn't name it, but it looked fierce and unforgiving.

"Now I have a question for you," he declared.

"All right."

"Why are you really here?" He stepped away from the bar, slowly, his drink still in his hand. "Dressed like that?"

The shadows in the room seemed to grow suddenly darker. "I told you. I—um—came by to give you one more chance to back out."

"You couldn't have done that with a phone call?" He lifted the glass back to his mouth, his gaze never leaving her face. She watched his lips part and subconsciously opened her own.

She ignored the question. "As for my dress, I had to go to a formal dinner meeting at the pier."

He didn't say anything for a while, just stared at her with an expression that made it clear he wasn't buying it. Why had she shown up here? She'd fully intended to call him.

She cleared her throat. "Well, I should go. I see now I've interrupted you while you were working."

"It can wait." He moved closer, bringing the scent of his distinctive cologne with him. "Right now I'm more interested in getting to the bottom of this."

"Bottom of what?"

"Your visit."

She felt a stinging warmth on her skin, not sure if it was embarrassment or something else. "I—I already told you. What else do you want to hear?"

"I want to know the real reason you're here. Standing in my living room, in a dress that seems to have been created to reduce a man to tears."

He stared at her as she stood immobile. Angel watched as his eyes traveled over her shoulders, lingering at her chest. A curl of heat meandered its way through her center.

"Is it as smooth as it looks?" he asked in a whisper.

She heard herself gasp. "Wh-what?"

He took large steps toward her. Close, so close. "The dress. Is the velvet as smooth as it looks?" She froze as his hand came up to touch her. He ran a finger over the low collar of the dress, moving provocatively toward the center, where it dipped lower between her breasts. She tried not to react, even as her breathing grew heavier.

She strained for a casual laugh that came out more like a nervous cackle. "Come on, R.J., you think there was some ulterior motive to my coming here like this?"

She tried to step away, but he moved to block her. She could feel his heat over her skin. She tried not to breathe. One deep breath and her chest would come in agonizing contact with his.

"You explain it to me, then, Angel," he challenged. "Tell me why you're here to ask me something you could have asked on the phone. Wearing that."

"It's just a dress, R.J. Nothing more."

He lifted his eyebrows. "Oh, it's so much more. Let me ask you something. Was it the dress you were intending to wear all along to your business dinner? Or was it a spur-of-the-moment decision?"

She tried not to gasp in acknowledged surprise. It had been a last-minute decision. Subconscious, but last minute.

It was time to bring out the defensive artillery. "Aren't you flattering yourself just a little?" God, she hoped she sounded convincing. "I came here to merely talk to you, to make some sort of agreement that we're both fully committed to this trip. Now that I've done that, I think I'll leave."

"And that's it? That's the only reason you're here right now?" He paused as his eyes made another slow, discomforting journey over her.

She cleared her throat. "R.J., you're being silly."

"Am I? Am I being silly when I read desire in your face? I know that desire, Angel. I'm the last man on earth who would mistake that look in your eyes."

She swallowed. "There is no 'look.' I'm stressed out and I'm tired. My shoes were killing me the whole way here." She stared at him defiantly, trying to quell the effect his closeness was having on her. "Exhaustion. That's what you're seeing. Nothing more than pure physical exhaustion."

He gave her a look that clearly said, *The lady doth protest too much*. "You walked here?"

"I needed the air." She could use a large swallow of it now.

"That's a long distance for heels."

"You're not telling me anything my feet don't know."

A knowing look settled across his face. "So you felt the need to walk, in the dark, to offer an apology that could have been delivered on the phone."

"Like I said, I needed some air. It did me a lot of good. It's just too bad my feet didn't agree with the decision."

He bent down then, quickly and unexpectedly. She tried not to jump as warm strong fingers wrapped around her ankle.

Images flashed through her mind, and all she wanted to do was join him down there. On the carpet, feeling the weight of his body on hers. She yanked her foot back with too much force and nearly toppled over backward. "R.J., please don't, I'm fine."

He didn't come up from his crouched position. "Your feet are starting to swell, and your right heel is loose."

Now things were getting romantic, Angel thought drily. It was hard to determine whether to laugh or cry at her predicament. Or should she just give in and ask for what she wanted…?

She gave her head a quick shake. "I—I'll be fine. We'll talk tomorrow. Sorry to have disturbed you."

"We're not finished yet."

As far as she was concerned they were. She twirled around to make a dash to the door, away from the danger of this conversation.

"Angel, just hold on." His voice had grown more gentle, but it was still a demand. "Don't you think you owe me an explanation?"

The last question broke her control. How could he ever expect her to explain this senseless attraction that seemed to consume her? Clutching her purse to her middle like a protective shield, she tried to suck in a calming breath. "I shouldn't have come here. This whole thing is going to be difficult enough. Let's just see how we can best get through the next couple of days and this trip. We don't need to rehash the fires of old attraction."

"If you really meant that, you wouldn't be here, sweetheart."

"I told you, I realize now that I shouldn't have come."

"But you did."

She felt tears of frustration and swore they would not fall. "Why are you doing this?"

He moved quickly, so fast she could have sworn she felt the air move around her. She felt herself being pulled up against him. "I agreed to become involved because I assumed you were being straight with me. You said you needed help with a small business matter and that only I fit the job requirement. If there's more between us than that, I need to know about it."

"I don't know why you're so worked up over a simple visit."

He gently but effectively pushed her up against the wall, then followed to lean up against her. It was sweet agony to feel his weight against her again, to have his heat on her skin.

"Let's just call it precaution, darling."

She wanted to fling her anger at him, wanted to wound him with harsh words and strong denials. She wanted to scream that there was nothing between them. But the lies wouldn't form on her tongue. Instead, the truth started to roll out. "Do you want me to admit it? Is that it? Do you want to hear that I still yearn for you, that I've missed your touch every day since you left?" Thoroughly disgusted with herself at the complete lack of control, she tried to quell the shaking.

"Is that what you want from me?"

R.J.'s eyes grew wide. Then instantaneously turned darker.

"What did you just say?" His lips were so tight and his voice so low that she almost wondered if she'd imagined the words.

Suddenly it was all too much: the pressure of the last few days, the threat of losing her business. Confronting her dangerous attraction to a man she should have forgotten long ago. Afraid to stay in his presence a moment longer, she yanked herself out of his grasp and ran to the door.

"Angel, wait."

"No. I'm leaving now, R.J." A rock had appeared right above her throat. It was painful and choking.

"Don't. Not yet, please. Not like this."

She wasn't listening anymore. Everything she did in his presence seemed to take a wrong turn. Her vision blurred as her eyes began to sting. All that mattered now was to leave his apartment as soon as possible. She gripped the doorknob so tight her hand hurt.

"Angel, I didn't mean to be so hard on you. You—you just threw me off."

She had thrown *him* off? Her life had become an out-of-control ride on a speedy Tilt-A-Whirl since he'd shown up in her office a few days ago.

"I'm sorry I keep disrupting your life," she said over her shoulder. "Once this is over, it will never happen again." The last word came out on a sob, and she despised herself for it. How pathetic could she be?

"That's not what I meant. For God's sake, would you just hang on?"

She couldn't. She yanked the door open. The hallway swam in front of her, and she started to run as she felt him closing in behind her.

"Angel, please. Give me another second."

"R.J., not now!" she said, afraid to turn around. She ran past the elevator, not wanting to wait.

"Sweetheart, I'm sorry I snapped. Would you just wait—?"

She hurried down the hallway, cursing herself as a coward. But for all her successes and all her accomplishments, she didn't have the strength to face the man behind her.

The loose heel of her shoe wobbled, but she ignored it. She was almost at the stairway. The only important thing right now was to get out of here.

She reached the emergency stairs and yanked open the door, R.J. hard on her heels.

"Damn it, Angel. You're going to tumble down those steps. Would you please just stop?" He was near pleading now, the urgency thick in his voice.

But she couldn't stop. She couldn't even slow down.

"Angel, I'm not going to follow you. All right? Just slow down before you hurt yourself."

She didn't heed him. Her heel gave another twist, and she inadvertently took two steps at a time. Her foot landed on the hard stone and shot a jolt of pain through her already sensitive ankle. She stumbled but managed to right herself. R.J.'s gasp was audible from behind her, even though it was obvious he wasn't pursuing her any longer.

She saw the exit sign and hiccupped with relief. Just a few more steps. When she pushed the door open, cool air finally hit her like a smooth, satin curtain. She stopped on the sidewalk to catch her breath.

"Angel, please," she heard him say behind her several moments later.

How could she let him see her cry this way? It was bad enough he'd read her so well, bad enough he had figured it out before she could even admit it to herself. No, she had to get away from him. She ran to the curb, desperate to find a taxi.

Her heel finally gave way. She felt herself plunging toward the ground and braced for the inevitable pain of impact with the hard concrete. Before she could even cry out, strong arms gripped her at the waist and stopped her fall.

It took a moment to regain her breath, then she said the first words that came into her head. "Nice catch."

He remained silent for a beat. "Yeah, you were."

God, it felt right. Being in his arms felt like being home. All she could think about was the feel of him.

"I—I guess I totally lost that heel."

"You lost the whole shoe."

Despite herself, she let out a small laugh.

She moved to disengage herself, and he shook his head. "Uh-uh. You can't walk like that."

What was the alternative? Suddenly, he picked her up and turned around back toward his building. She didn't protest. Her husband was carrying her back to his hotel room in the middle of the night. And she wasn't going to protest.

Strangers stared at them, but she hardly noticed. The old sensation that they were the only souls on earth manifested itself like habit. She gave in to the urge to snuggle into his chest.

They seemed to be moving in slow motion through the stairway.

"I'm sorry."

She looked up and brought shaky fingers to his lips.

"Don't. Please don't apologize."

"I need to. I don't know what came over me. But you showed up, and you looked so damn—" He let out a frustrated breath. "So much like the way I remembered. And it—"

Intuitively, she knew they had both moved toward each other.

Anticipation froze her muscles. Nothing moved but her heart. Even time seemed to stop.

He pulled back from her suddenly, a quiet moan on his lips.

"Angel?"

"Yes?"

"I'm taking you back upstairs."

CHAPTER SIX

HE INTOXICATED HER. Why else would she be allowing this to happen? Savoring it?

She was still cradled in his arms when they stepped back into his hotel suite. He dropped his forehead on hers and slowly started to lower her to the floor. She clutched at his shoulders, savoring his heat as she traveled down the length of him.

This was the way it had always been between them, so much fire it was a wonder their souls hadn't scorched. He nuzzled against her as he settled her onto her feet, and she thought she'd never realized such pleasure.

Until he set her down and a shooting pain shot through her calf. Angel gasped.

"Don't tell me—your foot?" R.J. said above her.

She nodded, clenching her teeth against the hurt.

"Here, sit down." He gently maneuvered her onto the sofa. "Let me take a look. I've had quite a few injuries in my lifetime." Angel knew the reasons for that. R.J. had grown up on some of the toughest streets of metro Boston. He'd been in more than his fair share of fights, an aspect of his life he refused to talk about. She could hardly blame him. He softly touched her ankle with gentle fingers.

"It's swollen even more, but it doesn't appear sprained." He wrapped his hand around the top of her foot, applying gentle pressure. The innocent massage sent fire up her leg. Full-blown kisses from other men had elicited less desire.

"R.J., you don't have to do this."

"I just want to reduce the swelling." He continued to

massage her ankle. “I’ll have the bellboy bring up an ice pack in a minute.”

She tried not to imagine his hand moving higher, his palm slowly moving over her calf, around her knee, up toward her thigh.

She couldn’t stand it anymore.

She braced her hands at his shoulders to stop him. “R.J., really. Don’t. I don’t need an ice pack either.”

He looked up at her, then his gaze dropped first to where her right hand was on his shoulder. Then followed it to her left hand. She realized how tightly she was squeezing him.

She hadn’t meant to grab him so intimately. But it was impossible to move, to let go.

He reached up and gently touched her cheek. “It’s okay,” he whispered.

She felt her lips part, felt herself move closer to him. It felt so easy, so natural. “R.J., I—I’ve really missed you.”

A sad smile formed on his lips. “Me, too, Princess. Me, too.”

“It’s been such a long time.”

“I know.” His thumb moved on her cheek. “I didn’t think I’d ever see you. Let alone be made to act like your loving husband again.”

They both stilled at the words. Hearing the actual term seemed to drive home the enormity of what they were about to do. To actually travel overseas together where they would pretend they’d never even separated.

R.J. stood suddenly. “We have quite a few days ahead of us, don’t we?”

Such an understatement. What in heaven’s name was she doing? Why was she letting her attraction rule her again? Their circumstances were complicated enough. She shouldn’t be here. She shouldn’t be admitting to having feelings for him.

R.J. had his head tilted back, his eyes shut. He looked utterly drained.

Reality had hit them both.

She cleared her throat. Did he realize how difficult it was going to be traveling with him, pretending to be his woman? All the while knowing that none of it meant anything. Not to him.

"I'm not sure I'll be able to act the part," she admitted.

R.J.'s lips pursed into a tight line. When he looked back down at her, all hint of gentleness had left his eyes.

"I'll call you a taxi," he declared. "Try to stay off that ankle until the swelling goes down."

"I—I will," she answered, faltering at the sudden change in him.

"I'll instruct the bellboy to come help you when the cab arrives. Now, if you'll excuse me, I realize I do have a lot of work to do."

She watched dumbfounded as he walked away. It was regret. He was angry for letting himself come so close to her again. Well, so be it. It was fine with her if he wanted her to leave.

He turned back to her suddenly, and she nearly jumped. "Oh, and Angel?"

"Yes?"

"I'm sorry I lost myself a minute ago. I won't let things go this far again."

She bit down on her lip, anger completely numbing any pain she may have felt in her foot. She gave him a stiff nod in response.

What did she expect? She was twenty-seven years old and still hadn't learned to manage her overzealous hormones when it came to her ex-husband. Dressing up for him, albeit unintentionally, taunting him. She had to get a handle on her attraction. Before it was too late.

His next words just drove it home. "Do me a favor and don't pack that dress."

* * *

R.J. watched from his window as the bellboy assisted Angeline into her cab. He cursed himself as the car pulled away from the curb and drove into traffic.

He'd almost lost control. And the pretending hadn't even started yet.

I'm not sure I'll be able to act the part.

How could he have been so stupid? That's all this was supposed to be—the two of them acting, for a business deal. He'd almost lost himself again. Just because she'd worn that dress. First he'd lashed out at her, then he'd been ready to ravish her right there on the sofa. He'd spent years disciplining himself, working toward his goals. Now he couldn't contain himself because of a damn dress.

Her father's words echoed in his head. *"I hope you're smart enough to stay away from her. Sign those damn divorce papers already. So she can move on to someone more suitable."*

R.J. gripped his glass tighter in his hand. To think, for a split second upon accidently running into him, R.J. had thought that maybe Richard Scott was cornering him to make peace. Perhaps he would even commend him on how far R.J. had come since he'd become his son-in-law.

Foolish. Why had he expected anything like acceptance from a man like Richard Scott when his very own father had never given him anything of the kind? Why had R.J. expected anything but scorn?

And why had he expected it of the man who'd once even tried to bribe him out of his daughter's life?

R.J. walked over to the bar and slammed his glass down. What remained of his drink splashed over the side onto the rich glossy wood. She was right. This was simply a part he'd be playing.

Then he'd remove himself from her life for good. Or

Angeline would never have a chance to reconcile with her father.

This wasn't going to be a reunion between them. She'd asked for his help, and he was still such a fool for her he'd agreed to give it. Hell, he'd done more than that. He was actually going to travel to the supplier's estate with her. But he had his motives. She'd lost everything because of him; her inheritance, standing, her father.

But there was no excuse for letting Angel get under his skin the way she had tonight. Why had she shown up here? She didn't know what she wanted. In one breath she was talking about how much she'd missed his touch and in the next she was reminding him they were doing nothing but playacting for the sake of her business.

It couldn't be anything more.

Sure, he was no longer the outclassed lowbrow he'd been when they'd first met. But he didn't have the bloodlines her friends and family required. As her father had unequivocally explained at their unexpected meeting, that wasn't something he could work hard to achieve. No matter how hard he tried.

For some unknown reason fate had brought them together once again. Maybe his life had become too peaceful. Maybe he was becoming too complacent. And some unknown force had said: let's see how you deal with Angeline Scott again all these years later.

R.J. let out a small laugh. That's what it was. This was all a big joke. A joke on him. Well, he wouldn't forget again. He'd remember from now on that they were both only playing a part.

"Angel, wake up."

"Hmm?"

"Wake up, we're landing. Final destination, we're here."

A warm hand gently caressed a path down her cheek,

and she turned her face into it. R.J. was touching her. She was snuggled close up against him.

A small sound of pleasure escaped her lips through the caverns of sleep.

"Oh, Lord," she heard a strangled voice say. She moved her lips into the hand that was now cupping her face.

Funny, her dreams had never felt so real before. She didn't want to wake up from this one. A curl of heat slowly kindled inside her rib cage. The harsh jolt of the wheels touching down shocked her awake. Angeline shook the cobwebs out of her head and forced herself to move. Her surroundings slowly started to register.

So it hadn't been a dream.

"I guess I was asleep," she said groggily.

"You say and do some interesting things in your sleep. I'd forgotten."

She was practically sprawled on top of him. "I—I'm sorry." Though it almost hurt to pull back to her own seat, she forced herself.

"For?" he asked.

"For collapsing on top of you like that. I hope I didn't make you too uncomfortable."

He swallowed, tension etched in his face. "Not in the way you think." His words put her at a loss for her own. The plane came to a sudden and jerky stop.

She barely noticed when the speaker above them crackled and then came fully to life. "Ladies and gentlemen, your flight crew welcomes you to Tels, Mondolavia. Please go to your left as you enter the airport. We look forward to serving you again."

R.J. dropped his hand and stood. Moving with his usual efficiency and competence, he pulled their bags from the overhead compartments.

"I guess the adventure begins," he remarked as he stepped aside to let her into the aisle.

"I guess."

After a brief stop at the gate, they made their way to the airport exit. She heard someone shouting for them as they walked outside.

"Angeline, R.J. Welcome, welcome." It was Tavov.

"Tavov!" She felt a genuine smile. "So nice to see you again."

"Yes, same to you." He motioned for them to follow him to a waiting car at the corner.

Angeline slowly took in her surroundings. The sun appeared bright in the sky, but the temperature outside was comfortably warm. Lush hills surrounded the airport. The air smelled faintly of the sea.

A comfortable silence filled the space of the luxury vehicle when they started the drive. The road curved around hills and cliffs. In the distance, the water gleamed. Finally, they turned onto the small road that lead to the Bay's estate. A large iron gate came into view. Tavov waited at the entrance while a man in tan overalls ran out to let them in. He tipped his head in greeting as they drove past.

With all the stress over securing the deal, she'd nearly forgotten how lovely the Bay's property was. The large white house with pillars stood majestically at the end of the road. Angel found herself distracted by the Greek-style mansion and the lush landscape surrounding it. She noticed the brilliant greenery as they all got out of the car. Nowhere else had she seen grass quite that color of jade.

The front door flew open, and Mila stepped outside. Waving, she walked toward them as Tavov and R.J. emptied the trunk of their bags.

"Angeline, R.J. So great to see you again."

"Hello, Mila." Angel accepted the other woman's hug, then watched as she embraced R.J., as well.

"Come, let's get you settled."

They followed Mila through the large foyer. The walls

were adorned with colorful Middle Eastern art. Thick silk rugs covered wooden floors.

"We've put you in a suite on the second floor," Mila said over her shoulder as they followed her up a winding staircase.

A suite. R.J. looked over his shoulder at her. They hadn't had a chance to discuss their living arrangements. Of course the Bays would expect them to be comfortable in a one-bedroom suite.

If she had any luck whatsoever, there would be a large couch in addition to the bed.

"This is it." Mila indicated a door on their left. Angel crossed her fingers as the other woman opened the door. They entered a charming, spacious room. Angel took stock of her surroundings. Sliding glass doors leading to a balcony offered a majestic view of the beach and ocean. Two wooden rocking chairs sat on opposite corners, on either side of the glass doors. A large bed with an ornate burgundy cover faced the balcony. There was a colorful silk Turkish rug covering the center of the wooden floor, clearly handmade.

The room was beautiful. But there was no couch. That finger-cross thing never did seem to work.

"Through that door is the washroom." Mila pointed. "And right next to it is the closet."

Angel realized it immediately. R.J.'s expression told her he did, too. Far from being lucky in any way, by some strange stroke of misfortune, the layout of the small suite was uncannily similar to that of their first shared apartment as newlyweds.

Images flooded her mind. Her eyes darted toward the bed, and the visuals tripled in intensity.

She looked back to find R.J. watching her. A warm flush

reached her cheeks. He must have known exactly where her thoughts had drifted. She didn't bother to look away.

"What do you think?" Mila was asking, motioning to the room in general.

"It should do just fine." R.J. smiled, but Angel didn't miss the hardened timbre that had reached his voice.

Angeline turned away from the bed and walked over to the balcony.

"Mila, the view is breathtaking. We'll be more than comfortable. Thank you."

Mila practically beamed in pleasure, apparently taking her responsibility as hostess seriously. "In that case, I'll let the two of you freshen up. Why don't you meet us downstairs for afternoon tea when you're ready?"

Angel watched as Mila shut the door behind her. R.J. had walked over next to her to stare out over the balcony.

"I just can't believe all this." What had she gotten the two of them into?

She removed the elastic holding her ponytail in place. Hard to believe, but she was actually feeling a slight ease in the tenseness of her shoulders. Even given R.J.'s close proximity.

She turned to look at the bed. "I suppose we'd better figure out our sleeping arrangements."

"There's nothing to talk about. I'll find a way to make myself comfortable on the floor."

"That hardly seems possible."

"I've slept in worse conditions. Way worse."

Still, she didn't want him to have to sleep on a hard floor. Especially tonight, following the long trip they'd taken. But what other choice was there?

"R.J., we could take turns. We're in this together, it's only fair. Why don't I sleep on the floor tonight?"

He turned quickly. "I have yet to make a woman uncomfortable while spending the night with me. I don't intend to start with my Brahmin wife."

The sexual innuendo stopped her heart briefly. And exactly how many women fell into that category anyway?

The last thought triggered an angry response. "This may be hard for you to believe, but I have 'roughed it' in the past."

It wasn't a bald-faced lie, although most people's definition of roughing it probably couldn't be held comparable to hers. Still, she'd gone camping, hadn't she? Even if it was in a well-equipped cabin with all the worldly comforts in the luxurious backdrop of the Swiss mountains.

The corner of his mouth lifted. All right, so it was a bald-faced lie.

"Go ahead and laugh," she told him.

He did. And he looked so sexy, so incredibly appealing. Suddenly all she wanted to do was to touch him, to have him hold her.

"Angel, you sleep on the bed. Believe me, the hardness of the floor is the last thing I'll be thinking about tonight."

She didn't have to guess what he meant. This would be the first night in three years they'd been so close together. Only a few feet apart with the sensuous sounds of the ocean drifting into the room. Five days pretending to be really married, together twenty-four hours a day. She shivered slightly. She had to stay focused on the issue here. Getting Mila and Tavov to sign the supply contract and going back to Boston with a clear plan for growth. She could handle a few awkward days to achieve that.

She turned away and made for the bureau chest behind her. "Well, perhaps we could find you a blanket or something. That throw rug, as beautiful as it is, is not going to do much for your back."

She pictured him sprawled out on the floor asleep and furiously started rummaging through the drawer's contents. There didn't seem to be anything in there besides a thin afghan.

He was behind her all of a sudden and grabbed her hand gently. "I'll be fine on the floor, Angel."

She stilled at the contact and looked up to meet his eyes in the mirror above the chest. The awkwardness of their surroundings hung unspoken between them.

"The room looks so familiar." She wasn't sure she had meant to say it out loud.

"Yeah, it does."

Did it bring back memories for him, too? Memories of the intimate, unguarded moments they'd shared?

"I've thought of that first apartment often," she admitted.

"Some things are better forgotten."

She looked up at him, saw the familiar yet frustrating curtain guarding any emotion in his eyes.

"Perhaps you're right," she said. But there were some things a woman could never forget. That was the apartment he'd carried her into as his wife, and they hadn't left the bedroom until the next afternoon. It was there where they'd talked about all their dreams around the ragged breakfast bar in the center of the kitchen.

But it was also the same apartment where they'd had their harshest arguments.

"It never occurred to me we wouldn't be moving out of there together," she found herself admitting.

He nodded slightly in the mirror above her. "Me neither. But we both made our decisions. Right or wrong."

Would he ever understand? She turned back around and leaned against the bureau. "I guess we'll always disagree on the importance I placed on starting my own business."

The raised eyebrow suddenly fell into a straight line. "Is that what you think?"

She shook her head. He looked away from her, up toward the ceiling.

"I told you how important it was for me to start this business venture, R.J. But all that mattered to you was getting away. You couldn't wait to leave Boston."

He lifted his hand in the air impatiently. "I had no business in Boston anymore. Not after college. And especially not after we started to grow apart."

"We were still close in a lot of ways when things started to fall apart."

He swallowed. "Being compatible in bed can only take a couple so far, Angel. Every time I moved in your circles, it just made me realize what a mistake—" He stopped midsentence.

She tried to ignore the hurt. *Mistake.* There was that word again. Damn him. What they'd felt for each other had not been a mistake. Ever.

"R.J., I had no circles."

He let out a short laugh. "No? What about all the country club boys? The ones who hovered around you like hornets. The same ones who looked at me like I was dirt every time I had the audacity to touch you, even after we were married? What about all the debutantes who looked at you like you'd lost your head?"

"Those were your friends, too. From the football team and from class."

He laughed at that. "Angel, those so-called friends never treated me as more than a wannabe. But when you were around, instead of shunning me outright, they just ignored me. All of them, except, of course, for Shanna."

"I—I just can't believe that."

He laughed again, a humorless, empty sound. He was mocking her. "Face it, with very rare exception, anyone at all close to you hated that you chose me."

"Well I seem to recall several of the females in my so-called 'circles' flirting shamelessly with you, sometimes right under my nose."

"Yeah?" He stepped closer to her, and all the air seemed to have sucked out of the small room. "Even as they propositioned me they made it clear I shouldn't harbor any delusions of grandeur. But they were just being who they were." Her confusion must have shown on her face because he continued. "At least those women were straight with me, Angel. With them I knew from the beginning exactly where I stood."

"What are you saying? That what you got from me wasn't real? That somehow our marriage wasn't real?"

"I'm not saying a thing. The time to say anything about it all is long gone. We were just too young, and too naive, to get married."

He turned from her suddenly and thrust a hand through his hair. "Listen, this is useless. It's gonna be hard enough staying here in such close quarters. Let's just forget about slamming out the past, okay? In the end, it's simple. Our worlds didn't belong together."

It wasn't okay. How could he say those things, think those things? "You think it was senseless of us to fall in love?"

R.J. started to rub his eyes. "It hardly matters. Why don't we just wipe the slate clean, all right? Starting here, starting now. I promise to do whatever I can to make this easier between us." But she noticed he wasn't answering her.

"We have to act and sound like a true married couple after all," he continued when she was silent.

Sure, like a married couple who held hands, who touched each other affectionately. Who shared the same hopes and dreams. Not to mention shared the same bedroom.

Well, he was wrong about her; she'd tried damn hard to make it work between them.

Hadn't she?

CHAPTER SEVEN

SOMETHING WAS DEFINITELY crawling up her leg.

Angeline shook out her left foot, kicking several blades of long grass in the process.

Whatever it was, it was very persistent. She'd swatted it away several times already. There was barely enough light to study her leg if she wanted to look down and identify her tormentor. She didn't.

"Maybe it wasn't such a good idea to go wanderin', huh, missy?" she admonished herself. *Great.* It was never a good sign when she started talking to herself. But she'd just wanted to get away on her own for a while. Just to clear her head.

The luscious, fragrant bushes of Mila's Bloom had beckoned her, and she'd decided to walk around the orchard. Only problem was, now she was lost. And by herself. The shrubs had grown higher than she remembered, and the house was no longer visible.

Now what?

It felt like she'd been in the fields for hours even if her watch told her it was less than twenty minutes. How long did this shrubbery go on anyway?

She suddenly felt a chill. Even with the full moon above, the evening had suddenly grown inexplicably dark. Like a forgotten room that had been shut off from the rest of the house after its occupant had passed away.

The tickly itch traveling up the back of her knee returned. This time it went clear up to her thigh. Angeline gasped in horror. Who would have thought that she'd had the ability to jump and swat at her leg at the same time?

The circus must need some kind of talent like that. If this whole tea business thing didn't work out… She shook her head at the silly thoughts and continued moving.

Something grabbed her.

Panic darkened what little light the moon afforded. Angel struggled to pull herself out of the strong grip that had suddenly gotten hold of her. There was a large, male hand wrapped around her upper arm.

"Calm down, it's just me." The unmistakable voice came from behind her ear.

The hand slowly removed itself, and she hurled herself around. "What do you think you're doing sneaking up on me like that?"

"I could ask you what you're doing out here wandering alone."

She was going to ignore that question. As well as his patronizing tone. "Jeez, R.J. You nearly scared the logic out of me!"

"Again, I ask what you're doing out here. In the dark, by yourself."

Angeline huffed in frustration. Her heart still thudded with fear. "I just needed some time and some air. To think."

"Didn't look like a stroll. It looked more like you were karate chopping some of the plants."

"Ha, ha. I was just about to make my way back."

He quirked an eyebrow. "Is that so? You weren't lost at all?"

"Most definitely not."

"Right." Skepticism laced his voice. "Were you checking out the crop, making sure it's all still worthy of your investment?"

She sighed, utterly weary now after all the excitement. "Was that a jab? I just want to grow my business, R.J. I'm starting to get tired of trying to justify that to you."

He crooked a finger under her chin. It was an innocent

yet oddly sensual action. Under the evening sky, amid a field of aromatic grass with the sounds of the ocean in the distance. Having him touch her in such circumstances was risky. “Angel, you don’t have to explain your determination to me. I know firsthand how powerful that is in you.”

“I know you didn’t mean that as a compliment, but in the interest of harmony, I’m going to take it as one.”

“By all means.” He stepped aside and gestured for her to go forward. “So, lead the way.”

“Ah…me?”

He nodded at her solemnly. “Yes. You know…because you’re absolutely not lost.”

“Very funny.”

“Will you admit it?”

She waited without answering, tapping her foot.

He finally broke the silence with a laugh. “I knew it.”

“Don’t get cute with me, Robert James Davet. I’d rather not stay in this grass any longer than I have to.”

“It was your decision to come out here, Princess.” He rubbed his chin. “Now, admit you were lost or I won’t show you the way.”

“But there are bugs in here,” she hissed.

His only answer was to cross his arms in front of his chest.

“Great,” Angel muttered. “I’m in one of the most beautiful parts of the world and instead of enjoying it I’m making myself a late-night snack for a swarm of insects.”

“All to break out into the herbal tea market.”

She sighed. “It would mean so much more than that. It would mean a huge expansion.”

Suddenly, the air grew serious. “Let’s assume everything goes smoothly on this trip. You get the deal for the exclusive distribution rights. The expansion goes through, the new tea is an instant phenomenon.”

Angel closed her eyes, imagining that very scenario.

"And every one of my employees will be secure for the foreseeable future. That's all I'm hoping for."

He nodded. "It does sound great. But then what? There's still a loose end."

"Which is?"

"What are you going to tell the Bays when we finally go through with the divorce?"

The question brought a chill to her insides. Divorce. Finally. Of course, she'd known all along that's where her life was headed. She'd be a divorced woman eventually. She and R.J. had just been too busy to move forward with finalizing and before she knew it, three years had gone by. Still, to hear him say it outright somehow jolted her in a way she didn't want to examine.

She gave a small shrug. "There will be only one thing to say, I suppose."

"And that would be?"

"That despite our furtive attempts, we couldn't find a way to make it work."

At that point, at least, she'd be telling the Bays the truth.

Tavov and Mila appeared to have retired for the evening. R.J. shut the door of the suite quietly behind him. He looked up to find Angel gazing nervously at the bed.

They still hadn't worked out their final sleeping arrangements.

He started to reassure her of his intentions when she suddenly jumped. High.

"Oh my God, it's on my neck!" Angel started desperately swatting at her hair.

"What? What's the matter?"

"It's crawling into my hair." There was a note of sheer terror in her voice.

"What is?"

"I'm sure I don't know." She sounded near hysterical. "I

assume it's a bug. A large, hairy, slimy bug! It must have crawled on me in the fields."

"Angel, come here and I'll take a look," he tried to say in his most calm, least amused voice. It wasn't easy.

"Get it out, now, please," she shrieked.

The head of a successful distribution business and here she was hysterical over a small bug. "Angel, sweetheart. Just calm down and let me look. But please try not to make any more noise. You're going to have Mila and Tavov wondering what I'm doing to you in here."

He gently pulled her by the shoulders and turned her around. Lifting her hair up, he tried to peer through the mass of tresses to examine her scalp.

"There's nothing there."

"Don't tell me that! I can feel it."

"I don't see anything," he insisted, trying to reassure her.

"Of course you don't, it's inside my hair." She resumed the frantic swatting.

"Look, just relax. Here, let me." He cupped the back of her neck, plunging his fingers into her hairline. *Mistake.* He could feel her pulse racing beneath his hand.

"Is it gone?"

It quickly became a struggle to catch his breath. "I don't see or feel anything."

"Please just make sure."

He moved his hand around, trying to ignore the soft, silky feel of her hair across his forearm. A light, citrus scent drifted to his nose. She still used the same shampoo.

She stopped moving, and they both stilled. He had to clear his throat before he could continue. "There's nothing crawling on you, Angel."

"Are you certain?"

Why was it becoming so hard to breathe? "I'm certain," he managed to croak out.

She didn't answer right away, still breathing heavily. "I guess I must have imagined it."

All right, you've checked. Pull your hands off her now. But he couldn't bear to, it was too hard. Her pulse quickened under his palm.

"I guess so." His hand seemed to move on its own. He plunged his fingers farther into the silkiness of her hair and felt her shudder. Soft, she was so soft. Her hair, her skin. His calloused hand felt as if he was running it through a cloud. With zero control, he pulled her closer, her back snug against his chest.

A cricket chirped in the distance, as if to issue a warning cry. He didn't heed it, just gave in as he allowed his lips their slow descent.

She inhaled sharply, and it was all he needed. He tried to bargain with himself, one small kiss, just to see if her skin still held the same warmth. But he knew that was a lie. He had no doubt it would.

He was right. Nothing could have prepared him for the sweet torment that assaulted him as he let his lips fall on the back of her neck. He heard her groan and responded by yanking her closer. Her back was up against him completely. Fire spread through his shirt, then moved lower.

He couldn't stop himself from nuzzling closer into her neck. Even as he cursed himself, he splayed shaky fingers on her abdomen. There was no hiding her effect on him now. She let her head fall back as he moved the kisses around her neck.

He had to stop. But as insane as this was, it felt too right. Besides, he couldn't have stopped if he wanted to. Not when she was leaning into him and uttering those maddeningly erotic sounds under her breath.

She reached behind her and pulled his head closer. His hand moved up, meeting soft, yielding flesh. His fingers burned at the touch of her skin. He started to lower the collar of her dress. He wanted to expose her to him, to run his hands over her breasts, to feel her and taste her like he had so often in the past.

He shouldn't be touching her like this. He shouldn't be wanting her like this. Men like him didn't belong with ladies like Angeline Scott. God, he knew from experience how devastating the results could be of such a foolish union.

Somehow he managed to pull himself away and forced himself to step back. He'd done it again.

Angel turned to look at him and wrapped her arms around herself. "What just happened, R.J.?"

"Something that shouldn't have happened. An error in judgment."

He rubbed a palm across his face and forced himself to calm down, to squash the unwanted urges.

"Well, it did happen, and so did the incident in your apartment back in Boston."

He let out a small laugh. "I guess I need to learn how to stop making the same mistakes, don't I?" He heard himself echo his father's words.

Angel flinched. "It's not that simple. And I, for one, would like to talk about this."

"I don't think there's anything to talk about."

She spread her arms. "How can you say that? This is the second time we've lost control with each other."

She was right, but there was no point in analyzing something that shouldn't have happened in the first place. "What exactly are we supposed to discuss?"

She squeezed her eyes shut. "Don't you have anything to say?"

"Not really. Except that it won't happen again."

"You're so certain?" she asked. "Can you just turn your feelings off like that? Is it that easy?"

"Easy isn't always—"

"Yeah, I know," she interrupted, impatience laced in her

voice. "Easy isn't always better. Well, difficult isn't necessarily right either."

"I suppose with rare exception."

"No, there's nothing rare about it. Why can't you just trust me enough to tell me what you're feeling?"

He took a deep breath. How absurd, to think he could just say it all to her. To tell her that he'd learned long ago that he couldn't just grab what he wanted. Everything had its price, everything had to be fought for. And sometimes the casualties were too high to risk. Why couldn't she understand that?

"What exactly is it that you want from me?" he asked her.

When she responded, the punch had gone out of her voice. "I just want to know, I guess. To understand. Every time you touch me, it's the way it was. I know you feel it, too. But then you just shut yourself off. How can you do that so well?"

"Angel, it's not too difficult to understand. We both learned the hard way that we're too different. We don't want the same things. You're charities and society balls, I'm South End litter. An intense attraction is not going to change that."

"Are you sure you know me so well?"

"I know what you were born into, the legacy you should be a part of. And I also know how our marriage came between all of that."

"You can't believe any of that matters to me."

"You say that now. How do you know you're not going to wake up one morning and resent that you lost your rightful inheritance because of an impulsive decision you made when you were barely an adult?"

"Falling in love with you was not impulsive. You know," she started. "Shanna said something to me right before this trip."

"What was that?"

"She said the only two people who can break up a relationship are the two people in it."

He knew she was waiting for a response. But suddenly he was just too tired to come up with one.

"Angel, it's late. We're both very tired. Not to mention jet-lagged. We'll talk in the morning."

"No. In the morning you'll just come up with a sugar-coated way to brush everything aside. Just this once, I want you to talk to me instead of pushing me away."

He didn't want this, didn't need to be thinking about all this right now. Her look told him she wasn't in any mood to drop the matter.

"Don't you understand?" he blurted. "We can't forget that people as different as you and me will never really mesh. We're from two completely different worlds."

"And therefore we should have never gotten married? Is that it?" She crossed her arms in front of her chest and shook her head slightly. "What a double standard you have, R.J. Do you have any idea how pompous that would sound coming from, say, someone like me? Someone who grew up with money. What makes you think it's okay for you to come to a conclusion like that?"

"I guess it's one of the few luxuries my background afforded me." He knew his tone held the warmth of a glacier.

"So, just how far do you think such a generality should go?" she pressed.

He shook his head. "What do you mean?"

"Where would you draw the line? Just at marriage? Or any emotional involvement?" What in the world was she getting at?

She stepped up to him, her finger pointed at his chest. "Is it all right to share a purely physical attachment? What if there's no emotional tie? Then is it okay?"

Now they were moving into dangerous territory. Way

too dangerous. "What the hell are you talking about? Is what okay?"

She shrugged. "A casual toss in the hay for instance. Is it all right for us to sleep together, as long as that's all we do?"

She'd shocked him. But he recovered quickly. Before allowing himself to realize what he was about to do, he was in front of her. In an instantaneous movement, he had her by the shoulders and pulled her closer.

"Is that an offer, Angel?"

Suddenly the topic at hand was very different. "I just want to make sure I understand you correctly," she said slowly.

"First let me make sure I understand. Are you offering a no-strings-attached little romp? Something to add to the excitement factor of this trip?"

She started chewing her lip. "I'd like to know exactly where you draw the line between your rules and your feelings."

"Acting on our feelings is what got us into trouble years ago." Even as he said it, he pulled her closer. "We don't want to do it again."

"Why not?" she demanded. "Didn't we agree that the only taboo was any emotional involvement?"

He lowered his head, speaking into her lips. "I'd just like to be clear. Is the respectable and ever so proper Angeline Scott offering her soon-to-be ex-husband a casual fling?"

She swallowed. "It appears so."

"It better be more than appearance, Angel. You'd better be damn sure you're prepared for me to take you up on it."

"What makes you think I'm not?" As good as she was at bluffing, he knew her too well.

But he wasn't feeling terribly merciful. "What if I call your bluff? Right here. This very moment. Will you still be as sure?"

"You know I'm a woman of my word, R.J."

"I know you used to be."

He kissed her then, a hungry kiss. One meant to take everything and give nothing in return. She responded with longing. She wanted him. He could feel how much.

He stopped finally, shaking with desire. "Well, you've definitely changed. Such a worldly proposition. Apparently you've done some growing up in the last few years."

"I don't see why we can't be adult about this." She cleared her throat, looking him straight in the eye.

"Adult." He smiled, then took his hands off her. It took all his will, but he reluctantly let her go. "Go to bed, Angel." He turned and made his way to the door before he could regret it.

"Wait, where are you going?"

He didn't bother to turn back around. "Out."

Angel watched the door shut and wanted to throw something at it. Sheer will prevented her from going after him. That and pride. She wasn't going to beg, had come way too close to it just now. She turned and faced the balcony doors. The night had grown dark now, so dark the world beyond the railings appeared to be a limitless empty space.

She'd said she was open to a casual fling. Until the words had left her mouth she wouldn't have believed it. Why had she made such an empty offer? She would have given up so much if R.J. had taken her up on it. She would have given up her heart. The moment he touched her again intimately the already fragile shell around her heart would have crumbled. She knew that was the last thing R.J. wanted.

Why was he trying so hard to deny that he was at least physically attracted to her if nothing else? It didn't matter. He didn't want to get close to her again. So why had she done it?

Silly question. She knew the answer. Because when it came to R.J. she was oh, so ready to take whatever she could get. No matter what the consequences to her pride. He meant that much to her. He always had.

Shanna had been so wrong that night back when they'd indulged in all the junk food. R.J. had left for the West Coast because he'd wanted to. Not to give her an out, not because he'd felt guilty in any way. He'd wanted to move to Silicon Valley, and he was going to do it with or without her. He was an enormously successful businessman now. But he still didn't seem to want their marriage to continue. Just today he'd asked how she was going to break the news of their divorce to the Bays when it happened.

That told her everything she needed to know.

Angel walked over to the balcony doors and pressed her forehead against the glass. She would go crazy if she kept thinking about it, if she kept thinking about him.

Her skin was still on fire, and her breasts felt heavy with the want of his touch. But she would try to ignore all that. As unlikely as it was, she'd try to get some sleep. She'd put her head on the pillow and close her eyes.

And she'd pray that she had the strength to deny her feelings come tomorrow. Deny them as strongly as R.J. insisted on denying his.

R.J. stepped slowly into the suite and winced when the floor creaked loudly. He held his breath for a beat, waiting to see if Angel shifted.

No hint of sound came from the bed a few feet away, and he finally let out his breath. He didn't want to wake her. He didn't want to pick up where they'd left off. Didn't know if this time he'd be strong enough to walk away.

Shutting the door quietly behind him, he thought about what she'd said earlier. His wife had done some maturing since they'd parted. He couldn't get over how up-front she'd been. He'd known, hadn't he? When she'd shown up at his suite back in Boston, looking so utterly seductive, he'd harbored no illusions about what her true intent was.

Angeline Scott apparently missed the kind of rough-house, tumbledown lovemaking they'd once shared. Now that was all she wanted from him. She wasn't even shy about admitting it.

So very tempting. What kind of man would that make him if he took her up on it? Knowing that any kind of reconciliation was out of the question. Not if there was any chance of Richard Scott taking his daughter back into the fold.

A chilling thought raced into his brain. What if she didn't miss such physical enjoyment at all? All this time they'd been apart, maybe she had found such release regularly elsewhere. With other men?

He squeezed his eyes shut. It was no business of his. It hadn't been for three years. But the thought came close to physical pain. It took all he had to try to force it out of his mind.

His gaze focused on the outline of her leg. Long, shapely, the white sheet draped seductively around it. He imagined going up to her. Pulling the sheet up and running his hands over the smooth skin, up her leg. Higher.

He thought about the sensuous heat in her eyes as she woke and saw him. He thought about settling over her, feeling her arms go around him, touching his bare back.

Damn. R.J. moved back to lean against the door, and this time the creak was louder.

It would be so easy to go to her. He wanted to so badly. But he wouldn't. Maybe she could be casual about resuming a physical relationship, but there was no way he could be. Not that he hadn't had casual flings himself. He just couldn't with her. Never with her.

He started to settle himself on the floor. No need to bother with a comforter or any padding, he figured. He wasn't going to get any sleep anyway.

CHAPTER EIGHT

ANGELINE STEPPED OUTSIDE into the gentle, warm air of the veranda where Mila, Tavov and R.J. were already seated around the table. A soft morning breeze caressed her bare arms and legs and ruffled the sundress she was wearing. In the distance, she could hear the gentle waves of the sea. Bright sunshine accented the brilliant green of the lush plants surrounding them.

"I hope I haven't kept you waiting," she said, addressing all three at the table. She picked up her dining napkin and sat down, trying to ignore the fluttering in her stomach caused by R.J.'s stare. Dear God, the man only had to look at her and her stomach did jumping jacks.

She'd woken in the middle of the night to find him sleeping on the floor. It had taken all she had not to pull him into bed with her. This morning he had showered silently and beat her downstairs.

"Not at all," Mila answered her. "We've just been discussing the upcoming wedding."

Tavov leaned over and patted his wife's hand. "Mila's very excited. Let me tell you a wedding around these parts is a grand affair."

"Yes indeed." His wife nodded. "There'll be beautiful music, of course a ton of food. The whole village is set to attend. Everyone is just so excited."

Angeline picked up a pastry from the large tray in the center of the table, a filo dough pocket stuffed with various cheeses. Steam rose from the hot center as she broke it open.

Taking a bite, she felt a pang of envy for the bride. How

lucky to be looking forward to the rest of your life with the man you loved. She looked over at R.J. and found him staring at her. For a moment she could do nothing but hold his gaze. She had so anticipated their own marriage. By no means was it a grand affair. Just two people so in love they couldn't wait to take on life together.

Mila's voice broke through her thoughts. "I really think you'll enjoy the celebration, Angel. We're going to have folk dancers dressed in traditional costume. They're the best in the area. And you and I will be able to help with the henna ceremony before the reception."

"The henna ceremony?" Angeline asked, intrigued.

"Yes, it's tradition. A craftswoman from the village will brand the young bride's hands with decorative patterns using dark red henna. It's absolutely beautiful. Such a shame it fades in a few weeks.

"The women will do that while the men tease the groom about the chains of married life." She smiled at Tavov. "All the while, they'll be relentlessly filling his glass with ouzo."

R.J. shifted again, and Angel stole a glance at him. He seemed bothered.

"Sounds like a real fete," R.J. declared then, before turning back to Tavov. "I think I'll take you up on the tour of the grounds you offered earlier. If now is a good time."

Angel felt an urge to throw the pastry at him. He was clearly trying to get away. From her.

Tavov nodded. "Yes, yes of course. Whenever you're ready."

"I'm ready right now," he said as he finished off the rest of his breakfast.

The two men stood and made their way toward the orchards. Angeline watched R.J.'s retreating back and then turned to see Mila smiling at her.

"I can tell by the way you're looking at your husband, as if you'd like to chase after him, that this trip is just what the two of you needed. I knew I was right about that. You love him very much, don't you?"

Angeline tried not to gasp out loud. She could only nod. Adoration was definitely not the reason she wanted to chase after R.J. right now.

"It's obvious you and R.J. are committed to each other," Mila continued, oblivious to Angel's true mood. "After all, every marriage has its difficult moments. I think you're the perfect example for the young bride and groom. They're really looking forward to meeting you."

The grin faded quickly. The perfect couple? They weren't even a real couple.

"Um—thank you," was all she could mutter.

Mila suddenly smiled wider. "You know, I have the perfect idea."

Oh, no. Another one of Mila's great ideas. Angel knew she was going to regret what was coming next. "What's that?"

"You and R.J. can offer the young couple a public toast after the nuptials. You know, along with their family and friends."

"Us?"

"Yes of course. Some words of wisdom from a seasoned marriage to one about to bloom."

Angel swallowed. Such a toast would be the most hypocritical thing she'd ever done. There had to be a way to get out of it. But she couldn't see one.

"I—uh— But there must be other people more connected to the couple who would like to do the honors." She knew it was a weak argument.

"Nonsense. It's a rare treat to have newfound friends from so far away attend such a joyous occasion. Besides, what better than to have the lucky tidings of our guests from America to bestow the same good fortune you yourself have enjoyed."

Angel wondered how often in the span of a few days she could be made to feel so horrible. She had no choice but to accept Mila's request. What possible reason could she give to refuse?

"We'd love to do it," she answered. R.J. was going to want to throttle her when he found out.

"That settles it, then," Mila said, rising. "Now, why don't you come with me while I go talk to the chef?"

"Actually, Mila, I was hoping I might be able to walk along the grounds a little. The plants are so lovely to look at."

"Yes, they are, indeed. Even after all these years, every time I look out there, it still takes my breath away." Her eyes grew distant before she sharply turned back to her. "Why don't you wait a few minutes and that way I can accompany you?"

Angel shook her head. "No need to entertain me, Mila. I know you must be terribly busy. I'll enjoy the solitude anyway."

"All right, then. I shall find you for lunch or even run into you sooner perhaps."

Mila nodded and turned to leave, her full-length skirt swirling around her ankles.

"Um, Mila?" Angel stood.

"Yes, dear?"

"Speaking of the plants, would it be terribly harmful to unearth one of them? Perhaps one of the smaller ones?" she asked.

"Certainly."

"Thank you. The scent is just so soothing. I was thinking how nice it would be to have it sit in a vase in our suite while we are here."

"That smell is like no other in the world," Mila agreed. "There are some younger, smaller plants on the southwest corner. You can unearth one of those. I'll go find a vase for you."

"Thank you," Angel replied. Heaven knew she could use all the soothing and calming of her nerves that she could get whenever she and R.J. were alone in that room together.

"Mila told me I could find you here."

Angel looked up from her crouched position on the ground. R.J. stood above her, his shoulders silhouetted against the bright rays of the sun. Shadow completely darkened his face. He looked like a mythical Greek god, come down from the heavens.

She brushed the dirt off her hands. "Yes, well. Here I am."

"Nice hat," he said with a smirk.

Angeline blew on the netting of the large safari hat Mila had lent her. "Yes, well it keeps the bugs off my face."

He crouched down beside her. "What's that smell?"

She deliberately misread his question. "The plants. They're very floral."

"I don't mean that. What's that awful, antiseptic-like smell?"

"It must be the dirt. It's somewhat damp."

He leaned closer to her and took a sniff. "Darling, I think it's you. New perfume?"

Angel turned and gave him her most vile look. "I'm wearing bug spray, all right? A really strong bug spray. Mila gave it to me."

"It is indeed strong." He didn't even try to hide his smirk. "What are you doing out here anyway?"

She resumed her digging. "I'm removing one of these plants."

"Any particular reason?"

"I just wanted one, that's all." She didn't need to see his face to feel his smirk.

"What for?"

"Just because they're nice. I thought it might brighten up our suite. Don't you think?"

She started digging at the dirt furiously now. The plant root didn't seem to want to budge.

R.J. shrugged, then crouched down beside her. "Well, the plant doesn't seem to want to cooperate in your efforts to dislodge it."

She rubbed her nose with the back of her hand through the netting. Sweat and dirt were starting to cling to her skin. "Nonsense, I've almost got it loosened." Of course, he was right. The plant was barely budging, despite all her efforts.

"If you say so." He absently rubbed a thumb on her nose through the netting, removing a smudge she must have put there.

Truth was, she was ready to give up just before R.J. had appeared. She'd been in her crouched position for who knew how long, and her knees were starting to ache.

He sighed and settled himself next to her on the ground. "Here, let me help."

"I can do it." She pushed his hand away, suddenly annoyed, though she'd be hard-pressed to say why. Probably from the effort of trying to ignore his closeness and the damp heat around them.

"You said you'd been trying for a while. Just let me help."

She didn't want his help. Didn't need him so close to her, rubbing his arm against her leg. She just wanted to dislodge one little plant. She yanked harder than she should have and ended up falling back on her bottom.

R.J. shook his head. "Why are you so damn stubborn?"

"I am not the one who's stubborn."

"Oh, no? You're sitting in the hot sweltering sun. You have dirt all over you, including on your face." He leaned over and wiped another smudge off her cheek. "But you refuse to let me help. Face it, Angel, you're stubborn. Always have been."

"Fine." She stood with a grunt, unable to bear his closeness any longer. "Go ahead, remove it."

He took another deep breath and got to work on the plant.

"The excitement certainly seems to be buzzing around the estate," she ventured by way of an attempt at conversation. She still had to somehow tell him about this toast she'd just agreed they'd give.

He gave her a brief glance over his shoulder. "You're talking about the wedding."

She dropped to her knees again next to him. "The anticipation about it is almost palpable in the air."

His shoulders lifted in the briefest of a shrug. "Well, I, for one, think it's a bit much."

"Like how?"

"Like do they really need to have over two hundred guests? What's wrong with a small, quaint wedding with close family and friends?"

"How can you say that? Mila and Tavov both said the whole village has been talking about it for months, since the happy couple got engaged, in fact."

He rubbed his eyes wearily. "That's right. I'm sure it will be a loud, crowded, boisterous affair resulting in mass quantities of aching heads the next morning." He stopped tugging on the plant and looked up at the sky. "Exactly the kind of events I usually stay away from. You wouldn't understand."

She wanted to shake him.

"You're right. I don't understand," she said with as much indignation as she could muster. "I think you sound downright heartless." All right, so that was below the belt. But she didn't know what else to say in the face of his negativity.

He suddenly let go of his hold on the plant and braced

his forearms on his knees. "What is the big deal about a large wedding? All that matters is that they both say 'I do' and move on. Doesn't it?"

She gaped at him. Move on? This was the most momentous day of these two people's lives so far. R.J. was making it sound like a dental appointment.

"That's one view. A completely boorish, insensitive one," she said.

"Well, it's the one I subscribe to." He turned his attention back to the plant.

"I can't believe you're being so detached about a young couple's declaration of love and commitment."

"I'm just being practical."

"Well, I think you're being narrow-minded and stiff." She tried to sound as bothered as she was.

"And I think all of you are being fanciful and getting overworked about a simple wedding." He wiped at the sweat on his brow with his forearm. The disdain in his voice had her heart thumping.

She shook her head, flabbergasted at his apathy. "How can you be so negative about this? What kind of toast would you be able to give with an attitude like that?"

He looked up at her. "Huh? What toast?"

Uh-oh. She hadn't meant to spring it on him that way. "Mila wants us to offer the couple a public toast after the nuptials. You know, the old toasting the new."

He looked at her like she'd grown another head. "She wants us to do what?"

"I know what you're going to say and don't bother. I had no choice but to agree to it."

"How the hell are we going to pull that off? Without laughing out loud?"

"I guess we'll just have to demonstrate extraordinary restraint."

The hurt must have sounded in her voice. He let out a

breath and rubbed some dirt off his hands. "Sorry. But you gotta admit we have no business toasting such an occasion. I especially don't."

"Why?"

He let out a laugh. "Let's just say my own parents' marriage was an utter insult to the institution. Not to mention our own little effort at holy matrimony."

"You don't really talk much about your parents."

His lips tightened into a firm line. "No, I don't."

And he clearly wasn't going to start now. She hesitated, faltering slightly at the vehemence in his voice.

"Those are not reasons to shun weddings and marriages in general. Haven't you ever had any fun at a wedding ceremony?"

"No." He looked away suddenly. "What about the fiasco your friend Joanne's wedding turned out to be for you? Because of me."

"Joanne had a very pleasant wedding. I had a great time with you."

"Yeah? And it didn't bother you? Not even a little bit?"

"What?"

"Angel, don't play coy. You know exactly what I'm talking about."

"The fact that I was dropped as a bridesmaid? R.J., I was never bothered by that. She just changed her mind about the size of the wedding party. There's nothing wrong with that."

"Is that what you told yourself?"

"What?"

"Come on Angel, she changed her mind about you as a bridesmaid right around the time you married me. You're trying to tell me there's no connection?"

"Of course not. Unexpected glitches come up when planning such events. I understood that. Adjusting a wedding party is not that uncommon."

"Joanne's sudden decision was just a bit too convenient."

"That's just ridiculous." She'd had no idea back then that he'd felt this way. He'd apparently hid so much from her.

"Is that what you really think?" he asked. "Or are you just being blind to your friend's snobbery? You can't tell me you weren't even the slightest bit resentful of me. After all, it was just one more nudge away from your rightful life."

Angel felt her confusion and hurt rapidly convert to anger. "You really think that? That something so silly as a place on someone's wedding party would affect the way I feel about you?"

"It was just more icing on the cake, wasn't it? First your father cuts you off. Then, I can't afford to give you a real wedding. You have to settle for a silly nonevent in a dingy chapel on Roxbury Street. Then you're shunned at one of your best friend's wedding."

She felt the foolish tears and prayed they wouldn't fall. Tears of pain, tears of anger. How shallow did he think she was?

"That 'silly ceremony' was one of the happiest moments of my life, R.J. I'm sorry you couldn't see that."

The look he gave her was one of sheer utter surprise. "Did you think I was faking how happy I was?" she demanded.

"Angel, you had a tendency to tell me what I wanted to hear."

"All I've ever told you is the truth."

He stood up in frustration, his disbelief clear in his stance. "You were happy about turning your wedding day into a fifteen-minute field trip? You were happy about having it rubbed in your face by your best friends that you'd obviously wasted your life and married someone so beneath you?"

She couldn't respond, outraged that he could think so low of her.

"You're telling me none of that mattered to you?" he

demanded. "How about how you suddenly lost touch with them all after we were married. All but Shanna."

"We were all busy. Starting new careers. Joanne became pregnant. None of it was intentional."

"That's the reason you stopped associating with your lifelong friends? Busy lives? Not because you'd married someone who would never really fit in at the yacht club events? Someone who'd never swung a golf club, sailed a boat? You're saying none of that had anything to do with how you and your friends suddenly grew apart."

She stepped closer and met him eye to eye. "I'm saying none of that mattered. All that ever mattered to me was being with you." She accentuated every word, daring him to challenge them.

His lips formed a curve that wasn't a smile. "That's what you tried to tell yourself, wasn't it?"

"It's what I believed." She knew she was about to go out on a limb. "It's what I still believe."

He touched her then. The gentlest brush of fingertips across her chin. "My sweet Angel," he whispered. "What I would have given to have that be enough."

She grabbed his wrist, holding it next to her face. "It could have been. It *should* have been." Dear God, why didn't he see?

"R.J., you meant so much more than silly society weddings. You meant more than anything. We did. The two of us."

His noncommittal silence infuriated her. He honestly discounted her loyalty that much. To think that things as trivial as an informal wedding and the shunning from her so-called friends would have made her resent him.

"Why can't you believe that?" She whispered the question, yearning to understand.

His eyes searched her face, but he didn't answer. Finally, he sighed and leaned back over the plant. "If you grab the bottom, I'll yank from the top. It should be enough to pull it out."

That was it. The look in his eyes told her he wasn't going to let her in any further. How could he have hidden such feelings from her? Dear God, she'd been walking through her marriage blind. She'd have done so much differently if he'd only been honest with her. It might have made a difference.

It might have saved her marriage.

She silently lowered herself back over the plant and did as he instructed. Unable to look at him, she gave the plant a forceful yank full of all the frustration and fury she was feeling. This time, the plant slid easily out, finally defeated.

CHAPTER NINE

"THEY'RE AGONIZING."

"I beg your pardon?" R.J. stood up from the table as soon as Mila entered the sitting room.

"She means the tea leaves." Angel was a step behind her. She'd changed into a light black cashmere sweater and a long silk wraparound skirt that hugged her hips provocatively. He tried not to let his eyes run down the length of her legs.

"That's right." Mila smiled at him. "You were staring into the press pot. I thought you might have been watching the tea transform as it brewed. The tea leaves change shape as the water saturates them. It's called the agonizing of the leaves."

Agonizing. He could relate. Angel gave him a knowing look and quirked an eyebrow.

R.J. pulled out the chair Mila was headed for and then waited for her to sit down. He moved toward Angel's chair, but the look she gave him was more effective than a slap on the hand. Their conversation earlier in the field hadn't been forgotten.

"So what have you two been up to all day?" Mila asked.

"Nothing exciting," he answered and thought about how incredibly wrong that statement was.

Excitement and adrenaline were still running through his blood. Her words had replayed in his mind, words that were too tempting. Too dangerous. Words that weren't reality. She might be able to fool herself. But there was no fooling him. It *hadn't* been enough that they'd cared for each other.

They were two breeds that didn't mix. He'd made his peace with that. How dare she try to make him question that now? She was playing with fire, tampering with conclusions made long ago. And now she sat there, looking as innocent as a missionary.

"Did Angeline tell you you're to speak at the wedding?" Mila clapped her hands together. "I've talked to the couple about it, and they're terribly excited."

Angel dropped her spoon with a clang, and he felt some of his anger ebbing. He'd almost forgotten all this was putting a lot of strain on her, too. He suddenly felt like a heel for the way he'd been behaving. Hell, he had to admit it was more than part self-defense. She just had to understand that they couldn't rehash the past anymore. Things could not go any further between them. He had to spend nights alone with her, for God's sake.

"I mentioned it to him earlier," Angel directed at Mila. "He was terribly happy about it." She glared at him.

Angel's tone most definitely did not match her words. Mila lifted curious eyes at the two of them, then resumed sipping her tea.

R.J. cleared his throat. "I'm just not one for public speaking, that's all. It sort of makes me nervous," he embellished.

Angel let out an unladylike snort from across the room. "That's really amazing coming from a high-level, respected CEO."

"Yes, well, it's completely different."

Angel set her cup down. "I find it fascinating, Mila, that a man who can be so successful within the cutthroat business of corporate security can be so deathly afraid of certain things."

"For God's sake." R.J. stood up. He'd have to be a fool not to understand her double meaning.

"Is there a problem?" Mila lifted an eyebrow.

No problem at all. I just don't know whether to shake my ex-wife silly or carry her upstairs.

"None whatsoever," Angel said drily.

"Are you certain, dear?" Mila asked.

"Absolutely. Why do you ask?" Angel's voice dripped with honey. The eyes boring into him told another story, however.

"Is that some kind of new American trend, then?"

R.J. looked down at the clear glass cup Angel was holding and knew immediately what Mila was referring to. He bit back a smile. Angel blinked.

"Is what?" Angel asked.

Mila leaned closer. "I'm wondering why you put both milk and lemon into your tea. Is it a new American thing to drink it curdled like that?"

Angel glanced down into her cup and wrinkled her nose. She recovered quickly. "Not yet it isn't. But who better than me to start one?"

She smiled so wide, R.J. figured it must have hurt her jaw.

Mila wasn't buying it. She kept looking back from Angel's smiling face to R.J. He just shrugged.

"I see," Mila finally said. "I think I'll go have my tea downstairs on the veranda."

"Wait." Angel stood. "I'll join you."

Mila lifted her hand. "No, dear, I don't think you should." With that she turned and walked out of the room.

"I think that was a subtle hint that she thinks we need to talk." R.J. walked over to the table.

"Yes, well, unfortunately Mila doesn't know any better, does she?"

"On the contrary. I think she's a very wise woman."

Angel sat back down with such a thud he felt himself move to catch her in case she actually missed the chair.

She started to chew her lip. The small action made her lips look so damn kissable.

"R.J., we're doing it again."

He had to refocus. "Doing what?"

"We're messing up."

"How so?"

"Mila is obviously aware there's something not right between us. Tavov is probably suspicious also."

He walked to her and lifted her slowly by the elbow. "Come on."

"Where are we going?"

"We shouldn't be talking about this here."

He guided her toward the balcony adjoining the sitting room. It overlooked the side of the house. Across them over the horizon, the sun was making a slow dip into the water. Angel moved over and leaned her elbows on the edge of the railing.

God he wanted to go to her. He wanted to pull her toward him, to tilt her head back and drink his fill of her. Their exchange in the fields earlier once again repeated in his mind. The desperate look in her eyes when she'd told him he'd been the only thing that mattered. For one split second there he had believed it. Had wanted so desperately to believe it. It had taken everything he had not to pull her into his arms. To hell with her father's cruel demands. But he couldn't.

So he was acting distant instead.

He felt a sudden pang of guilt. For his behavior, he told himself. Not for his reasons. He had to stay strong and reject his attraction. His strength and his resolve had served him well in adulthood. He was a far cry now from the scared, mousy little boy hiding from his violent father. He needed to pull on all the strength he could muster to do the right thing here.

Of course, Angel didn't know any of that, and it hardly

mattered now. She deserved a chance to fully move on, to find someone more suitable so that she could reclaim her rightful position as the sole Scott heir.

On that reminder, he forced himself to remain where he was. He watched as a group of men on the grounds below them started setting up the party-style tents. Others were stringing streamers on the plants and trees along the perimeter.

"Look, we knew things would be a little awkward." He tried not to laugh at the understatement. "But we have to be more careful, judging from Mila's reaction in there just now."

"You're right. And she told me after breakfast that it appeared we were making amends to each other."

"Right, so no more repeats of what just happened in there. Agreed?"

"Agreed. We'll have to act very different," she said without looking up, a slight hesitation in her voice.

He was doubtful, too. Playacting as the loving couple was easier said than done lately. But how the hell was he supposed to convincingly act like the man who still made love to her at night? When all he could focus on was the desperate need to do so and the clear knowledge that it would be wrong.

"Our actions as of late have been less than convincing, but we can work on fixing that," he repeated with more conviction than he felt.

"Certainly." She blew a bang off her forehead. "How?"

How the hell did he know? "Uh—I should probably hold your hand more often."

"I suppose that would be good."

"And I should probably put my arm around you more often."

She nodded emphatically. "Right. And I should pretend to enjoy it."

He snapped his head to look at her. Fury and disappointment rocketed through him until he noticed the small lift at the corner of her mouth. She actually had the nerve to tease him at a time like this.

"See if you can manage to do that," he said drily. "That should allay some of their suspicions."

"And definitely no more arguments," she said, much more serious.

She stared at him. "I just have one question."

Oh, no. "What's that?" he asked, though he really doubted he wanted to answer.

"You're usually Mr. Logical, always focused on the facts. You usually immediately home in on the most reasonable scenario. Why is it that you only appear irrational when it involves me?"

The question caught him off guard. Why exactly did he get so scattered when it came to her? Why did he still feel any sense of responsibility toward his estranged wife?

He turned away from her to walk to the other side of the balcony. "Very good question, Princess. Trust me, my life would be so much easier if I had an answer."

Before she could ask him to expand on that surprising comment, R.J. suddenly stopped in his tracks and turned to her.

"Looks like we have a chance to do some damage control," he whispered.

Damage control? What in the world was he talking about?

Sheer shock replaced her confusion as he gently lifted her chin. The breath caught in her throat, and she was afraid to look up at him, afraid of the sudden change in the conversation.

And then he was kissing her.

Dizziness assaulted her, and he must have noticed. He

lowered his hands on her arms and held her closer. The sweet contact with his lips never wavered.

She didn't know why he was suddenly doing this, didn't care. All that mattered now was that he not stop.

She noticed movement in the corner of her eye. It hit her then. Tavov had stepped onto the balcony; he was watching them. R.J. was putting on a show. He was kissing her only for Tavov's benefit.

The hurt opened fire on her heart. All of a sudden it was too much: their arguments, his demands, the tension. And the taste of him, his heat up against her.

Something snapped. She pulled her arms out of his grasp and lifted them around his neck. His sharp intake of breath didn't even make her hesitate. She stepped closer to him, feeling the rock of muscle that lined his frame.

"Oh, we need to be so much more convincing than that…" she spoke low into his ear. "A real wife," she continued, "would be much closer to her husband as he kissed her."

"Angel—" His cautionary warning died on his lips when she rubbed against him.

His arms went slack, then came around her again, tighter this time. A small voice whispered in the back of her brain. She knew she shouldn't be doing this. She shouldn't be baiting him this way.

But somehow her mouth and body wouldn't obey the logic.

"And she'd do a lot more of this."

She boldly touched her tongue to his lips to demonstrate. One of them moaned, she couldn't tell who. Maybe they'd done it in unison. His mouth pressed against hers fiercely, punishing. But the bruising kiss was more than welcome. She needed to see him moved, needed to know that at least some small spark of affectionate passion remained between them. Needed to have him touch her for her, not for the benefit of an audience.

A movement to her left told her Tavov was leaving. R.J.'s quick glance said he'd noticed it, too.

But their kiss didn't stop. His palm splayed at the small of her back, and he hauled her through the miniscule breath of space between them. Waves of pleasure rocked through her at the contact. She became more adventurous and trailed the tip of her tongue along his lips. Finally, he opened his mouth and forcefully took her in. She thought the taste of him would drive her wild. And she wanted it to, wanted to push herself to the edge of sanity and bring him there with her.

This was what her dreams had been about. This intensity she'd never forgotten. She savored the taste of him on her tongue, the feel of him against her body. She was shaking from the inside out. He wanted her. His kiss told her he always had.

He yanked her away suddenly. "What the hell?" he bit out, fury vibrating through his whole body.

It had backfired. She'd tried to elicit some response from him and instead she was the one quaking with desire. He grabbed her by the elbow and led her away from the balcony doors. All traces of gentleness were gone as he pushed her up against the wall.

What a mistake. He'd never been a man to be pushed. Somehow, she made herself meet his gaze.

"Don't play games with me, Angel."

She tried to move away, and he slapped both his palms against the wall on each side of her face. She flinched as he leaned closer, his breath hot up against her skin.

"I already told you not to push for something you're not sure you're ready to give."

She'd hurt him. R.J. attacked only when he was wounded.

Briskly, he took her by the arm and pulled her into the suite, shutting the balcony door behind them.

She cleared her throat. "I—I'm sorry. I know you don't want me to—"

His eyes narrowed, and he cut her off. "It's not about what I want." He cursed under his breath. "The whole problem is how badly I want you still." He rammed a hand through his hair. "But this can't happen between us."

Angel wanted to crawl into a hole in the ground. How many times could she throw herself at this man only to be turned down?

She had to ask the question that had been plaguing her. Couldn't avoid it any longer. "Is there someone else?"

He hesitated a brief moment, as if weighing his response. Finally, he rubbed a palm down his face. "No, there's no one else."

She couldn't help the surge of relief that shot through her. But R.J. still looked downright anguished. "Then what is it? I know there are things you're keeping from me. Things you've never let me in on. I wish you'd just trust me enough to do so now."

He studied her face. "I was trying so hard not to rehash the past on this trip."

"But it keeps coming up, doesn't it? I get it, you're still angry."

"Angry?"

"Yes. That I didn't come with you when you asked. I understand that." She took a deep breath. "I thought you'd come back."

"Oh, Angel. Sweetheart."

"The truth is, I didn't come with you because I thought you'd be back for me. I was so wrong."

He studied her face. "Maybe you're right. Perhaps it is time to come clean about some things."

"Please."

"Right before I got the job offer in Silicon Valley, your father paid me a visit."

Angeline's heart stopped for an instant, then started beating double time. This wasn't going to be something she wanted to hear. "What did my father have to say?"

"He had an offer for me."

"I don't understand." But as she said the words, the realization dawned on her. The offer was a bribe.

"He said he'd make it worth my while to take the job in California. He wanted to pay me to leave. To leave you."

Suddenly, all the pieces fell into place. R.J.'s admission answered so many questions, solved so many unanswered little mysteries: R.J.'s sudden interest in moving far away. For a job he'd barely been interested in when he'd first been offered it.

"I see," she said, trying to process it all. "That explains a lot."

"I didn't want to tell you."

"I wish you had. I could have told you right away that I don't blame you. I'm glad it worked out so well for you."

He blinked. "What are you saying?"

She swallowed past the sickening wave of nausea that had suddenly gripped her. "I'm saying it's okay. I mean, look at all you've accomplished with it."

"Wait. You think I took it. You think I took his money."

That's clearly what he was telling her, was it not? "Isn't that why you left?"

"Is that who you think I am?"

"You mean…you didn't?"

"Of course I didn't" He'd raised his voice. His eyes grew a deeper, darker shade.

He was the one getting angry? "Is that supposed to make me feel better? You didn't take my father's money, but you left anyway. Without telling me anything about what was happening."

"I knew things would never work out. Not with your father's ever-present shadow looming over us. I figured we would either take the leap and both leave, or I'd give you a chance to reunite with the only family you have. I left it in your hands."

"Unbeknownst to me." And *he* was her family by then. He was her husband.

"Your father was willing to pay me a large sum of money to stay away from you. That's the kind of man he thinks I am." He exhaled a heavy breath. "And you seem to think I'm the kind of man who could take him up on it."

She stepped right up to him, jabbed a finger at his chest. So hard her knuckle hurt. "You don't get to play the wounded party here. By keeping me in the dark about this, you made a major decision for both of us."

"Would it have made a difference in the end? If you'd known?" He grabbed the offending hand and held it in his own. "I couldn't stay there after that."

"You should have come to me. I could have explained it."

"Explained what?"

"That my father pays for everything. It's how he gets his way," she bit out. "But you made it so easy for him. You gave him exactly what he wanted, and he didn't have to pay a dime."

Angeline stood and waited as a breath of a wave slapped around her toes, the water refreshingly cool.

The sea air massaged her face. The effect should have been peaceful, but her heart was still racing, pounding against her chest. She'd abruptly left R.J. alone on the balcony in a desperate attempt to get away. Somehow, some way, she had to get her mind around what he'd just told her.

The damning secret he'd kept from her for three long years.

She heard soft footsteps behind her and realized her respite would be short-lived, however. It appeared R.J. had followed her.

"I need to talk to you," he quietly said behind her. His voice was tight. He drew a breath. "I'm sorry."

"Are you apologizing for what just happened, or what you've been keeping from me all this time?"

He blew out a breath. "Either. Both."

She bit down on the scathing response that came to her lips. What good would that do? What's done was done. "Apology accepted."

"That's it?"

"What else?"

"You have to understand something, Angel. I'm not sure I'd do anything differently if given the same reality today. I did what I thought was best."

Dear heavens. He honestly believed that. "Then there really is nothing else to say, is there?"

She plastered an insincere smile on her face. "Hey, listen. It's okay. Right now, we're business partners, right? Not your everyday garden-variety type but business partners just the same. Let's just focus on that for the time being." She herself had to, or she might just lose her mind on this trip.

It was hard to read his expression.

He nodded once. "Right. Partners."

"Partners," she repeated, trying not to choke on the word.

She turned and started walking again, afraid to look into his eyes any longer.

He continued behind her. "Was there something else?" she asked.

This time he smiled. "Yeah, actually."

"What is it?"

"I think we should leave for a while."

She shook her head, confused. "Leave?"

"Yeah, I think we should get away from the orchards. You know, do some sightseeing or something." The smile turned into a boyish grin. Its effect on her felt like a blow in the stomach.

"Sightseeing? Now?"

"What better time?"

"I thought you said this wasn't a pleasure trip. That we had to do what we came here for and leave."

He looked up toward the horizon. "Yeah, I know. But it occurs to me that we could use the distraction. Let's face it, staying here under Mila and Tavov's watchful eye continuously, it's starting to feel like being in a zoo exhibit or something."

"What about Mila and Tavov?"

"I told them we wanted to take in the sights. And that we didn't expect them to chaperone us, that they were doing enough already."

"They bought that?"

"Not really. I had to insinuate that we wanted to have some time to ourselves, without others around."

"You didn't!"

"Don't worry, I was diplomatic about it."

"I'm sure you were. What did you have in mind?"

They continued walking. Angel let the water lap around her ankles and drench the hem of her long skirt.

"You were right about the island," R.J. said. "It is one of the prettiest areas in the world. The city is supposed to be amazing. Restaurants, shops, a bazaar that could compete with the Grand Bazaar in Istanbul. I think we should go explore it all."

Her breath caught. He hadn't forgotten what she'd said on the flight over here. Though she knew better than to think it was more than an apologetic gesture.

"R.J., you don't need to placate me. I'm a big girl." She wiggled her toes in the water.

"That's not what I'm doing. I just think it would be good to get away for a while, and the city is only about an hour away by car. So why not?"

Why not? Because it sounded like a dream to her, like a fantasy she'd not dared to hope for during the last few years. What would she have given to be able to spend the day with R.J. just a few short weeks ago? Now she was being offered the chance to, even if it was just to assuage his guilt. If she was smart she'd turn him down. Heaven knew her heart wasn't ready for such an experience, not after the conversation they'd just had.

Then again, she certainly could use the distraction.

"I think you should tell Tavov and Mila we've changed our minds," she told him.

He lifted his eyebrows. "You don't want to go?"

"I mean that we've changed our minds about going alone."

His expression shifted. "You'd rather not go alone with me." He turned before she could answer. "I'll go tell them you'd like them to come."

She reached out to touch his arm. "No, not them."

"Then who?"

"Reid and Kaya."

Understanding settled over his features. "The bride and groom."

She nodded. "I think they probably could use the chance to get away, too. And they could show us around like true natives. I know you've been there before, but they've got the insider's track."

He studied her. "It means that much to you to spend this time with them?" he asked.

She nodded, hoping he wouldn't guess as to just why. If R.J. got the opportunity to spend just a few hours with the young couple, if he could just witness firsthand how excited they must be about getting married, maybe it might make the whole idea of toasting at the wedding a bit more palatable. Especially after the conversation they'd just had.

He shrugged. "Why not? It might be fun. Though I'm gonna warn you it's been a while since I've been out on any kind of double date."

"It *will* be fun. Just give me a half hour to get ready."

"All right," he agreed. "I'll go see about securing a vehicle."

She turned away to stare at the water before speaking. "I'm glad you were finally straight with me."

He didn't say anything, his only response a soft sigh before walking away.

R.J. paid the cabbie and turned to join Angeline and the other couple already at the entrance of the expansive shopping bazaar.

He'd learned about the place when he'd been doing research after the meeting in Angel's office back in Boston. It was one of the biggest indoor bazaars in the world.

He wasn't sure why he was doing this, why he'd even brought it up. But the past few days had just been so tense. They definitely needed the time away. He certainly did, anyway. At least they'd be able to relax a little, away from Tavov and Mila's all-too-observant stares.

He looked up to see a wide smile on Angel's face. With a wave of her hand, she gestured him over to where she stood with Reid and Kaya. He knew when he looked at her what his motivation had been; the joy that was in her eyes right now. He'd been able to put it there quite effortlessly years ago. This little jaunt was a small price to pay to see it there again.

Reid and Kaya were smiling, too, their hands clasped. They couldn't have been older than early twenties. Kaya had the same coloring Angel did, her hair slightly less wavy than Angel's unruly curls. Reid was one of the few blond men he'd seen in this part of the world. He had a small frame and was only slightly taller than his average-height fiancée.

R.J. approached the small group. "Is everyone ready?"

Three happy voices answered him in unison.

"Then let's go spend some money," he said as he placed his palm on the small of Angel's back. It occurred to him that such displays were not necessary now that they were away from the orchard, but it was becoming more and more natural to touch her this way.

Chaos descended as soon as they entered the arched doorway. Hundreds of people bustled past them, and the noise of intense bartering filled the air. Even the decorative artwork on the walls and high arched ceiling seemed busy and detailed.

Kaya turned excitedly to Angel. "We have to look at the jewelry first," she urged. "I bet you've never seen so much shiny gold in one place before."

"I was afraid this would happen," Reid said, his voice suffering. "R.J., we'll never get out of here if the ladies start in on the jewelry. Do you know how many gold stores there are in here?"

"The shine in this part of the bazaar alone is giving me a good indication," he answered.

A teenager breezed past them carrying a dangling tray with small glasses of hot tea swinging to and fro. Miraculously, not a drop seemed to spill.

"I think starting with the gold is a terrific idea," Angel said, smiling wide.

"Hold on to your wallet, my good man." Reid winked at him over Kaya's head. "You're about to buy your wife some baubles."

He felt Angel stiffen slightly next to him. It was natural for Reid to assume that R.J. would be the one making the purchases for her. In reality, aside from her wedding ring, he'd never actually bought her any piece of jewelry. He'd never been able to afford anything worthy of her back then, though he'd always known that someday… And he'd been right. He finally could afford such things. Now that it was too late.

"Well, then. Shall we get started?" Angel offered. "Kaya, lead the way." She gestured in front of her.

"Oh, she knows the way all right," Reid teased.

Kaya pulled her hand out of her fiancé's hand long enough to give him a mock slap on the wrist.

"You really don't want to make me too upset with you in here, do you?" She was giving as good as she got.

Reid gave an exaggerated shudder. "Not on your life. Lead the way, my darling." He stepped aside and bowed.

Angel's throaty laugh shook through R.J. The young couple had such an easy manner between them. He couldn't remember sharing that with any woman. Only Angel had come close, and he hadn't really let it happen. He'd never allowed such camaraderie to occur. *He'd* never allowed it. Despite Angel's warmth, despite her sense of humor. He'd never really let his guard down long enough. It was hard not to feel sorry for that now. He took a deep breath. There was no use questioning any of it.

She'd thanked him for being straight with her. Only there was so much more he didn't ever want her to find out.

The three of them followed Kaya as she made a beeline to one of the merchant booths on the other side. The whole window seemed to glisten like one big treasure chest of gold. He turned to catch a glimpse of Angel. In the dark lighting of the hall, bright yellow from the gold reflected in her eyes, accentuating their distinctive hazel color. He tried not to let the sight take his breath away.

The women were immediately approached by two clerks on the other side of the displays. Neither wasted anytime picking out what she wanted to try on. He couldn't believe he was actually enjoying himself. For all practical purposes, he was being made to shop for jewelry. For the life of him, he knew that should bore him to tears. But quite the opposite, he couldn't remember the last time he'd enjoyed himself so much. Tom, his longtime friend and current business partner, would have a field day if he could see him now. Tom would have to see this to believe it.

Close to twenty minutes later, they were finally out of the store. It was hard to tell which woman had done more damage.

"Did you save any money for the ride home?" he teased Angel. The other couple was walking ahead, immersed in their own world.

"This—" Angel lifted the parcel in her hand "—is a wise investment."

He gave her his best smirk. "Is that what you think?"

"I know it for a fact," she said. "This is high-quality fourteen- and twenty-two-karat gold. You can't find it in the States at these prices."

"What I heard," he began, not ready to stop teasing her, "is that everything in this place is marked up a couple hundred percent."

"Oh, please." She gave him a disdainful look. "What kind of businesswoman do you think I am? I know that. I bartered and negotiated my heart out for these deals."

"I noticed the clerk looked a little exhausted by the time he rang you up."

"I think he was glad to get rid of me."

"It was wonderful," Kaya chimed in as they caught up. "I've never seen anyone haggle so hard. These are some of the best prices I've ever paid."

"Must be hard to be married to a woman who drives such a hard bargain," Reid taunted good-naturedly.

"Absolutely," R.J. agreed quickly. "But it also has its advantages."

"Next store, you can help me seal some bargains, then," Reid said as he stopped to assist his fiancée in putting on one of her recent purchases.

"Be glad to," Angel said. "Actually, R.J., they had some great watches and men's rings. I think a lot of them would have appealed to you."

He lifted a curl of hair that had strayed out of her chignon.

"I'm not much for wearing jewelry, but thanks anyway."

Her expression suddenly turned serious. "Is that why you didn't hold on to your wedding ring?" she asked low enough for only him to hear.

That wasn't a question he'd been expecting. He searched for an answer, something that wouldn't tell her too much.

She suddenly raised a hand to her mouth. "I—I'm sorry," she stammered. "I don't know where that came from."

She appeared as shocked by what she'd said as he was.

"It's all right," he said lamely, still unsure how to respond. What was he supposed to say? Tell her truth? That he had held on to it? That he had it on him even now, and every day since it had been given to him? He couldn't do that.

"Come on, you two." Kaya's excited voice interrupted their mutual discomfort. "We haven't even covered a fraction of territory in here yet."

He gently cupped Angel's elbow and guided her forward. Thank the stars for Reid and Kaya. Asking them to come along had been a good idea after all.

A few stops later, they were at the door of a large rug and afghan store. This time, the men decided to hover outside while the ladies ogled the merchandise.

"We're really glad you're here to share in our wedding," Reid said.

The wedding. Reid and Kaya had talked about it constantly since the four of them had left the orchard. The more time he'd spent with the other couple, the harder it was to remain jaded or cynical about their upcoming nuptials.

Hell, he'd realized two stores ago that was Angel's intent all along. R.J. suspected she'd invited the other couple along for that very reason. She'd known damn well that he'd have second thoughts about raining on their parade in any way once he got to know Reid and Kaya. And damned if Angel hadn't been right. Damned if he hadn't fallen for it.

He peeked inside the store at her. Angel was traipsing barefoot on a thick, ornate rug. The appealing scene made him feel barbaric enough to want to wrap her neatly up in the carpet, throw the bundle over his shoulder and carry her outside. Then he could wrap himself around her and kiss her with all the want and desperation these past few days had evoked.

He tried to curb his frustration by reminding himself it was almost over. Just a few more days. Once they got through the distraction of the wedding, they could get a signed contract for Angel and head back to Massachusetts. After that, he and his ex-wife would finally go their separate ways. For some reason, that thought didn't have the calming effect it should have.

"R.J., did you hear me?" He looked up to find Reid watching him curiously.

R.J. tried to shake out the cobwebs. "I'm sorry, did you say something?"

The other man let out a small laugh. "You seem a little preoccupied."

"Just admiring the vastness of this place," he lied.

Reid looked at him, then shrugged. "I said it looks like the ladies are about done. What do you say we all grab some dinner?"

"That sounds like a great idea. Any longer with the two of them in here and even this place might run out of merchandise."

Angel and Kaya chose that moment to step outside. "Angeline, I don't know how you do it," Kaya was saying.

She turned to the two men. "Angeline got that man to go down seven hundred dollars on a handwoven silk rug."

"Don't be too impressed," Angel insisted. "He must have marked it up at least twice that amount when he saw an American approach."

"Still," the other woman insisted, "they're usually much more stubborn than that."

"Well, even watching all this haggling from a safe distance gave Reid and me a huge appetite," R.J. joked. "Are you ladies through tormenting these poor merchants yet?"

Angel laughed. "Just giving them a taste of their own medicine. It's good for them once in a while."

"Well, we men are worn out. What do you say to some dinner?"

She stepped closer to him. "I, for one, would love to have dinner with said men." She turned back to Kaya. "What about you, partner?"

R.J. noticed Reid's arm go affectionately around his fiancée's midriff. The two of them looked so happy, and so right together. The excitement practically shone from both of them. Excitement about their upcoming nuptials no doubt.

Kaya nodded her agreement. "I know exactly where we can go. This place has the tastiest *doner.* It's a Middle Eastern dish. The perfect combination of lamb and beef, seasoned just right. And on Thursdays and Fridays they have an elaborate show. Both male and female belly dancers."

"Sounds like my kind of place," Angel said. R.J. couldn't help but give her a wary look. Why did she want to watch male dancers? The only one he could picture doing an erotic dance was her.

"Be sure to pay close attention to the dancing, Angeline," Kaya said as the four of them walked out of the bazaar and hailed a taxi.

"Why?" Angel asked.

"Because I'm going to show you how to do it at our wedding," Kaya beamed. "I'm going to show you how to belly dance for your husband."

R.J. didn't bother to suppress his groan.

CHAPTER TEN

"COME ON, ANGELINE. Curve your hips a little more," Kaya ordered with a laugh. The young bride was teaching her a basic belly dancing move. At least she was trying to.

The marriage ceremony performed earlier had been breathtakingly touching, even though part of it had been recited in a dialect Angel hadn't understood. But it had sounded sacred and poetic.

Now the reception was fully under way, with loud pounding music, lively dancing and a lot of food and drink.

"Kaya, I would have to be double-jointed to curve it any more than this."

"All right." The other woman laughed. "I suppose that's good enough."

"It will have to be, unless I want to throw my back out."

"Look, there's your husband. We will start now. Remember what I told you." Kaya winked at her.

"Got it." Angeline quickly lifted the veils up to cover her face. The fluttering in her stomach wasn't nervousness. She was just playing a game.

Still, it was a risky game. She and R.J. had been nothing more than civil toward each other the last couple of days, ever since the evening they'd spent in the city. They behaved like lovers during the day, then he quietly settled himself down on the floor to sleep at night. She'd offered to share the bed, purely platonically. But he'd refused each time. Still, the friendliness was much better than the cold distance he'd insisted when they'd first gotten here. She didn't want to jeopardize that.

But what was the harm in a little flirting? They still had to be convincing for Mila and Tavov, didn't they?

She turned to look for him in the crowd. Her heart fluttered as she laid eyes on him. He was so striking and handsome. He was at least half a head taller than anyone else there. He looked the epitome of dashing. He looked so darn sexy. He looked dangerous, he looked…downright preoccupied.

Her heart did a little flip when she realized he was looking for her.

Finally, their eyes caught. For one small moment, the world between them seemed to shift. She couldn't turn away from his stare, and the expression on his face held her spellbound. It was broken when he broke eye contact and started making his way toward her.

"What's this?" R.J. reached her just as the last scarf was securely fastened.

"It's the bridal rites."

He lifted one eyebrow, a smile creasing the corners of his mouth.

"The bridal rites, huh?"

"That's right. It's a way to honor the wedding. All the couples are supposed to kiss at the sound of the chime." As soon as the words left her mouth, the ringing of a nearby bell sounded.

"There it is. You're supposed to kiss me now."

"Yeah?" He lifted an eyebrow and rubbed his chin. "How do I know it's really you under there?"

"You'll know as soon as you kiss me," she couldn't help but taunt him.

R.J.'s expression didn't change, but something shifted in his eyes, and the fluttering in her stomach increased.

"In that case…" He slowly removed the scarf.

She knew her breath had just stopped as she watched

him lean closer. Some magnetic force lifted her arms to link her fingers behind his head.

Soft at first, gentle and sweet. His mouth slanted over hers comfortably. He paused long enough to give her a smile, then returned. She ventured to touch his lips with her tongue.

Then fire quickly took over. It molded them together, branding them. His hand splayed at the small of her back, and desire rocketed through her whole being.

He was kissing her the way he had during all those heat-filled needful moments years ago. In an instant, she was back to being the young college student who had fallen so deeply in love with him.

Finally, R.J. broke away. It was hard to tell which one of them was breathing faster. The crowd had gone past the ceremony. Everyone but the two of them had resumed celebrating.

Kaya's joyous peal of laughter brought Angel's attention back to the dance floor.

"She's beautiful, isn't she?" Angel asked. "I don't think I've ever seen a more beautiful bride," Angel whispered as she watched the younger woman swirl around the installed wooden dance floor.

R.J. didn't respond right away. She looked up to catch him watching her. Something in his eyes took her breath away.

"I have," he said in a heated whisper.

He reached out to touch her, his fingers stroking her jaw. The noise of the loud reception around them turned to a faint humming in her ears.

"*My* bride," he added, his tone possessing.

His words shattered her emotions. She lifted shaky fingers to his face. "I—I can't help but think how excited I was the day we were married," she confessed. "Every time those two kiss, I remember how in love we were."

"I've never forgotten." He seemed surprised that the words had left his mouth.

His thumb continued to rub her jaw gently. Her eyes loaded heavy with tears. Tears of regret at what they'd once had and lost.

She searched his eyes for answers. "How did it happen, R.J.? How did we let it slip out of our hands?"

"I wish I knew, darling, but I don't."

Did that mean he was as sorry as she was that it had? Or was this just sentimental rambling brought on by memories forced to the surface.

The emotion in his eyes looked genuine, but she wished she knew for sure. One thing she did know, she'd been fooling herself for years. Her feelings for R.J. went way beyond the physical, way beyond mere attraction.

"There you two are."

Angel jumped back as if stung. She'd forgotten where they were. Tavov and Mila we're walking toward them. Mila had the smile of a royal queen on her face.

"It seems this romantic mood has affected everyone," Mila teased.

Angeline dared a look at R.J. He was staring at her. Fire still burned in his eyes, stoking the one burning in her.

"Come, you two." Tavov motioned. "We're going to stop the music long enough for a couple of more toasts, including yours."

She managed to finally tear her gaze away from R.J.'s heated stare. "That, um, sounds lovely."

Mila stepped to her and took her arm into her own. "Come, our guests are all looking forward to hearing from you."

Angeline nodded, and awareness ran down her spine as she walked away with Mila. She knew R.J. was still watching her.

What was she doing? She'd just managed to shatter any

peace she may have obtained. Then realization of the truth erupted within her chest. She was still in love with him. She always had been. All those years of pretending they'd had nothing but chemistry between them had been such a ruse. Her pretense now stared her in the face. Nothing she could say or do from now on would allow her to deny it anymore. She'd loved him since she'd laid eyes on him. Without a doubt, she wanted him. And he wanted her.

Was that enough?

She shook her head briskly as Mila led her away. What a silly question. Of course it was. Her foolish heart would settle for anything he gave her. That's how blindly in love she was. Something had shifted between them tonight. They had both acknowledged their mutual attraction. And that they'd both felt sentimental for all they'd lost. But she was almost certain for him that's all it was.

She harbored no illusions that he felt as strongly for her as she did for him.

In a few short hours they'd be back in the suite alone. Their spoken words of sentiment still between them. The question was, was she ready to do something about it?

Mindlessly, she followed R.J. up the steps to the portable stage. Another man was already at the microphone offering his best wishes.

Angel didn't hear him. How in the world was she supposed to go back to her carefully crafted life after this? The one belief that had helped her move forward was the knowledge that it would take only a matter of time to get over a youthful attraction. Now she would have to acknowledge the pain for what it was—her heart breaking, slowly and irreparably, with each and every day, most likely without end.

"We're being called forward, Angel."

"What?"

"It's our turn to toast the bride and groom. And offer wise words of guidance." He seemed to have a barely veiled grip on his control. Was he as floored as she was? Or was it just all this acting starting to take a toll on him, as well?

Letting him guide her toward the center, she pasted what she hoped was a convincing smile on her face. Suddenly, the true force of what she was about to do hit her. She felt the eyes of hundreds of people, waiting for her to say something. People who had no reason to suspect she was being anything less than sincere.

"Well, Angel?" R.J. prompted.

"Huh?"

"What's your answer?" For some odd reason, she felt her nervousness go down a notch at the sound of his voice.

"I'm sorry, I didn't hear your question."

"Would you like me to go first?" he asked.

What a godsend. "Y-yes, thank you. I guess I should have been better prepared. It's a little different from a business presentation, isn't it?"

He merely tipped his head in answer.

"I'm sure I'll come up with something concrete by the time you finish." She hoped she would.

"It's okay. I'm not exactly sure what I'm about to say myself."

She watched as he took the microphone from the bride's waiting cousin. The crowd seemed to grow even quieter as R.J. cleared his throat.

"First of all," he began, "I'd like you all to know what a terrific honor this is for both me and my wife." Angel swallowed at the last word.

"We were honored to be invited, and we are even more pleased to be able to personally give our regards to the couple."

The crowd had grown completely silent, hanging on R.J.'s every word.

"I know everyone's got a lot of celebrating to do, so I'll be brief. To our honored couple, I'd just like to say…remember always what has brought you here together to this day. No matter how little, remember every detail that has endeared you to each other."

Angel felt herself chewing her lip. It would be so easy, so terribly tempting to believe his words actually held some meaning for the two of them.

R.J. continued. "Never take for granted the love you have for each other. It is a gift that few people are ever lucky enough to find. It's apparent when looking at the two of you that you have done so. So remember the little treasures, remember the starlit nights, the slow dances when it's just the two of you on the dance floor. Remember how the other person's smile takes your breath away." He stopped to clear his throat, and Angeline felt her eyes sting. What she wouldn't give to have those words come from him directly to her.

But she had to be logical. She had to realize that fate was playing a cruel, harsh joke on her. Forcing her and R.J. to utter words that may have been true years ago but had long ago lost their merit. She blinked the tears out of her eyes as R.J. resumed his speech.

"And finally," he continued, "always remember, nothing matters but the two of you and what you've found in each other." He lifted his glass before completing. "Good luck and best wishes." The crowd stood silent for the briefest of seconds and then roared their applause.

Angel was too stunned to move—let alone speak. She felt R.J.'s hand at her elbow nudging her toward the crowd. He handed her the microphone.

She cleared her throat and winced as the sound tore through the air. "Well, that's going to be quite a tough act to follow.

"Again, we are both so very pleased that you have made us part of such a joyous occasion. My husband pretty much put it best. Fate has brought the two of you together. The love you share for each other has culminated in this very special moment. It stands stronger than time. True love transcends pride, wealth and—" she turned to look fully at R.J. "—background."

At the last word, she had to turn away from him.

"So from this day forward, let your affection for each other be the power that guides you. Let nothing or no one ever tell you it's any less than it is. R.J. and I will always remember how strong your bond is. Good luck and best wishes."

The band struck up behind her as the crowd cheered, but Angeline stood frozen where she was. Adrenaline pumped through her, and it had nothing to do with public speaking.

"Nice words," R.J. whispered in her ear.

"Thanks. For a moment I wasn't quite sure what I was going to say. I'm glad it's over."

He was about to respond when he was interrupted as Tavov clapped a hand on his shoulder.

"R.J., good speech. There's someone here I'd like you to meet."

"Please, go on," she urged before he could refuse. She didn't feel much like celebrating.

He appeared out of nowhere. Angel shook the sleep off and sat up. She could see R.J.'s silhouette through the darkness. He had the advantage. The bed was bathed in moonlight while he stood protected by the black cover of the night.

"R.J.? Are you all right? I've been so worried." She glanced at the mounted clock on the wall. "It's almost dawn.

He didn't answer, didn't move.

She removed the covers and started to get out of bed. "Where have you been? You've been gone for hours." She realized too late her state of disarray. Her pajama top had shifted off her shoulders, exposing most of her neckline and chest. She knew R.J. had noticed.

She drew the covers protectively back around her.

"I was trying to stay away," he whispered. "Away from this room, away from you." She heard him suck in a deep breath. "But I couldn't do it. I'm not strong enough."

His voice sounded off, strange. She could barely make out his shape. Some internal battle he was fighting was evident in his tone. He moved closer, and Angeline felt her heart beating furiously in her chest. It was fear and anticipation all at once. Her hands stilled, fingers wrapped tightly around the blanket.

"I tried so hard not to come back here. Because I knew I wouldn't be able to help myself if I was back in this room with you. But here I am."

She swallowed, willed herself to speak. "Where'd you go?"

"I've been wandering the beach for hours. I think I may have walked to the next city over before turning around."

Angel resisted the urge to stand and hug him; he'd been wandering in the chilly dark night. "We knew this wasn't going to be easy. Pretending to be married, I mean."

He shook his head. "That's been the easy part. Pretending I can resist you is what I can't stand anymore."

She knew it was really him, knew she wasn't dreaming. But the voice she heard now didn't belong to the man she'd known before. This sounded like a man whose last hold on control had just snapped.

"What caused all this?"

He let out a small laugh that sounded wounded and bitter. "Everything. The wedding, how happy Reid and Kaya seem to be starting their lives together. Our toast. Even watching Mila and Tavov, seeing how happy they still seem after all these years." He paused for so long she thought he wasn't going to speak again. But then added, "And watching you. Pretending you're still mine. Trying to ignore the way you affect me."

She bit down on her lip. "And how do I affect you, R.J.?"

"Like no one else ever has. Apparently three years apart hasn't changed it."

Her breath caught at his admission.

"But you have to tell me," he continued. "I'll walk out of here right now if you want me to. God knows, it's the sane thing to do. But if that's what you want, you'd better tell me now."

She couldn't form a response, couldn't bring herself to speak. It took all she had to resume breathing. Finally, she summoned the ability to utter his name.

"Come here," he bade. The gentlest of demands, as if he'd finally allowed himself to voice a silent wish.

Her limbs wouldn't move. Heavens, she wanted him, wanted to feel him around her, embracing her. Over her. Yet an overwhelming force held her where she was, unable to move past the crossroads she was being offered. If this was the wrong move, she knew without a doubt that this time her heart would never recover.

"I need to be certain, Angel." She heard his scratchy voice through the darkness. "I need to be sure this is what you want. Show me." He paused to take a deep, tortured breath.

Suddenly, without preamble or warning, she felt her own slim grasp on control snap.

Somehow she managed to move, though she wouldn't have thought it was possible. The hardwood floor felt cold on the soles of her feet, but the sensation barely registered. The universe consisted of nothing but the man before her. The man she knew she would always love. True to form, he was making sure it was completely her decision.

Automatically, she placed one languid foot in front of the other. He stepped closer to her, and the moonlight finally illuminated the hard, sharp features of his face. The harsh reality of what she was about to do hit her when she fully saw his face.

And then she could go no farther. Only the length of a small room stood between them. But it may as well have been miles. Nothing and everything held her back. Fear, desire, desperation, doubt. All of it warred within her, freezing her in her spot. Even in his cry for her, she could feel part of him holding back. Perhaps the most important part.

But what was the point in fighting? She couldn't deny she wanted him. Would always want him.

Her need for his touch roared like wildfire in her ears. She reached out her hand, asking silently for reassurance.

R.J. quickly breached the area between them. The contact was sudden, savage. She knew the world had stopped. At least it had for her.

He grabbed her by the waist and pulled her fiercely up against him. The kiss was clumsy at first. Then sheer familiarity took over. She savored the taste of him.

He thrust forceful fingers through her hair. Several tangled strands caught, causing a flash of pain. It didn't matter. He kissed her deeper, and she couldn't help the groan that escaped her.

Finally, he was here. And he was going to make love to her.

CHAPTER ELEVEN

HE'D LEFT HER. Angeline knew instinctively that R.J. had moved off the bed. The comfortable warmth that had enveloped her till morning, even in sleep, had disappeared. Squinting in the dawn's light, she made out his silhouette on the balcony.

He looked deep in thought.

Don't panic, he's simply processing. No way he's about to break your heart again.

But her mouth had gone dry.

"Watching the sunrise?" she asked with false cheeriness as she stepped outside. The rigid hold of his back stoked her fears.

This was not going to be a fun conversation.

He didn't look at her, just kept staring straight ahead at the water. The rays of the infant sun turned the sky a majestic red along the horizon. R.J. had pulled on only his pajama bottoms, his upper body bare despite the chill. Her gaze fell to his chiseled arms. Arms that had held her into the morning. Surrounded her and loved her.

There was no mistaking the tension in his shoulders.

He didn't look at her when he spoke. "I'm afraid I let all the excitement of last night get to me."

"Is that all that was? The only reason you made love to me was due to the excitement of the wedding?"

"Yes."

She knew better. "I don't believe you. You said a lot of things last night. Things that just don't jell with what you're trying to tell me right now." She stepped closer.

"That was just the heat of the moment, Angel."

Ouch. That dart had hit its mark. But she wasn't going to fall for it. This was nothing more than R.J. trying to battle his demons alone. As usual. "I don't believe that either. Please tell me why you're pulling away."

"This is exactly why I should have stayed away from you last night. We don't need this distraction right now."

"The obvious fact that we still have feelings for each other is a little more than a distraction, R.J. What are we going to do about it?"

"Nothing. We're going to go back to the States and pretend none of this ever happened."

"And move forward with the divorce?"

He tilted his head slightly in agreement. He couldn't mean that. How could he still want the divorce after what had been happening between them on this trip? "We're as different as two people can be, Angel."

She couldn't seem to get through to him. "Why do you still believe that? As far as we've both come?"

"I can say it because it's true. I can declare we're different because while you were out boating with your wealthy friends as a teenager, I was defending myself from my old man. And I usually got a jaw full of loose teeth for it."

Angel felt the breath leave her. "I—I'm sorry. I know you'd had a rough childhood—but you never told me the specifics."

"What was I supposed to tell you? Was I supposed to discuss my life in the projects with my beautiful, privileged Brahmin wife? Was I supposed to tell her how my old man got off on seeing other people suffer, particularly my mother? Was I supposed to explain how I watched her wither from disease and die of cancer in a shelter while he gambled away the little money we had? Money she scraped together by cleaning houses and scrubbing toilets, by the way. In houses owned by people like you."

"I'm so sorry," she repeated, unprepared for the onslaught of emotion pouring from him.

"What do you think about your husband now?" he demanded.

She swallowed the lump that had formed in her throat. "I respect him more than ever."

His eyes narrowed on her. "What?"

"You heard me," she said, firmly. "Look at all you've accomplished despite all that. Look at the life you've built for yourself."

"None of that changes where I came from."

"And what does that mean? Why does it even matter anymore where you came from? You've always been the same strong, bright, talented man you are right now." She'd grown frustrated now. He could be so obstinate. "I see ladies from run-down homes and squalid backgrounds change their lives all the time. It's what the Works program is all about."

"It's not the same thing," he argued.

"Only because what you've done is even more extraordinary." She took a fortifying breath to try to settle her nerves. "No one wants you to forget," she urged. "I certainly don't. You should be so proud of yourself, R.J., for having come as far as you have."

She watched as his hands tightened on the balcony railing. "What about what I did to you?"

Huh? "I don't understand."

He turned to her, his eyes darkened with an emotion she couldn't name. "I cost you everything, Angel. I'm the reason your father won't speak to you. The reason you've lost touch with your friends. I'm the reason you'll be denied your rightful inheritance and your stature as a Scott. You've lost everything because of me."

"My father and I have had a strained relationship since I

was a child. It began when my mother left. As for the rest, you can't mean to think any of that matters to me."

"But it should."

She had to laugh at his logic. Until she heard his next words.

"Those are all things that should matter to you, Angel. Because this isn't going to work between us. We don't have a chance."

No, she certainly didn't feel like laughing anymore. Maybe she wouldn't ever again, in fact. "What do you mean?"

"Simple. I'm not husband material. My move to the West Coast was just a start. I haven't stayed in one place for more than a couple months since I left Boston. Don't you see?" He turned from the railing to fully face her. "I don't want to be tied down. Not to any one place. Not to any one person."

CHAPTER TWELVE

WHY THE HELL hadn't he stayed away from her last night? Because he was a selfish bastard who'd ignored everything but his own needs.

R.J. reached down to adjust the shower knob. Turning it, he braced himself for the punishing pulse of hot water.

What a mistake. He'd had to hurt her. She would never understand why they couldn't get back together. Angel could claim all she wanted that her relationship with her father had been strained for years, but the fact was they'd *had* a relationship until he entered the picture.

He couldn't bear the responsibility of being the final knife that ultimately severed their bond, tenuous as it may have been.

Nothing he'd told her had been a lie. It was truth that he was gone for several months at a time. Often not even in the country. What kind of a husband could he be given his lifestyle? Certainly not someone worthy of causing the kind of loss that Angeline had to endure because she'd married him. The best thing he could do for her would be to sever all contact. And move forward with the divorce once and for all.

At least this fiasco of a trip had opened his eyes to what he needed to do. Best thing now would be to wrap it up.

He had to leave. As soon as he could.

He turned the shower knob even farther, the water almost at scalding now. He would just tell her that a business matter had come up that needed his immediate attention. Hell, that would actually prove the point he'd just made. She couldn't count on him or depend on him to follow through.

And she would see right through it.

No matter. For her own good, he couldn't be around her any longer.

Angeline couldn't seem to make herself move off the balcony. She had no idea how long she'd been standing there listening to the running of R.J.'s shower. She'd barely noticed when the water had shut off and he'd moved about the suite getting dressed.

She couldn't speak to him. She didn't know what to say.

She'd been his wife, but she'd never known about the horrors he'd lived through growing up. He hadn't trusted her enough to share any of it with her. Just like he hadn't trusted her enough to tell her about her father's attempted bribe.

She had to take him at his word now. He just declared to her that he wasn't one to feel close to anybody. He had no interest in being tied down. R.J. had clearly never felt about her the way she had felt toward him.

She certainly wasn't going to beg him to reconsider. He'd done enough by agreeing to this trip.

Shutting her eyes, she inhaled deeply. This wasn't the end of the world. She'd find a way to live her life. She'd throw herself in her responsibilities at TeaLC and with the Works program, and soon, hopefully, this wretched pain in her chest would turn to a dull ache that she might even be able to ignore.

She could do it. She could learn to somehow love him yet live without him.

She finally turned around and stepped back into the gloomy darkness of the suite. Her eyes fell on the unmade bed. Walking over to it, she ran her hands over the tangled sheets. Memories assaulted her, further stretching her already tight emotions. Her gaze shifted to the floor, where the casual white shirt R.J. had been wearing lay crumpled on the floor. Without thinking, she reached for it and put it on. The fabric smelled of him. She rubbed her arms and hugged the material close.

She couldn't bear to take it off. She'd hide it with a spring sweater. She needed to feel near him. And if the best she could settle for was to wear his shirt for the day, then she'd take what she could get.

After all, healing didn't happen overnight, did it?

Angel spent the morning roaming the grounds, trying to clear her scrambled mind. It didn't help. But one thing was certain—she had to tell Mila and Tavov the truth: that TeaLC wasn't going to be run by a family operation after all. It would just be her. They had a right to know. The farce had gone far enough. And she was just tired. Tired of pretending, tired of the half-truths she'd been sprouting to get this deal. Maybe Mila and Tavov had grown to care for her enough that it wouldn't matter and they would hopefully give her the deal anyway. If not, well, she would have to figure out how to grow the business some other way.

As for the prospect she didn't want to think about—if she had to sell, she'd make sure to negotiate the best deal she could for her employees. But she would exhaust every other option first. Every possible loan, every potential investor. None of the choices were ideal. More investors meant more decision-makers who might want to phase out the expensive Works program.

She vowed not to let that happen.

R.J. was already in the suite when she made her way back. There was no missing his closed suitcase in the corner of the room.

"You're back," she announced as she entered the room, careful to keep all emotion out of her voice.

"Just got in."

"Tavov and Mila are expecting us for lunch."

He drew in a breath and looked away. "Actually, I need to talk to you. I'm not going to make it for lunch. Or dinner."

"I don't understand," she lied. She understood all too well, and her heart sank to her stomach.

"I'm leaving."

Her chest felt as if she'd just gone over a steep drop. "The plan was that we would leave in three days."

"I'm afraid I'm needed back for an emergency a major client is having."

Right.

"I see," was all she could manage.

Don't beg him, whatever you do, don't plead for him to stay.

He'd made his decision very clear. No point in telling him now that she was about to admit to the Bays the entire truth. What did it matter? He wasn't even going to stay.

"But I didn't want you traveling back alone."

A small spark of hope ignited deep within her heart. "I don't understand."

"I've made arrangements to fly Shanna here. She should be arriving tomorrow. The two of you can fly back to Boston when you're ready."

"I guess you've thought of everything."

"We said we'd come together, and we did. Mila and Tavov aren't suspicious. You'll get what you need."

If she was lucky. And even if everything he said proved true, she knew she'd still feel like her world had fallen apart.

CHAPTER THIRTEEN

SHE WAS SUCH a pansy. She couldn't even watch him leave. Angeline stopped in the middle of the rows of tea plants and breathed in the spicy aroma.

He'd be on his way off the plantation now. An overwhelming cloud of sadness shrouded her. Her emotions were all her fault. R.J. had been more than fair with her. He'd gone along with the plan, helped her with the deception, and he'd been honest with her from the beginning. Yep, he'd stuck to his part of the deal perfectly. She'd been the one to let the closeness of it all go to her head. She'd been the one who'd let daydreams cloud her visions.

And now he was leaving. He probably hated himself for letting things go as far as they had. He'd said all along that he wanted nothing to do with her. Pretty soon, the whole business deal would likely go bust, too, as soon as she sat down with Mila and Tavov this afternoon.

She had to tell them.

It was past time to come clean about everything. Past time to let them know that she and R.J. had been pretending all along. Given how much she'd lost, the least she could do was be honest with the people she had grown to care for.

Mila and Tavov had a right to know who exactly they were doing business with. Or not doing business with.

No herbal tea supply, no expansion, no growth in sales.

No R.J.

She closed her eyes against the pain. This time hurt almost more than the first time she'd lost him. Almost.

She'd let him walk out of her life then, too. It had settled nothing. And here she was, years later, experiencing it all over again.

She hugged her arms across her chest, bracing against the tightness in her heart. A small object in the pocket of the shirt she was wearing pressed against her wrist. R.J.'s shirt. She still hadn't taken it off.

Curious, she took off the sweater to look inside the shirt pocket. A shimmer of bright gold reflected out at her. She took the object out.

A thin rope chain with a gold band dangled from her fingers. Her mind went numb when she realized what it was. R.J.'s wedding band, the original one she'd given him five years ago. The one he'd told her he'd gotten rid of.

He *had* kept his ring.

The implications were almost too much to fathom. He hadn't been able to forget her. Not only had he kept his wedding ring, he still wore it around his neck. All this time, all these years. He'd wanted a token of their love with him always.

Her vision blurred as she stared at the gold. He'd been so good at keeping his feelings from her. Maybe he didn't even want to truly face them himself. It appeared neither one of them was over their breakup.

What was she going to do about it?

Stand by and let the worst loss in her life repeat itself? Without so much as a true answer? Didn't she owe it to herself to at least try to find out exactly what R.J.'s feelings were? Didn't she owe it to both of them? He insisted on being stubborn and distant. But he cared enough to drop everything to participate in a farce of such grand proportions. And he cared enough to want to keep his old wedding ring with him at all times.

She clutched the chain in her palm. Maybe, despite all that, he truly wanted to forget her and go on with his life. Maybe it didn't go any deeper than a genuine affection. But one thing was certain. This time she was going to find out. Her whole future depended on it, and she refused to leave it up to chance or pride. R.J. wasn't the only one intent on not letting history repeat itself.

She owed it to both of them to tell him straight out—ask him not to let her father, or anyone else, come between them this time.

She turned on her heel to find R.J. and get an answer once and for all. She turned to make her way back to the house. It was time to end the doubts. Time to get to the bottom of everything once and for all.

She hadn't taken more than two steps when the putrid smell of smoke hit her nostrils. Then she noticed the flash of deep orange light just a few feet away.

Before the fear even registered, she turned to try to run through the thick and heavy foliage. A fire.

The Mila's Bloom fields were ablaze. And the flames would reach her at any moment.

He had no reason to feel guilty. R.J. grabbed the last of his things from the room he and Angel had shared for the past several days. Zipping up his overnight bag, he paused to look around once more at the room. The same room they had spent days in as man and wife.

The phoniness of it all sent a wave of bitterness through him. He knew Angel would get the deal she had come down here for. He'd played his part well.

Aside from falling for his wife again, that is. There was that one small glitch.

He swore out loud. Whom was he kidding? He'd never fallen *out* of love with her. Still, he could leave now with a clear conscience. The contracts were about to be signed, and Shanna was on her way to escort Angel back.

There was no reason for him to stick around. He'd only

hurt her further if he stayed. All he'd ever managed to do was confuse her, and hurt her in the process.

She was a Scott. A true Boston Brahmin. She had certain obligations. People had expectations of her. None of which involved marriage to a hood from the projects of South Boston.

He'd contact Richard Scott as soon as he returned to the States. To let him know he was moving forward with the divorce and that Richard should make plans to contact his estranged daughter. The rift between them had gone on long enough. It was time for Angel to resume her rightful place in the world she'd been born into.

What a mess. He was deeply in love with a woman from one of New England's most prominent dynasties. But he wouldn't allow that love to cost her everything she'd known her whole life.

That's why he had to leave now.

He debated conducting another search for an object that seemed to have disappeared.

You've lost it. It's gone.

If he delayed much longer he'd miss his flight. Besides, maybe it was a telling sign that he'd misplaced his original wedding band. Still, to have lost it after all this time. But he had to let it go. There was no more time left to look for it. He had to let *her* go, too.

He'd already bidden farewell to the Bays and had packed everything else. Angel had disappeared. It was better this way. This time she was the one being logical about things. There was no reason to prolong their leave-taking.

Rubbing a palm down his face, he walked over to the phone. It was time to call for his ride to the airport. He picked up the receiver, then dropped it back into the cradle at the sound of a knock on the door.

Damn. Not right now. He just needed to get out of here. The sooner, the better.

"Yeah?" He knew he sounded curt.

"It's Mila. May I come in?"

What did she want? They'd already said their goodbyes.

"Sure," he answered, despite what he was thinking. "But I'm afraid I don't have much time."

"I see you're packed," Mila said as she breezed into the room.

"Yep. Just about to leave." He threw his toiletries case in the carry-on bag.

"It's too bad you got called back to your office. The four of us could have celebrated signing the contracts tonight." She moved over to the bed and sat down, watching him with probing eyes.

"Angel will have to do enough celebrating for both of us. I've been away long enough," he said, somewhat terse. He didn't want to be rude. He just wanted to get as far away from here as possible.

Mila seemed intent on delaying that.

"I hardly think that's possible," she said. "It's clear from the way she looks at you how much she enjoys your company. She seems to light up when the two of you are together."

Apparently, he and Angel were pretty good actors after all. They had Mila believing wholeheartedly they were a happy young couple still in love. Then again, they weren't acting 100 percent of the time, were they?

"That sounds a little exaggerated," he said and zipped up his garment bag.

"I don't think so. You get a little spark in your eye as well when you look at her, you know."

Man, this was the last thing he needed to be hearing right now. "She is my wife," he managed to say.

"I think it's marvelous."

"What's that?" he asked. Where was all this leading?

"Well, between all of us, we seem to cover the whole range of happy couples."

"Not sure what you mean, Mila."

"Well, there's Reid and Kaya, representing the newest of the group. They've just started the dawn of their life together. You and Angel are in the middle of the spectrum, so to speak." She paused a moment. "How long did you say you've been married?"

There didn't seem to be any way to avoid answering her question. "About six years," he told her. But we've been apart for three, he added silently in his head.

Mila nodded. "Then there's me and Tavov. We're clearly the most seasoned of the group. Do you know we've been married twenty-three years?"

He had to give that the credit it was due. "That's amazing, Mila. And impressive."

She smiled wide. "Yes, and to think no one thought it would last."

His curiosity stirred. "Yeah?"

"Oh, yes. Everyone was convinced we didn't have enough in common. You see, when we met, Tavov had nothing but his dreams. My parents had worked hard all their lives to give me a safe, secure life. They didn't think I should risk my future with someone who had nothing."

R.J. had stopped packing, fully interested in the story now.

Mila continued, a faraway look in her eyes. "But I knew exactly how happy he could make me. I believed in him. We invested every penny of my trust fund toward these orchards. I had every faith that no matter how the investment turned out, Tavov was meant for me. And I was right. Even if he hadn't discovered and cultivated such a popular product, all I really needed from him was the love he's shown me all these years. Of course, we've had our problems, everyone does."

R.J. was starting to get the distinct feeling there was a message intended for him. But why?

Mila stood up off the bed. "Well, that's enough useless musing from an old woman." She walked over to him and placed a motherly palm on his cheek. "I wish you could stay a little longer."

She moved to the door and left before he could respond.

His thoughts shifted to Angel. He had to see her once more. He honestly didn't know if it had anything to do with what Mila just said. But he couldn't leave just yet, not with things as they were.

Hell, he just had to look into her eyes one more time. All logic aside.

He walked over to the balcony to see if he could spot her on the grounds. A small glow coming from the fields caught his eye.

He squinted in the light to make out exactly what it was. Clarity and horror struck at once. There was no way to jump down the three stories. He turned and started running downstairs.

God, don't let her be in the tea fields.

"Tavov," he bellowed, not pausing to see if he was within earshot.

"My goodness, man." Tavov ran toward him. "What's the matter?" Mila followed on his heels. All three of them finally reached the front door step.

"The fields," R.J. called out. "There's a fire. Call for help. Now!"

"My crop," Tavov wailed as he ran out the door behind him. "It's on fire. The whole field will go up in minutes."

"Angel!" R.J. yelled out her name even as he prayed she wasn't in there. But his sixth sense told him otherwise. He heard a faint sob behind him and realized Mila had followed him to the edge of the field.

It was impossible to see more than a few feet into the

fields. It appeared the flames had fully engulfed the center. If that was the case, and Angel was in there…

No! Not like this. God, he couldn't lose her. Especially not like this.

"Angel," he yelled louder. "Answer me!"

He quickly took off his jacket and shirt, subconsciously considering how flammable the material was.

"R.J.," Mila's despondent voice cried out to him. "What are you doing? It's no use."

He moved closer toward the fire.

"R.J., stop!" This time it was Tavov. "It's destroyed. There's nothing you can do. Where are you going?"

"Just stay back," R.J. ordered and turned to make sure they had obeyed.

There was no time to explain. Besides, they would try to stop him. After all, he had no clear proof that she was in there. But his gut told him she was. And for now, that was all he needed.

He choked as clouds of black smoke hit his lungs. He'd had to escape and jump from blasts before. But he'd never actually been inside a fire. What if he failed?

His father's voice chose that moment to ram through his panicked brain.

"You're too big for your britches, boy. Sooner or later you're gonna fail. You think you're good enough to do anything. You're not."

He had to be. He had to be good enough for this. He had to get her out of there. Or die trying.

"Angel!" He looked around, his vision almost completely obstructed now. The hairs on his skin started to singe. He was running out of time. What if she was on the other side of the field? There were rows and rows of plants. She could be anywhere.

And then he knew. Or he hoped he knew. He ran to the other side of the field. He had precious little time.

Please, let her have gone there.

He was only a few feet from the spot where they had both struggled to unearth the one plant. The same spot where he'd given in to the urge to finally touch her. Where she'd made him laugh as she shuddered in fear and disgust at the many bugs he was making her sit in.

He wasn't the kind of man someone like her deserved.

Or so he had thought. Now, with death staring him in the face, he almost laughed at that. It was up to him to become that man, and for her, he would.

If only he found her in time. He'd tell her all that. He'd tell her everything.

CHAPTER FOURTEEN

ANGEL TRIED TO curb the panic surging through her. She had to think. Rapid tears ran down her face. Flames danced around her, courting her like a demonic partner. She wasn't afraid of dying. At least she didn't think so. She was afraid of the agonizing pain.

Could a person willingly force herself into a catatonic state? She was out of options here.

Options. Choices. Choices she'd had, and the paths she'd chosen. All of it flashed before her eyes in an instant. She felt a sob emerge through her as she gagged. If she'd have the chance to do it over again, she'd do it so much differently. She loved him. And he loved her. She would make him see that. Somehow she'd make him understand.

If given the chance, she'd show him he meant more to her than anything else. Definitely more than returning to her life as Richard Scott's daughter and sole heir.

She choked out another sob as the thick smoke burned through her sinuses and throat. Consciousness slowly edged away, and she welcomed the comfort of darkness.

She could almost hear him. Could almost hear his voice calling out to her. But she knew it was a dream. Knew it was too late.

She managed to utter his name. And then the darkness started to press heavier and heavier. She felt the hard ground beneath her and realized she didn't remember falling.

Coughing. Someone was coughing. Was it her? It was just so hard to try to concentrate.

Suddenly, miraculously, she felt herself lifted. Someone was here. Someone was helping her.

She could only pray she wasn't imagining it.

The burning light was different this time. She could still taste the smoke in the back of her throat, but it didn't burn as strongly. Angel fought to open her eyes, not sure if she really wanted to.

This light *was* different. It was coming from a lamp above her.

Did heaven have lamps?

"Well, look who's finally stirring."

And apparently heaven had greeters who sounded just like Shanna.

Angeline tried to speak, but dryness stilled her tongue. "W-water..."

Someone touched plastic to her lip, and she opened her mouth as cool, smooth liquid slid down her throat. It hurt like hell to swallow. She forced herself to open her eyes completely, slowly letting the brightness seep in.

A familiar face hovered above her. She felt a smile form on her lips.

"N-not heaven," she croaked out.

"Well, I'm not sure how to take that comment."

Angel felt a comforting hand gently take hold of her wrist.

"Shan."

"Shh..." the other woman cooed. "I'm here, darling. I'm right here. But you take it easy, okay?"

"'Kay..."

"More water?"

Angel tried to nod but only managed a slight lift of her head. The plastic touched her lips again, and she sipped from it slowly. Exhausted from the small effort, she sank her head deeper into the pillow.

"Alive," Angel muttered, more to seek validation of her unexpected state.

Shanna nodded above her. "Yes, darling. You're alive. And you're going to be fine."

"S-sorry."

"Well, you should be." Shanna's voice broke. "I distinctly told you when you left not to play with fire."

Angeline did her best impression of a laugh. "Y-you m-meant R—" She stopped. It took several moments before she could resume. "R.J." She finally managed to finish.

Shanna nodded. "Yes, yes, of course." She then turned and left the room.

Angeline felt too tired to try to figure out why Shanna had left. And the burning sensation in her eyes was intensifying. Closing her lids slowly, she allowed herself to drift back to sleep, not even hearing the excited voices of the three people when they entered the room.

"You know they're going to start charging you rent here if you don't wake up soon." R.J. tried to sound casual as Angel slowly roused herself from sleep. As jokes went, it was a pretty lame one. And her startled eyes told him she hadn't really heard it.

She tried to sit up, and he immediately reached to help her. "Whoa, there. Take it easy."

"What are you doing here?" She spoke very slowly, and he felt his chest tighten at the thought of all the pain she must be in. He sat on the edge of the bed near her pillow and gently took her into his arms.

"We've been waiting for you to wake up again. Who knew it was going to take you another whole day?"

"We?"

"Yeah, Shanna's here, too. And my business partner, Tom. He flew her personally in the jet when they heard what had happened."

"You flew back?" she asked him.

"He never left," Shanna's voice boomed cheerily from the doorway.

Angel's confusion showed on her face. Shanna moved closer to the bed.

"How are you?" Shanna reached for Angeline's hand and sat beside him on the side of the bed.

"I--I guess I'm fine."

Angel turned questioning eyes back to him. He trailed a finger down her cheek. He had to touch her. To make sure she was really there. "I came back to talk to you. One more time, I figured, before I left for the States. I saw the fields on fire and realized you must have been in there."

"B-but how?"

R.J. shrugged.

"Isn't it just like a man?" Shanna gave him a mocking glare. "Leaving out the best details. He just knew, Angeline. And he managed to find you. Luckily, by then you'd managed to get yourself far enough away from the smoke."

R.J. watched as Angeline's mouth came open. "You saved me?"

He touched a finger to her lips. He didn't need or want words of gratitude. She'd never understand fully that he'd jump into hundreds of fires for her if he had to.

She acknowledged the gesture with a slight movement of her head. "What happened? How did it start?"

R.J.'s arms tightened around her. "No one really knows. Probably one of the celebratory candles from the wedding made its way to the field. Or someone dropped a cigar that smoldered until it finally caught flame."

Her lips tightened. "Is everyone okay?"

"You were the only one near the fields. No one else was injured. And the doctor Mila and Tavov had check you out said you were very lucky."

She dropped her gaze, and he could anticipate her next question.

"The crop?"

He'd been right.

He tightened his lips, not wanting to dump the bad news on her. But she was going to find out sooner or later. "I'm sorry," he replied finally.

"All of it?"

"I'm afraid every last plant was destroyed before they could put the fire out."

She shut her eyes tight. "H-how are Mila and Tavov taking it?"

"They're just glad no one was hurt," he tried to reassure her.

He could see her desperate effort to try to compose herself as she processed the news. "There isn't even one bush left? Nothing with which they can replant from?" she asked, her voice shaky.

He blew out a deep breath. "Angel, don't do this to yourself."

"Please, R.J. I need to know. Is there any possibility something was salvaged?"

He rubbed his face and stood. "I'm afraid not, sweetheart. The fire destroyed every single plant on the Bays' property."

Desolation filled her eyes, and he could do nothing but give her the full finality of it. "The Bays told me there's nowhere else it can be found. It only grows on this soil. And every last plant is gone."

Her reaction to this last bit of news confused the hell out of him. Her eyes grew wide, but not with sadness this time. Then a slow smile spread across her face. He watched in shock as the grin turned into all-out laughter. He decided to ring for the doctor when her laughter grew even louder.

"No, no. I'm okay. I think things may turn out okay, after all." R.J.'s look told her he clearly thought she'd lost it.

"Angel, I just told you that the Bays lost every single last plant."

She smiled again. "Maybe not," she said. "Maybe not."

"It's wonderful to see you up and about again, dear." Mila stood from where she was kneeling and brushed the dirt off her knees.

"How's the soil prep going?"

"Fine, fine. Luckily, the ground was moist enough that it wasn't damaged too deeply. And thank the heavens you had that plant in your room. I shudder to think what we'd have lost if you hadn't had the impulse to want one in your room. With the way Mila's Bloom divides and spreads, we might have a small harvest within a couple of seasons. Not much, but that will change with time." She gave her a wide smile. "That would certainly make your product much more exclusive initially."

Then Mila scanned Angeline with concerned eyes. "But enough about that. How are you feeling? Will you be able to make your trip tomorrow?"

"I think so. It's R.J.'s company's private plane. I'll have the three of them to take care of me."

As if on cue, Tom and Shanna materialized out of the fields. Shan had streaks of dirt around her cheeks and nose. Tom was fast on her heels. They both looked annoyed.

"Look, stop pestering me. I don't need your help," Shanna was insisting.

"Why are you so damn stubborn? All I did was carry some lousy water for you."

They stormed right past Angeline and Mila as Shanna replied in a huff, "You're the stubborn one. Even though I said not to, you yanked those buckets right out of my hands.

If you're planning to play hero, forget it. Been there, done that." She threw her hands in the air.

Angeline watched them descend toward the house and turned to give Mila an inquisitive look.

"They've been acting like that since they got here," the older woman said.

Angel smiled. "Looks like it's going to be an interesting flight." Her attention returned to the matter at hand, and the heavy weight once again settled inside her chest.

"Mila, I—I need to discuss something with you and Tavov before we leave. I meant to do this before—" she paused and let out a breath "—before everything happened."

"Tavov had to go purchase some materials. Why don't the two of us talk until he gets here?"

Angel started chewing her bottom lip. "I was kind of hoping to tell you both at once."

Mila reached and took her hand. She started leading her to the wooden park bench a few feet away.

"I think it might be better if us girls chatted a little bit first," Mila insisted.

Angel sat down on the bench with a thud, then shifted uncomfortably as her thighs hit the hard surface. She hadn't suffered any serious burns, but her skin was still tender. It was like she'd fallen asleep under the sun.

For several hours, near the equator, in the nude.

She shook her head and berated herself for the negative thoughts. She'd been very lucky.

"All right, then," she began. "What I'm about to say isn't going to be easy."

Mila gave her an understanding look. It was enough encouragement to just spill it all out.

"Mila," she started again, "the ugly truth is that R.J. and I weren't really together when I told you we were. I mean, at first we were. We were originally, but when we told you that we were, we weren't."

Mila's expression didn't change. "I mean," Angel tried to continue, realizing she wasn't making any sense, "we were, but we were officially separated."

God, this was harder than she had thought. "We lied, Mila. I lied, so that Tavov would at least start negotiating. R.J. was just trying to help me. Then we were going to tell you, but I never mustered up enough courage to do it." She was rambling. She thumped her palm to her forehead. "I'm not making any sense, am I?" She must not be because Mila wouldn't still be sitting there so calmly if she was.

"Let me try this again." She turned to face the other woman, then felt a reassuring squeeze on her hand.

"It's all right dear, I think I understand."

"No, you can't really…"

"Angeline, dear, I do. I know all about it. I've known for a while now."

Angel blinked. Once, twice. Mila's hand patted hers. "But you never said anything."

"I felt you needed to tell me yourself. After you and R.J. had worked out your—how do you Americans say it? Issues? Hmm?"

"How long have you known?"

"I wasn't sure until the morning after the wedding."

"What gave us away?"

"You mean besides the longing that was so apparent in each of you? I could see that both of you were keeping yourselves at a distance. But the looks you stole when you thought the other wasn't looking… The real giveaway was your argument on the balcony that morning. Tavov and I were right below. We heard most of it."

Angel put a hand through her hair and looked out at the sea. "Oh my God, Tavov heard it, too?"

"He and I spoke about it. We both agreed to let you two

settle it between yourselves before having to deal with us. Then it appeared you'd never get a chance when R.J. announced he was leaving. We also agreed that you hadn't actually ever lied to us. You were a married woman. And you both admitted to having problems that morning in Boston when I stopped by to check on you."

She'd never thought of it that way. Mila's words served as a figurative balm on her guilty soul. Much like the one she had to apply every few hours on her abused skin.

"Still, we should have told you that we knew. Please, please forgive us," Mila pled and squeezed her hand.

Now, that was irony. Mila was asking for forgiveness from *her*. The heavy weight on her heart finally lifted. "Only if you return the favor."

"It's hard to believe we've only been living in this suite for a week." Angeline stared out at the view from the balcony and felt R.J.'s hands on her upper arms.

"Something tells me you're ready to leave." She allowed herself to lean back into him. He felt so solid, so secure.

"I wanted to come out here one last time." She turned to face him.

She rested her cheek against his chest. Still unable to believe he was here with her, holding her.

The avalanche of emotions running through her were hard to put into words. But she had to try. "We've been given another chance. I'd like to take it. A lot of things went wrong with us, R.J. But there's so much more that's so right. We need to look at *our* lives together, moving forward. Our future together is what matters now. Not what the past was, not what anyone else thinks."

He pulled her tighter against him and stroked her cheek with gentle fingers. "I know, sweetheart. Life is too precious to live it without you. I'm tired of going through the motions. I don't plan on making the same mistakes again."

A comfortable silence ensued, and she took advantage of it to merely savor the feel of his arms around her.

He rubbed his chin against the top of her head as he spoke. “And you don’t have to worry about keeping TeaLC solvent until the next full harvest. I already have my finance people working on transferring the funds.”

She stepped back to stare at him. “I don’t want you to—”

He cut her off. “I am technically your partner, Angel. In every sense now. Let me invest in my own company.” He smiled, then corrected, “Our company, that is.”

“Thank you.” It was all she could think to say, the emotion welling inside her close to choking her up.

“You’re welcome.” He gave her one last squeeze. “We better get going. I know TeaLC has been missing its leader for quite a while.”

She slowly pulled out of his embrace to look at him. “That will take care of itself when Shanna gets back.”

He lifted an eyebrow. “I don’t understand.”

“I’ve turned over the reins to its new CEO. Shanna deserves it. She knows the business as well as I do. She’s already got the plans drawn for the launch of the newest product once the harvest is ready—Angel’s Brew.”

He smiled wide. “She’s a genius.”

“Besides, I’m much better at launch and development than I am at maintenance management.”

He narrowed his eyes. “What exactly does that mean?”

“I’ll be too busy to manage TeaLC.”

“Busy doing what?”

“Focusing on what I’m good at.” She touched a hand to his cheek. “And working on what I haven’t been so good at in the past.”

“Meaning?”

“I’m going to try to take TeaLC Works national.”

She’d come to the decision last night, surprised it hadn’t occurred to her before. “To pitch the idea to other major corporations. I can show them exactly how to recruit from women's shelters and how much of a philanthropic effect it can have on the community.

"And if you let me, while I'm doing that, I'd like to work on being your wife."

As her answer, she felt herself being picked up and thoroughly kissed.

"Is that a yes?"

"I think it's about time we had a real honeymoon," he said with a laugh.

"You mean you'd actually be willing to risk another trip with me?"

He set her down and rubbed his jaw. "Mmm, maybe not. We don't actually have to go anywhere. It's really not necessary. Especially given what I want to do for most of our honeymoon."

"And what would that be?" she asked before realizing what a loaded question it was.

He gave her a wicked wink, and she had to laugh. "But aside from that." He cleared his throat, and his eyes suddenly turned serious. Slowly, she let him take her in his arms and hold her close.

"I just want to hold you. I just want to dance."

She tilted her head to look up at him, the surge of emotion almost too much for her heart to handle. "We get in trouble when we dance together. You said so yourself."

"Mmm-hmm," he agreed. "I know. Why don't we start now?"

* * * * *

If you enjoyed this book, don't miss
MISS PRIM AND THE MAVERICK MILLIONAIRE,
the debut novel by Nina Singh. Available now!

If you can't wait to read another fake relationship
romance then make sure you treat yourself to
THE MILLIONAIRE'S REDEMPTION
by Therese Beharrie.

“We’re not giving up now,” Brenna said. “Don’t even think it.”

“But are you…?”

“We are doing this.” Her eyes had stars in them. “And we are taking home the prize.”

“Brenna…” She smelled of flowers and fresh-cut grass. Travis really wanted to kiss her.

“Do it,” she whispered, clearly reading his mind. “We need to do it. How can we pretend that we’re headed for forever when you’ve never even put your lips on mine?”

Was she right? Did he really *need* to kiss her to make their fake relationship seem real? All he could think was that he’d never kissed her—and he *had* to kiss her.

He lowered his head a fraction closer and she surged up.

His mouth touched hers.

With a sigh, she let go of his shirtfront. Her hands slid up to clasp the back of his neck. “Travis…” She stroked his nape with her soft fingers as she whispered his name, kissing it onto his lips.

So good. So right. She tasted of honey, of ripe summer fruit—peaches and blackberries, watermelon. Cherries. She tasted of promises, sweet hopes and big dreams. She tasted of home.

Someone yelled, “Kiss her, cowboy!”

Neither Travis nor Brenna paid their hecklers any mind. The brims of their hats collided. His fell and then hers. Neither of them cared.

* * *

Montana Mavericks:
The Great Family Roundup—
Real cowboys and real love in Rust Creek Falls!

THE MAVERICK FAKES A BRIDE!

BY
CHRISTINE RIMMER

First Published in Great Britain 2017
By Mills & Boon, an imprint of HarperCollins*Publishers*
1 London Bridge Street, London, SE1 9GF

Special thanks and acknowledgement are given to Christine Rimmer for her contribution to the Montana Mavericks: The Great Family Roundup continuity.

ISBN: 978-0-263-92314-8

23-0717

Our policy is to use papers that are natural, renewable and recyclable products and made from wood grown in sustainable forests. The logging and manufacturing processes conform to the legal environmental regulations of the country of origin.

Printed and bound in Spain
by CPI, Barcelona

Christine Rimmer came to her profession the long way around. She tried everything from acting to teaching to telephone sales. Now she's finally found work that suits her perfectly. She insists she never had a problem keeping a job—she was merely gaining "life experience" for her future as a novelist. Christine lives with her family in Oregon. Visit her at www.christinerimmer.com.

For MSR,
always.

Chapter One

It was a warm day for March. And everyone in Bee's Beauty Parlor that afternoon had gathered at the wide front windows to watch as Travis Dalton rode his favorite bay gelding down Broomtail Road.

The guy was every cowgirl's fantasy in a snug Western shirt, butt-hugging jeans, Tony Lama Boots and a black hat. One of those film school graduates from the little theater in nearby Kalispell, a video camera stuck to his face, walked backward ahead of him, recording his every move. Travis talked and gestured broadly as he went.

"My, my, my." Bee smoothed her brassy blond hair, though it didn't need it. Even in a high wind, Bee's hair never moved. "Travis does have one fine seat on a horse."

There were soft, low sounds of agreement and appreciation from the women at the window—and then, out of nowhere, Travis tossed his hat in the air and flipped to a handstand right there on that horse in the middle of the street.

The women applauded. There was more than one outright cry of delight.

Only Brenna O'Reilly stood still and silent. She had her arms wrapped around her middle to keep from clapping, and she'd firmly tucked her lips between her teeth in order not to let out a single sound.

Because no way was Brenna sighing over Travis Dalton. Yes, he was one hot cowboy, with that almost-black hair and those dangerous blue eyes, that hard, lean body and that grin that could make a girl's lady parts spontaneously combust.

And it wasn't only his looks that worked for her. Sometimes an adventurous woman needed a hero on hand. Travis had come to her rescue more than once in her life.

But he'd always made a big deal about how he was too old for her—and okay, maybe he'd had a point, back when she was six and he was fourteen. But now that she'd reached the grown-up age of twenty-six, what did eight years even matter?

Never mind. Not going to happen, Brenna reminded herself for the ten thousandth time. And no matter what people in town might say, she was not and never had been in love with the man.

Right now, today, she was simply appreciating the view, which was spectacular.

Beside her, Dovey Jukes actually let out a moan and made a big show of fanning herself. "Is it just me, or is it *really* hot in here?"

"This is his, er, what did you call it now, Melba?" Bee asked old Melba Strickland, who'd come out from under the dryer to watch the local heartthrob ride by.

"It's his package," replied Melba.

Dovey snickered.

Bee let out her trademark smoke-and-whiskey laugh. "Not *that* kind of package." She gave Dovey a playful slap on the arm.

"It's reality television slang," Melba clarified. "Tessa told me all about it." Melba's granddaughter lived in Los Angeles now. Tessa Strickland Drake had a high-powered job in advertising and understood how things worked in the entertainment industry. "A package is an audition application and video."

"Audition for what?" one of the other girls asked.

"A brand-new reality show." Melba was in the know. "It's going to get made at a secret location right here in Montana this summer, and it will be called *The Great Roundup*. From what I heard, it's going to be like *Survivor*, but with cowboys—you know, roping and branding, bringing in the strays, everyone sharing their life stories around the campfire, sleeping out under the stars, answering challenge after challenge, trying not to get eliminated. The winner will earn himself a million-dollar prize."

Brenna, who'd never met a challenge she couldn't rise to, clutched the round thermal brush in her hand a little tighter and tried to ignore the tug of longing in her heart. After all, she'd been raised on the family ranch and could rope and ride with the best of them. She couldn't help but imagine herself on this new cowboy reality show.

True, lately, she'd been putting in some serious effort to quell her wild and crazy side, to settle down a little, you might say.

But a reality show? She could enjoy the excitement while accomplishing a valid goal of winning those big bucks. A few months ago, Bee had started dating a handsome sixtyish widower from Kalispell. Now that things had gotten serious, she'd been talking about selling the shop and retiring so she and her new man could travel. Brenna would love to step up as owner when Bee left.

But that would cost money she didn't have. If she won a million dollars on a reality show, however, she could buy the shop and still have plenty of money to spare.

And then again, no. Trying out for a reality show was a crazy idea, and Brenna was keeping a lid on her wild side, she truly was. *The Great Roundup* was not for her.

She asked wistfully, "You think Travis has a chance to be on the show?"

"Are you kidding?" Bee let out a teasing growl. "Those Hollywood people would be crazy not to choose him. And if the one doing the choosing is female, all that man has to do is give her a smile."

Every woman at that window enthusiastically agreed.

First week of May, a studio soundstage,
Los Angeles, California

Travis Dalton hooked his booted foot across his knee and relaxed in the interview chair.

It was happening. *Really* happening. His video had wowed them. And his application? He'd broken all the rules with it, just like that book he'd bought—*Be a Re-*

ality Star—had instructed. He'd used red ink, added lots of silly Western doodles and filled it chock-full of colorful stories of his life on the family ranch.

He'd knocked them clean out of their boots, if he did say so himself. And now here he was in Hollywood auditioning for *The Great Roundup.*

"Tell us about growing up on a ranch," said the casting director, whose name was Giselle. Giselle dressed like a fashion model. She had a way of making a guy feel like she could see inside his head. *Sharp.* That was the word for Giselle. Sharp—and interested. Her calculating eyes watched him so closely.

Which was fine. Good. He wanted her looking at him with interest. He wanted to make the cut, get on *The Great Roundup* and win himself a million bucks.

Travis gave a slow grin in the general direction of one of the cameras that recorded every move he made. "I grew up on my family's ranch in northwestern Montana." He was careful to include Giselle's question in his answer, in case they ended up using this interview in the show. Then they could cut Giselle's voice out and what he said would still make perfect sense. "My dad put me on a horse for the first time at the age of five. Sometimes it feels like I was born in the saddle."

Giselle and her assistant nodded their approval as he went on—about the horses he'd trained and the ones that had thrown him. About the local rodeos where he'd been bucked off more than one bad-tempered bull—and made it all the way to eight full seconds on a few. He thought it was going pretty well, that he was charming them, winning them over, showing them he wasn't shy, that an audience would love him.

"Can you take off your shirt for us, Travis?"

He'd assumed that would be coming. Rising, Travis unbuttoned and shrugged out of his shirt. At first, he kept it all business, no funny stuff. They needed to get a good look at the body that ranching had built and he kept in shape. He figured they wouldn't be disappointed.

But they wanted to see a little personality, too, so when Giselle instructed, "Turn around slowly," he held out his arms, bending his elbows and bringing them down, giving them the cowboy version of a bodybuilder's flex. As he turned, he grabbed his hat off the back of his chair and plunked it on his head, aiming his chin to the side, giving them a profile shot, and then going all the way with a slow grin and a wink over his shoulder.

The casting assistant, Roxanne, stifled a giggle as she grinned right back.

"Go ahead and sit back down," Giselle said. She wasn't flirty like Roxanne, but in her sharp-edged way she seemed happy with how the interview was shaking out.

Travis took off his hat again. He bent to get his shirt.

"Leave it," said Giselle.

He gave her a slight nod and no smile as he settled back into the chair. Because this was serious business. To him—and to her.

"Now we want to know about that hometown of yours." Giselle almost smiled then, though really it was more of a smirk. "We've been hearing some pretty crazy things about Rust Creek Falls."

Was he ready for that one? You bet he was. His town had been making news the past few years. First came the flood. He explained about the Fourth of July rains that wouldn't stop and all the ways the people of Rust Creek Falls had pulled together to come back from the worst disaster in a century. He spoke of rebuilding after the waters receded, of the national attention and the sudden influx of young women who had come to town to find themselves a cowboy.

When Giselle asked if any of those women had found *him*, he answered in a lazy drawl, "To tell you the truth, I met a lot of pretty women after the great flood." He put his right hand on his chest. "Each one of them holds a special place in my heart."

Roxanne had to stifle another giggle.

Giselle sent her a cool look. Roxanne's smile vanished as if it had never been. "Tell us more," said Giselle.

And he told them about a certain Fourth of July wedding almost two years ago now, a wedding in Rust Creek Falls Park. A local eccentric by the name of Homer Gilmore had spiked the wedding punch with his special recipe moonshine—purported to make people do things they would never do ordinarily.

"A few got in fights," he confessed, "present company included, I'm sorry to say." He made an effort to look appropriately embarrassed at his own behavior before adding, "And a whole bunch of folks got romantic—and that meant that *last* year, Rust Creek Falls had a serious baby boom. You might have heard of that. We called it the 'baby bonanza.' So now we have what amounts to a population explosion in our little town. Nobody's complaining, though. In Rust Creek Falls, love and family is what it's all about."

Travis explained that he wanted to join the cast of *The Great Roundup* for the thrill of it—and he also wanted to be the last cowboy standing. He had a fine life working the Dalton family ranch, but the million-dollar prize would build him his own house on the land he loved and put a little money in the bank, too.

"I'm not getting any younger," he admitted with a smile he hoped came across as both sexy *and* modest. "One of these days, I might even want to find the right girl and settle down."

Giselle, who had excellent posture in the first place, seemed to sit up even straighter, like a prize hunting dog catching a scent. "The right girl? Interesting." She glanced at Roxanne, who bobbed her head in an eager nod. "Is there anyone special you've got your eye on?"

There was no one, and there probably wouldn't be anytime soon. But he got Giselle's message loud and clear. For some reason, the casting director would prefer that he had a sweetheart.

And what Giselle preferred, Travis Dalton was bound and determined to deliver. "Is there a special woman in my life? Well, she's a…very private person."

"That would be yes, then. You're exclusive with someone?"

Damn. Message received, loud and clear. He wasn't getting out of this without confessing—or lying through his teeth. And since he intended to get on the show, he knew what his choice had to be.

"I don't want to speak out of hand, but yeah. There is a special someone in my life now. We…haven't been together long, but…" He let out a low whistle and pasted on an expression that he hoped would pass for completely smitten. "Oh, yeah. *Special* would be the word for her."

"Is this special someone a hometown girl?" Giselle's eyes twinkled in a way that was simultaneously aggressive, gleeful and calculating.

"She's from Rust Creek Falls, yes. And she's amazing." *Whoever the hell she is.* "It's the greatest thing in the world, to know someone your whole life and then suddenly to realize there's a lot more going on between the two of you than you've ever admitted before." Whoa. He probably ought to be ashamed of himself. His mama had brought him up right, taught him not to tell lies. But who did this little white lie hurt, anyway? Not a soul. And to get on *The Great Roundup*, Travis Dalton would tell Giselle whatever she needed to hear.

"What's her name?" asked Giselle. It was the next logical question, damn it. He should have known it was coming.

He put on his best killer smile—and lied some more. "Sorry, I can't tell you her name. You know small towns." Giselle frowned. She might be sharp as a barbwire fence, but he would bet his Collin Traub dress saddle that she'd never been within a hundred miles of a town like Rust Creek Falls. "We're keeping what we have together just between the two of us, my girl and me. It's a special time in our relationship, and we don't want the whole town butting into our private business." *A special time.* Damned if he didn't sound downright sensitive—for a bald-faced liar. But would the casting director buy it?

Giselle didn't seem all that thrilled with his unwillingness to out his nonexistent girlfriend, but at least she let it go. A few minutes later, she gave the cameraman a break. Then she chatted with Travis off the record for a couple of minutes more. She said she'd heard he was staying at the Malibu house of LA power player Carson Drake, whose wife, Tessa Strickland Drake, had deep Montana roots. Travis explained that he'd known Tessa all his life. She'd grown up in Bozeman, but she spent most of her childhood summers staying at her grandmother's boardinghouse in Rust Creek Falls.

After the chitchat, Giselle asked him to have a seat outside. He put on his shirt and grabbed a chair in the waiting area next to a watercooler and vending machine. For the next few hours, he watched potential contestants come and go.

It was past six when they called him back in to tell him that he wouldn't be returning to Malibu that night—or anytime soon, as it turned out. Real Deal Entertainment would put him up in a hotel room instead.

Travis lived in that hotel room for two weeks at Real Deal's beck and call. He took full advantage of room service, and he worked out in the hotel fitness center to pass the time while he got his background checked and his blood drawn. He even got interviewed by a shrink, who asked a lot of way-too-personal questions. There were also a series of follow-up meetings with casting people and producers. At the two-week mark, in a Century City office tower, he got a little quality time with a bunch of network suits.

That evening, absolutely certain he'd made the show, he raided the minibar in his room and raised a toast to his success.

Hot damn, he'd done it! He was going to be a contestant on *The Great Roundup*. He would have his shot at a cool million bucks.

And he would win, too. Damned if he wouldn't. He would build his own house on the family ranch and get more say in the day-to-day running of the place. His older brother, Anderson, made most of the decisions now. But if Travis had some hard cash to invest, his big brother would take him more seriously. Travis would step up as a real partner in running the ranch.

Being the good-time cowboy of the family had been fun. But there comes a point when every man has to figure out what to do with his life. Travis had reached that point. And *The Great Roundup* was going to take him where he needed to go.

The next morning, a car arrived to deliver him to the studio, where he sat in another waiting area outside a different soundstage with pretty much the same group of potential contestants he'd sat with two weeks before. One by one, they were called through the door. They all emerged smiling to be swiftly led away by their drivers.

When Travis's turn came, he walked onto the soundstage to find Giselle and Roxanne and a couple producers waiting at a long table. The camera was rolling. Except for that meeting in the office tower with the suits and a session involving lawyers with papers to sign, a camera had been pointed at him every time they talked to him.

Giselle said, "Have a seat, Travis." He took the lone chair facing the others at the table. "We have some great news for you."

He knew it—he was in! He did a mental fist pump.

But then Giselle said, "You've made the cut for the final audition."

What the hell? *Another* audition?

"You'll love this, Travis." Giselle watched him expectantly as she announced, "The final audition will be in Rust Creek Falls."

Wait. What?

She went on, "As it happens, your hometown is not

far from the supersecret location where *The Great Roundup* will be filmed. And since your first audition, we have been busy…"

Dirk Henley, one of the producers, chimed in, "We've been in touch with the mayor and the town council."

"Of Rust Creek Falls?" Travis asked, feeling dazed. He was still trying to deal with the fact that there was more auditioning to get through. He couldn't believe she'd just said the audition would be happening in his hometown.

"Of course, of Rust Creek Falls." Giselle actually smiled, a smile that tried to be indulgent but was much too full of sharp white teeth to be anything but scary.

Dirk took over again. "Mayor Traub and the other council members are excited to welcome Real Deal Entertainment to their charming little Montana town."

Travis valiantly remained positive. Okay, he hadn't made the final cut, but he was still in the running and that was what mattered.

As for the final audition happening at home, well, now that he'd had a second or two to deal with that information, he supposed he wasn't all that surprised.

For a show like *The Great Roundup*, his hometown was a location scout's dream come true. And the mayor and the council would say yes to the idea in a New York minute. The movers and shakers of Rust Creek Falls had gotten pretty ambitious in the last few years. They were always open to anything that might bring attention, money and/or jobs to town. Real Deal Entertainment should be good for at least the first two.

Dirk said, "We'll be sending Giselle, Roxanne, a camera crew *and* a few production people along with you for a last on-camera group audition."

Giselle showed more teeth. "We're going to put you and your fellow finalists in your own milieu, you might say."

Dirk nodded his approval. "And that milieu is a very atmospheric cowboy bar with which I'm sure you are familiar."

There was only one bar inside the Rust Creek Falls town limits. Travis named it. "The Ace."

"That's right!" Dirk beamed. "The Ace in the Hole, which we love."

What did that even mean? They loved the name? Must be it. No Hollywood type would actually *love* the Ace. It was a down-home, no-frills kind of place.

Dirk was still talking. "We'll be taking over 'the Ace'—" he actually air quoted it "—for a night of rollicking country fun. You know, burgers and brews and a country-western band. We want to see you get loose, kick over the traces, party in a purely cowboy sort of way. It will be fabulous. You're going to have a great time." He nodded at the other producer, who nodded right back. "I'm sure we'll get footage we can use on the show."

And then Giselle piped up with, "And, Travis..." Her voice was much too casual, much too smooth. "We want you to bring your fiancée along to the audition. We love what you've told us about her, and we can't wait to meet her."

Chapter Two

Fiancée?

Travis's heart bounced upward into his throat. He tried not to choke and put all he had into keeping his game face on.

But…

Fiancée? When did his imaginary girlfriend become a fiancée?

He'd never in his life had a fiancée. He hadn't even been with a woman in almost a year.

Yeah, all right. He had a rep as a ladies' man and he knew how to play that rep, but all that, with the women and the wild nights? It had gotten really old over time. And then there was what had happened last summer. After that, he'd realized he needed to grow the hell up. He'd sworn off women for a while.

Damn. This was bad. Much worse than finding out

there was still another audition to get through. How had he not seen this coming?

Apparently, they'd decided they needed a little romance on the show, a young couple in love and engaged to be married—and he'd let Giselle get the idea that he could give them that. He'd thought he was playing the game, but he'd only played himself.

He tried to put on the brakes a little. "Uh, Giselle. We're not exactly engaged yet."

"But you will be." It was a command. And before he could figure out what to say next, Giselle stood. "So, we're set then. You'll be taken back to the hotel for tonight. Pack up. Your plane leaves first thing tomorrow."

Travis had come this far, and he wasn't about to give up now. Somehow, he needed to find himself a temporary fiancée. She had to be outgoing and pretty, someone who could ride a horse, build a campfire and handle a rifle, someone he could trust, someone he wouldn't mind pretending to be in love with.

And she had to be someone from town.

It was impossible. He knew that. But damn it, he was not giving up. Somehow, he had to find a way to give Giselle and the others what they wanted.

Real Deal Entertainment had a van waiting at the airport in Kalispell. The company had also sent along a production assistant, Gerry, to ride herd on the talent. Gerry made sure everyone and their luggage got on board the van and then drove them to Maverick Manor, a resort a few miles outside the Rust Creek Falls town limits.

Gerry herded them to the front desk. As he passed out the key cards, he announced that he was heading back to the airport to pick up the next group of finalists. They were to rest up and order room service. The producers and casting director would be calling everyone together first thing tomorrow right here in the main lobby.

Travis grabbed Gerry's arm before he could get away. "I need to go into town." *And rustle up a fiancée.*

Gerry frowned—but then he nodded. "Right. You're Dalton, the local guy. You can get your own ride?"

"Yeah." A ride was the least of his problems.

Gerry regarded him, narrow eyed. Travis understood. As potential talent, the production company wanted him within reach at all times. He wouldn't be free again until he was either culled from the final cast list—or the show had finished shooting, whichever happened first.

Travis was determined not to be culled. "I'm supposed to bring my fiancée to the audition tomorrow night. I really need to talk to her about that." *As soon as I can find her.*

Gerry, who was about five foot six and weighed maybe 110 soaking wet, glared up at him. "Got it. Don't mess me up, man."

"No way. I *want* this job."

"Remember your confidentiality agreement. Nothing about the production or your possible part in it gets shared."

"I remember."

"Be in your room by seven tonight. I'll be checking."

"And I'll be there."

Gerry headed for the airport, and Travis called the ranch. His mother, Mary, answered the phone. "Honey, I am on my way," she said.

He was waiting at the front entrance of the Manor when she pulled up in the battered pickup she'd been driving for as long as he could remember. She jumped out and grabbed him in a bear hug. "Two weeks in Hollywood hasn't done you any damage that I can see." She stepped back and clapped him on the arms. "Get in. Let's go."

She talked nonstop all the way back to the ranch—mostly about his father's brother, Phil, who had recently moved to town from Hardin, Montana. Phil Dalton had wanted a new start after the loss of Travis's aunt Diana. And Uncle Phil hadn't made the move alone. His and Diana's five grown sons had packed up and come with him.

At the ranch, Travis's mom insisted he come inside for a piece of her famous apple pie and some coffee.

"I don't have that long, Mom."

"Sit down," Mary commanded. "It's not gonna kill you to enjoy a slice of my pie."

So he had some pie and coffee. He saw his brother Anderson, briefly. His dad, Ben, was still at work at his law office in town.

Zach, one of Uncle Phil's boys, came in, too. "That pie looks really good, Aunt Mary."

Mary laughed. "Sit down and I'll cut you a nice big piece."

Zach poured himself some coffee and took the chair across from Travis. In his late twenties, Zach was a good-looking guy. He asked Travis, "So how's it going with that reality show you're gonna be on?"

Travis kept it vague. "We'll see. I haven't made the final cut yet."

Zach shook his head. "Well, good luck. I don't get

the appeal of all that glitzy Hollywood stuff. I'm more interested in settling down, you know? Since we lost Mom…" His voice trailed off, and his blue eyes were mournful.

"Oh, hon." Trav's mom patted Zach gently on the back. She returned to the stove and added over her shoulder, "It's a tough time, I know."

"So sorry about Aunt Diana," Travis said quietly.

Zach nodded. "Thank you both—and like I was sayin', losing Mom has reminded me of what really matters, made me see it's about time I found the right woman and started my family."

Travis ate another bite of his mother's excellent pie and then couldn't resist playing devil's advocate on the subject of settling down. "I can't even begin to understand how tough it's been for you and your dad and the other boys. But come on, Zach. You're not even thirty. What's the big hurry to go tying the knot?"

Zach sipped his coffee. "You would say that. From where I'm sitting, Travis, you're a little behind the curve. All your brothers and sisters—and more than a few cousins—are married and having babies. A wife and kids, that's what life's all about."

"I'll say it again. There's no rush." Well, okay. For him there kind of was. He needed a fiancée, yesterday or sooner. But a wife? Not anytime soon.

Travis's mother spoke up from her spot at the stove. "Don't listen to him, Zach. If a wife is what you're looking for, you've come to the right place. There are plenty of pretty, smart, marriageable young women in Rust Creek Falls. Marriage is in the air around here."

Travis grunted. "Or it could be something in the water. Whatever it is, Mom's right. Marriage is nothing short of contagious in this town. Everybody seems to be coming down with it."

Zach forked up his last bite of pie. "Sounds like Rust Creek Falls is exactly the place that I want to be."

It was almost three in the afternoon when Travis climbed in his Ford F-150 crew cab and went to town.

He drove up and down the streets of Rust Creek Falls with the windows down, waving and calling greetings to people he knew, racking his brain for a likely candidate to play the love of his life on *The Great Roundup.*

Driving and waving were getting him nowhere. He decided he'd stop in at Daisy's Donut Shop—just step inside and see if his future fake fiancée might be waiting there, having herself a maple bar and coffee.

He found a spot at the curb in front of Buffalo Bill's Wings To Go, which was right next door to Daisy's. As he walked past, he stuck his head in Wings To Go. No prospects there. He went on to the donut shop, but when he peered in the window, he saw only five senior citizens and a young mother with two little ones under five.

Not a potential fiancée in sight.

Trying really hard not to get discouraged, he started to turn back for his truck. But then the door to the adjacent shop opened.

Callie Crawford, a nurse at the local clinic, came out of the beauty parlor. "Thanks, Brenna," Callie called over her shoulder before letting the door shut. She spotted Travis. "Hey, Travis! I heard about you and that reality show. Exciting stuff."

"Good to see you, Callie." He tipped his hat to her. "Final audition is tomorrow night."

"At the Ace, so I heard. We're all rooting for you."

He thanked her and asked her to say hi to her husband, Nate, for him. With a nod and a smile, Callie got in her SUV and drove off.

And that was it. That was when it happened. He watched Callie drive off down the street when it came to him.

Brenna. Brenna O'Reilly.

Good-looking, smart as a whip and raised on a ranch. She'd taken some ribbons barrel racing during the three or four summers she worked the local rodeo circuit. She was bold, too. Stood up for herself and didn't take any guff.

But he'd always considered himself too old for her. Plus, he kind of thought of himself as a guy who looked out for her. He would never make a move on her.

However, this wouldn't be a move.

Uh-uh. This would be…an opportunity.

If she was interested and if it was something she could actually handle.

Brenna.

Did he have any other prospects for this?

Hell, no.

He had less than three hours to find someone. At this point, it was pretty much Brenna or bust.

By then, he was already opening the door to the beauty shop. A bell tinkled overhead as he went in.

Brenna was standing right there, behind the reception counter with the cash register on it, facing the door. She looked kind of surprised at the sight of him.

Before either of them could say anything, the owner, Bee, spotted him. "Travis Dalton!" She waved at him with the giant blow-dryer in her left hand. "What do you know? It's our local celebrity."

Every woman in the shop turned to stare at him. He took off his hat and put on his best smile. "Not a celebrity *yet*, Bee. Ladies, how you doing?"

A chorus of greetings followed. He nodded and kept right on smiling.

Bee asked, "What can we do for you, darlin'?"

He thought fast. "The big final audition's tomorrow night."

"So we heard."

"Figured I could maybe use a haircut—just a trim." He hooked his hat on the rack by the door. "So, Brenna, you available?"

Brenna's blue eyes met his. "You're in luck. I've got an hour before my next appointment." She came out from behind the counter, looking smart and sassy in snug jeans, ankle boots and a silky red shirt. Red worked for her. Matched her hair, which used to be a riot of springy curls way back when. Now she wore it straight and smooth, a waterfall of fire to just below her shoulders.

She waited until he'd hung up his denim jacket next to his hat then led him to her station. "Have a seat."

He dropped into the padded swivel chair and faced his own image in the mirror.

Brenna put her hands on his shoulders and leaned in. He got a whiff of her perfume. Nice. She caught his eye in the mirror and then ran her fingers up into his hair, her touch light, professional. "This looks pretty good."

It should. He'd paid a lot to a Hollywood stylist right before that first audition two weeks ago. "I was thinking just a trim."

She stood back, nodding, a dimple tucking into her

velvety cheek as she smiled. “Well, all right. You want a shampoo first?”

What he wanted was to talk to her alone. He cast a glance to either side and lowered his voice. “Say, Brenna…”

She knew instantly that he was up to something. He could tell by the slight narrowing of her eyes and the way the bow of her upper lip flattened just a little. And then she leaned in again and whispered, “What’s going on?”

He went for it. “I was wondering if I could talk to you in private.”

Her sleek red-brown eyebrows drew together. “Right now?”

“Yeah.”

“Where?”

He cast a quick glance around and spotted the hallway that led to the parking area in back. “Outside?”

She folded her arms across her chest and tipped her head to the side. “Sure. Go on out back. I’ll be right there.”

“Thanks.” He got right up and headed for the back door, not even pausing to collect his jacket and hat. It wasn’t that cold out, and he could get them later.

“What’s going on?” Bee asked as he strode past her station.

Brenna answered for him. “Travis and I need to talk.”

Somebody giggled.

Somebody else said, “Oh, I’ll just bet you do.”

Travis kept walking. It was okay with him if everyone at the beauty shop assumed he was finally making a move on Brenna—because he was.

Just not exactly in the way that they thought.

Outside, he looked for a secluded spot and settled on the three-walled nook where Bee stored her Dumpster. It didn't smell too bad, and the walls would give them privacy.

He heard the back door open again and stuck his head out to watch Brenna emerge. "Psst."

She spotted him and laughed. "Travis, what *is* this?"

He waved her forward. "Come on. We don't have all day."

For that he got an eye roll, but she did hustle on over to the enclosure. "All right, I'm here. Now what is it?"

He had no idea where to even start. "I...I have a proposal."

Her eyelashes swept down and then back up again. "Excuse me?"

"This... What I'm about to say. I need your solemn word you won't tell a soul about any of it, or I'll get sued for breach of contract. Understand?"

"Not really." She chewed on her lower lip for a moment. "But okay. I'm game. I won't tell a soul. You have my sworn word on that." She hooked her pinkie at him. He gave it a blank look. "Pinkie promise, Trav. You know that is the most solemn of promises and can never be broken."

"What are we, twelve?"

She made a little snorting sound. "Oh, come on."

He gave in and hooked his pinkie with hers. "Satisfied?"

"Are *you*? Because that is the question." She laughed, a sweet, musical sound, and tightened her pinkie against his briefly before letting go.

"As long as you promise me."

"Travis. I promise. I will tell no one, no matter what happens. Now what is going on?"

"How'd you like to be on *The Great Roundup*?"

She wrinkled her nose at him. "What? How? You're making no sense."

"Just listen, okay? Just give me a chance. I…well, I really thought I had it, you know? I thought I was on the show. But it turns out they want a young couple. A young, *engaged* couple. And the casting director sort of asked me if there was anyone special back home and I sort of said yes. And then, all of a sudden, they tell me there's one final audition, that it will be at the Ace and I should bring my fiancée."

Brenna's eyes were wide as dinner plates. "You told them you were *engaged*?"

"No, I didn't *tell* them that. They assumed it. And now I need a fake fiancée, okay? I need someone who doesn't mind putting herself out there, if you know what I mean. Someone who's not going to be afraid to speak up and hold her head high when the cameras are rolling. Someone good-looking who's familiar with ranch work, who can ride a horse and handle a rifle."

Brenna grinned then. "So you think I'm good-looking, huh?"

"Brenna, you're gorgeous."

"Travis." She looked like she was having a really good time. "Say that again."

Why not? It was only the truth. "Brenna, you are superfine."

And she threw back her red head and let her laughter chime out. He stood there and watched her and thought how he'd known her since she was knee-high to a gnat. And that she was perfect, just what he needed to make

Giselle happy—and earn him his spot on *The Great Roundup*.

But then she stopped laughing. She lowered her head and she regarded him steadily. "So say that it worked—say I go to the Ace with you tomorrow night and we convince them that we're together, that we're going to get married. Then what?"

"Then you belong to them for the next eight to ten weeks. First while they run checks on you and make sure you're healthy, mentally stable and have never murdered anyone or anything."

"You're not serious."

"As a rattler on a hot rock. And as soon as all that's over, we start filming. That's happening at some so far undisclosed Montana location. We're there until they're through filming."

"But what if I get eliminated? *Then* can I come home?"

He shook his head. "Everyone stays. So they can bring you back on camera if they want to, and also because if you come home early, everyone who knows you will know you've been eliminated. They want to keep the suspense going as to who the big winner is until the final show airs. Also, when the filming's over and you come home, you and I would still be pretending to be engaged."

"Until?"

"The episodes where we've each been eliminated have aired—or the final episode, where one of us wins. The show airs once a week, August through December. Bottom line, you could be my fake fiancée straight through till Christmas."

She leaned against the wall next to the Dumpster

and wrapped her arms around herself. "Wow. I…don't know what to say."

He resisted the burning need to promise her that they would win and that she was going to love it. "It's a lot to take in, I know."

She slanted him a glance. "I'd have to check with Bee, see if she'd hold my station for two months."

He refused to consider that Bee might say anything but yes. "I get that, sure."

"And then there's the money. I heard the winner gets a million dollars."

"Actually, once you get on the show, there's a graduated fee scale. The million is the top prize, but everybody gets something."

She leaned toward him a little, definitely interested. "Graduated how?"

"The first one eliminated gets twenty-five hundred. The longer you stay in the game, the more you get. For instance, if you last through the sixth show, you get ten thousand. And if you're the last to go before the winner, you get a hundred K."

She actually chuckled. "Good to know. So, Travis, if we're in this together, I say we split everything fifty-fifty."

He'd figured on giving her something, but he'd been kind of hoping she'd settle for much less. After all, he had big plans for his new house, for the ranch. He cleared his throat. "Would you take twenty percent?"

"Travis," she chided.

"Thirty?" he asked hopefully.

"Look at it this way. If they like me and want me on the show, you double your chances to win. Not to mention, the longer we both stay on, the more we both make." She spoke way too patiently. He found himself wistfully recalling the little girl she'd once been, the little girl who'd considered him her own personal hero and would have done anything he asked her to do, instantly, without question. Where had that little girl gone?

"True, but I'm your ticket in," he reminded her. "I'm the one who worked my ass off getting this far, you know?"

"I see that. And I admire that. I sincerely do. But without me, you won't make the cast."

She was probably right. He argued, anyway. "I'm not sure of that."

Brenna was silent, leaning there against the wall, her head tipped down. The seconds ticked by. He waited, trying to look easy and unconcerned, playing it like he didn't have a care in the world. Too bad that inside he was a nervous wreck.

Finally, she looked up and spoke again. "I'm trying not to be so impulsive in my life, to settle down a little, you know what I mean?"

Their eyes met and they gazed at each other for a long count of ten. "Bren. I know exactly what you mean."

She gave a chuckle, sweet and low. "I kind of thought that you might. The thing is, playing your fake fiancée on a reality show is not exactly what I would call settling down. And what are the odds against us, anyway? How many will end up competing with us?"

"I think there are twenty-two contestants total, so it's you and me and twenty others."

"Meaning that however we split the money, odds are someone else will take home the big prize."

He pushed off the wall, took her by the shoulders and looked deeply into those ocean-blue eyes. "First rule.

Never, *ever* say we might not win. We *will* win. Half the battle is the mental game. Defeat is not an option. Winning is the only acceptable outcome."

She got it, she really did. He could feel it in the sudden straightening of her shoulders beneath his hands, see it in the bright gleam that lit those wide eyes. "Yeah. You're right. We *will* win."

"That's it. Hold that thought." He let go of her shoulders but held her gaze.

She said, "We really would be increasing our chances, the two of us together. Together, we can work out strategies, you know? We can plan how to handle whatever they throw at us."

"Exactly. We would have each other's backs. So what do you say, Bren?"

"I still want half the money." A gust of wind slipped into the three-sided enclosure and stirred her hair, blowing a few fiery strands across her mouth.

He smoothed them out of the way, guiding them behind her ear, thinking how soft her pale skin was and marveling at how she'd grown up to be downright hot. It was a good thing he'd always promised himself he'd never make a move on her. Add that promise to the fact that he'd sworn off women and he should be able to keep from getting any romantic ideas about her.

"Travis?" She searched his face. "Did you hear what I just said?"

"I heard." He ordered his mind off her inconvenient hotness and set it on coming up with more reasons she should take less than half the prize.

Unfortunately, he couldn't think of a single one.

So all right, then. His new house and his investment in the ranch would be smaller. But his chances of winning had just doubled—*more* than doubled. Because Brenna was a fighter, and together they *would* go all the way to the win.

"Fair enough, Bren. Fifty-fifty, you and me." He held up his hand.

She slapped a high five on it. "I'll be right back."

He caught her before she could get away. "There's more we need to talk about."

"Not until I get the okay from Bee, we don't." She glanced down at his fingers wrapped around her upper arm.

He let go. "What will you say to her?"

"That I might have a chance on *The Great Roundup*, but to try for it, I need to know that she'll let me have my booth back on August 1."

"Good. That's good. Don't mention the engagement yet. We still need to decide how to handle that."

She let out another sweet, happy laugh—and then mimed locking her mouth and tossing away the key. "My lips are sealed," she whispered, then whirled on her heel and headed for the back door.

Five endless minutes later, she returned.

"Well?" he asked, his heart pounding a worried rhythm beneath his ribs.

Her smile burst wide open. "Bee wished us luck."

"And?"

"Yes, she'll hold my booth for me."

He almost grabbed her and hugged her, but caught himself in time. "Excellent."

"Yeah—and is there some reason we need to hang around out here? Let's go in. I'll give you that trim you pretended you needed."

He heard a scratching sound, boots crunching gravel. "What's that?"

He signaled for silence and stuck his head out of the enclosure in time to see the back of crazy old Homer Gilmore as he scuttled away across the parking lot toward the community center on Main, the next street over.

Brenna stuck her head out, too. "It's just Homer."

They retreated together back into the enclosure. He asked, "You think he heard us?"

She was completely unconcerned. "Even if he did, Homer's not going to say anything."

"And you know this how?"

"He's a little odd, but he minds his own business."

"A *little* odd? He's the one who spiked the punch with moonshine at Braden and Jennifer's wedding two years ago."

"So?" The wind stirred her hair again. She combed it back off her forehead with her fingers. "He never gossips or carries tales. To tell you the truth, I trust him."

"Because…?"

"It's just, well, I don't know. I have this feeling that he looks out for me, like a guardian angel or a fairy godmother."

Travis couldn't help scoffing, "One who just happens to be a peculiar old homeless man."

"He's not homeless. People just assume he is. He's got a shack on Falls Mountain he stays in."

"Who told you that?"

"He did. And he's not going to say anything. I guarantee it. Now, let's go in and—"

Travis put up a hand. "Just a minute. A couple more things. Starting tomorrow night, we're madly in love.

You'll need to convince a bunch of LA TV people that I'm the only guy for you."

"Well, that's a lot to ask," she teased. "But I'll do my best."

"You'll need to make everyone in town believe it, too—including your family. They all have to think we're for real."

"Trav, I can do it." She was all determination now. "You can count on me."

"That's what I needed to hear."

"Then, can we go in?"

"There's one more thing..."

"What?"

"It's important tomorrow night that you be on. You need to show them your most outgoing self. Sell your own personality." When she nodded up at him, he went on, "I did a lot of research on reality shows before I went into this. What I learned is that the show is a story, Bren. A story told in weekly episodes. And a good story is all about big personalities, characters you can't forget, over-the-top emotions. What I'm saying is, you can't be shy. It's better to embarrass yourself than to be all bottled up and boring. Are you hearing what I'm saying?"

"Yes, I am. And let me ask you something. When have you ever known me to be boring?"

Her various escapades over the years scrolled through his mind. At the age of nine, she'd gotten mad at her mom and run away. She got all the way to Portland, Oregon, before they caught up with her. At twelve, she'd coldcocked one of the Peabody boys when she caught him picking on a younger kid. Peabody hit the ground hard. It took thirty stitches to sew him back up. At sixteen, she'd rolled her pickup over a cliff because she never could resist a challenge and Leonie Parker had dared her to race up Falls Mountain. Only the good Lord knew how she'd survived that crash without major injury.

The more Travis thought of all the crazy things she'd done, the more certain he became that Brenna O'Reilly would have no problem selling herself to Giselle and the rest of them. "All right. I hear you."

"Good. 'Cause I'm a lot of things, Travis Dalton. But I am *never* shy or boring."

The next night, Real Deal Entertainment had assigned Gerry to drive the finalists to the Ace in the Hole.

All except for Travis. They let him make a quick trip to Kalispell in the afternoon and then, in the evening, he drove his F-150 out to the O'Reilly place to pick up his supposed fiancée.

Brenna's mom answered his knock. Travis had always liked Maureen O'Reilly. She loved her life on the family ranch, and her kitchen was the heart of her home. She'd always treated Travis with warmth and affection.

Tonight, however? Not so much. When he swept off his hat and gave her a big smile, she didn't smile back.

"Hello, Travis." Maureen pulled back the door and then hustled him into the living room, where she offered him a seat on the sofa. "Brenna will be right down."

"Great. Thanks."

She leaned toward him a little and asked in a low voice, "Travis, I need you to be honest with me. What's going on here?"

Before he left Brenna at the beauty shop yesterday, they'd agreed on how to handle things with her parents and his. Right now, Maureen needed to know that there was *something* going on between him and her middle daughter. The news of their engagement, however, would come a little bit later. "Brenna and I have a whole lot in common. She's agreed to come out to the audition at the Ace with me tonight."

"What does that mean, 'a whole lot in common'?"

"I care for her. I care for her deeply." It was surprisingly easy to say. Probably because it was true. He did care for Brenna. Always had. "She's one of a kind. There's no other girl like her."

Maureen scowled. She opened her mouth to speak again, but before she got a word out, her husband, Paddy, appeared in the archway that led to the kitchen.

"Travis. How you doin'?"

"Great, Paddy." He popped to his feet, and he and Paddy shook hands. "Real good to see you."

"Heard about you and that reality show."

"Final audition is tonight."

"Well, good luck to you, son."

Maureen started to speak again, but Brenna's arrival cut her off. "It's show business, Dad," she scolded with a playful smile. "In show business, you say 'break a leg.'"

Travis tried not to stare as she came down the stairs wearing dark-wash jeans that hugged her strong legs and a sleeveless lace-trimmed purple top that clung to every curve. Damn, she was fine. Purple suede dress boots and a rhinestone-studded cowboy hat completed the perfect picture she made.

Again, Travis reminded himself that she was spunky little Brenna O'Reilly and this so-called relationship they were going to have when they got on the show was just that—all show. Brenna didn't need to be messing with a troublesome cowboy like him.

And he knew very well that Maureen thought so, too.

Still, he could almost start having *real* ideas about Brenna and him and what they might get up to together pretending to be engaged during *The Great Roundup.*

Brenna kissed her mom on the cheek and then her dad, too. She handed Travis her rhinestone-trimmed jean jacket and he helped her into it.

They managed to get out the door and into the pickup without Maureen asking any more uncomfortable questions.

"It's time," she said in a low and angry tone as he turned off the dirt road from the ranch and onto the highway heading toward town. "Scratch that. It's *past* time I got my own place." Rentals in Rust Creek Falls were hard to come by. A lot of young women like Brenna lived with their parents until they got married or finally scraped together enough to buy something of their own. "Bee offered me her apartment over the beauty shop. She's been living in Kalispell, anyway, with her new guy. So when we win *The Great Roundup*, I'm moving. I love my mom, but she's driving me crazy."

"*When we win.* That's the spirit." As for Maureen, he played the diplomat. "Your mom's a wonderful woman."

Brenna shook her head and stared out the window. He almost asked her exactly what Maureen might have said to upset her—but then again, it was probably about him and he wasn't sure he wanted to know.

The rest of the ride passed in silence. Travis wanted to give Brenna a little more coaching on how to become a reality TV star, but the closer they got to town, the more withdrawn she seemed. He started to worry that something was really bothering her—something more than annoyance with her mom. And he had no idea what to say to ease whatever weighed on her mind.

The parking lot at the Ace was full. Music poured out of the ramshackle wooden building at the front of the lot. They were playing a fast one, something with a driving beat. Travis drove up and down the rows of parked vehicles, looking for a free space. Finally, in the last row at the very back of the lot, he found one.

He pulled in and turned off the engine. "You okay, Brenna?"

She aimed a blinding smile at him. "Great. Let's get going." Shoving open her door, she got out.

So he jumped out on his side and hustled around to her. He offered his hand. She gave him the strangest wild-eyed sort of look, but then she took it. Hers was ice-cold. He laced their fingers together and considered pulling her back, demanding to know if she was all right.

"Let's do this." She started walking, head high, that red hair shining down her back, rhinestones glittering on her hat, along the cuffs, hem and collar of her pretty denim jacket.

He fell in step with her, though he had a scary premonition they were headed straight for disaster. She seemed completely determined to go forward. He was afraid to slow her down, afraid that would finish her somehow, that calling a halt until she told him what was wrong would only make her turn and run. Their chance on *The Great Roundup* would be lost before they even got inside to try for it.

They went around to the front of the building and

up the wooden steps. A couple of cowboys came out and held the door for them. Both men looked at Brenna with interest, and Travis felt a buzz of irritation under his skin. He gave them each a warning glare. The men tipped their hats and kept on walking.

Inside, it was loud and wall-to-wall with partiers. Travis had never seen the Ace this packed. He spotted a couple of cameramen filming the crowd. Over by the bar, he caught sight of old Wally Wilson, a fellow finalist who'd grown up on the Oklahoma prairie and ridden the rodeos all over the West. Wally was talking the ear off one of the bartenders. And another finalist, that platinum blonde rodeo star, Summer Knight, was surrounded by cowboys. He knew it was her by the shine of her almost-white hair and that sexy laugh of hers.

"Come on." He pulled Brenna in closer so she could hear him. "We'll find the casting director, Giselle. I'll introduce you."

She blinked and stared at him through those now-enormous eyes. What was going on with her?

She looked terrified and he had no idea what to do about it.

Brenna *was* terrified.

She was totally freaking out. Brenna never freaked out.

And that freaked her out even more.

She'd been so sure she knew how to handle herself. She *did* know how to handle herself. She was bold. Fearless. Nothing scared her. Ever.

Except this, the Ace packed to bursting, the music so loud. All these people pressing in around her, a casting director waiting to meet her.

And Travis.

Travis, who was counting on her to win them both a spot on *The Great Roundup.*

Dear Lord, she didn't want to blow this. She would never forgive herself if she let Travis down.

"There's Giselle." Travis waved at a tall, model-skinny woman on the other side of the room. The woman lifted a hand and signaled them to join her. "This way." His fingers still laced with hers, he started working his way through the crowd, leading her toward the tall woman with cheekbones so sharp they threatened to poke right through her skin.

"Wait." Brenna dug in her boot heels.

He stopped and turned back to her, a worried frown between his eyebrows. "Bren?" He said her name softly, gently. He knew she was losing it. "What? Tell me."

She blasted a smile at him and forced a brittle laugh. "Can you just give me a minute?" She tipped her head toward the hallway that led to the ladies' room. "I'll be right back." She tugged free of his grip.

"Brenna—"

"I need to check my lip gloss."

"But—"

"Right back." She sent him a quick wave over her shoulder and made for the hallway, scattering *Excuse mes* as she went, weaving her way as fast as she could through the tight knots of people, ignoring anyone who spoke to her or glanced her way.

When she reached the hallway, she kept on going, her eyes on the glowing green exit sign down at the end. She got to the ladies' room and she didn't even slow down. She just kept right on walking down to the end of the hall.

And out the back door.

Chapter Three

The heavy door swung shut behind Brenna, and the racket from inside dimmed a little. She'd emerged into a loading area, with the packed dirt parking lot spread out beyond. Under the light of a few lamps on tall wooden poles, the rows of empty cars waited, not a soul in sight. Brenna shivered at the eeriness of it after the crush of people inside.

With no idea what to do next, she kept walking, her arms wrapped tightly around herself, her head tipped down, not knowing where she was going—until she ran right into someone coming the other way.

"Whoa, now…" said a raspy male voice.

She blinked and looked up—first at the dirty top half of a union suit. The shirt was frayed around the wattled neck of an old man with bristly gray whiskers and thinning, scraggly white hair. "Homer," she said in a dazed whisper. "Homer Gilmore."

The old man smiled, showing crooked, yellowed teeth. "If it isn't Brenna O'Reilly. Where you headin' in such an all-fired hurry?"

"I was just…"

"Runnin' away?" he finished for her.

Homer was famous in Rust Creek Falls for a number of reasons. He made moonshine that made people throw off their inhibitions. He tended to show up when you least expected him. And he *knew* things. Travis might scoff at her for saying it, but that didn't make it any less true. Homer really could read things about people. He always seemed to know intuitively what folks were going through.

She started to deny that she was running anywhere. "I was just—"

"Scared, is what you were. And that is not like you."

"I got—"

"Stage fright. I know. Sometimes it happens."

"Homer, how do you—"

"Know things?" He only laughed, a sound every bit as ragged and rusty as the rest of him. And then he lowered his head. Brenna followed his gaze to his gnarled right hand, in which he held a jar of clear liquid.

"Homer, is that—"

"Just what you need about now? Yeah, Brenna. It is."

She looked up into his watery eyes again. "But I don't want to get—"

"Drunk? Uh-uh. You won't be. This is just a little magic for you, that's all. A little nudge in the right direction for this one time. Look at me, Brenna." His voice was softer now. She could just wrap it around her, it sounded so soothing and good. She looked right into his eyes.

"Say what you're thinking," he instructed.

And she did. "I'm still afraid, but it's okay. I'm bigger than my fear."

"That's right. That's the spirit." He held out the jar. "Take one long drink, Brenna O'Reilly. And then get back in there and show them what you're made of."

She took the jar and unscrewed the lid.

Travis was getting really worried.

And not only about the fact that Giselle kept shooting him dirty looks and mouthing, "Where *is* she?" across the crowded dance floor at him.

He was worried about Brenna. She'd looked so upset when she took off for the restroom. He shouldn't have let her go like that. He should have gone with her, made sure she got there safe, made sure she was okay.

She'd seemed so cocky and confident yesterday, so completely *Brenna*, out there behind the beauty shop. He'd really believed she could handle anything *The Great Roundup* could throw at her. So he'd gotten her into this.

Travis had pulled some crazy stunts in his life, but one thing he'd always done right was to look out for Brenna O'Reilly. He'd protected her from more than one potential disaster.

Not tonight, though. Something was really bothering her, and he knew it. And still, he'd let her leave his side.

It was an error in judgment on his part, and he needed to rectify that. He needed to stop standing here like a damn fool and go after her.

He started for the hallway that led to the restrooms. People pushed in around him, and he just pushed back. Nodding, forcing a smile when anyone spoke to him, he kept going until he reached the hallway, where a line of women waited to get into the restroom. Brenna was not among them.

He was just trying to decide whether or not to barge into the ladies' room shouting her name when the door all the way down at the end of the hallway opened—and there she was.

"Brenna!"

She tipped her chin high so he could see her face clearly under the brim of her hat. She spotted him—and she smiled, a bright, glowing smile. Hot damn, she was gorgeous.

And apparently, she'd gotten over whatever had been bothering her.

"Travis!" She gave him a jaunty wave and started toward him.

"'Scuse me, ladies." He eased his way between two women at the front of the restroom line and went for her, not stopping till he stood in front of her a few feet from the door. "Brenna, are you okay?"

She grinned up at him. "Never better." She really did seem fine now, brimming with her usual bright confidence.

But he had to be sure. He leaned close and said for her ears alone, "We don't have to do this. I can take you home."

She reached up and got a handful of the front of his shirt. "We're not giving up now. Don't even think it."

"But are you—"

She cut him off by jerking him down to her and lifting her mouth to within an inch from his. "We are doing this." Her eyes had stars in them. "And we are taking home the prize."

"Brenna..." She smelled of flowers and fresh-cut grass. He really wanted to kiss her.

"Do it," she whispered, clearly reading his mind. "We need to do it. How can we pretend that we're headed for forever when you've never even put your lips on mine?"

Was she right? Did he really *need* to kiss her to make their fake relationship seem real for Giselle and the others? Hell if he knew. All he could think was that he'd never kissed her—and he *had* to kiss her.

Finally. At last.

He lowered his head a fraction closer, and she surged up.

His mouth touched hers.

With a sigh, she let go of his shirtfront and her hands slid up to clasp the back of his neck. "Travis..." She stroked his nape with her soft fingers as she whispered his name, kissing it onto his lips.

So good. So right. She tasted of honey, of ripe summer fruit—peaches and blackberries, watermelon. Cherries. She tasted of promises, sweet hopes and big dreams. She tasted of home.

Someone up the hall a ways let out a whoop, while someone else yelled, "Kiss her, cowboy!"

Neither Travis nor Brenna paid their hecklers any mind. The brims of their hats collided as they deepened the kiss. His fell and then hers, but neither of them cared.

That kiss went on forever.

And still, it was too short.

She ended it, finally, by dropping back down to her heels again. Dazed, reluctant to lose the hot spell of her kiss, he opened his eyes to find her staring up at him, her mouth as plump and red as the cherries she tasted like.

"Brenna..." he whispered like some kind of long-gone fool. At that moment, her name was the only word he knew.

She gave a low laugh and dipped to the floor, grabbing both their hats and passing him his. He slid it on his head as she held out her hand. "Come on, cowboy. Let's go have ourselves some fun."

How did she do it?

Travis had no idea.

But that night, Brenna was a natural, a reality TV show dream come true.

He took her to Giselle first. She shook Giselle's hand, leaned in close and whispered something.

Giselle laughed out loud. In the weeks he'd been dealing with her, Travis had never seen Giselle laugh.

It went on like that all night. Brenna was sexy and funny and so good at pretending to be in love with him, he almost believed it himself. She rubbed up against him and pulled him down to whisper naughty things in his ear. And the way she smiled at him? You'd have thought he was the only guy in the place.

All the other guys wanted to dance with her, but Travis kept her close. After the way he'd lost her there at first, he wasn't letting her out of his sight again tonight.

She was so relaxed and easy, mugging for the cameras, but not too much. Just enough to be charming and playful and fun. She was drinking Coca-Cola, hadn't had a single beer. Still, he couldn't help wondering if she'd knocked back a little liquid courage when he wasn't looking.

Once he even whispered, "Are you drunk?"

She laughed that magical, joyful laugh of hers. And then she kissed him—a deep, wet, amazing kiss that made him acutely aware of exactly how long it had been since he'd had sex with a woman.

And the way she felt in his arms when they danced?

So good. Just right. He could almost start wishing the night would never end.

At a little past midnight, with the band on a break, Giselle signaled them over again. She had two of the cameramen with her that time.

Travis knew what the casting director was up to. They were getting interviewed, an on-the-fly interview to test them both, to see if they had chemistry up close and personal, and to find out if Brenna could really shine with the camera focused right on her.

Giselle asked, "Brenna, how long have you two been together?"

Travis wanted to grab her and whisper that no matter what, she was amazing. If they made it or not, he'd owe her forever for this fine night at the Ace.

But then Brenna laughed. And he knew that she had them. "How long have Travis and I been together? Not nearly long enough, if you ask me." She grabbed his arm and snuggled up close. "I have loved Travis Dalton since I was six years old," she said dreamily. "That was the day that my mom let me ride my new bike on the Cedar Street sidewalk while she was shopping at Crawford's General Store. It was the day that Angus McCauley pushed me off my bike and then rode away on it. I called Angus some bad names, but he didn't come back. So I sat down on the sidewalk and burst into tears..."

It seemed to Travis at that moment that the whole

place had gone quiet. People pressed close, but only so they could hear better as Brenna told them how Travis had appeared out of nowhere that day.

"He came like a knight in shining armor—except, you know, in dusty boots, jeans and a snap-front shirt." She looked up at him with a glowing smile.

He brushed her lips with his, the light kiss so easy and natural, exactly right. He looked at the nearest camera. "I hate to see a little girl cry."

Brenna went on with her story. "He picked me up and asked me if I was hurt. I showed him the scrape on my elbow where I'd hit the sidewalk when Angus pushed me down. Travis looked at it, all serious and frowning. He said, 'You are a very brave little girl. Stay right here. I'll get your bike.' And he did just that. Not five minutes later, he came back around the corner of Cedar and North Buckskin Road, walking my bike. I ran to meet him, and that was when I told him I loved him and would marry him someday."

"What did he say to that?" Giselle asked downright breathlessly.

Brenna let out a put-upon sigh. "He acted like I hadn't said it. He did that a lot for the next twenty years or so."

"She was too young for me," Travis insisted, as he'd done more than once during the twenty years in question.

Brenna made a face at him. "The second time I said I loved him, I was eight and he was sixteen. That time, as it so happened, he'd just saved me from drowning in Rust Creek. I said, 'Oh, Travis. I love you and I can't wait to marry you!' He just wrapped me in a blanket and drove me home. And then, when I was ten..."

He knew what was coming and couldn't hold back a groan.

She nudged him with her shoulder. "Aurelia won't mind. Remember, she got married and moved to Sioux Falls?"

Giselle, looking more eager than Travis had ever seen her, prompted, "So tell us what happened."

"I caught them kissing, Travis and Aurelia."

"Oh, no!" Gerry, the production assistant who stood at Giselle's elbow, gave Travis a dirty look.

"Oh, yes," said Brenna. "And okay, I was only ten, but still it destroyed me. It was in the summer, out at the county rodeo. Aurelia and Travis were both eighteen. Aurelia was so annoying. She had breasts and everything. I took one look at the two of them squishing their mouths together and felt my poor heart break clean in two."

"Heartbreak?" Travis teased her. "Come on, admit it, Brenna. You were mad, not heartbroken."

She gave a sniff, her cute nose in the air. "That was not anger, that was pure heartbreak, just like I said. Heartbreak that caused me to pick up a rock and throw it at Aurelia. I hit her in the shoulder."

Travis elaborated, "Aurelia let out a yelp you could hear all the way to Kalispell." He scolded Brenna gently, "You hit her pretty hard."

"Well, I was upset and it seemed to me at the time that she deserved it."

He shook his head. "You always did have a good arm on you, even when you were ten."

"I remember she called me an evil little brat. And I turned to you and said, 'Travis Dalton, what is the matter with you? You're supposed to be waiting for *me*.' I reminded you that I was already ten and it wouldn't be long now—or it wouldn't *have* been."

"Except that you were so mad—"

"Correction. Brokenhearted. I was so *brokenhearted*, I ended it between us."

"Bren. Come on. You were *ten*. I was eighteen. There was nothing to end."

She put her finger to his lips. "Shh. *I'm* tellin' this story." And then she spoke to the camera again. "I said that on second thought, I hated him and I wasn't going to marry him, after all, no matter if he crawled on his knees to me through razor blades and broken glass."

He leaned in and told the camera confidentially, "She was always a bloodthirsty little thing."

"Maybe. Now and then." Brenna let out a rueful sigh. "Especially when the guy I love goes and breaks my heart." Slowly, she grinned. "But then, look at us now." She grabbed Travis closer. He went willingly. "Travis Dalton, I forgive you."

"For…?"

"Not taking me seriously when I was six and breaking my poor heart when I was ten."

He would have delivered a clever comeback for that one, but she went and offered up her sweet mouth. Comebacks could wait. He claimed her lips in another long, bone-melting kiss that brought a volley of applause and appreciative laughter from the circle of contestants and locals surrounding them.

When he lifted his head, she said, "Finally together, forever and ever."

It was the perfect moment, the one Travis had been waiting for.

He dropped to his knees, reached in his pocket and

took out the ring he'd slipped in there before driving out to the O'Reilly place to pick her up that night. That ring, bought in Kalispell that afternoon, had cost him more than half of his hard-earned savings. But he'd spent that money anyway, because the ring was as beautiful as she was and because it was important that they come across as the real thing.

"Travis!" Brenna stared down at him through shining ocean-blue eyes. "Oh, Travis…" Those fine eyes shone even brighter with her tears. Damn, she was amazing. "That is the most beautiful ring I have ever seen."

"I was hoping you might think so." And he really was getting into this, maybe more than he should. "Brenna O'Reilly," he said with feeling, "I love you and you are the only woman in the world for me."

"Oh, Trav. I love you, too."

God. The way she looked at him. He didn't care if it was all an act. Nothing lit him up like the glory of her smile. "Marry me, Brenna."

"Yes, Travis. Yes!"

"Hot damn!" He slipped the ring on her finger, jumped to his feet and threw his hat in the air. Everyone with a hat followed suit. Hats went flying everywhere. To a thundering rumble of excited applause and a torrent of catcalls and triumphant shouts, Travis grabbed Brenna close in his arms and kissed her again for all he was worth.

"Brenna," Giselle said as soon as Travis and Brenna had been congratulated by half the partiers in the place, "you think you could give us a few minutes alone?"

Brenna looked a little stunned. She turned to Travis. "Trav?"

He slid his hand down and clasped hers. "I'll go with you."

Giselle gave a shrug. "Suit yourselves." She pointed her index finger at the ceiling. "One moment." The finger dipped down. "Do not move from this spot." She turned and consulted with two of the cameramen, putting her eye to one viewfinder and then the other, evidently checking out footage that had already been shot. Then she gestured at various contestants around the Ace. The cameramen moved off, seeking their assigned targets. "All right then," said Giselle. "This way, you two."

The band started up again as Travis and Brenna followed the casting director and her assistant to the long hall that led to the back door. Giselle took them past the restrooms, finally opening the last door before the one that led out. "Here we go." She ushered them into a small space with a desk, a battered couch and two chairs. Apparently, she'd made arrangements to have the room available.

The pounding beat of the music receded to a dull roar as Giselle shut the door. She gestured for Travis and Brenna to take the two guest chairs while she claimed the big chair behind the desk. Roxanne, with one of those tablet phones, took the minion position at Giselle's shoulder, stylus at the ready.

"I'll get right to the point." Giselle rocked back in the chair. "Brenna, the camera loves you. And we like you. We like you a lot." She held up her thumb and index finger with a half inch of space between them. "You're this far from being on *The Great Roundup*—both you and your handsome fiancé here."

Bren felt for his hand again. He grabbed hers and held on tight.

Giselle asked wryly, “So, am I safe in assuming that you *are* interested in being on the show?”

Brenna’s head bobbed up and down. “I am interested. Definitely.”

“We’ll have to arrange for some other test footage—what we would have wanted to see in your package. Can you ride a horse?”

“Oh, yes, I can.”

“How about roping?”

“I was raised on a ranch. I’m not a champion roper, but I have the basics down.”

“Well, all right then, it can all be arranged. We’re going to put you up at Maverick Manor with Travis and the rest of the finalists. There will be contracts to sign, more interviews and a series of tests and a background check.”

“Yes. I’m ready.”

“You’re saying you’re in?”

“Yes, I am.” Bren straightened her shoulders. “I want to do this.”

“All right, then.” Giselle gave a slow nod. “You’re ours. You would potentially be here in Rust Creek Falls at Maverick Manor for a couple of weeks. And then, if you’re chosen for the final cast, you’ll go on location until filming is complete.”

Brenna squeezed Travis’s hand. “I want to do it.”

“Wonderful.” Giselle doled out one of those almost smiles of hers.

Brenna raised her free hand—like a kid in class getting permission to speak. “But…”

“Go on.”

"Well, I need to go home tonight. I could be at the Manor by noon tomorrow, if that's all right. But first I need a little time with my family. I need to catch them up on all that's, um, going on."

Giselle sat back in her chair and rocked a moment. "All right. Go home, talk to the family and pack your bags. We'll expect you at Maverick Manor at twelve noon tomorrow, to stay."

"I'll be back tomorrow, early, to talk to your folks and then to drive you to the Manor," Travis said.

Brenna sat with him in his pickup in front of the ranch house. All the windows were dark. Her mom had left the porch light on, though. It cast a golden pool of light that reached to the bottom of the front steps. Beyond that, the night took over.

Brenna touched the stone of her gorgeous engagement ring. Even in the dark, it glittered. They weren't really engaged, but still, the ring already seemed to her like a good-luck charm. The feel of it on her finger soothed her somehow. "I can tell them about the engagement on my own. You don't need to be here for that."

"Are you kidding? Your dad and brothers would come looking for me with blood in their eyes if I wasn't there with you to share the big news."

"Oh, come on. They would not."

"I should be there. I *will* be there."

"Travis, stop. It's not even real."

"But they have to *believe* it's real. You know that."

Her throat felt tight. She coughed into her hand to clear it. "Okay. I know you're right. But are you sure you can leave the Manor again? Don't they *own* you, like Giselle said?"

"Bren…" He reached out as though he would touch her, caress her—but then he caught himself and dropped his hand. She couldn't help wishing he'd carried through. This pretending to be engaged to him was pretty confusing. Already, she found it too easy to forget that it wasn't real. "They're giving me a little leeway," he explained. "Because they want both of us and I'm helping them to get you on the show." He took her hand and cradled it between his two big rough ones. "Are you having second thoughts?"

She whipped her hand free and bopped him lightly on his rock-hard chest. "No, I am not. No way. I *want* this job, and I aim to get it."

He gave her his sexiest grin. "That's what I needed to hear. Come on, I'll walk you in."

"It's not necess—"

"Shh. Don't say that. Of course it's necessary. You're my bride-to-be, and I am the luckiest man on the planet. A lucky man like me is honored to walk his girl to her front door."

That did make her chuckle. "I think you could charm the habit off a nun."

"Brenna, you know I would never do such a thing—because that would be disrespectful to a woman of God. And because I am already spoken for."

"Oh, Travis. You've got one silver tongue on you."

"Stay right there."

"Why?"

"I'll come around and open your door."

She laughed again and shook her head at him. But she waited, let him walk around the front of his crew cab, pull her door wide and offer his hand. She took it and felt like a queen as he helped her down.

They went up the front steps and stood under the porch light.

He leaned close, bringing his manly scent of soap and leather and a hint of pine. "I think I should kiss you. And I think you should let me."

"And why is that?" she whispered back.

"We're engaged, remember? An engaged man will always kiss his sweetheart good-night." He'd left his hat in the pickup, and the porch light cast his eyes into darkness, gave a bronze sheen to his almost-black hair.

"But, Travis, we're only engaged when someone is looking."

He tipped up her chin. "And you never know, someone could be watching us right now. We can't be too careful." His lips brushed hers, so lightly, back and forth. His beard, which he kept trimmed short enough that it bordered on scruff, scratched a little in the sexiest sort of way.

Too soon, he lifted his head.

She longed to grab him, pull him in closer, demand a *real* kiss good-night.

But she didn't. It *wasn't* real, and she had to remember that.

She heard whining on the other side of the door. Her mom's dog, Duchess. She needed to go in before the dog started barking. "See you tomorrow."

"I'll be here at eight." Everyone would be up long before that. On a working ranch, a lot got done before breakfast. "Don't say a word until I get here."

"Oh, please. It's Rust Creek Falls. Remember, you live here? Everyone is bound to be talking about what happened at the Ace tonight. You took a knee and I took your beautiful ring. That's huge news. Somebody's probably already called my mom."

"In the middle of the night?"

"As if the gossip grapevine keeps regular hours. Besides, she has a cell phone. Someone could have texted her. She gets up at five. One look at her phone and she'll be pounding on my bedroom door."

"Don't be so negative. It's all going to be fine."

"Oh, Travis. I really hope you're right."

"How about this? I'll be out here in my truck at 5:00 a.m., ready whenever you need me."

Now she wanted to grab him and kiss him again for being willing to do that—but no. It wouldn't be right to ask that of him. "Are you crazy? It's already after two."

"Good point. So I might as well just stay. I'll be right over there." He pointed at his waiting pickup. "It won't be the first time I slept in my truck. Then I can run in and rescue you when your mom starts yelling."

"You act like it's a joke, but you know my mother. She's got the biggest heart in the county, but she likes things slow and steady. You and me and what we are up to? About as far from slow and steady as anyone can get."

"I'll be here. Don't worry."

"No. That's not right. I shouldn't have said anything. Eight o'clock is fine. Now go on." She put on a smile and made shooing motions with her hands. "Go back to the Manor and get some sleep."

Just to make sure he didn't stay anyway, she waited to go in until she'd watched him drive off.

A volley of sharp taps jarred Brenna awake.

And then her mom's voice demanded, "Brenna O'Reilly, open this door."

Brenna groaned and put her pillow over her head. "Go away, Mom."

"Open. Now. I mean it!"

Brenna peeked out from under her pillow at the bedside clock—4:55 a.m.

Her mother knocked again. Loudly. "I need to talk to you. Open this door now!"

No doubt about it. Her mother had heard the big news.

Chapter Four

"Brenna!"

"Ugh. Fine." Brenna threw back the covers, stalked to the door and yanked it wide. "What?"

"I just got a call from Mary Dalton. She wanted to know if I knew that you and Travis got engaged last night."

Brenna raked her tangled hair off her forehead and leaned on the door frame. "Mom. Can you just calm down a little, please?"

"I'm perfectly calm!"

"You don't seem very—"

"Oh, Brenna," her mother cried and grabbed the hand Brenna had just used to push her hair back. Maureen made a strangled sound as she gaped at the ring Travis had slipped on her finger last night. "It's…beautiful." Maureen's voice trembled, threatening tears.

Brenna gently pulled her hand free. "Mom," she said softly. She started to reach for a hug.

But Maureen nipped that impulse in the bud. "Travis?" she demanded. "Honestly? I mean, I know he's handsome and charming and all the girls love him. I know you've had a crush on him since you were practically in diapers, but...*Travis*?"

Brenna felt annoyance rise again. She straightened and folded her arms across the extra large Bushwacker T-shirt she wore for a nightgown. "You don't have to say his name like that. It's just rude."

"Rude? You're engaged to Travis Dalton out of the blue and *I'm* being rude? This is so..." Maureen ran out of words, but then quickly regrouped. "This is everything you've been saying you weren't going to do anymore. It's impulsive and crazy and— Oh, Brenna. You promised. After Juárez, you said you'd learned your lesson at last."

Juárez. Brenna felt a stab of shame, though what had happened there wasn't really her fault. Still, Juárez had been awful, and her dad had had to come and bail her out of jail. After Juárez, she really had been trying to keep a lid on her natural propensity to end up in situations that some might call risky.

But this wasn't risky. This was actually about settling down, about owning her own business and getting her own place. And no way was she letting it slip through her fingers.

Her mother wasn't finished. "What about working hard and keeping both feet on the ground? What about learning to look before you leap? Travis Dalton is a great guy and I'm very fond of him, you know that.

Who wouldn't be? But we both know he's not a settling-down kind of man."

"Mom. I love you," she said through clenched teeth. "I've made some mistakes and I admit that I have. But I'm also twenty-six years old and perfectly capable of making my own decisions about how to run my life."

Her mother opened her mouth to argue some more—but then her dad called up the stairs, "Maureen, Brenna! Travis is here."

Brenna stiffened. How much had the men heard—and had poor Trav slept outside in his truck, after all?

Maureen shut her mouth over whatever she had been going to say. And then she called down, "We're coming!"

Brenna yanked on a pair of jeans and followed her mother down to the front hall.

Her dad must have come in from doing his morning chores. In stocking feet, he stood by the door with Travis, who wore the same clothes he'd had on last night. Both men looked really uncomfortable. Yep. No doubt about it. They'd heard what had been said upstairs.

Brenna went right to Travis. Why shouldn't she? They were supposed to be engaged, after all. He put his arm around her. She leaned into his warmth and strength and liked being there probably more than she should have. "You didn't go back to the Manor, did you?" she chided.

He kissed the end of her nose. She loved that—even if the gesture did cause her mother to suck in a sharp breath. "I drove around the first bend in the driveway and waited for you to go in," he confessed.

"You shouldn't have."

"I wanted to be here. And I think it's a good thing

I stayed." He squeezed her shoulder, pulling her even tighter into the circle of his arm. And then he faced her parents. "Maureen, Paddy, I guess you've already figured out that Brenna has made me the happiest man alive and agreed to be my wife. I realize this might seem a little sudden, but—"

"A *little* sudden?" Maureen sniffed.

Travis didn't miss a beat. "I love your daughter and I hope you will see it in your hearts to wish us well." Dear Lord, the man was *good.* He should have been an actor, no doubt about it.

Her dad, always an easier sell than her mother, gave a slow nod. "Well, now." He hooked his arm around her mom. "It's never too early in the morning for good news, right, darlin'?"

"Oh, Paddy." Her mother elbowed him gently in the side. She let out a tired-sounding sigh. "Let's all go on in the kitchen. I'll make some coffee and we can talk."

"Good idea," said her dad. With a hard huff of a sigh, her mom left them. That was when Paddy took a step forward and offered Travis his hand. They shook. "You be good to my girl, now."

"I will, sir. You have my word on it."

Her dad held out his arms. Brenna went into them, feeling dewy eyed and grateful to both of her parents. Her mom could drive her crazy, but there'd never been any shortage of love in the O'Reilly house. "You be happy," Paddy whispered in her ear. "You hear me?"

"I love you, Dad. So much." She hugged him back, good and tight.

Ten minutes later the four of them sat around the old kitchen table, each with a comforting mug of morning coffee to sip. Too soon, her older sister, Fiona, would be coming downstairs and her brothers, Ronan and Keegan, would appear from the barn, ready for breakfast.

Brenna wanted to tell her parents her other news before her siblings joined them. Travis must have been thinking the same thing, because when she glanced his way, he threw her an opening.

"I suppose you've both heard that I've made the finals in the national auditions for *The Great Roundup*..."

Brenna's mom looked a little pinched around the mouth. "Lately it seems like that show is all anybody in town ever talks about."

"Everyone's excited about it," said her dad.

If only Fallon were there. Brenna missed her younger sister desperately right then. Fallon had always understood her, was always on her side. But just a week before, Fallon had married the love of her life, Jamie Stockton. Fallon, Jamie and his adorable triplet toddlers were all off in Florida on a Disney World honeymoon.

Travis kept sending her questioning looks, waiting for her to either share her news or signal that she wanted him to do it. He was being much too wonderful, but she needed to step up and deal.

She drew a deep breath. "Mom. Dad. We have something else we, um, can't wait to tell you." She tried to inject excitement into her voice, but somehow it came out sounding squeaky and scared.

And why shouldn't she be scared? Running off for weeks to do *The Great Roundup* was every bit as wild and outrageous a plan as suddenly getting engaged to Travis. It fell squarely into the Brenna Does More Crazy Things category.

Her mother would not be thrilled.

A frown creased Maureen's brow. "What now?"

Brenna made herself say it. "It just so happens I'm a finalist to be on *The Great Roundup*, too."

Her mother sat very still. She did not say a word. Her dad knocked back a big gulp of coffee.

Swiftly, eager to get it over with now, Brenna told them what had happened at the Ace in the Hole the night before—that not only had Travis proposed, the casting director had said Brenna would be perfect for the show. "And so I'm moving to Maverick Manor for the next week or two. There will be more interviews before I find out for certain if I've made the final cast list."

"B-but what about your *job*?" her mom sputtered.

"Bee says she'll hold my booth for me."

"But this is just crazy." Maureen had more questions. A thousand of them.

Brenna answered them patiently.

Until her mom finally just gave up. "You'll do what you want to do. You always have." Wearily, as though she bore the weight of the world on her shoulders, Maureen pushed herself to her feet. "Let's get the breakfast started. You'll at least have a last home-cooked meal before you run off with Travis to be on TV."

At a little after eight, way ahead of schedule, Brenna's suitcases were packed and stowed in Travis's truck. Her older sister and brothers had all wished her well and she and Travis were on the road, headed for a stop at the Dalton Ranch before surrendering to the watchful custody of Giselle and crew.

"You're way too quiet." Travis glanced over at her.

She put on a wobbly smile for him. "It's my mother.

I love her so much, but there's just not enough room in that house for the both of us. I need my own place."

"And you'll get it when we win *The Great Roundup*." He took her hand, tugged it across the console and pressed his lips to the back of it. She didn't pull away. So what if no one was watching? His lips were so warm and his short beard felt silky, but a little scratchy, too. He made everything better, always had. He said, "All things considered, I thought it went well."

Shaking her head, she took her hand back. "You always did look on the bright side."

"That's me. Chock-full of happy thoughts."

She admired the ring he'd given her. How could she help it? "I know you spent way too much on this ring."

"You're worth it."

"I give up." She let her head fall against the seat back. "There's just no wrecking your positive attitude."

He laughed, a deep, manly sound that sent a sweet little shiver dancing all through her. "Come on. Your eyes are sparkling as bright as that ring you're wearing. You know as well I do that what we're doing...well, it's who we are. We're the ones who take the dares, the ones who go for the gold ring against all the odds. This is what we were born to do. And your mom? No matter how much she begs you to be someone you're not, she loves you for your guts and your gumption. Don't you doubt for a minute that she loves how you shine."

Brenna's throat clutched at his words. "Trav. That was beautiful."

"It's only the truth." He turned the truck into the long driveway that led to his parents' house. "Now brace yourself. We'll deal with my family and then we'll head for Maverick Manor, where the room service is 24/7 and all the mattresses have pillow tops. If you're lucky, you'll get to sneak in a nap before Giselle comes knocking, ready to make you a star."

The visit with Ben and Mary Dalton went pretty well. If Travis's parents had their doubts about this engagement, they also had the grace to keep it to themselves. There were hugs and well-wishing all around.

Ben said, "Proud of you, son."

Mary warned, "You'd better treat this sweet girl right."

Travis wrapped his arm around Brenna, pressed a kiss to her temple and promised that he would.

At Maverick Manor, Gerry had already arranged for Brenna's room—next to Travis's, with an adjoining door between. "Because we know you two will want to be close." Gerry mimed a racing heartbeat with a hand against his chest—and then burst into "People Will Say We're in Love" from *Oklahoma*.

He belted out two verses, standing right there in the hallway. And then he blushed. "Musical theater. Always my first love. I played Curly at Kansas City Rep back before I decided to move to LA." He drew his shoulders back. "I may not be tall, but I have a tall presence. I mean, Tom Cruise is only five-seven, right?"

"Right." Brenna gave him a big smile. "And your voice is amazing."

"Thank you." Gerry granted her a regal nod. Then he stuck the key card in the reader and swung the door wide. "Milady. Your chamber awaits."

Brenna put her stuff in the drawers and then fell across the wide bed. It was a pillow top, just as Travis had promised. She kicked off her boots, closed her eyes and slept for five full hours—until Travis tapped on the door between their rooms.

She let him in and they ordered room service. As they ate, he gave her more tips on how to handle Giselle, what kind of footage they were going to want on her and what to say at her psych evaluation.

The next days were busy ones. Brenna rode a horse and roped a calf for the cameras. She gave more interviews and Skyped with network executives. She met the other finalists and liked most of them, especially Roberta Hinckes, who was in her midforties and coming off a bad divorce from some corporate bigwig who'd dumped her for his executive assistant. Tall and slim with thick brown hair, Roberta was not only levelheaded and smart, she was gorgeous. The guy who'd traded her in for a younger model had to be a complete fool.

Travis, meanwhile, made friends with Steve Simons, who had lost a leg from the knee down in Iraq. The former soldier was black and heartthrob handsome. He'd just turned thirty. The four of them—Travis and Brenna, Roberta and Steve—hung out every chance they got.

On Friday, six days after Brenna first checked in at the Manor, all forty-six finalists were ordered down to the conference room. Twenty were sent packing.

Travis, Brenna, Steve and Roberta, along with Wally Wilson and Summer Knight, the rodeo star, were among the twenty-six finalists still in the running.

Travis touched the back of Brenna's hand. She laced her fingers with his and held on tight. They were so close now. Only four more finalists would be eliminated. Brenna just knew that she and Trav would both make the cut. She felt it in her bones.

"I won't congratulate any of you yet," said the field producer, Roger DelRay, who would be going with the final cast when they left for location to begin filming. "We'll be meeting with a few of you privately to discuss certain necessary contract clauses before the final four cuts can be made."

Brenna leaned close to Travis. "'Necessary contract clauses'? What does that even mean?"

"Got me."

When Roger dismissed them, Giselle's assistant grabbed Brenna's arm as she and Travis were following the others out of the conference room. "This way, you two," Roxanne said. "We have a few things we need to go over with you."

Brenna kept hold of Travis's hand as Roxanne led them into a smaller meeting room. Giselle, Roger DelRay and another producer were there, along with a tall, intense-looking bearded guy Brenna hadn't met before. There were blue file folders waiting on the table in front of two of the chairs.

"Welcome, you two," said Roger. "We would like you to meet Anthony Locke. He'll be directing *The Great Roundup.*"

Anthony Locke shook their hands. "Let's have a seat, shall we?"

Giselle led them to the chairs in front of the blue folders.

"Travis, Brenna," said Locke, "we're all beyond sold. You each have the skill sets to excel in the challenges that will face you in the show—which means you each have a good chance to stay in the game once filming is under way. The camera loves both of you, and your chemistry together is off the charts. We want you both."

We're in! Brenna groped for Travis's hand again. As his strong fingers closed around hers, she somehow managed to suppress a gleeful shout of triumph.

"So let's get right down to business here," said Roger. "Your contracts are in front of you. Most of what you'll find there isn't going to surprise you. Travis, you've already signed your confidentiality agreement. Brenna, we'll need one from you, and it's in the folder before you."

Travis had already explained to her that all the contestants had to agree to total confidentiality concerning the show until after the last episode aired at the end of the year. That meant that even when filming ended and they all went home, they still wouldn't be able to tell anyone what had happened during shooting. No one could know who won, who lost, who came close—not until the series played out on national TV.

"I understand about the confidentiality clause," said Brenna.

"Excellent," said Roger. "And I'm sure you're both wondering why we've called you in together."

Travis made a low sound in the affirmative. Brenna nodded.

Roger smiled indulgently. "The truth is, you two have an extra clause in your contract that none of the other contestants will have to sign. It's on page twelve. We'll need you to take the agreement to your rooms with you and read it over carefully. You would both have to sign the clause, so talk it over with each other. Should either of you be eliminated early, the clause will most likely not be activated." Roger gave a smug little snort. "Because, frankly, if you're eliminated early, who's gonna care? Thus you'll note that the clause is activated at the sole discretion of Real Deal Entertainment. Meaning we decide to activate. Or not."

Brenna wasn't getting it. She sent Travis a sideways glance. He looked as confused as she felt.

Roger kept talking. "On a brighter note, if you both last on the show, if you both keep coming out ahead in the challenges, if we feel, as filming continues, that America will end up falling as hard for you young lovebirds as we at Real Deal have, then we're throwing you a wedding." He beamed at them proudly.

Brenna almost choked. "Urgh," she squeaked. "Did you just say…a wedding?"

"Yes, you heard me right, Brenna. If all goes as we hope it will, you and Travis will be married on camera at the end of the show."

Chapter Five

Married?

They would have to get married on the show?

A numbness stole through Brenna.

No. She couldn't do it.

It was one thing to pretend they were engaged. An engagement, after all, could be broken by a simple and private decision, just between two people. With an engagement, all you had to say was that it didn't work out.

But marriage? A real, legal marriage, before God and a national audience? To break a marriage, you had to do a lot more than just decide to call it off. They would have to divorce each other. Or at least get an annulment.

Yeah, okay, she'd made a few questionable choices in her life, but she'd always been absolutely certain that when she got married, it would be forever. She might be the wild child of her family, but she still shared a bedrock foundation of O'Reilly family values.

A temporary marriage was simply a bridge too far.

Her stomach felt hollowed out, and her brain refused to function. She tried to pull her hand free of Travis's hold.

He didn't let go. He said to Roger and the others, "We would need to talk to our lawyer first."

Our lawyer? What lawyer? Brenna didn't have a lawyer. Or did he mean his dad, Ben, who ran a law office in town?

Bad idea. Ben, like the rest of Trav's family and hers, thought that she and Travis were *really* engaged. It wasn't right to put their secret on poor Ben. She sent Travis a frantic look. He gazed back at her steadily. Cool as they came.

Brenna got the message. If she was going to freak out, she should do it in private. First rule of reality TV: save the drama for the cameras and never let the suits see you sweat.

Was that two rules?

Whatevs.

And okay. Maybe not Ben, but seeing a lawyer for this problem wasn't a bad idea. Some of the other finalists were pros at the reality show game. They had agents and lawyers advising them on their every move. Well, she and Travis had a right to a little legal advice, too—like how bad would it be to sign the marriage clause and then not follow through if it came to that?

She sucked in a slow breath and put on her game face. "Yes." She backed Travis up. "Our lawyer would have to advise us on something like this."

Roger nodded. "That's wise. Call in your attorney. We'll need your decision by tomorrow at noon."

They took their blue folders and went straight upstairs from the meeting. Brenna wanted to break something. She wanted to throw back her head and let out a scream.

Travis followed her into her room. The second the door clicked shut, she whirled on him. "We can't get married, and no way are we calling your dad about this."

"Bren," he said, using a soft, coaxing tone suitable for soothing riled horses. "Slow down. First things first."

She eyed him sideways, ready to bolt. "What things?"

He tipped his head at the small table by the window. "We sit down, we read what it says on page twelve and then we discuss."

She glared. "Discuss? There's nothing to discuss. We're not getting fake married, because you *can't* get fake married. If we get married on *The Great Roundup*, it will be for real and then we'll end up having to get a divorce. Trav, I don't want to be someone who's gotten divorced. Especially not when I haven't even *really* been married."

Instead of answering her, he turned and walked away.

"Where are you going?" she demanded.

At the table, he set down the blue folders, one at each of the two chairs. "Come here. Sit down."

She folded her arms protectively across her middle and aimed her chin high. "Not doing it. Just not."

He came toward her again, his blue eyes holding hers, a slight smile curving those sexy lips of his. "Bren."

"I just don't feel right about it, Travis. I really don't."

He took her by the shoulders and dipped his dark head close. "One step at a time. There's no win in just rushing to a negative conclusion."

"I can't help it. Negative is how I feel. I hate this. Hate. It. Am I making myself clear?"

He squeezed her shoulders. "Stop freaking out. We'll

read what it says in the contract and then we'll call Ryan and find out what our options are."

"Wait a minute." She blinked up at him. "You mean Ryan Roarke?"

"Yep."

She had to admit that calling Ryan wasn't a half-bad idea. Ryan was married to Travis's cousin Kristen. The couple lived in Kalispell now, and Ryan had a small practice there. But before he came to Montana, Kristen's husband used to be a lawyer in LA. "I think I heard he was in entertainment law when he lived in California..."

"Exactly. He's an expert on just this sort of thing."

"*If* he's available on zero notice."

"He's a good guy. He'll come right over if he possibly can."

Ryan had experience. A marriage clause in a reality show contract wouldn't be all that shocking to him. Somehow, it didn't seem quite as bad to consider consulting with Ryan as it would be to have to face Travis's dad.

"Bren," Travis said again, so softly. "We really need to run the contracts by a professional, anyway. And Ryan will be bound by attorney-client privilege. He's not telling our secrets to anybody."

"I know that."

"Come here." He pulled her close. She surrendered to his offer of comfort, sliding her arms around his lean waist and laying her cheek against his hard chest. "One step at a time," he whispered and stroked a hand down her hair.

She breathed in his woodsy scent. "Right. Okay. We call Ryan and we ask for his help."

* * *

"My advice, if you sign," said Ryan, "is that you need to be ready to follow through with the on-camera wedding."

Travis glanced at Brenna. She didn't look happy, but at least she seemed calmer now. For a while there he'd been afraid she might run out the door and keep running all the way to the O'Reilly place, taking their chance at *The Great Roundup* along with her.

Brenna said, "What if we sign and then *don't* follow through?"

Ryan lifted a shoulder in a half shrug. "Expect a lawsuit. One you will lose. The terms here are very clear. If Real Deal Entertainment chooses to activate this clause, you're legally bound to do what you agreed to do. You have to marry on the show and then remain legally married until March 31 of next year."

"The final show's airing around Christmas—or I think that's the plan, anyway," Travis said. "So that we have to stay married until spring makes sense, I guess. They would want us married for at least a few months after the whole country gets a front-row seat at our wedding."

Ryan focused on the contract in front of him again and then looked up. "It doesn't require that you live together, though. That means you can essentially go your separate ways as soon as filming wraps."

"That's such a relief," muttered Brenna, clearly meaning it was anything but.

Ryan raked a hank of dark hair off his forehead. It fell right back across his brow. "Just curious. What happens if you tell them you're not willing to sign this clause?"

"Best guess?" asked Brenna. At Ryan's nod, she continued, "There are four of us still to be eliminated from the cast of the show. If we don't sign the marriage clause, Trav and I will be two of the four who have to go."

"But you don't know that for certain. I'm just saying there are unknowns in this equation. Maybe they're bluffing you and they plan to hire one or the other or both of you even if you won't sign on for a wedding. You could bluff back."

Travis glanced across at Brenna. Those sea-blue eyes were waiting. She slowly shook her head. He took her meaning as clearly as if she'd spoken aloud—and he agreed with her, too. If they didn't sign on to be married, this adventure was over.

After Ryan left, Travis suggested, "Let's go downstairs to the Manor Bar. At a time like this, what you need is a big burger and a double order of fries." When she only shook her head again, he came up with a second option. "Or we can call Steve and Roberta, see if they want to hang out for a while."

Brenna sank to the side of her bed. "You go ahead. I need a little time, you know, to think this over."

He wanted to coax her some more, see if he could snap her out of this dark mood of hers. Even if this was the end—and damn it, he hoped not—he hated to see her so down.

"Please," she said. "Just go."

So he left her. He worked out in the basement gym to take some of the tension off. When he came back upstairs, he found a Do Not Disturb sign on her door.

He had a shower and then called Steve. They met up with old Wally Wilson and a couple of other finalists for burgers and fries in the bar. After the meal, they went up to Wally's room and played poker till a little after eleven.

When Travis returned to his room that time, he found the Do Not Disturb sign still hanging on Brenna's door.

Well, all right then. If she wanted to brood all night, fine. He was done trying to cheer the woman up. He left her alone.

After changing into sweats and a T-shirt, he stretched out on the bed and channel surfed for a while. Somehow, he managed to resist the temptation to knock on the door between their rooms. At some point, he must have dropped off to sleep.

He jerked awake to the sound of someone tapping on the interior door.

"Trav?"

He blinked to clear the sleep from his brain. "Brenna?" Was he dreaming?

More tapping. "Travis, can I come in?"

He jumped up so fast he tripped over his boots, which he'd dropped at the side of the bed. A string of curse words escaped him as he grabbed the bedpost, barely keeping himself from landing face-first on the floor.

"Trav?"

"Coming!" Flicking the lock, he hauled back the door. Her side was already open.

She stood there in the same Bushwacker shirt she'd been wearing the morning he took her from her parents' house. Her hair was a wild red tangle around her pale, serious face.

She swallowed hard. And then, out of nowhere, she said, "I got arrested in Juárez."

He tried to think of what to say to that. She looked so fragile right then, like if he touched her she might shatter into a million little pieces and he'd never get her put back together again. He was still trying to figure out how to offer her comfort when she opened her mouth and the story just came spilling out.

"I wasn't even supposed to *be* in Juárez, you know? It was a trip with my girlfriends to El Paso." She rattled off three names he vaguely recognized, girls who had gone to Rust Creek Falls High. None of them lived in town anymore. "It was a reunion trip, me and my girls from back in school. Leonie lives in El Paso now, so we all met up there. We were hanging out, seeing the sights. I fell asleep in the backseat and the next thing I knew, it was dark and Leonie was parking the car not far from this Juárez dive."

He got the picture. "You'd crossed the border while you were sleeping?"

"Exactly. I started to argue that we shouldn't even be there. Marlena said they were going in and I could sit in the car if I wanted to. And I…well, the street was dark and I didn't want to sit there alone. But it was more than that. You know me. We were already there and it was kind of dangerous and exciting…"

He took her sweet face between his two hands. "Hey. It's me, Travis, you're talking to here."

"Oh, Trav…"

"I get it. You don't have to explain. You didn't want to sit out in the car in the dark—and you were curious, so you went in with them."

She held his eyes. "Yeah, I went in. And at first it was fine, not much different than a Friday night at the Ace, just with everyone speaking Spanish and Tejano music on the jukebox. But then it turned out some kind of a drug deal was going down. There was shouting and then shooting. The police showed up and hauled everyone in the place to jail."

He let his hands trail down to her shoulders and then took her arm. "Come on." She let him pull her to the edge of his unmade bed, and she sat when he gently pushed her down. "Were you hurt?"

She shook her head. "We were all okay. Just terrified. They kept us in that jail for three days, in a big holding cell full of desperate-looking women. I got questioned a few times. They were trying to figure out who was in on the drug deal, I think. Finally, they let us make a phone call each. And in the end, my dad and Ronan had to fly down and bail me out. It was awful. I've never seen my dad so disappointed in me. And my mom…she didn't speak to me for weeks. Because, you know, we are O'Reillys. And an O'Reilly doesn't get herself arrested in a Juárez dive bar. That just doesn't happen. After that, I swore off adventure and taking chances. I promised myself and my family that I was settling down."

He put his arm around her and pulled her close to his side. Truth was, he liked how she fit there—maybe too much. "And now here you are, running off with troublesome Travis Dalton to be on a reality show."

"Yeah." She sagged against him, her head tipped down. "You said it." But then she looked up at him. Now those eyes blazed blue fire. "I want it, Trav. I really, really want it. I want to be on *The Great Roundup* with you. I want us to win a million bucks."

He smoothed a hand down her sleep-scrambled hair. It snapped with electricity under his palm. Damn. They were doing this. They were *really* doing this. "I hear you. I get you. I do."

"I want it enough that I'm willing to sign the marriage clause, willing to go through with the wedding if we have to." Her eyes were enormous oceans of blue. "Because if we have to get married, that means we win, right—or at least that we get really close?"

"That's right. That is exactly what it means." But now he felt wary. Now that she knew what she wanted, his conscience had suddenly decided to kick in. He couldn't help wondering if this was the right thing to do.

She saw the change in him. "Uh-uh. Don't you back down now, Travis Dalton. Don't you dare."

"I just want you to be sure, that's all."

"I *am* sure."

"I want it bad, too, but you have to be all in with this. If they make us get married, we'll be going through with it. And then, next spring, we'll be getting a divorce. And not only do O'Reillys *not* get arrested in Juárez dive bars…"

"An O'Reilly does *not* get divorced," she finished for him. "I know it. It's all I've been thinking about all day and all night. And you know what? I still want this. I want to get on that show and I want to win. And that is why we are doing this."

His heart beat a triumphant tattoo under his ribs. "You're certain, then?"

"I'm positive. Tomorrow we tell them we're signing the marriage clause."

At noon the next day, Travis and Brenna signed their contracts.

At three, the final four contestants were eliminated. Brenna and Travis, Steve, Roberta, Wally and Summer Knight all made the cast.

Roger, the field producer, gave a little pep talk, finishing with, “Congratulations to all of you. Relax and rest up tomorrow, get in touch with your loved ones and share your big news. On Monday, you’ll all be going on location. And on Tuesday, filming begins.”

Rest? Brenna couldn’t rest. That night, she did a lot of pillow punching and no sleeping. She couldn’t stop second-guessing her choice to sign the marriage clause.

In the morning, she looked bad, with some serious dark circles under her eyes, but she hadn’t changed her mind about her ultimate choice. The show would be the experience of a lifetime—and a way to finance her plans for the future.

Also, well, who could say what would happen? Even if she or Travis won, the show’s story could change and they wouldn’t have to get married, after all. As of now, though, her choice had been made and she was through stewing over it. She showered and dressed and put on more makeup than usual—enough to cover the evidence of her restless night.

Travis, on the other hand, looked fresh and ready for anything when she opened the inner door to him. Apparently, second thoughts hadn’t messed with *his* sleep.

He breezed into her room. “I could eat a side of beef. Let’s order up some breakfast.” He grabbed the room service menu off the table. Really, the man ate like there was no tomorrow and remained lean, his muscles sharply cut, not an ounce of fat on him.

“Where do you put it all, that’s what I want to know?”

Travis only chuckled and picked up the phone.

An hour later, their plates were empty. They sat at the table enjoying second cups of coffee, trying to decide how to spend their last day at the Manor.

There was a tap on the door. Assuming it would be Steve or Roberta, Brenna jumped up to answer.

She opened the door to find her sister Fallon on the other side. With a happy cry, she reached for a hug, then stepped back and pulled her baby sister into the room. "It's *so* good to see you. When did you get back from Florida?"

"Yesterday."

"You didn't call."

"I thought I'd surprise you." Fallon spotted Travis. "Hey, Travis."

He got up and hugged her, too. "How was Disney World?"

Fallon, tall and slim as a willow wand, her hair a riot of O'Reilly-red curls and her china-blue eyes shining bright, had never looked happier. "The kids ran us ragged." The triplets were just fourteen months old. "We loved every minute of it." She gave Trav a radiant smile that wavered a little when she added, "I understand congratulations are in order."

"Thanks." Travis played his part so perfectly. He reached out a hand and Brenna went to him, tucking herself up close to his side as though she was born to be there. And truthfully, sometimes she could almost believe that he actually did love her, that they were finally *really* together and nothing could ever drag them apart. He pressed a kiss to her temple, his lips so warm and soft. "I snagged the pot of gold with this one, that's for sure—and I'll get out of here and let you two catch up."

"It's good to see you, Travis," said Fallon as he turned for the inside door to his room.

He paused in the doorway. "You, too. You look great,

Fallon. I can see that married life is working for you. My best to Jamie."

"I'll tell him you said hi."

With a last nod, Travis went into his room, pulling the door shut behind him.

"Coffee?" Brenna offered. "There's some in the carafe."

"Sounds perfect."

Brenna got her sister a clean cup and they sat down together. "There's toast," she offered. "And blackberry jam."

"Just the coffee." Fallon took the cup Brenna handed her and raised it toward the door to Travis's room. "He's such a charmer."

"Always and forever," Brenna agreed.

"Mom told me a cute story. You know Abby Fuller?"

"Yeah, Marissa Fuller's nine-year-old." Marissa was widowed with three girls. Abby was the oldest.

"Abby's adorable," said Fallon. "All three of those little girls are. Anyway, Marissa told Mom that Abby thinks Travis is dreamy—Abby's word, I kid you not. Abby says she's going to marry herself a cowboy someday…if she can't marry the lead singer of 2LOVEU." The sisters laughed together. "Remind you of anyone?"

"Oh, yeah. Brings back precious memories." She saw herself at six, when Travis brought her bike back after Angus McCauley stole it. "I planned to marry a cowboy, too."

"A certain cowboy."

"Yep."

"And just look at you now."

"That's right." Fake engaged to be legally married—and divorced come the spring.

Fallon frowned. "What's wrong?"

"Are you kidding? Not a thing."

Fallon sipped her coffee. "Downstairs, I asked for you at the front desk. A short guy with a big smile appeared."

"Gerry, the production assistant."

"He was sweet. He said he could have guessed that we were sisters and of course I could see you. He gave me your room number." She set down her cup. "So. Lots going on with you, huh? *The Great Roundup*, for real?"

Brenna shared her news. "We found out yesterday that we made the final cut. We go on location tomorrow."

"Oh, my gosh. Seriously?"

"That's right. We're in. It's a big step—but also just the beginning. We've got six weeks of filming to get through."

"You have to tell me everything as soon as you get back."

"Sorry, can't do that." She explained about the confidentiality agreement.

"That's no fair. Your own sister has to wait to find out what happened?"

"You know if I could tell anyone, it would be you." Brenna wanted to grab her and hug her all over again. "Oh, Fallon. It's so good to see you."

"You are amazing," her sister said. "I admit I've envied the way you throw yourself into life. You've always been ready for anything. I used to wish that I could be as brave as you."

Brenna got misty-eyed. She sniffed. "Don't you dare make me cry—and I noticed you said 'used to wish.'"

"Well, as it so happens, my life is turning out to be

pretty amazing, too." Fallon had loved Jamie Stockton all her life. And now she was married to him. "I'm so happy, Bren. I can't tell you."

"I'm glad."

Fallon reached across the table. Her soft fingers brushed Brenna's. "Just…be careful, okay?"

Brenna tried to keep it light. "Me? Careful? Never gonna happen."

"I think Travis is a great guy, you know that. And he seems really crazy about you…"

"But…?" Brenna drew out the word.

"I know you've had a thing for him for years. And I'm glad it's working out for you two. But, well…"

Brenna couldn't stand it. "Look. I know what you're going to say. He's thirty-four and I'm his first serious relationship." *Or I would be, if it wasn't all just for the show.* "Not to mention, he's got that rep as a player, right?"

"I'm your sister. It's my job to say the hard stuff—or in this case, to make *you* say it." Fallon gave a weak laugh.

"Well, okay then. You've done your part. And please don't worry about me. I can handle myself, and I know what I'm doing. *The Great Roundup* is a once-in-a-lifetime opportunity, and there is no way I'm passing it up."

Fallon stood. She stepped around the table to Brenna's side.

Brenna looked at her sister. "What?"

Fallon pulled her to her feet and looked directly into her eyes. "Bren, what is really going on here?"

Brenna lied without flinching. "I don't know what you're talking about."

"Oh, honey." Fallon stroked her hand down Brenna's

hair. "I notice you haven't told me how much you love him."

Okay, so she'd blown it. At the moment, she felt crappy enough about the whole thing that she didn't even care. She straightened her shoulders. "That Friday night at the Ace, the night he asked me to marry him? That night I said it a lot of times. You can ask anyone."

"But you're not saying it now, to me. Is this whole engagement thing just a stunt to get you on the show?"

Brenna didn't answer. She hated lying to her sister. And right now, she just wasn't going to do it. Let Fallon think what she wanted.

"You're not answering me," Fallon accused softly. When Brenna still said nothing, Fallon grabbed her in a tight hug. "Bren, please just be careful," she whispered. "Be careful and try not to get hurt."

Chapter Six

At six on Monday morning, Gerry tapped on Brenna's door.

"Top o' the mornin' to ye, Brenna, m' love. I need to see your suitcases and go through all the drawers in your room."

"Uh. Because?"

"My darling, some items are not allowed on location. If you have any of those, they'll be boxed up for you and available as soon as filming wraps."

"Items such as…?"

"Ropes, tack, compasses, fire starters, anything you might use in a challenge. All contestants use the equipment provided on-site. Weapons, drugs, narcotics. Video games, iPods. Medications you didn't get approved ahead of time. The list goes on."

"What about my phone?"

"You can bring it on location, but you'll turn it in there. We'll keep it charged for you and return it to you for approved phone calls and other special circumstances—and just FYI, it's all in the contract, my sweet."

She vaguely remembered all that. "All righty, then." She let him in and he went through all the drawers, both of her suitcases and her makeup kit, too, confiscating a bottle of aspirin, her old iPod and her iPad. He bagged and labeled them, stuck them in the pack he had with him and then went and knocked on Travis's door.

Once she was packed, dressed and ready to go, Travis joined her in her room and they ordered up some breakfast.

As they ate, they went over the series of simple signals they'd worked out. A tug on the left ear meant one thing, on the right, another. On set, they would be wearing body mics. Anything they said would be recorded, so they needed ways to communicate without words until they could steal a little privacy for a real conversation.

Their signals memorized, they left their rooms for the last time.

"This is it," Travis warned. "From now on, assume we're being filmed and recorded at all times. We're madly in love and engaged to be married. Play that for all you're worth and don't say or do anything to give our game away."

She clutched his arm and gazed up at him adoringly. "I love you with every fiber of my being and I can't wait to be your wife."

He gave a nod of approval. "Sell it, Bren."

"Oh, just you watch me."

* * *

Downstairs, they loaded their gear into a large, no-frills white van and Gerry drove them and half the contestants the twenty-five miles to High Lonesome Guest Ranch. The other half of the cast followed an hour later in an identical van. The whole idea, Gerry said, was to transport the contestants without drawing attention to them and giving away their supersecret shooting location.

In a rolling valley surrounded by mountains blanketed in thick evergreen, the ranch had been leased to Real Deal for the duration of filming. Gerry said the owners were in the process of converting the place from a working ranch to a guest facility. They were still building guest cottages and doing finish work on various interiors and wouldn't open for business until next spring. Real Deal had gotten an excellent rate for the exclusive use of the property during filming, and High Lonesome would reap the benefit of all that free publicity for its opening season.

It was a beautiful site, acres and acres of gorgeous land, all those tall trees with a few craggy, snow-capped, cloud-ringed peaks looming in the distance. There were stables, two barns and a series of linked corrals and paddocks. Green pastures dotted with patches of bright wildflowers were home to a herd of grazing cattle. Besides a number of cozy log cottages, the property boasted a fancy main lodge.

Inside the lodge they got their room assignments. Again, Brenna and Travis ended up side by side with a connecting door.

Summer Knight had the room on Travis's other side, so they rode up in the elevator together. Summer dimpled and fluttered her eyelashes at Travis, the way she'd done every chance she got during their stay at the Manor. Brenna tried not to be too aggravated with the woman. Summer flirted with all the guys, even old Wally Wilson and the seventeen-year-old Franklin twins, Rob and Joey, who had joined the cast with their father, Fred.

"Don't let her get you alone," she teased Travis a few minutes later, after they'd dropped their bags on their beds and opened the adjoining door. "She might try anything."

He moved in close. "Jealous?"

She was, just a little. And that annoyed her almost as much as Summer did. "Let Summer put a move on you and you'll find out."

He actually smirked. "You can't fool me. You're jealous. I kind of like that."

Saying she wasn't would only serve to convince him that she was. So she rolled with it. "As your adoring fiancée, it's my job to act jealous—of Summer, especially."

"Why Summer?"

"She's a man-eater."

"And you know this how?"

"Oh, please. Take my word for it. And stay away from her."

"Or…?"

"Really? Seriously? You're doubling down?"

Now he put on his wounded face. "Oh, come on. You know I was only kidding."

"I do?"

"As your husband-to-be, I would never even look at another woman."

"Travis. Get real. You were pretty much born to flirt."

He faked a look of pure longing. "Not since you stole my heart."

She pantomimed gagging with her hands to her throat as the phone by the bed rang. He picked it up. "We'll be right down," he said and hung up. "They want us in the lobby—and we have to bring our phones."

Downstairs, production assistants bagged and tagged their cell phones. Then Anthony Locke and Roger Del-Ray welcomed them all to High Lonesome and introduced them to the show's host, Jasper Ridge, who would narrate the various challenges and run the eliminations.

Jasper clearly had a thing for black. He looked like some old-time bad guy, in black jeans, a black shirt, a black bandanna and a black hat. When he tipped his hat, the hair underneath was patent-leather black, too. He had actual sideburns and a black handlebar mustache.

"Enjoy today and tonight at the lodge. But remember," Roger warned them all, "*The Great Roundup* is not a luxury vacation. Starting tomorrow, you'll be living outside—mic'd up and on camera twelve to eighteen hours a day." He introduced some of the crew, including the story editor, associate directors and various assistants.

"Hospitality services will keep a buffet available until ten tonight in the dining room." Roger pointed toward a hallway. "Through there. Spend the day getting acquainted with the property. Check out the canteen. Ride the horses if you want to. Stable grooms are there to help you. Everyone take a backpack." He indicated the stacks of them on a long table against an interior wall. "Fill them with the basics in clothing and toiletries. Just what will fit in the packs. Everything else you'll turn in to the concierge desk before call time tomorrow."

A couple of assistants passed out call sheets that showed who had to be where at which times for the next day's work. A glance at her copy told Brenna they were mostly for the crew, who had a somewhat staggered schedule. For the cast, it was pretty much show up in the lobby at 5:00 a.m. armed with your full pack and ready to roll.

After they were dismissed and they stowed their backpacks upstairs, Brenna and Travis took a tour of the ranch with Steve and Roberta.

They checked out the available horses, looked over the equipment in the tack room and visited the canteen, a glorified tent set up out of sight of the lodge. Inside the canteen, long tables were piled with foodstuffs, cooking utensils, a few basic tools and various outdoor gear, including tents and camping stuff.

After lunch, they chose horses, tacked them up and rode out to get a better look at the property.

Brenna was impressed by Steve's abilities. Though he'd lost his left leg below the knee and wore a prosthesis, she'd never guess it to see him on a horse. He'd been raised on a West Texas cattle ranch, where his dad, stepmom and three little half brothers still lived.

When Brenna complimented his riding skill, Steve flashed his gorgeous smile. "Six weeks out from my last surgery, soon as I got my doctor's approval, I moved back to the ranch and started riding again."

Roberta knew her way around a horse, too. She might have been living in the city for the past twenty years, but she'd grown up on a horse ranch near Santa Barbara.

Brenna realized they'd both present some serious competition.

It was past six when they returned to the stables. They took care of their horses and went in to eat.

Later that evening, Wally Wilson got out his battered old guitar—the rules allowed musical instruments as long as they weren't amplified or electronic. The old man sat by the big stone fireplace in the lodge's great room and played country songs that had been popular back when Brenna's folks were kids.

It was nice, kind of homey, with everyone gathered around the fire. Some knew the words to the old songs and sang along.

Travis led Brenna to a club chair by the window. Brenna played her part, sitting crossways on his lap, letting her boots dangle over the chair arm. She rested her cheek against his shoulder. As he idly stroked her hair, she settled in with a contented sigh and decided that reality TV wasn't bad, really. Not bad at all.

There were no cameras that she noticed at first, but Anthony Locke and his minions must have seen the opportunity and grabbed it. She looked over and spotted a cameraman in one corner and a guy with a boom mic homing in on old Wally. And now that she was paying attention, she noticed the cameras mounted in the rafters.

She must have stiffened, because Trav leaned down to kiss the top of her head and asked, "What is it?"

She snuggled her face into his neck and pretended to kiss him there. He smelled so good, of leather and man. "Cameras," she whispered. "Everywhere."

He chuckled as though she'd said something really amusing. "Get used to it," he whispered back.

"It's creepy."

He tipped up her chin. They shared a long look. Oh, really, she could pretend to be Travis's girl for the rest of her life, easy-peasy. He kissed her, his warm lips so soft, his beard thrillingly scratchy. "Embrace the creepy."

"More reality show wisdom?"

"You said it."

"Next you'll be reminding me that I signed on for this."

Travis said nothing. He just kissed her again.

"Get a room!" one of the Franklin boys heckled. Somebody else snickered.

Brenna smiled to herself as she settled her head back on Travis's shoulder. If she had to play a bride-to-be who couldn't keep her hands off her man, at least she got to do it with the best kisser in Montana.

At five the next morning, they all gathered downstairs in the lobby to get their body mics. The mics came in two pieces connected by a wire—a microphone, which you hooked to your shirt or pinned in your hair, and a transmitter, which went in a pocket. The mics could record a whisper at three feet away. Contestants were expected to wear them throughout the working day.

Before they went outside, Roger introduced the wranglers—crew members who wrangled the cast. Dressed in jeans, boots and dark shirts, the wranglers would help to keep track of who was doing what and where, all while keeping themselves mostly invisible. They wore headsets to get instructions from Roger, Anthony and the story editors. They would also consult off camera with the judges when it came time to determine winners and losers.

Hospitality served them all breakfast outside at picnic tables. And then, as the sun came up, with the cameras rolling, Anthony had the contestants grouped at the entrance to the canteen. Brenna, next to Travis, played her part for the camera, holding his arm, glancing up at him adoringly, staying in good and close.

Jasper emerged from within and started talking. It was an intro to the show. For the benefit of the TV audience, Jasper explained the rules that all of the contestants had already read and agreed to. There were to be major challenges and minor ones. If you won a minor challenge, you got some small perk. If you won a major challenge, you got immunity from elimination in the next round.

And if you didn't have immunity and the judges gave you the lowest score on a major challenge? Bye-bye.

Jasper introduced the judges, three old cowpunchers, each with a hat bigger than the one before. The one with the biggest hat explained in a lazy drawl that points would be given for skill, daring, teamwork and the successful accomplishment of each major challenge. The points didn't accumulate. Once the judging of any given challenge was over, everyone still in the game started fresh. All you had to do was survive each major challenge to remain in the running.

As Jasper talked, the wranglers ran around whispering directions in people's ears. Apparently, one of them told Summer Knight to cozy up to Travis, because the rodeo star popped up out of nowhere on Trav's other side.

Like a shark gliding through deep water, the woman

had gotten to him without a sound. Brenna sensed movement in her peripheral vision. When she glanced around Travis, there was Summer, up close and personal, flashing him a big, flirty smile.

Brenna considered not reacting. But then the whole point was the drama, right? Where was the drama if she just let it go?

She grabbed Travis's hand.

"What?" he whispered, which was a total crock on every level. He knew exactly what. And his whisper might not disturb Jasper's endless monologue, but their body mics picked up every slight sound they made. Brenna just shook her head and dragged him around Fred Franklin and the twins to the far edge of the group.

When she stopped, Travis pulled his hand free of her grip—but only so he could slide his arm around her neck and pull her in close. He kissed her cheek, a sweet little peck that she enjoyed way too much. "'Fess up, baby," he said softly in a country twang. "You're jealous. You know you are. But you don't need to be. 'Cause, darlin', all I see is you."

Sheesh. He should put that line to music.

She almost laughed but caught herself and put on a sulky little glare instead.

Objectively, she got that this was just what the director had been going for. Jasper was a pretty good talker. He made all that information as interesting as possible. But come on, listening to rules and instructions was a snooze. A little drama on the side would liven things up.

She was just starting to feel smug that she'd thwarted the man-eater. But no. Here came Summer again, slipping into position on Travis's other side. They ought to play the theme music from *Jaws* wherever that woman went. Summer flashed a radiant smile—first at Brenna and then right at Travis.

Brenna simply couldn't let that move stand. She had her pride, after all.

She ducked free of Travis's hold and slid around to his other side. "'Scuse me," she whispered, all innocence, and eased herself between her fake fiancé and the man-stealing rodeo star.

Summer only sighed and turned her eyes front, suddenly totally enthralled as Jasper described their first task on the show: they would each be creating their own immunity bracelet. After each major challenge, the winner would put on his or her bracelet, thus acquiring immunity from elimination during the next major challenge.

They got to work braiding bracelets out of strips of leather using colored beads for decoration. Brenna was pretty good at it. She and Fallon had played around with making leather bracelets back in their teens. Plus, as a hairdresser, Brenna knew how to get a tight, even braid. She added purple and turquoise beads in various shapes and sizes to jazz her bracelet up a little and had it finished in no time.

Trav was another story. Judging by his lumpy-looking effort, crafting with leather wasn't something he'd ever tried. He got a look at Brenna's bracelet and gave her the sexy eyes. "Gee, Bren. How 'bout helping me out a little here?"

She showed him how to hold the leather strings with even tension and suggested he use azure-blue beads. "Because they match your eyes."

He gave her that smile that could melt panties at

fifty paces and leaned in for a quick kiss that somehow stretched out into something longer. And deeper.

Seriously, forget bracelet making. Maybe she and Trav could stand here kissing for the next hour or two. They could call the show *The Great Romance Roundup.* And forget the ranching challenges. It could be all about kissing and togetherness, about deep, meaningful sharing and beautiful declarations of undying love.

Was it wrong to feel this good when she was kissing him? His lips played over hers. She reached up a hand and stroked the hair at his temple. He pulled her closer into the circle of his lean arms.

About then, though, it started to seem way too quiet around them. Brenna broke the kiss and opened her eyes to find everybody watching and more than one camera aimed at them.

Trav seemed to shake himself. "Bracelets, right? We're making bracelets..."

She laughed and took his bracelet from him. "Okay, pay attention, now."

He caught on quickly. Roberta signaled Brenna. Brenna went to give her a hand.

An hour later, she'd helped seven other contestants make their bracelets. Wally Wilson had some experience with leatherwork, too. He'd taken Brenna's lead and pitched in to give pointers to anyone having trouble.

Wally ended up helping Summer, who shamelessly flirted with him the whole time. Actually, it was kind of cute watching Wally flirt back. He had that cowboy way about him, both shy and courtly at the same time.

As soon as everyone had completed a bracelet, Jasper emerged from the canteen carrying a large, shallow wooden box intricately carved with Western scenes. He raised the lid to reveal twenty-two labeled slots, one for each contestant. One by one, he called them forward to lay their bracelets in the box.

It was all very solemn and ceremonious. And when the box was filled, Jasper closed the lid and handed it off to one of the wranglers, who disappeared with it back into the canteen.

"Next task," announced Jasper. "Set up camp."

Jasper made a big show of inviting them into the canteen, where the piles of equipment had been arranged on the tables and labeled with their names, one for each cast member. The married couple, Leah and Seth Stone, had one pile labeled with both their names. So did Travis and Brenna.

That was when it hit her. They were sharing a tent.

When Brenna turned those turquoise blue eyes on him, Travis expected her to look freaked. But in fact, on the surface, she seemed fine with the tent arrangements.

And why wouldn't she be? They were lovers, after all, and engaged to be married. Of course they would want to be sleeping together.

But Travis knew she didn't like it. It was one thing to have adjoining rooms with a door to shut between them. But it was another altogether to sleep side by side every night in the close confines of a tent.

Because in real life they simply weren't *that* intimate.

He wrapped an arm around her waist, hauled her close and nuzzled her ear. "We got lucky, darlin'," he whispered, for the benefit of their body mics.

And they *had* gotten lucky, at least in terms of the tent itself. He'd expected they would have to sleep out in the open. A tent was a bonus.

But Brenna still seemed too subdued when he let her go, so the next time she glanced his way, he tugged on his left ear, their signal for *Let's talk as soon as possible.*

Actually the talk signal was intended for emergencies, when one of them had some urgent bit of info to communicate to the other. But he didn't have a signal for *Please don't freak out. I'll explain why the shared tent is a good thing as soon as we're alone.* So he worked with what he had.

"Gotcha," she said. He took that to mean she'd understood the signal. They grabbed their gear.

The tents went up in a wide circle on a large, mostly cleared space a quarter mile from the canteen. Furnishings were minimal: bedrolls, sleeping bags, their packs and a battery-powered lantern for each tent. Each contestant had a camp chair to call their own.

Once the shelters were up and ready, they all pitched in together to build the community campfire in the center of their little tent village. Like putting up a tent, building a campfire was a basic skill for all of them. They worked together smoothly, everybody pitching in. There were a few slackers, especially Dean Fogarth, a sandy-haired cowboy in his early twenties who spent a lot of time trying to impress Summer. But the job wasn't big enough or difficult enough for anyone to care much if Dean didn't do his part.

Wally and a couple of the other guys prepped the flat, open spot in the center of the tent circle. They cleared away debris and brought buckets of gravel up from the side of the nearby creek for better drainage when it rained and to keep the heat from sterilizing the ground beneath the blaze. Most of the women, Brenna included, began gathering firewood.

Travis helped by hauling rocks to make the fire ring. Through a cluster of trees out of sight of the camp, he found a nice stash of granite boulders at the base of a rock slide. He was hefting the first one to carry back to the campsite when Brenna popped out from behind a cottonwood.

He almost dropped the rock on his foot. "What the—"

She signaled frantically for silence and then waved her hand for him to follow her. He put down the rock and trailed her deeper into the grove of trees. When she stopped, she unclipped her mic from her hair, tugged it out from under her shirt and put it in her back pocket. She gestured for him to do the same.

A quick glance around showed no cameramen, no cast members and zero wranglers. Moving the microphone to a pocket would probably mute the sound enough that they wouldn't be heard if they whispered. And as the mic would still be operating, it would take the sound techs a while to realize that something wasn't right.

Travis stashed his mic. "What?" he whispered, in a hurry to know what was so all-fired important she needed to tell him right now.

She blinked. "What do you mean, what? You signaled that you had something to tell me that couldn't wait."

He winced. "Sorry, I just wanted to reassure you."

"Reassure me of what?"

"That there's an upside to sharing a tent. If we keep it low, we'll probably be able to talk every night—you know, make plans. Strategize."

She looked at him the way his mom used to, back when he was little and did something only a wild-ass, irresponsible kid would do. "You pulled your left ear. That means you've got something you *have* to tell me ASAP."

"Uh..."

"Travis Dalton." She puffed out her cheeks with a hard breath. "There's no emergency, is there?"

"I thought you were upset."

Her expression softened. "Well, that's kind of sweet—and honestly, I'm okay."

"Sure?"

"Positive."

He suggested, "Because we could tell them we need separate tents, that sex before marriage is against our beliefs."

She burst out laughing—and then clapped her hand over her mouth to keep too much sound from escaping. Finally, she whispered, "The way we've been going at each other? No one's going to believe we're a couple of innocent virgins. And even if we were, well, there's no reason we couldn't share a tent and keep our hands to ourselves. I mean, in the old days, engaged people used to share the same bed. It was called bundling. They would put a board between them so that—"

"Stop. I know what bundling is. And no board is going to keep two sex-starved kids apart."

"They had integrity back then."

"And a bunch of unplanned pregnancies, I'll bet. You should start worrying."

"About?"

"You're so hot," he teased, just to watch her cheeks turn pink. "What if I can't control myself?"

She did blush—just a little. And then she scowled to cover it. "Save the shameless flattery for the cameras." She reached out and grabbed him by the shirtfront, yanking him close. "And don't mess with the signals."

She was one hundred percent dead-on right about that. They couldn't afford to risk pissing off the powers that be over nothing. And she was really cute when she was mad. "Yes, ma'am." Her skin had the sweetest flush on it. He admired the pale freckles scattered across the delicate bridge of her nose. "And come to think of it, there's a good chance they've mounted a camera in these trees somewhere. Don't look around. You'll give us away."

She stiffened and kept her eyes locked with his. "Fine." He bent a little closer. "What are you up to?" Her whisper sizzled with suspicion.

"Ask yourself, what do lovers do when they manage to steal a moment alone?"

And then she smiled. "Got it." She lifted her head up that extra inch so their lips could meet.

Yeah.

Kissing Bren. He was getting way too used to it. And it felt too damn good, dangerously so.

But he'd never been the kind of guy to let a little danger stop him. He had a part to play, after all. He ran his tongue along the sweet seam where her soft lips touched. With a sigh, she let him in.

He took shameless advantage, tasting her deeply. She sighed again, like she couldn't get enough.

Really, they were so good at this kissing thing. Too good. More and more lately, he forgot that she was still little Brenna O'Reilly and he'd always vowed never to make a move on her. Somehow, the longer they pretended to be crazy in love, the harder it got to stop his mind from spinning fantasies about what it might be like, the two of them, together. For real.

He imagined taking it further, maybe letting his hand slide up from where he clasped her waist—up over the slim shape of her beneath her soft plaid shirt, up and up, until he cupped her breast. He would tease her nipple with his thumb until it got hard and tight and he could feel it even through her bra.

Damn. He really needed to dial it back. He was getting excited—and she knew it, too. A sharp gasp escaped her. For one delicious second, she surged even closer, pressing her hips to the growing hardness at his fly.

And then she yanked those soft hips away. Breaking the kiss, she stared up at him. He tried to force an easy grin when all he really wanted was to pull her back good and close, cover those fine lips again and kiss her some more.

He would kiss her all over, take her down to the mossy ground under the cottonwoods and not let her up until he'd had a real taste, a deeper taste. A taste that included every smooth, pretty inch of her.

Still staring wide-eyed, she let go of his shirt. Her breathing was agitated. But she was still Bren. In a split second, she pulled it together, giving him a crooked grin and advising, "I think you'd better pull your mic out of your pocket now and get back to hauling boulders."

A couple of hours later, the community campfire had a ring of boulders all the way around and a fire laid, tepee-style, all ready to go. Wally did the honors, striking a storm-proof match from the boxes that had been provided in their piles of equipment. The dried leaves inside the tepee of sticks caught fire.

Dinner was canned chili, which they heated over the fire along with mini hot dogs, also from a can. Real Deal provided all the water anyone could drink, offered in ten-gallon watercoolers. For cleanup, they carried their pots and plates to the creek down a gentle slope west of the campsite. And when nature called, a pair of porta-potties rigged up to look like old-time outhouses waited on the far side of the stream.

After dinner, they relaxed by the campfire. But the day's work wasn't done. One by one, they were called for OTFs—individual on-the-fly interviews.

"You pulled Travis away from Summer this morning outside the canteen when she moved in close to him," Roger said to Brenna when it was her turn. "And then, when she followed you and Travis to the edge of the group, you got between her and your fiancé. Why?"

It was after nine at night. Brenna sat in a camp chair just outside the canteen. The camera was on her. Roger was a disembodied voice beyond the circle of light.

Behind her they'd set up what they called a green screen so they could digitally add the background later. They'd lit the night around her in a sort of golden glow, and she assumed that if any of this interview made the show, she would appear to be sitting in front of a campfire.

"Summer's a big flirt," she said. "If she comes after my man, she'll be dealing with me."

"Is that what you were doing this morning?"

She nodded. "That is exactly what I was doing."

"You seemed real calm, real purposeful, when Summer moved in on Travis, but how were you feeling inside?"

"When Summer put her move on Travis at the canteen this morning, I tried to keep a smile on my face, but inside I was angry."

"Do you have a message for Summer?"

"I do." Brenna looked directly into the camera and played her part for all she was worth. "Watch yourself, Summer. Nobody likes a man-stealing tease."

Travis ducked into their darkened tent. "Alone at last," he whispered.

"Find any recording equipment?" she asked. He'd gone out to pee—and to check the perimeter for hidden recording devices. They'd already painstakingly checked their packs, the tent, their sleeping bags and bedrolls and the lantern as well, and found nothing. But you just never knew.

"I couldn't find anything suspicious nearby," he said. "But we should keep it down, just in case." He closed the tent flaps and got into his sleeping bag next to her. Only then did he take off his clothes, pulling each item out of the sleeping bag as he removed it.

Surprisingly, it was fine, cozy. Just her and Travis, finally able to whisper what was on their minds at the end of the day. She couldn't believe that the idea of sharing a tent with him had made her nervous at first. She didn't feel the least bit edgy now. There was nothing to be nervous about—not as long as she didn't let herself dwell on that smoking-hot kiss he'd given her that afternoon.

"I would kill for a bath about now." She pulled a hank of hair in front of her nose. "I smell like a campfire."

He chuckled, the sound low and rich in the darkness. "They've got some sort of outdoor shower setup by one of the barns, so eventually we'll get a turn at those. But still, you need to get used to that grubby feeling. It's only going to get worse."

"Where are the makeup people and hairdressers when a girl needs them?"

"You wear your own clothes and do your own makeup. That's why they call it reality TV."

"Yeah, well. As for makeup, I was lucky to fit blusher, mascara and lip gloss in my pack. But my hair…" Late in the afternoon, the wind had come up and a light rain had fallen. Her hair was no longer smooth and straight. "Ugh. I have no words."

"Your curls came back. I like 'em." She felt his hand on her head, a light caress and then gone. "Springy."

Warmth slid through her at his touch. And not only his touch. Sometimes he said the sweetest things. "I'm braiding it tomorrow. In fact…" She sat up and reached for her pack.

"What are you up to now?"

"I'd better braid it now or it will be nothing but tangles by the morning."

"In the dark?"

"Piece of cake." She felt for her comb, brush and a hair elastic and began brushing it in sections, working out the snarls.

He shifted in his sleeping bag, rolling over to his back. She could see him well enough to watch him put his hands behind his head. "What do you think about Roberta and Steve?"

She switched to her comb to ease out a bad tangle. "I have to say, the way she looks at him…"

A low chuckle from Trav. "And the way *he* looks at *her*. Pow. That's attraction."

Though he probably couldn't see her do it, Brenna shook her head. "Roberta's divorce just became final. It was really bad, she said. That bastard destroyed her. She loved him, and he just traded her in like a car with too many miles on it. She told me she's swearing off men forever."

"But Steve's a great guy."

"Trav, get real. She lives in California, he lives in Texas. She's forty-five, he's thirty. And didn't I just tell you she's swearing off men forever?"

"Some barriers are just made to be broken."

She winced as she forced her comb through another tangle. Really, maybe Travis was right. Up to a point, anyway. "Hmm. Well, on second thought, maybe a fling would be good for both of them."

"Good for their game, too." Meaning their story within the show.

To succeed on a reality show, you not only had to come out ahead in the challenges, you needed a strong emotional game so viewers would root for you. Or love to hate you. After all, good drama needed bad guys as well as good ones.

Travis added way too casually, "And speaking of the game, Summer came after me again while I was hauling rocks."

Brenna felt a little stab of something unpleasant—a certain tightness in her belly. She refused to call it jealousy. "Before or after you and I talked alone?"

"After."

Brenna started braiding swiftly, tugging the sections

of her hair harder than she needed to, hard enough that it hurt a little. "Came after you how?"

"I was working a boulder free of the rock slide. She came up behind me and slapped my ass."

"What in the— You're kidding."

"Nope. When I told her to knock it off, she laughed and took hold of my arm. Caught me off balance and I ended up practically falling on top of her. I grabbed her to steady her…"

The silence in the tent seemed to echo. Outside, very distinctly, Brenna heard the lonely hoot of an owl. She prompted, "And?"

He made a slight throat-clearing sound. "Brenna, you know that it's the story that counts and it's our job to play it and play it good. That's all she's doing, playing her part."

"And what are *you* doing, Trav?" She slipped the hair elastic off her wrist and wrapped it three times around the end of her braid, giving it a final snap for good measure.

"Bren—"

"That was wrong, what she did, slapping you like that. Why are you defending her?" She shoved her comb and brush back into her pack.

"Why are *you* so pissed off all of a sudden?" he demanded. Unfortunately, it was a very good question. One she wasn't going answer—not even to herself. He added, "All I care about is keeping us strong in the game."

The game. Right this minute, she hated the damn game. And that was kind of scary, given that this whole thing was a game—one that she really did want to win, one that had only just begun.

"I'm going to ask you one more time, Travis. You grabbed her to steady her. What happened next?"

Another silence. Somewhere out in the night, that lonely owl hooted.

"She kind of…toppled against me."

"Shc toppled?"

"Yeah."

"And then?"

"And then, out of nowhere, she grabbed me around the neck and smashed her mouth on mine."

Chapter Seven

"You kissed her," Bren accused in a tiny whisper.

Travis felt like the run-down heel on an old, dirty boot—disreputable and in need of immediate replacement. Kissing Summer had been nothing like kissing Bren. With Bren, he was sorely tempted. With Summer, it was…a calculated transaction. Part of the game.

He opened his mouth to say that of course he hadn't kissed the woman. She'd kissed *him*, and he'd pulled away immediately. "I…" The lie got stuck in his throat, and the truth just slid around it and escaped. "I hesitated. I didn't kiss her back, but for a second or two, when she jumped at me, I didn't push her away, either."

"Why not?" Her whisper was soft, carefully controlled. But she wasn't happy with him. Her disappointment had weight that dragged on his heart. "Are you going to throw me over for Summer, Trav? Is that your game now?"

"Of course not—but yeah, I *was* thinking of the game. I was running through my options. Trying to decide what the best move would be. To let it go on a moment for the drama, or to push her away fast and remind her that I'm engaged."

"Oh, great." Meaning it seriously wasn't. "Now I get to play the jilted fiancée. Everybody back home can watch you mess me over on network TV." She zipped her pack, the sound sharp and furious.

"Of course I'm not jilting you. My alliance is with you."

"Coulda fooled me."

"You're overreacting."

"Oh, I don't think so. I think it's crap what you did, Trav. I think playing Summer's game is the cheap way to go." That hurt. It hurt bad. And she wasn't done yet. "We're supposed to be partners."

"We *are* partners."

"And yet you think it's a good idea to run around behind my back with another woman."

"What are you talking about? It was a couple of seconds with her mouth on mine. Nobody was running around. And I'm *telling* you what happened. How is that behind your back?"

"What about our *Great Roundup* wedding? Does the *game* require that I marry a cheater in front of the world?"

"Of course not."

"If you say 'of course not' one more time, I'm going to scream."

He had the most terrible feeling—that he was losing her. Which made no sense. He'd never even *had* her, and he never would.

"Bren, I swear to you, it was just a split second that I let her kiss me, and then I took her by the shoulders and pushed her away. I told her to back off, that I was engaged and in love with my fiancée and she should try looking for a guy who might actually be interested."

A full ten seconds passed as she absorbed that information. "At least you said that," she gave out grudgingly at last. "Finally."

"I'm not messing around on you, Bren. I would never do that."

"Oh, come on. You've spent your whole life messing around."

Now he was the one letting the silence stretch out. What she said was the truth, as far as it went. So why did it wound him to hear her whispering it at him in the dark?

He answered her honestly. "Well, I think that depends on your definition of messing around. Have I spent time with a lot of different women? Yes. Have I ever cheated? Never. And I never tried to make time with somebody else's girl. I may be the troublesome Dalton who never settled down, but I *am* a Dalton, and a Dalton doesn't cheat."

She didn't say anything. Not for a really long time. Instead, she slid down into her sleeping bag and settled on her side with a long sigh. At least she was facing him. He decided to take that as a good sign.

Then she asked, her whisper softer than ever, "What did Summer do next?"

He didn't want to tell her. But he'd stuck to the painful truth so far. It seemed pretty pointless to start lying now. "She said she'd be waiting when I changed my mind. And then she picked up the armful of sticks she'd gathered and headed for camp."

"I can think of several unattractive names to call Summer Knight."

"It's the game they handed her. She plays it or she's out."

"If I were her, I would come up with a *better* game."

"I have no doubt." He wanted to reach over, brush her shoulder, stroke her hair. But right now, he didn't dare. He kept his hands to himself.

"Trav?"

"Hmm?"

"Did Roger pull you out for an OTF after Summer kissed you?"

"Yeah."

"What did you say?"

"I said that *she* had come after *me*, that it shocked the hell out of me when she kissed me, that I had zero interest in Summer Knight, that I had never led her on and never would. And that you were the only woman for me."

He seemed to have trouble breathing until she finally spoke. "Well, all right." And then she said, "If you do change your mind about how you want to play things—"

"I won't." He said it louder than he should have. And he meant it, absolutely.

"I was only going to say that I would really appreciate it if you'd let me know first."

"You're right. We're a team. I screwed up and I'm sorry. She kissed me and I started calculating options—but I swear all I did was hesitate. I didn't kiss her back."

"She'll consider your hesitation proof that she's making headway with you."

"She's not."

"Be prepared for her to come after you again."

"Next time—if there *is* a next time—she won't catch me off guard. And I *won't* hesitate. I'll tell her to get lost in no uncertain terms."

In the morning, after eggs and bacon cooked over the campfire, the first major challenge began. The last of the season's calves, born a couple of months before, needed branding and vaccinating. It was to be a humane procedure, Jasper announced.

"Here on the High Lonesome, dehorning is done shortly after birth, as is the castration of male calves." Jasper granted them all a wide, cheerful smile that was distinctly at odds with his gruesome subject. "You won't be dealing with either procedure in this challenge." Made total sense to Brenna. Dehorning was painful for the animal and best done right after birth. As for neutering, no matter how humanely that job was done, it wouldn't make for pretty TV, and the calf wouldn't enjoy it, either.

Jasper kept talking. "And instead of the hot-iron method, we'll be freeze branding, which causes only a momentary sensation of extreme cold and no physical harm or scarring. The hair is frozen off and grows back a lighter color, so the brand is clearly visible from across an open pasture." Once he explained all that, he added, "Before you get started, you'll need to choose your boss."

They voted on that. Fred Franklin, the twins' dad, won the vote. In his late forties, with a steady, confident manner, Fred had a ranch near Buffalo, Wyoming. He knew how to run a branding crew.

Most modern ranchers used four-wheelers to gather the calves and a chute to run them through, with a calf table at the end to hold them in place for the brand.

Not on *The Great Roundup.* They went at it old-school, on horseback.

The gathering and separating of calves from their mamas took forever.

There were reasons. Most of the contestants had experience herding cattle on horseback, but usually it was a job you did on a horse you knew. For the show, they had to use the horses they were given. Brenna got lucky with a great little sorrel mare named Ladygirl. Ladygirl was quick and agile. She would have made a fine barrel horse. Not only did she have the right conformation for a barrel racer, Ladygirl was eager to please and smart, too. That mare had the will to win.

But some of the other High Lonesome horses were understandably skeptical of the strangers riding them. They balked and got fractious. And more than one of the contestants took advantage of the situation, stealing any opportunity to spook another rider's mount.

With filming going on the whole time, cameramen got in the way. Locke kept hollering, "Cut!" so that he could move his minions into position to get a better angle on this or that shot.

Plus, whenever one cowboy got into it with another over some imagined slight or other, Roger would pull the combatants aside for OTFs, where he badgered them about what had happened and how it made them feel.

On the brighter side, Fred made a great boss. He had no problem with letting women do "men's" work. He made sure everyone had a chance to get in on the job, starting with setting up portable panels to form a corral, gathering the two hundred cow-calf pairs in that pasture and driving them into the corral on horseback.

Next, they hooked ropes to the corral panels and used the horses to drag the panels tighter, overlapping them to make an alley leading out.

The cows were more than happy to head for the opening and get free. Brenna and Joey Franklin stationed themselves on foot in the alley, letting the cows go through but turning back the calves. Travis and Steve, both skilled ropers, took positions at the exit and caught any calves that got by her and Joey.

When they stopped for lunch at midday, they had stew and hot bread served up by the hospitality crew.

A few of the men complained at the complete absence of beer. "What's a good branding without the beer?" Dean Fogarth groused.

Trav didn't let him get away with that. "You have enough trouble staying on your horse as it is, Fogarth. The last thing you need is a belly full of beer."

Dean scowled and muttered that the damn horse was a goosey little bugger—and right then the big triangle chuck wagon bell that hung on one of the posts holding up the canteen started clanging.

The bell signaled their first mini challenge. They all had a choice: finish their stew or answer the challenge and get a chance to win some nice little reward.

Brenna considered the possible prizes. A dinner at the lodge, maybe, or a night in a real bed…

She went running with the rest of them—and regretted her decision as soon as she learned that the challenge was to sew buttons on a shirt.

Brenna sucked at sewing. Her mom had taught her

the basics, but she'd never had much interest in getting better at it.

The wranglers passed out the shirts, the buttons and the needles and thread. Each shirt had three buttons missing. You had to replace them and you got points for speed and skill.

Brenna got all three buttons on, eventually. But the finished product was far from stellar. They were four-hole buttons and the thread that showed through was lumpy and uneven. Her tie-off should have been smooth and flat, but it was a hard ball of tangled thread. And Trav's buttons didn't look much better than hers.

Roberta and Steve were a whole other story. They both finished fast. You couldn't tell the buttons they'd sewn on from the ones that had been on the shirts when they started. Brenna felt glad that one of them would surely win.

But no. Summer won. She had the fastest time and the best-looking finished product, at least according to the judges. She laughed and fluttered her eyelashes when Rusty Boles, the judge with the biggest hat, named her the winner. For a prize, she got two hours in a luxury room at the lodge. She could take a long bath and soak the cares of the day away—or watch TV, order up something to eat from hospitality services and have a nap on a real bed.

"Sometimes life is so unfair," Brenna muttered out of the side of her mouth.

Trav put his arm around her and nuzzled her dusty hair. She leaned into him, enjoying his attention way too much. But, hey, never-ending PDAs were a big part of their game. He nibbled her ear. "Disappointed?"

"How did you guess?"

"You're wearing your sulky face."

She stuck out her lower lip and sulked even harder. "I want a bath. And Roberta should have won."

"The judges disagree."

"The judges are such fools. And look at her." She glared at Summer, who was whispering something in Rusty Boles's ear. "Her eyes might pop out of her head if she bats her eyelashes any harder."

Trav nuzzled her hair again. "Meow…"

She playfully shoved him away. "I am never catty." At his low chuckle, she shook a finger at him. "And you'd better watch yourself."

"Or…?"

"You never know the things that I might do."

"Wow, Bren. I'm quaking in my boots."

She leaned in close and pressed a kiss to his bearded jaw, her spirits lifting just from trading a few fond insults with him. "Remember," she warned. "We share a tent, and you have to sleep sometime."

They got half the calves branded and vaccinated that day. Trav and Steve stuck with roping, riding into the knots of milling, bawling calves, setting their ropes for a calf to step into place, then pulling the rope tight on the hind legs and dragging the animal toward the wrestlers, who flipped it and held it in position to get vaccinated, have its ear tag checked and take the brand.

Brenna tried branding and found she had a talent for it. The brands stood in coolers of dry ice. When they stopped bubbling, they were ready to go. Freeze branding was a little trickier than hot branding. She had to hold the frozen iron steadily in place for a good thirty seconds to make sure she killed all the hair pigment cells. She had four other wrestlers on her team to hold the calves steady, and she quickly got the rhythm of the task. Roberta, who'd gone to veterinary school before her cheating dirt-ball ex showed up to mess with her heart, did the vaccinating.

The afternoon stretched into early evening, but they kept after it. Finally, at a little past seven, as the shadows from the mountains crept across the land, Anthony called an end to shooting for that day.

They all turned in their body mics and staggered back to their circle of tents for dinner from a can. Once she'd filled her belly and done her part cleaning up the dishes down at the creek, Brenna grabbed her pack from the tent and headed for the two outdoor showers Real Deal had provided at one of the barns.

Summer, Trav and a few others had been called to the green screen by the canteen for OTFs. Almost everyone else was at the showers, waiting in two lines for a turn in one of the corrugated metal stalls. They discussed the day just passed and the first elimination that would be coming up tomorrow after the remaining calves were branded.

Inside the stall at last, Brenna found there was just one faucet—cold. And she didn't even care. It felt like heaven to wash off the grime. She lathered her hair and rinsed as fast as she could, shivering the whole time. Once she'd dried off, she put on clean clothes and her dusty boots, gathered her things and let the next person have a turn.

Halfway back to the campsite she heard an odd choking sound. Pausing in midstep, she listened—and there it was again, coming from somewhere off to her right, away from the circle of firelight.

And then she heard the sound a third time. A sob, definitely. Someone was crying.

Brenna changed direction, moving as quietly as she could across the rolling, shadowed ground, following the painful, stifled sounds.

Behind a rocky outcropping away from all the other buildings, she found Leah Stone, who was half of the only married couple in the show, crouched behind a boulder. Leah sobbed softly, her head in her hands.

Brenna hesitated. Leah wouldn't have come out here alone in the dark if she wanted company. She and her husband, Seth, mostly kept to themselves. Brenna had hardly shared two words with the woman.

Probably better to just go. As silently as possible, she backed up a step.

But then Leah let out the saddest little moan. It kind of broke Brenna's heart, that lonely, unhappy sound. Really, she couldn't just sneak away without at least making sure Leah was all right.

She took a step forward and then another. By then, she was only a few feet from the crying woman.

Leah must have heard something. Her head shot up. "Who's there?"

Sheepishly, Brenna wiggled her fingers in a wave. "Leah. Hey."

"Oh, God. Brenna..."

"I'm sorry. I should go—"

"No. I... Um. I just..." Leah slowly shook her head. And then, with another sob, she planted her face in her hands again.

Brenna set everything but her towel on one of the boulders and dropped down beside the other woman. "Hey. Hey, now..." She wrapped an arm around Leah.

Leah sobbed harder and huddled closer. Brenna wrapped her in a full hug. “Hey, hey.” She stroked Leah’s back and smoothed her hair. “It’s okay. It’ll be okay.”

“Oh, no. I don’t think it will. I really, really don’t.”

Brenna wanted to argue, to promise that it would all work out. But she didn’t even know what *it* was. So she settled for making soft, reassuring sounds and holding Leah good and close.

Finally, Leah spoke again. “I just wanted a little time, you know, to myself.”

“I get that.” Brenna tipped up Leah’s chin. “You want me to go?”

Leah sniffed. “No, stay. Actually, it feels kind of good to have someone to lean on.”

“Here.” Brenna used her towel to gently wipe Leah’s tear-streaked face. “Sorry, the towel’s kind of damp.”

“It’s cool, though. Feels good.” With a ragged little sigh, Leah rested her head on Brenna’s shoulder. Brenna reached back and put the towel on the rock behind them. She thought of Fallon, of how she could always get her sister to say what was really bothering her. “Spill.”

“Hmm?”

“That’s what I say to my sister when I know she wants to tell me what’s on her mind but she’s trying to be all brave and self-sufficient and not put her troubles on me.”

“I *don’t* want to put my troubles on you, Brenna. I hardly know you.”

“I get that. But sometimes a girl just needs to talk, right?”

“True, but—”

“Come on. Say it.”

“Well, can I trust you? I mean, we are in competition.”

"Yes, we are." Brenna started to promise that she would keep Leah's confidence. But that wasn't strictly true. She admitted, "Whatever you say, I'll most likely share it with Travis, because I tell him everything." At least, when it came to the show, she did. "But he'll keep it to himself, and I'll never tell anyone else."

"I believe you." With a shaky inhale, Leah lifted her head again. "Too bad Big Brother is always watching." She peered into the darkness, as though she might suddenly spot a hidden camera hanging from a tree.

Brenna shrugged. "I doubt they're recording us here. But you're right. You never know."

Leah put her head back on Brenna's shoulder again and whispered, "I don't think my husband loves me."

"Oh, Leah." Brenna gave the woman a good, tight squeeze.

"I don't think he ever did."

"No…"

"Um-hmm." Leah lifted her head and stared up at the star-scattered sky. "His family's farm was right next to ours. His parents and mine were best friends. I fell in love with him when I was eight. And I never stopped. Who *does* that?"

Brenna smiled to herself, thinking of her six-year-old self declaring undying love to Trav. "Sometimes you just know when it's right." She felt the smile melt right off her face. "Even if *he* doesn't."

Leah gave a sad little nod. "I was always the one pushing him to be with me. We were together straight through high school and when he enrolled at Iowa State, so did I. Everybody expected us to get married, and that worked for me. So we did. And now, after ten years of marriage, he's… Oh, Brenna. He never *talks* to me. He's distant, like a stranger. I thought that getting on this show, having this adventure together, might rekindle the flame, you know? But now I'm afraid there was no flame to start with, at least not for him."

Brenna tried to think of something helpful to say. "Have you talked to him about it?"

"I've tried. I get nowhere. He says everything's fine." She sat up a little straighter. "And I can't believe I'm telling you all this. I don't even *know* you."

Brenna met Leah's eyes and said gently, "I do understand how you feel."

"Because of Travis? You…you think Travis doesn't love you?"

I know he doesn't love me. But she couldn't tell Leah that. Her loyalty to Trav and to the win had to come first. "I'm just saying I get it, that you have your doubts. I, um, have them, too." It was the truth, though not in the way that Leah would assume. Sometimes, especially in the past few days, Brenna wondered if she was getting too attached to her fake fiancé. Sometimes she dreaded the end of the show. Because however it ended, even if they won a million bucks and she could buy the beauty shop from Bee, it wouldn't be easy. They would have to pretend to be engaged for months. And what if Real Deal decided to activate the marriage clause?

Uh-uh. Seriously. She really shouldn't even let herself go there.

Leah asked, "So what do you do when you start doubting?"

"Honestly?"

"Please."

"Denial. Total denial."

Leah actually laughed. "Oh, come on. You're not serious."

"Oh, yes, I am. I tell myself not to think about it. I focus on the moment, on staying in the game. I…keep close with Trav, keep the lines of communication open and remind myself that we're in this together." That didn't sound so bad, did it? And really, it was all true. As far as it went.

"I remember at the final audition at that cowboy bar, the Ace in the Hole?"

"Oh, God." At least the darkness hid her blush of embarrassment. "I really put on a show that night, didn't I?"

"You were great."

"Right."

"I mean it, you *were*—and I remember you said you fell in love with Travis when you were six years old."

Brenna face-palmed. "I have such a big mouth."

"No, really. It was charming and heartfelt, everything you said."

"I went a little crazy that night." *With the help of Homer's magic moonshine.*

"I think you just said what was in your heart. There's nothing wrong with that."

"Leah?" A man's voice—Seth, no doubt—came from the other side of the rocks behind them. "Leah, you out here?"

"Shh." Leah signaled Brenna for silence. And then she leaned close and whispered, "Thank you." Her soft lips brushed Brenna's cheek. "You've made me feel so much better."

"But I only—"

"Leah?" Seth called again.

Leah called back, "Coming!" She leaned into Brenna again and pitched her voice extra low. "Don't you ever doubt Travis. A person only has to watch him watching you to know you're everything to him. That man loves you like nobody's business."

All of a sudden, *she* wanted to cry.

And then Leah swept to her feet. "I'm here, Seth!" She slid around the outcropping and vanished from sight.

"You kissed Summer yesterday, Travis," said Roger. "Why?"

Travis sat in front of the green screen bombarded by golden light, knowing the cameras were picking up every move he made, every slight change in his expression. Two days into filming and already he hated the damn OTFs. And come on, hadn't they already covered this ground yesterday? "Summer kissed *me* yesterday. You'd have to ask her why she did that. I'm in love with my fiancée, and I told Summer so."

"It looked to us like you *almost* kissed Summer back."

"I'm only interested in one woman. That's Brenna O'Reilly. Summer should know that."

"Summer's had her eye on you from the first."

"If Summer's had her eye on me, I didn't notice."

"She's a beauty. And so seductive. It's crystal clear she'd like to make time with you."

"I have a feeling Summer would like to make time with a lot of guys. She should pick one of them and leave me the hell alone."

"Why are you so riled up, Travis? Does Summer

pose more of a temptation for you than you're willing to admit?"

Travis had the urge to leap from his camp chair and go after Roger, bust him a good one right in the chops. But that would only be giving the producer exactly what he was after.

Which, come to think of it, was exactly what Travis was supposed to do. Play the game, get emotional. Start a fight.

But what was it Bren said last night? That Summer should play a *better* game?

Maybe *he* ought to take his fake fiancée's advice. Travis drew a slow breath and ordered his heart rate to even out. "I'll tell you what temptation is. My girl. *She's* a pure temptation. I waited a long time, years, to finally have my chance with Bren. At first, she was too young for me. And for way too long, as the good Lord and all of Rust Creek Falls knows, I was dead set on never settling down. I don't deserve her. I never did. But somehow she loves me, anyway. And so we're together now. No other woman can even compare. And yeah, I say that from experience. I've been with other girls. I've had my wild times. Now there's only one woman I want to get crazy with. That's why that woman has my ring on her finger. That's why I can't wait to make Brenna my wife."

When Travis got back to the tent, Brenna sat on her bedroll in her Bushwacker T-shirt, braiding that gorgeous red hair of hers by lantern light.

She gave him a soft smile as he ducked between the tent flaps. "How was the OTF?" She wore no bra. The T-shirt was several sizes too big for her, but it couldn't disguise the natural movement of her breasts beneath the worn fabric as she worked on her braid.

God, she smelled good, all clean and fresh. He bent close to get a whiff of her hair. Apples and honey. He wanted to touch it, to stroke his hand down and grab the end of that braid. He would give it a tug. She would laugh and slap at him, order him to stop. So he would capture her obstinate chin and tip her lips up to claim a long, sweet kiss.

Because that's who they were now. At least for the next six weeks or so. Brenna and Travis, deeply in love and planning on forever side by side.

"Trav?"

"Um?"

"The OTF?"

He grabbed his pack. "I've decided I hate OTFs."

She chuckled as she wrapped an elastic around the end of the finished braid. "Wait. Let me guess. They came after you about Summer again?"

"No surprise, huh?"

"Not even a little."

"The good news is I think I shut them up, at least for now. I told them all about you. How you're the only woman in the world for me."

She flipped her braid back over her shoulder. "My hero," she whispered in twangy drawl. "You're such a total romantic." She pretended to shiver with pleasure.

He shoved his pack against the side of the tent, took her by her strong, slim shoulders and pushed her onto her back, hiking a knee over her so he had her pinned between his thighs.

She blinked up at him looming above her on his

hands and knees and whispered, "Okay. What's the game?"

He bent his head and kissed her—a quick one, to start. Her mouth tasted like peppermint. She must have already brushed her teeth. "I need a shower."

She arched an eyebrow at him. "Not the answer to my question."

He tipped his head toward the lantern. "You've got the lantern on. Anyone outside can see our shadows in here…"

She got it then. Her mouth formed a soft O and her eyes shone the brightest, clearest blue.

He bent close again. "I think I need to kiss you—even if I do smell like the back end of a rode-hard horse."

She licked her pink lips. Damn. He couldn't wait to kiss them again. "It's very manly, how you smell."

"Manly. I'll take it."

With a happy little sigh, she lifted her soft arms and wrapped them around his neck. They felt so good there. He could almost wish she would never let go. "And of course you should kiss me," she whispered. "Because I've got the lantern on and anyone could be looking. And if they *are* looking, they need to see how we can't keep our hands off each other."

"It's a difficult job, all this kissing," he replied, straight-faced and solemn. "But it's *our* job, and we *have* to do it."

"Less talk." She made a growling sound. "More action."

He smiled at her and she returned it, right before he lowered his head and his mouth touched hers.

A soft, eager moan escaped her. And she opened so sweetly, letting him in.

Heaven and peppermint. She tasted so good. He wanted to lower his body to hers, press her down into the bedroll, reach for the hem of that faded T-shirt and slowly ease it upward, uncovering her slowly, inch by smooth inch…

Her fingers stroked his nape, and another moan escaped her. She breathed his name into his mouth. "Trav…"

His body burned. He ached, he was so hard and ready for her.

This was getting dangerous.

This was getting far too real.

"Come down here." She wrapped her hand around his nape and tugged a little. "You're too far away."

He was. Way too far. No doubt about it. He slid an arm under her and turned her as he lowered his body. Straightening his legs, he rolled them both to their sides.

"Better." She stroked the hair at his temples, rubbed his rough cheek. "I like your beard, the way you keep it short and scruffy. It's sexy. And it feels so good, a little scratchy and yet silky, too."

"That does it. I'll never shave again."

"Works for me."

He should stop. But he didn't want to stop. He kissed her some more as he trailed his hand up over the curve of her hip and down into the tender valley of her waist.

His hand was still on top of her shirt. He promised himself he would keep it there.

But then he cheated. Just a little. He ran his palm back over her hip again, going lower that time, down along the cool flesh of her bare thigh. Her skin felt so good, so smooth and perfect. *Mine.* The word filled his head. *Made just for me.* He curved his rough fingers around the tender cove behind her knee and tugged.

She giggled. He drank in the sweet sound as she took his cue, lifting her leg, wrapping it over his thigh. Her heel brushed his calf, burning like a brand even through the heavy denim of his jeans. He yearned to press himself hard and tight against her. To get rid of that T-shirt, strip off his dusty clothes and bury himself in the sweet heat of her body.

Somehow, he made himself break the mind-blowing, never-ending kiss. They stared at each other. He let his gaze wander, over her flushed cheeks and her swollen mouth and those eyes that glittered so bright, teasing him, inviting him.

"Do we have to stop?" she whispered. He made himself nod. "Why? Let's turn off the lamp, Trav. Let's see where this takes us."

He balled his hands into fists to keep from grabbing her again. "You're making me crazy."

She reached for the lamp. The tent went dark. "Are you sure that's a bad thing?"

Chapter Eight

"Right now, I'm not sure of anything." Travis uttered the words like a confession into the darkness between them.

But they were a lie. He was sure of one thing: he wanted her.

And that wanting was growing. Every hour he was near her, he wanted her more.

She was a handful, Brenna O'Reilly. Any man would have a hell of a time trying to tame her.

But then again, he didn't want to tame her. He wanted her *un*tamed. Wanted her just as she was and always had been—a little bit wild, sometimes kind of crazy. Beautiful. Strong. Willful and true.

She moved in the darkness. The sweet scent of her drifted closer. And then she framed his face between her two cool hands. "Think about it." Her breath touched his lips. "Think *real* hard."

"Bren." It came out on a groan.

And then she moved again—away from him, damn it.

He didn't realize she'd grabbed his pack until she shoved it into his arms. "Oof."

"Go on, cowboy. Have that shower."

"Bren..."

And she bent close and kissed him again, a sweet brush of her mouth on his. "Go." She gave a low laugh. "Before I grab you and have my evil way with you."

When he got back to the tent, the light was still off. He could make out the shape of her in her sleeping bag. He stripped down and slid into his own bag.

"'Night, Trav." Her voice was thick and lazy, hovering on the edge of sleep.

"'Night." His cold shower had taken the edge off his need for her. Now he just felt good to be lying there beside her in the dark.

He laced his hands behind his head and stared up into the darkness and thought about condoms. He had one, because even a guy who'd sworn off women should have the sense to carry a condom just in case. It was in his battered wallet in the bottom of his pack. One condom in a creased-up wrapper. It was probably out of date by now.

And that was probably a good thing. The next time kissing her threatened to get out of hand, he would just remind himself that you couldn't trust an old condom with a creased-up wrapper and he needed to behave himself.

Yeah. Right. Sure. That would work.

"Trav? You still awake?" Her sweet, sleepy voice tempted him out of the dark.

He gave her a low "Um" for an answer.

"I've been thinking..."

"Um?"

Her whisper went lower. "You may be right. About the sex? We probably shouldn't go there. We need to, you know, keep our heads on straight, focus on the game. Right?"

"You're right." They were just about the hardest two words he'd ever said.

"You're...okay with that?"

"I'm good," he lied. "Go back to sleep."

They finished branding the calves before noon the next day and filmed the first elimination in front of the canteen right after lunch.

Brenna stood next to Trav, who'd seemed kind of distant all day. Was he upset with her? Did he think she was a big tease or something, to be all over him one minute and then change her mind?

Did they need to talk it over?

Ugh. It had been hard enough telling him she'd had second thoughts. And now, to bring it up again?

Not her idea of a fun conversation.

But still. They needed to be strong together, as a team. And how could they be strong if there were simmering resentments between them? They had to keep straight, stay on point, be clearheaded and ready to face whatever the game threw at them.

So okay. In the interest of keeping things straight between them, if he still seemed distant tonight, she would bring it up to him and they would talk it out.

And then she spotted Summer maybe eight feet away, on the far side of Seth and Leah. The blonde kept sliding glances at Trav. Planning her next seduction attempt, no doubt. Brenna flashed the other woman a bright smile and leaned into Travis. He glanced down at her, and she tipped up her face for a quick kiss.

He gave it, brushing his lips across hers, lightening her heart, making her smile.

If he had been annoyed with her, he seemed to be getting over it.

When she slid another glance at Summer, the blonde was facing front, pretending to care what Jasper was saying.

Dag Dodson, the judge with the medium-sized hat, announced the three top scores in the branding challenge. "Steve Simon, Travis Dalton and Fred Franklin, step right up, please."

No one was that surprised when Jasper declared Fred the winner. They all applauded as the twins' dad claimed his immunity bracelet from the carved box. Fred had been the perfect boss—fair, considerate and firm, with a good handle on how the job should be done. Brenna would be proud to work for him anytime.

"And now," said Jasper, suddenly solemn as a preacher at a funeral, "it's time to say goodbye to one of you."

The three judges burst into a song. It was an oldie, by Woody Guthrie, "So Long, It's Been Good to Know Yuh."

Those old guys were good, too, in perfect harmony. They sang one verse and the chorus. Trav returned to Brenna's side as Rusty Boles whipped out a harmonica and played it soft and low and lonesome sounding.

The third judge stepped up to read the names of the

three lowest scorers. Brenna grabbed for Trav's hand. He wrapped his warm fingers around hers nice and tight. She really didn't think she'd end up in the bottom three, but she couldn't be sure.

And she was right. The judge didn't call her name.

Not surprisingly, Dean Fogarth was among the three. He got lucky, though. Another guy, a truck driver from Colorado, was the first to go. The judges sang another Woody Guthrie song, and the truck driver was sent to take down his tent, grab his gear and move to the lodge.

As one of the wranglers led him off, another clanged the chuck wagon bell.

Jasper laughed. "That's right, folks. It's your big chance to take a mini challenge. Who's in? Everybody? That's what I like to see."

It was a cooking challenge that time.

Skillet chili and corn bread. Each of them had to have their own recipe in their head or know how to fake it. With a flourish, Jasper gestured them all into the canteen, where their choices of ingredients were arrayed on two long tables, including several big bottles of Jack Daniel's whiskey—for the chili, supposedly.

Trav grabbed one of the bottles and then just stood there, at a loss.

Good thing Maureen O'Reilly made the best corn bread chili in three counties. And she'd taught her daughters well.

Trav looked at Brenna hopefully.

She put him out of his misery. "Yes, I can make my mother's chili."

"Score!" He waved his bottle gleefully.

"But her recipe doesn't call for whiskey."

"I'm not letting go of this bottle. See, I always cook with whiskey. Some of it even ends up in the food."

"Har-har. Just do what I do."

He wrapped an arm around her neck and yanked her close. "Damn, you're gorgeous." He laid a big smacker square on her mouth. "And you can cook. I am a lucky, lucky man."

She laughed and ducked away, feeling good about everything at that moment. He really didn't seem the least distant now. Maybe they didn't need to talk, after all.

Trav stuck close to her as they started on the mini challenge, grabbing the same ingredients she gathered, taking a space next to her at one of the prep tables, watching everything she did and then doing the same.

A couple of hours later, the judges started tasting.

Turned out old Wally Wilson used to cook for more than one outfit. The old man knew his corn bread chili. And he had experience making it over an open fire.

Wally won. His prize was a whole night at the lodge in a real bed.

He tipped his hat to the judges. "These old bones thank you kindly."

Travis's entry turned out burned on the bottom. But Brenna's chili was pretty darn good, if she did say so herself. They ate their entries for dinner. Brenna and Wally had plenty to share with Trav and the other bad cooks.

After the meal, Wally happily followed one of the wranglers off to claim his prize.

Not much of the Jack Daniel's had ended up in chili—which Brenna assumed had been the plan all along. She'd watched enough reality TV to know that when contestants got tipsy, good TV happened.

Everyone hung around the fire as night came on. They were unmic'd by then, but Roger had put a couple of cameramen on them, and there were also cameras mounted in the nearby trees. Nobody seemed to care that they were being filmed. Already, having a camera watching their every move had become normal for all of them, just the way that they lived.

They sipped whiskey from their tin cups as wranglers came to collect them, one by one, for their turns in front of the green screen.

When all the OTFs were done, most of the guys remained by the fire sipping whiskey, telling tall tales of their ranching and rodeo adventures. Roberta and Steve had gone off for a walk together. Brenna headed for the showers. When she got back, Trav showed no inclination to budge from his camp chair.

She thought about whispering to him that she needed to talk to him. But did she really? By afternoon, he'd seemed to be over whatever had been bothering him. No reason to ruin his buzz. They could talk later. Tomorrow night or the next.

Yeah, it might be a bad idea to leave him alone out there with the other men, a couple of the women she didn't know at all—and Summer. But she wasn't his babysitter, and she couldn't really blame him for wanting to get a little loose, shoot the breeze with the other guys.

Brenna ducked into the tent and shut the flaps. In the dark, she wriggled out of her clothes and into her sleep shirt and crawled into her sleeping bag.

Outside, she heard laughter from the men at the fire and thought of her childhood, of summer nights outside around a campfire, the glow of firelight warming the smiling faces of the ones she loved and—

A shout had her sitting straight up in her sleeping bag.

She scuttled to the tent flaps and peeked out.

Dean Fogarth and Randy Teasdale, a horse rancher from Idaho, circled each other on the far side of the fire. Dean threw a blow and connected. Randy landed on his butt in the dirt.

"Get up," growled Dean.

Randy grabbed Dean's boot and gave it a tug. Dean went down, too. The men rolled in the dirt together, grunting and punching each other.

Summer stood not far away, watching with an unreadable expression on her pretty face. The cameras were rolling.

Trav sat on Brenna's side of the fire, maybe twenty feet from their tent. Brenna threw a small rock and hit the back of his camp chair with it.

He twisted to look over his shoulder at her. "Hey, sleepyhead." He gave her a lazy, liquored-up grin.

"What's going on?"

He raised his tin cup to her. "Dean and Randy are havin' a li'l disagreement."

"Over Summer?"

Travis laughed. "How'd you guess? C'mon out, baby. Time to party."

Baby. Why did it sound so good when he called her that? She was definitely tempted to pull on her jeans and join him.

But no. Not tonight. She shook her head and retreated to the relative safety of the tent.

The fight went on for a while. She heard a whole

bunch of scuffling and a lot of angry swearing, words that were never going to make it onto network TV.

After the fight, somebody brought out a guitar. They all sang together—rowdy cowboy songs at first, "Friends in Low Places" and "All My Rowdy Friends Are Coming Over Tonight." Eventually they slowed things down and sang some great old ballads.

Somewhere in the middle of "Down in the Valley," Brenna dropped off to sleep.

"Bren? You 'sleep?" She felt a tap on her shoulder. "Bren?"

"Not anymore," she grumbled, rolling onto her back and blinking up into the darkness at the silhouette of Trav bending over her. "What time is it?"

A burst of whiskey breath hit her face. "Late. S'very, very late."

"Who won the fight?"

"I think they called it a draw. Summer got disgusted and stormed off."

"I don't really get it. What was the fight *about*, exactly?"

"Hmm. Two hotheaded drunk cowboys an' a flirty woman. 'Nuff said."

"Fascinating."

"As in you mean, it's not. Right?"

"Trav?"

"Um?"

"Time to lie down in your sleeping bag and get some sleep." She started to turn over.

"Wait."

"What?"

"Well, I got my boots off and got in my bag and then I jus' couldn't stan' not t' say 'night to you."

"You're drunk," she whispered gently.

"Unfort'nately, s'true."

"Well, good night, then." Again, she tried to roll back onto her side.

That time he held her in place with a hand on her shoulder. "Aw. Don' go…"

She stifled a chuckle. "Oh, Trav. You're going to be so sorry tomorrow."

She watched his white teeth flash in the darkness. "Oh, yes, I am. And you are so beaut'ful, Bren."

Something sweet and warm uncurled in her belly and she teased, "It's pitch-dark in here. You can't even see me."

"I don' need t' see you. I got you in here." He pointed in the general direction of his head. "Jus' how you look, with your skin like cream an' your red hair all sleek or, like lately, with it crazy curly so you gripe about it all the time an' put it in a braid down your back. With that bold smile on your mouth and those gold freckles so cute on the bridge of your nose. And those eyes, Bren. Where'd you get those eyes that are blue as the ocean sometimes and sometimes like a stormy sky?"

"Oh, Trav. What you just said? *That's* beautiful."

"What I'm tryin' to tell you is that I see you even when I don't see you. Does that make any sense? Nope," he answered his own question. "No sense at all. But it's the truth, anyway. You are burned in my brain. Like a brand, y'know?"

Like a brand. Her heart went to mush. She tried really hard to remember that he was drunk and he probably wouldn't recall any of this tomorrow. "You need to get some—"

"No. Lissen."

"Trav—"

"I shouldna got drunk, I know it. Ver' unprofessional of me. But I needed to blow off a li'l steam, you know?"

"It's fine. I get it. Now, just go to—"

"Bren. There's been no one for me. Not for over a year."

"Trav, you don't have to—"

"Jus' wait. Let me finish, 'kay?"

She was torn—curious about what he might reveal, and also oddly protective of him, of his privacy. In the morning, he might very well regret that the whiskey had loosened his tongue tonight.

"Yer quiet," he whispered. "So I'm gonna take that as a yes. Bren, you know how I've always been kind of busy with the ladies."

Busy with the ladies? She couldn't help it. She laughed.

"You laugh," he said with great solemnity. "But it's really not funny. I'm sick an' tired of bein' the hot player of Rus' Creek Falls. An' tha's why I haven' been with anyone in a year—not since this good-looking woman from Denver came lookin' for me."

The last thing she wanted was to hear about him and some other woman. "Trav, I—"

"Shh. There's a point to this. Jus' give me a chance to get there, will ya please?" He waited for her low hum of reluctant agreement before he went on. "This woman, she asked around town about me. Somebody gave her my number. We met up the next night, early, at the Ace. I asked her to dinner. And she said, 'Oh, honey. I don't need dinner. Le's jus' get a room.' I took her to a nice hotel I know in Kalispell. And afterward, when she was getting dressed to leave, she tol' me I was exac'ly as advertised, as good as her girlfriend said I would be."

"Oh, no." Brenna reached up in the darkness and put her hand against his beard-rough cheek. "I'm so sorry, Trav. What a horrible thing to say to you."

"Well, ackshually, she did mean it as a compliment. When I was younger, what she said wouldn'ta bothered me at all. I was jus' out for a good time back then, an' I didn' care what anybody thought. But lately, well, it had started to get so it wasn' much of a thrill, spendin' a night with a stranger. The past few years, I'd been wantin' more but not exac'ly sure how to go about gettin' it. A man acts like a player fer long enough, that's all any woman sees when she looks his way. An' that's why what that woman said that night was kind of a wake-up call. Y'know what I mean?"

She stroked the hair at his temple. "Tell me her name. I'll find her and beat the crap out of her for you."

He gave a low laugh. "You al'ays were a bloodthirsty li'l thing—an' I mean it. S'okay, really."

"You know you'll always be a hero to me."

He let out another big gust of whiskey-scented breath. "Thanks, Bren."

"It's the truth." And it was. It really was.

"An' y'know, a wake-up call ain't necessarily a bad thing. 'Cause I think it was time."

"Time?"

"Yeah, time to knock off chasin' women. And it hasn't been that tough, you know? I guess I've already had all the meaningless sex I'll ever need."

She almost laughed, but it really wasn't funny. He might be drunk, but she knew he was telling her something he wouldn't tell just anyone. He trusted her, and she treasured that trust. She cleared her throat. "Well, then. Good to know."

"An' I only said all that to tell you…" The sentence wandered off, unfinished.

"To tell me what?"

"Well, Bren, you said we *should* and then you said we *shouldn't*. An' I want you so bad I jus' want to give in, figure out some excuse to hold you and kiss you and not to stop there. I want to be with you when it's jus' you and me, alone, with nobody lookin'. Because it wouldn' be meaningless with you, Bren. With you, I know, it would be real."

Tears burned her eyes at such beautiful words.

But he wasn't finished. "Too bad there is no excuse, an' I need to remember that. We got a plan, and gettin' naked together ain't part of it. An' that's why I, well, I jus' wanna say, you were right the second time. We *shouldn't*."

His rough, warm hand touched her face, the lightest breath of a caress and then gone. She wanted to lift up, follow that touch, wanted him to *keep* touching her, wanted him to never, ever stop.

"It would be wrong," he whispered, "to go gettin' *really* intimate, you an' me. Reality TV is as *un*real as it gets and you 'n' me need to keep our heads about us. I know that. I get that. But that doesn' mean I'm not crazy for you, Bren."

"I'm…"

"Yeah?"

...crazy for you, too. She longed to say it. Because she was. Really, truly long-gone crazy.

Seriously, who did she think she was kidding for all

these years? She'd fallen for him when she was six years old. And all her later declarations to the contrary, she'd never stopped yearning to have him for her own. She could lie to herself all she wanted.

But lies wouldn't change the truth of the matter. She'd tried being with other guys. First with Davey Hart, her steady guy in high school. Davey had been her first, and she'd sworn she would love him forever. They broke up when he went off to college in Texas. It just hadn't been that hard to see him go.

And then there was Alan Schultz. She and Alan had even lived together in Missoula, while she went to cosmetology school. But when he ended it, she'd had to face the fact that she'd never really loved him.

Since then, there'd been no one. Why bother? Without the right person to do it with, she didn't care all that much about sex.

"Bren?"

"What?"

"You didn' finish. You said, 'I'm…' an' then you stopped."

"Go to sleep, Trav."

"Bren…"

"Go to sleep."

He loomed above her for a second more. Then, with a cheerful, "Okay," he flopped back to his own bedroll. He let out a groan and asked woozily, "How come the tent is spinnin'?"

"Close your eyes."

"Ugh. No. Bad idea."

Was he going to be sick? Dear Lord, she hoped not.

But then he whispered, "'Night, Bren." And he instantly started snoring.

She hiked up on an elbow and bent over him. "Trav?"

He just went on snoring, dead to the world.

So she dropped back to her side of the tent, closed her eyes and tried not to think about what had just happened.

Like a brand.

All these years she'd gotten along fine, she and her well-accustomed, comfortable denial. She'd told herself she was over him—that really, there was nothing to *get* over. It was a childhood crush, no big deal. He was an honorary big brother to her, a family friend with a strong protective streak when it came to her.

They understood each other, she and Travis. And what they understood was that nothing was ever going to happen between them. He couldn't be tamed. And neither could she.

They probably should have thought twice before faking an engagement to get on *The Great Roundup*. They probably should have considered that if there *was* any spark between them, pretending to be lovers who couldn't keep their hands off each other was no way to avoid starting a fire.

Now they were into it and into it deep. With a little help from his good friend Jack Daniel's, he'd admitted far too much tonight—and she had loved every slurred word of his beautiful, ridiculous declaration.

She'd loved it because she loved *him*.

"I love him." She mouthed the words into the darkness, careful not to give them sound, though the man snoring at her side probably wouldn't notice if she shouted them at the top of her lungs.

I love Travis Dalton. It was real and it was true, and there was no use continuing to deny it.

Did she think she could tame him?

Highly unlikely.

Was she going to get her poor heart broken?

Oh, it was very possible.

But did she want to take this fake love affair all the way to the end anyway, no matter how it all turned out?

Oh, yes, she did. If she ever hoped to have a chance with him, this was it, now, here at High Lonesome Guest Ranch on *The Great Roundup.*

And they didn't call her the bold, chance-taking, troublemaking O'Reilly for nothing.

She loved Travis Dalton.

She *wanted* Travis Dalton.

And one way or another, for however long it lasted, she was bound to have him.

Chapter Nine

Brenna planned to make her move the next day—and no, she didn't know exactly what that move would be. But she expected at least to have a real talk with him when they were alone in their tent at the end of the day.

Travis looked green when they got up at dawn. He'd done it to himself by answering what all the guys were jokingly calling "the whiskey challenge." Still, she felt sorry for him.

The Great Roundup didn't call a day off just because most of the men were hungover. They began the next major challenge right after breakfast.

The task? To cut and bale hay in a series of far pastures. Actually, haying involved more than just cutting and baling. There was also tedding—spreading the hay out in the field to dry. And windrowing—raking the spread hay into rows to ready it for baling.

They got to use machinery for this three-day process, taking turns on the tractors provided. All that first day Brenna worried that Travis might just keel over—or worse, roll a tractor and end up injured or dead. But somehow, he made it through and even managed to hold up his end.

And when they crawled into their bags that night, he was sound asleep before she could even think of how to begin to tell him that she'd changed her mind *again* about the two of them becoming lovers.

The haying challenge continued for two more days after that. An elimination followed. Dean Fogarth, who had somehow managed never once to get behind the wheel of a tractor during any part of the hay-making process, said goodbye that time. Travis won that challenge and claimed his immunity bracelet.

And that night, when Brenna got him alone, he was his old self again. They joked together and talked a little of what the next challenge might be.

But when she tried to bring up the two of them and how she'd like to take this fake relationship to a whole new level, he looked straight in her eyes and said, "I think we settled that, didn't we, Bren? I think we decided we shouldn't go there."

And what could she say to that?

She let it go that night.

And the next, and the next after that.

The challenges continued, one after another. They worked long days, driving cattle to higher pastures in the pouring rain. They slept out in the open two nights on the way up there, taking turns watching the herd, huddled under tarps against the downpour.

The sun came out when they reached their destination. Everyone cheered, including the crew, who'd struggled constantly to keep the cameras and sound equipment dry. Jasper announced the next challenge—to choose a partner and build a makeshift shelter out of what they could scavenge on the land.

Brenna and Travis got right to work. She sent him looking for a long, sturdy pole branch and prop sticks while she scouted locations. At the edge of the wide, rolling meadow, a trail wound up into the trees. She followed that trail until she came out on a rocky promontory jutting over a flat space. There, in the shelter of the cliff, she and Trav built a leaf hut lean-to, which she'd learned to make back in her 4-H days. The spot had good drainage, so they stayed reasonably dry that night.

The wind came up and the temperature dropped, so they stripped to their driest layer of T-shirts and underwear, zipped their bags together and slept all wrapped around each other. Brenna grinned to herself as she cuddled in close to him. She smelled like a lathered horse and her hair had bits of dirt and leaves in it. That night, having sex with him was the last thing on her mind. She felt only gratitude for the warmth of him all around her, for the strength in the arms that held her so close.

Brenna took the win on the shelter challenge—for choosing the best spot and knowing how to build the hut. After she'd put on her immunity bracelet, yet another contestant, a woman that time, went back to the lodge for good.

Jasper assigned two mini challenges that day. And the next morning, they headed down the mountain to their little tent village, which kept getting smaller after each elimination.

The days seemed to bleed together, one into the other.

They mended fences, burned weeds in ditches, went hunting for stray livestock and answered the endless mini challenges, from starting fires without matches to chopping wood, target shooting and doing laundry in the creek. Everyone complained that the mini challenge prizes had gotten chintzier. They were a camp pillow or an extra fry pan for cooking. By then, everyone longed for a night at the lodge. Too bad that lately the only way to get that was to get eliminated.

Brenna worked up her nerve and tried again to talk to Trav about the two of them. She got nowhere. Trav reminded her gently to focus on the win.

She decided that maybe he was right. Maybe, if she was going to make a play for him, she just ought to wait till filming was over and they were back home. Back home, at least he wouldn't be able to tell her she needed to keep her focus on the game.

By the last week of June, half the contestants had been sent to the lodge to stay. Bren and Trav, Roberta and Steve, Seth and Leah, Fred and the twins, Wally and Summer Knight remained in the game. Travis said they were all living proof that alliances made the difference. Everyone still in the running had someone they could count on.

"Except Wally and Summer," Brenna reminded him.

"Yeah, well, Wally gets along with everyone and Summer's good at the game."

Oh, yes, she was. Summer had the skill set to avoid elimination in a challenge. And she caused plenty of conflict, which didn't make her any friends but sure made for interesting TV.

The next day Seth Stone tumbled down a ravine and broke his leg, a messy compound fracture. They sent a helicopter for him from the hospital in Kalispell. The med techs took a stretcher down into the narrow canyon. They stabilized the injured leg and strapped him in for the ride up the steep bank to level ground. Travis, Fred, Joey and Rob helped to carry him up out of the ravine.

As they got ready to load him into the helicopter, Leah hovered close to him, clutching his hand. "I want to go with you."

He brought her fingers to his lips and kissed them. "Stick with it, sweetheart. Win it for both of us. I know it's what you want."

Leah's tears spilled over. "Seth, what I want is *you*. I love you so."

"I love you, too, honey. Always have, always will."

"You, um…you sure? Because lately, I…"

He searched her face. "What?"

She hesitated, but then he kissed the back of her hand and she busted to it. "Well, I wonder if maybe you're a little bit sorry that you married me, if maybe you have regrets that you were never really…free."

"Aw, sweetheart. Come here."

She bent closer and he asked, "What about you? Are you sad you never got your chance to be free?"

Leah gasped. "Of course not. You've always been the only guy for me."

"And you're the only girl for me. Honey, how could I be sorry? I've loved you since you were eight years old."

"Oh, Seth." She sniffed back tears. "Say it one more time."

"I love you, Leah Stone. There's no one else for me."

"Seth." She bent even closer and pressed her eager lips to his.

The cameras captured all of it. And Leah and Seth

could not have cared less that the cameras were rolling and everyone was watching. They had eyes only for each other.

After the med techs loaded the injured man onto the helicopter and took him away, Leah stood in the middle of the cleared space, looking up, watching the chopper vanish into the clear afternoon sky.

Brenna went to her. "Leah..."

With a cry, Leah grabbed on and hugged Brenna close. "He does love me," she whispered prayerfully. "He truly does."

"No doubt about it."

"I want to be with him. I *need* to be with him. I can't concentrate on winning when my husband needs me. I...I have to leave the show."

Brenna took both her hands. "Go talk to Roger. See what he says." Their body mics and the ever-present cameras had recorded every word. Brenna had a feeling that Roger, Anthony and the rest of them were loving the drama.

And that Real Deal Entertainment would let Leah go.

An hour later, after a final OTF in the middle of the cleared space where the helicopter had landed, a wrangler took Leah to the lodge to gather her and Seth's belongings. Brenna and Travis took down her tent for her. Gerry would drive her to the hospital in Kalispell.

The next morning Jasper gathered the remaining nine of them together for a one-day challenge.

They all got to show off their roping skills with a series of roping tricks, starting with the basics: coiling, building a loop, refining the loop and coils, swinging and catching. First, they roped a dummy. And by the end of the day, they each had to rope and tie a calf. The top ropers in the group—Trav, Steve, Wally and Fred—blew the rest of them away. But no one was a complete greenhorn at the job. Bren thought she was good enough to avoid elimination.

That night at the canteen, Trav won the roping challenge and claimed his immunity bracelet. Joey Franklin packed up and followed a wrangler to the lodge.

Now they were eight.

And the next day, everything changed. They met at the canteen for the morning's challenge and Jasper announced that they would be sent out in teams of two, each team to accomplish a different goal.

"And we want to switch things up a little," Jasper said with a wink. "This time, we'll be choosing your partners for you." He paired Brenna with Steve. Roberta got Fred Franklin. Old Wally and Rob Franklin were together.

And Travis got partnered with Summer.

Brenna told herself she would work hard with Steve and keep her mind off her own pointless jealousy. She wasn't even going to consider what Summer might get up to, given a whole day alone with Trav.

Yeah, Trav had refused to take what he and Brenna shared to the next level. But that didn't mean he would say yes to Summer. Bren and Trav had a strong alliance, she told herself. No way would he let Summer mess with that.

Brenna and Steve's challenge was to clean out one of the barns.

They got to work shoveling manure and clearing out moldy hay. They gathered rusty, abandoned tools into the empty crates someone had conveniently left piled against a back wall.

At noon, they stopped work for sandwiches provided by hospitality services—everyone but Travis and Summer. Wherever they were and whatever they were doing, apparently they couldn't afford to stop and return to the canteen for food.

At one, Steve and Brenna went back to the barn. The chuck wagon bell rang at a little after two. They were in pretty good shape in the barn, with most of the job done, so they both answered the mini challenge.

As did everyone else—except Summer and Travis, who were still off who knew where doing God knew what. The mini challenge was to make a pot of campfire coffee.

Steve came up beside Brenna, and as if he read her mind, he said, "They're probably too far out to ride in for a mini challenge."

Roberta leaned close. "Nothing to worry about, Bren."

Brenna put on a big smile. "Do I look worried?"

Steve and Roberta agreed that she didn't.

The coffee challenge went fast. Wally won, as he tended to do anytime campfire cookery was involved. Jasper said they could all have a ten-minute coffee break. "And what d' you know, folks? The coffee's fresh made." They each had a cup and then went back to work.

At the end of the day, when the rest of them were already gathered at the canteen, Summer and Travis finally rode in. Their clothes were wet and splattered with mud. Summer was laughing, flashing her dimples at Trav.

A two-man camera team and an assistant director

trailed after them. Film of their day's work would have been transmitted back to camp for the judges to view. The highlights would probably end up on the show.

Anthony signaled the newcomers to join the rest of them. Trav and Summer dismounted, and a couple of wranglers took the horses away.

Summer laughed again and wrapped both hands around Travis's arm. "Whoa, what a day, huh?"

Brenna knew her role too well by now. For the sake of the game and her part in the story, she really ought to do something—something lighthearted and cute, if possible. She ought to run to Travis, grab him away from Summer and kiss him senseless, maybe.

Or she could go raw, put on some sort of jealous display to keep the story moving—the story of lovebirds Brenna and Travis and that man-stealer Summer.

But no. It all felt way too real, and that wasn't fun.

Because she *was* jealous, and she hated that—despised it, even. She'd always been kind of a hothead, and she needed to keep a lid on that emotion. If she didn't hold herself in check, she'd put a whupping on the rodeo star. Just what she needed, to end up on national TV catfighting over Trav. Her mom would never forgive her.

Uh-uh. The game had turned too real. And for the moment anyway, Brenna refused to play.

Instead, she faced front and showed the cameras nothing. When Trav appeared at her side, she managed to give him what she hoped passed for a welcoming smile. He draped an arm across her shoulders and pulled her close to press his lips to her hair. She felt his breath across her skin, the wonderful, hard weight of his arm on her shoulder. He smelled of mud and man. Longing burned through her.

Somehow, she kept her expression composed. She laughed on cue when Jasper cracked a corny joke, sang along with the judges when they burst into a Tim McGraw song.

There was no winner that night, and no one got eliminated. Jasper announced that points would accrue in a series of daylong challenges and the next elimination would be called with no warning.

They were excused to rustle up dinner over the campfire, head for the showers and take turns at the green screen. Brenna's OTF was all about Summer and Trav and what she thought the two of them were doing out alone together the whole day long.

She answered in flat, short sentences: "I don't know" and "You should ask them."

"You seem upset, Brenna."

"I'm not upset in the least."

"Do you have anything you'd like to say to Summer?"

"I have nothing at all to say to Summer."

"Anything to say to Travis?"

She aimed a giant smile at the camera. "Travis, I love you more than words can ever say."

"You're pissed at me, aren't you?" Trav whispered.

He'd come back from the showers a few minutes before. They were alone in their dark tent. She couldn't stop thinking of Leah and Seth, of the love and honesty between them at the end.

"Bren?"

She turned her head away from him and closed her eyes. "Get some sleep."

"Come on."

"What."

"Just tell me. Are you pissed at me?"

"Just leave it, will you please?"

"Nothing happened with Summer. You gotta know that." He launched into a way too detailed description of what he and the blonde had done all day, including tracking a heifer who'd lacerated her teat on a barb-wire fence. "To make it all more fun, that heifer had run into a patch of blackberry canes. It was a mess." He fell silent.

Apparently, she was supposed to say something. "What do you want from me, Trav?"

"You know I've got no interest in Summer Knight."

"I know. Can I go to sleep now, please?"

"You know she does that—grabbing on to a man, blasting the movie-star smiles. It's all part of her game, and it does nothing for me."

Her game. Brenna was sick to the core of the damn game. "Why are we talking about this?"

"Because you're pissed at me, and I can tell you're pissed at me even though you keep trying to pretend you're not."

"I'm tired. I want to go to sleep. Can we just table this crap for tonight?"

A silence from him, a silence drawn tight as a wire. "Sure."

"Great. 'Night, then." With a loud sigh, she turned her back to him and closed her eyes.

Trav lay wide-awake in the dark for a long time.

What the hell was the matter with her, anyway? How

was he responsible for the tricks Summer pulled? Bren knew that Summer's behavior was in no way his fault. But still, Bren was mad at him.

Even if she wouldn't admit it outright.

He hated that she was mad at him. It made him feel out of sorts and angry right back, and edgy. Way edgy. Like he had ants crawling under his skin.

This whole thing was hard enough, being so close to her, knowing he couldn't reach for her. Not in the dark. Not when they were alone, just the two of them, and she smelled of apple-scented shampoo, so close he could reach out and gather her to him.

He could steal all the kisses he wanted when the cameras were watching, but not when they were alone. Because it wouldn't be right and he only had one out-of-date condom—and yeah, he now knew for a fact that the condom was out of date. Because even though he'd made it clear that they wouldn't be going there, he'd checked his wallet just to be sure. That condom had been ready for the trash two months ago.

Not that it mattered. He was never making love to her anyway, as he reminded himself at least a hundred times a night.

He turned on his side with his back to her, punched at the wadded-up T-shirt he was using as a pillow and shut his eyes good and tight.

The rules changed again the next day.

They stood outside the canteen as always, and Jasper laid out the new rules. "As I explained yesterday, today you will be judged and given points toward the next win and elimination. However, as an extra incentive to excellence, your day's work will also be a mini challenge. The winner today gets a night for two at the lodge. You'll stay in the Big Sky suite, finest suite in the house, *and* you'll share a gourmet dinner for two in the dining room.

"Each team will get four separate challenges. Teams will have until exactly 4:00 p.m. to tackle and complete these tasks. You will each be judged separately on how much you accomplish and how well you do each job, but you still have to work together to finish each task before moving on to the next one."

"If I win, do I get to choose who goes to the lodge with me?" Summer asked way too sweetly.

Jasper tipped his big black hat to her. "You do indeed."

"Wonderful." She flicked a flirty glance at Trav, followed by an evil grin at Brenna.

Oh, please. Brenna met those green eyes directly and refused to be baited.

This time, they drew their work partners and their job assignments from Jasper's hat. Brenna drew first. She unfolded the scrap of paper and read her new partner's name out loud. "Summer Knight."

Total setup. Just Roger and the writers, creating opportunities for sparks to fly. Brenna reminded herself that nobody had promised her this would be fair.

Summer stepped to her side and offered her hand. "Hey, partner."

Brenna made herself take it. "A pleasure to be working with you." She half expected lightning to strike her dead on the spot for telling such a whopping lie.

Trav drew next. He got Roberta. Steve drew Wally's name. And Fred ended up partnered with his son Rob.

Next, the partners drew the work assignments. Rusty

Boles offered Summer his upturned hat, and she drew out a folded slip of paper. Opening it, she read, "'One: clear mud and debris out of the east section of the west pasture ditch. Two: paint the exterior of the tool shed behind the blue barn. Three: paint the interior of same. Fourth challenge TBD as needed.'"

Brenna said, "I'm guessing there's some doubt we'll make it to the fourth task."

Summer sent her a mean little glare. "I am winnin' that night at the lodge, so don't you dare be a slacker."

Brenna considered how satisfying it would be to slap the woman silly, but she settled for a saccharine smile and said, "You certainly are motivated. I like that in a partner. If only you weren't so badly brought up, I'm thinking you and me would get along just fine."

Summer gasped. The whole group seemed to freeze in place, waiting for the fight to start.

Trav opened his mouth to speak, but Brenna shot him a glare and he kept quiet. She turned back to Summer and stared the blonde square in the eye. *Bring it on.*

But Summer turned to Jasper. "Can we get going? We've only got till four."

So Brenna wouldn't be taking Summer down this morning, after all. She couldn't decide whether she felt relieved or disappointed.

Jasper called Roberta, Wally and Rob forward. They drew the tasks for their teams.

Then Jasper announced, "Necessary tools and equipment are ready at the task sites. A task is not considered finished until you clean up after yourselves, which means returning all equipment and checking it in here at the canteen. Good luck, everyone." He pulled a pistol from the holster at his hip and aimed it skyward. "Ready, set…go!" The shot rang out.

They all took off running, each team in a different direction, followed by a scattering of cameramen and Anthony's assistants. Brenna and Summer beat feet to the west, jumping a pasture fence to get to the assigned ditch, where a wrangler waited with shovels, hoes and work gloves.

Summer pointed. "You start from that end and I'll start back there." She aimed her thumb over her shoulder. "We'll meet in the middle."

Seemed like a good plan to Brenna. Unless one of them came up against some obstruction too big to handle alone, they wouldn't even have to be near each other for most of the job. "Works for me." She took a pair of gloves, a shovel and a hoe and headed to her end.

Brenna worked hard and fast. She kind of hated to admit it, but Summer did, too. A couple of sweaty, dirty hours later, they had that ditch running again. Covered in mud and not even caring, they grabbed their tools and made for the canteen, where a wrangler logged in the equipment.

As soon as that was done, Brenna and Summer whirled and raced for the shed behind the blue barn. The wrangler waiting there had cans of blue paint, brushes, drop cloths, rags and a couple of lightweight ladders.

Thank God the shed wasn't that big. Even better, it was already scraped and primed. And there wasn't a separate trim color. Everything would be blue, including the door on the south wall.

Too bad they had to use brushes. That would take longer than spraying or rolling—not that Brenna's opinion of how best to do the job meant squat to anyone at this point.

They each took a wall and got going.

Three hours passed before the lunch bell rang.

Covered in mud from the first challenge and dotted with spatters of blue paint, Summer peeked around the corner of the shed. "You hungry?"

Brenna wiped a drip of paint off the end of her nose with the back of her hand. "Hell, no."

They painted through lunch. When the shed was covered in fresh blue paint, Brenna asked the wrangler, "Won't we need all this stuff to paint the inside?"

"Doesn't matter. It's part of the task to check in the equipment at the end of each job."

She considered calling the guy a few bad names, but she didn't want to waste the energy it would take. She and Summer slammed the lids back on the paint cans, grabbed everything but the ladders and made for the canteen.

The wrangler there reminded them that they needed to bring in the ladders, too. They raced for the shed, shouldered the ladders and hauled them back to the canteen.

Finally the wrangler checked them in—and then hit them with the news that they would need those ladders for the interior of the shed. "You can go ahead and take them back with you."

Summer made a growling sound. "There is crap and there is crap. And *this* is crap."

"Totally," muttered Brenna. She didn't like Summer, but the rodeo star spoke the truth, and Brenna felt honor bound to register solidarity on the issue of crap.

"Take 'em or don't," replied the wrangler. "It's up to you."

What could they do? They needed the ladders, even if they had to haul them back and forth across a pasture for no apparent reason other than to piss them off, wear them out and make them suffer. Because that made good drama. And reality TV was all about good drama.

Shouldering the ladders, they trudged to the shed. The wrangler was waiting for them inside with equipment identical to what they'd used on the exterior. Except that the paint was white.

Brenna looked on the bright side. At least the guy offered them bottled water.

They drank the water and got to work.

An hour or so later, the chuck wagon bell rang for a mini challenge.

Summer asked, "You going?"

"And win what? A camp pillow? No, thanks."

They kept painting until the interior of the shed was white. Again, it took two trips to the canteen to get everything turned in.

Spurs jingled as Jasper entered the canteen, a cameraman close on his heels. "Congratulations, ladies. It's five after three, and you've completed three tasks out of four." He gave them each a bottle of water. "Drink up, because you need to stay hydrated." As they guzzled the water, he continued, "And now for your fourth and final challenge..."

First, Jasper magnanimously announced that, due to the distance between the canteen and their final challenge, this time they would not be required to turn in their equipment, which consisted of a length of rope for each of them.

Outside, a pickup waited. They jumped in the back for a bouncy ride to their destination. A wrangler and a couple of cameramen went with them, filming them through the fifteen-minute trip.

Summer was a mess, spattered with mud, blue and white paint speckling her hair. Brenna knew she looked no better.

They stopped for the wrangler to jump out and open a gate, and then they were off across the pasture. Cows and their calves lifted their heads from the grass, ears twitching as they watched the truck go by. They crested a rise, and she spotted the crew below them on the bank of a muddy pond. One of Anthony's assistants and more cameras were waiting there to shoot their fourth challenge.

The pickup pulled to a stop. "Let's go," said the wrangler.

They all jumped down from the bed.

In the middle of the pond, on a small, soggy-looking scrub-grass island, two cows and their calves huddled, bawling unhappily. The muddy wranglers watching from the water's edge must have dragged the poor critters out there. And for the fourth challenge, it was Brenna and Summer's job to get them all safely back to dry land.

The sound guys stole several minutes of their time wrapping their body mic transmitters in plastic bags and taping the microphones behind their ears. "Try to keep your heads above water," one of them suggested.

Both Brenna and Summer laughed at that one.

"It's three thirty," announced the assistant director. "You have half an hour, ladies."

They looped their ropes around their necks and under one arm and waded in.

Their boots made sucking sounds in the muddy bottom as they slogged toward the island. Twenty feet from the bank, the bottom fell out from under them as the pond got too deep to stand. Brenna's boots dragged on her, but it wasn't too bad.

They were still a good two hundred feet away from the island—way too far to swim back to the shallows and use their ropes. Plus, roping presented some other problems. Calves followed their mamas, so they would need to rope the cows. No way could Brenna pull thirteen hundred pounds of unwilling beef into the pond.

That left plan B. Treading water, Brenna suggested, "We could swim around behind them."

Summer thought that over. "Nobody said we *had* to use the ropes."

"Exactly." Contrary to popular belief, cattle were smart, social creatures. They could swim just fine—when provided with the proper motivation. "But one of them could be a kicker," Brenna warned.

Summer grunted. "Time's running out. I say we take our chances."

"Okay, then. Let's do it."

Brenna went left; Summer went right. They swam around the island and climbed out behind the animals, who turned their heads to eye them with suspicion. Brenna moved toward one cow, while Summer advanced on the other one.

It only took a couple of well-timed smacks on the rump to get the mamas moving. Neither of them kicked, thank God. The cows bawled in annoyance, but they got in the water, their calves following close behind.

Piece of cake. The animals swam straight for the cameras. Summer and Brenna slid into the pond after them and swam for shore behind them. Both cows and one calf made it all the way to the bank without incident.

The second calf got stuck trying to get his footing when he reached the shallows. All it took was Brenna's boost on his bony behind and he was up and staggering toward his mama on the bank. He made it, too.

Brenna stood in a foot and a half of water, soaking wet with a soggy rope around her neck. Her hands braced on her hips, she called to the crew on the bank. "Did we make it in time?"

The assistant director gave her a thumbs-up.

She let out a whoop of triumph—right before Summer shoved her hard from behind.

Chapter Ten

Brenna's whoop turned to a startled cry. She staggered forward, barely saving herself from a face-plant in pond water. Whirling on the other woman, she flipped her wet braid back over her shoulder and demanded, "What the hell, Summer?"

Summer only stepped up—and shoved her backward, hard, with both hands.

Brenna went down, sprawling backward, the water closing over her—until she got her feet under her and popped upright again. She pushed at the constraining rope, getting it up and over her head, tossing it away from her as she sputtered, "What is the *matter* with you?"

Summer didn't answer. She tossed her rope off, too. And then she waded right up close to Brenna again and drew her arm back.

As Summer's open palm swung toward her, Brenna

realized that she was about to get bitch slapped and no one on the bank was going to do a thing to stop it. The cameras were still rolling.

Because a girl fight was exactly the kind of thing they loved on reality TV.

Brenna brought up her arm just in time to block Summer's blow, simultaneously reaching under with her free hand to shove the blonde in the chest. Summer windmilled her arms. With a screech, she toppled over on her butt. Muddy water went flying as Summer started to stand up.

Back in high school, Brenna's wild friend Leonie was constantly getting in fights. Leonie always said that once the other girl went down, your best bet was to make sure she didn't get up until she'd surrendered.

With a muttered, "No, you don't," Brenna jumped on Summer.

They rolled around in the shallows, hitting and slapping, pulling each other's hair, one going under, then rising, taking the upper hand and pushing the other beneath the surface. Summer was relentless.

But Brenna was bound and determined to end up the winner. And at last she did. Grabbing Summer by one wrist, she twisted the blonde's arm up hard against the small of her back. Summer gave a strangled-sounding moan.

"Up. Now." Brenna rose, pulling Summer with her. "Had enough?" she whispered in the other woman's ear.

"God, I really hate you!" Summer cried. "You're everybody's sweetheart, and it makes me want to puke."

Brenna almost laughed. All her life, she'd been the wild one, the one who inevitably managed to get herself in trouble. But somehow, on *The Great Roundup*, she got to be the sweet one. She clucked her tongue at Summer. "And here I kind of thought we were finally getting along."

Summer gave a smug little snort. "Fooled you, didn't I?"

From the bank, the assistant director signaled them forward.

Brenna commanded, "Start walking. Do not stop until we're both on dry land."

Summer and Brenna, dripping wet from head to toe, did a pair of OTFs right there on the edge of the pond. Summer acted like she'd won the fight, announcing that it was about time Little Miss Perfect ended up on her ass in a mucky pond.

Brenna played it breezy, smiling at the camera, waving her hand. "What can I tell you? Girls will be girls."

Once the interviews were done, crew and cast alike went directly to the canteen, where everyone else was waiting.

Trav took one look at Brenna and demanded, "What happened?"

"You should see the other girl." She flipped out a hand toward Summer several feet away.

"Whoa." He reached for her, pulling her close against his side.

As always, his touch, his very nearness, felt way too good. "Trav! You'll get mud and paint all over you."

He nuzzled her wet, filthy hair. "You're cute when you're dirty. And come on. Tell me what happened."

"Summer started a fight with me."

"But did *you* finish it?"

"Oh, you'd better believe I did."

"That's my girl."

My girl. She liked the sound of that way too much.

Jasper called for attention. The host gave a shorter-than-usual speech about which team had taken on what challenges. The judges sang a song and then the winner of the night at the lodge was announced.

The judge with the smallest hat said, "Brenna O'Reilly, step forward."

She couldn't believe it. She'd scored the highest of all of them, points that would go to keep her safe from elimination when this ongoing challenge ended. Best of all, she'd won the night at the lodge.

The judge gingerly patted her dirty shoulder and explained that she'd won because she and Summer, as a team, had been fast, focused and resourceful. They were one of two teams, with Trav and Roberta, who'd finished all four tasks.

But Brenna had made the highest score of all, digging out the ditch a little faster, painting that shed a little more expertly and coming up with the best way to get two cows and their bawling babies across a pond and back to dry land. The judge didn't mention the fight. But Brenna did kind of wonder how many points Summer had lost for starting a fight she didn't even manage to win.

Well, too bad for Summer. The rodeo star had gotten exactly what she deserved—a whupping. Brenna's mom would not be happy with her when the fight aired on national TV, but Brenna refused to feel bad for holding her own.

"Now, Brenna." Jasper wiggled his black eyebrows at her. "Who will you take with you for your luxury night at the lodge?"

Her gaze just naturally went to Trav. He looked so proud for her. She felt a delicious little flutter of anticipation under her breastbone. A night in a luxury suite with Trav. It sounded so tempting.

But it wasn't, not really. Because nothing would happen between them. All their hot, sexy loving was the fake kind, just for the cameras.

Ugh. She'd almost rather choose Roberta. They could order up some food, give each other mani-pedis and watch romantic movies.

But Trav was her partner in this big adventure, and she had her role as his adoring fiancée to play. They all needed to believe that she couldn't wait to be alone in a big bed with the man who owned her heart and made her body beg for more.

She asked, "Travis, will you spend a night at the lodge with me?"

He stepped forward and took her outstretched hand.

Jasper gestured grandly at the white van that waited to take them to the lodge.

The Big Sky suite was perfection, with a fancy sitting room and a giant bedroom, including a wonderful king-size bed with a carved headboard and pillows for days. Both rooms had huge windows looking out on mountain views crowned by wide slices of endless blue sky.

Their suitcases, which they hadn't seen for weeks now, waited in the bedroom, packed full of lovely clean clothes. Gerry had them change into flip-flops and took their dirty boots and socks to be cleaned.

Once they'd had a tour of the suite, they got to hand

over their body mics. The camera crew and director left them to clean up for dinner.

Alone at last, they stood in the middle of the sitting room, staring at each other.

"I can't believe we're here," she whispered—more in awe than in fear that there might be recording devices stashed nearby. There probably were, but she'd grown way too accustomed to all that by now.

Brenna pointed over her shoulder in the general direction of the gorgeous bathroom with its walk-in shower, jetted tub and twin sinks. "You go first, but make it fast. I want some quality time in that tub."

He grabbed the remote and turned on the big TV over the fireplace—at full volume.

She winced at the sound. "Trav!"

He waved her close and put his lips against her mud-spattered ear. "Check for cameras and recorders while I clean up."

She nodded and then yelled, "Turn it down!" just in case anyone was listening.

"Sorry." He punched the power button, dropped the remote on the coffee table and headed for the bathroom.

Brenna checked the living room first. She peered in every nook and cranny, looking for hidden cameras and tiny, nearly invisible microphones. She found none, but that didn't mean they weren't there.

She kept looking. In the bedroom, she pulled open the drawer of one of the twin nightstands—and found condoms of every size, flavor, style and color.

Brenna threw back her head and laughed. Apparently, Real Deal Entertainment wanted their contestants to practice safe sex.

A few minutes later, Trav emerged from the bathroom in a navy blue shirt, new jeans and dress boots. He looked so good and smelled all woodsy and clean. She felt a sharp tug of longing down inside her. Really, he was way too hot and handsome. It so wasn't fair.

His eyes asked, *Find anything?* She grinned, thinking about the drawer full of condoms. "What?" he demanded.

Let him find them himself.

She shook her head and headed for the bath.

Her shower took longer than she would have liked. The paint in her hair was especially stubborn.

Finally, she got all the paint off and sank into that beautiful tub. She soaked for an hour, then took her sweet time getting dressed for dinner.

Eventually, Travis tapped on the door. "Brenna, you okay?"

Leaning close to the mirror, she stroked mascara on her upper lashes. "Just a minute..."

"They're at the door, ready to take us to the dining room."

"Coming." She smoothed on cherry lip gloss and then stood back to check herself out in the mirror. "Not bad."

"Bren, we need to—" He blinked as she pulled open the door. And then his eyes went low and lazy.

Her heart leaped at that hot, hungry look on his face. Yeah, he kept insisting that he wouldn't make love to her. But right at that moment, she truly believed he wanted to.

He gave a low whistle. "Wow." She preened a little in her red dress that skimmed her curves just right and ended a few inches above her knees. He reached out and stroked a hand down her hair. "Straight and sleek again."

"Trav…"

He eased his hand up under her hair and wrapped it around the nape of her neck. Those rough, warm fingers felt so good against her skin, as though she'd been born to feel his touch. "So beautiful." He tried to pull her in for a kiss.

She resisted, dipping out from under his touch and asking, "Find anything…interesting?" Meaning cameras or microphones.

"Nothing," he replied.

She couldn't hold back a chuckle. "Did you happen to look in the drawer by the bed?"

He stifled a snort of laughter. "Oh, yeah." And then he leaned close again.

She didn't back away that time. He was so hard to resist. And judging by the blue fire in his eyes, he really did want to kiss her.

With a tiny smile, she let him reel her in. His warm lips brushed hers, and his neat beard tickled her just enough to send an eager shiver across her skin.

And then came the knock on the outer door.

Trav let her go with clear reluctance. "Dinner's waiting."

The table for two was in a private nook, with a white tablecloth, a floating candle, a rose in a crystal vase and the lodge's best china and silver. The perfect setting for romance. Over delicious food and a nice bottle of wine, they held hands across the table, now and then bending close to share more than one lingering kiss. He told her how much he loved her, and she said it right back to him.

But it was all for the cameras now that they were mic'd up again.

Travis didn't know that in her case it was true—and she wasn't going to tell him, not until they were back home again living in the real world. Maybe not even then.

Who could say what would happen? They needed to win a million bucks together. And then they could talk about what might happen next.

Oh, but she did love him, so much, more than anything. Her love felt all bottled up inside her sometimes, pushing at her rib cage, aching to bust out. She wouldn't let it, though, not now, not till all this was over. Maybe.

Or maybe not.

But the uncertain future aside, oh, she longed to be his lover for real—just the two of them in a room alone, with nobody watching. Brenna and Travis, doing whatever came naturally.

Even if she couldn't profess her love from the heart, she could have that, at least. And tonight was her best chance. Upstairs they had a real bed with actual sheets and piles of fat pillows. If ever a setting was made for seduction, the Big Sky suite was it.

And she was bold Brenna O'Reilly, the one who took chances. The one who stood tall, threw caution to the wind and went after what she wanted.

It was getting dark when Gerry ushered them back upstairs. The crew hung around to film them sharing steamy kisses at the door to the suite.

And then, finally, they got to take off their mics. A minute later, they were inside, with not a crew member in sight.

She turned the privacy lock and leaned back against the door with a long, happy sigh. "I thought they'd never leave us alone."

His blue eyes gleamed at her. She knew he wanted to kiss her again. He stepped in close. "I shouldn't…"

"Oh, yeah. You should." She lifted her mouth, offering it to him.

And he took it—leaning in, covering her lips with his, kissing her long and slow and deep.

She reached out, slid her hungry arms around his lean waist and gathered him into her, moaning when she felt him growing hard against her belly.

He pulled away too fast and looked down at her, eyes blazing, face flushed. "We have to watch it."

"Shut. Up." And she yanked him back to her again.

They kissed for the longest time, standing there against the door. His hands cradled her face, drifted down her arms and then back up again.

For the first time ever, he cupped her breasts. She melted inside and moaned against his mouth.

He pulled back, but then he leaned close again to whisper, "You know it's gotta be a setup, right? The big bed, the drawer of condoms?"

"Trav." She bit his earlobe. "Look at it this way. When are we going to get another chance like this?"

He kissed her again, a kiss that made her knees wobble and her heart dance. "You're sure?"

She felt a slow grin tip the corners of her mouth. "That was way too easy."

He leaned close once more and pressed his forehead to hers. He seemed to be trying really hard to control his breathing. "I can't stand it anymore, Bren. I want you too damn much."

"Exactly the words I've been longing to hear."

"You're sure?"

She pressed her cheek to his and whispered, "The answer is still yes. You can stop asking now."

He nuzzled her ear. "Even if the room was clean before, they could have put cameras in here while we were downstairs."

"So be it. How much can they show, anyway? It's prime-time network TV."

But he was insistent. "One more sweep. It can't hurt."

Reluctantly, they let go of each other to check the whole suite again.

Finally, she threw up her hands. "Nothing. Can we give it up now, please?"

"We can't be a hundred percent certain they're not filming us. And even if what they get doesn't end up on the show, it could turn up somewhere else. You realize that, right?"

"Trav, I have to tell you. At this point, I don't even care."

Travis loved that she wanted him enough to be reckless. But what would happen tonight was just between the two of them and he meant to keep it that way. "It won't kill us to be cautious."

Brenna groaned and glared up at him. "Travis Dalton, don't you tell me that you've changed your mind again."

He caught her stubborn chin. "Not a chance." He wanted her too much. More than any of the too many women he'd known. More than the win. More than his share of the prize money that would build him his own house and give him a real say on the family ranch.

Travis lowered his head and kissed her. She tasted so good, like heaven, with a hint of coffee and chocolate from dessert.

"You've got too many clothes on," she accused when he finally lifted his head.

He chuckled. "We'll get to that." And then he bent close again and whispered to her, explaining what they needed to do. "First, let's turn off all the lights..."

Once the lights were out, he closed the curtains in the bedroom. Faint light bled in from the big windows in the sitting area, just enough that they could move around without bumping into the furniture.

He took her hand and led her through the shadows to the side of the bed. They undressed each other slowly, punctuating the process with endless, tender kisses. When they were down to their underwear, he pulled back the covers. She got in, grabbing his hand and pulling him in after her. He settled the blankets over them before he reached for her.

She went into his arms eagerly, with a long, happy sigh. It felt so good to hold her. She curved into him, fitting just right, as though she was born to be there.

He cradled her close, his arms tight around her, her head tucked under his chin. It had been way too long since he'd held her like this—since the night in the lean-to at the high meadow. They'd had to sleep close that night to stay warm.

He pressed his lips to her silky hair and whispered, "Remember that night in the high meadow?"

Her lips brushed his throat. "Mmm-hmm. It was so cold. And I was so grateful to have you all wrapped around me."

He confessed, "I resented the morning when it came."

"Why?"

"Because I knew we were going back down the mountain and I might not get another chance to hold you all night long."

She tipped her head back and kissed him under the chin. "Travis Dalton, you are the sweetest man."

"Sweet?" He ran a finger down her slim, strong arm and loved the way her breath caught when he did it. "Are you kidding? I'm the one with the wild streak and the troublemaking ways, remember?"

"I thought that was me—and anyway, if you *are* a troublemaker, you're *my* troublemaker, at least for tonight, and don't you forget it."

He kissed the end of her nose. "And you are mine."

"Yes," she said, her whisper slightly breathless now. "All yours." She caught his hand and placed it on her breast, which was firm and pliant—perfect, even through the lace of her bra.

Now he was the one sucking in a sharp breath. "Brenna." He found her nipple under the lace and teased it a little.

Her hungry little gasp sent a bolt of hot desire shooting through him.

All these years and years he'd known her. Never had he dared to believe they would ever get here. In a big bed, just the two of them, with only a few scraps of fabric between them. He had never let himself even *think* about making love to her—well, not until lately. And now he couldn't *stop* thinking about it.

She amazed him, always had. And even more since he'd spent the past four and a half weeks with her. Not only was she the prettiest girl in Montana, she had imagination and resourcefulness, a great sense of humor, and the willingness to stay the course no matter how tough the task.

And she was kind. Generous, too.

"What *are* you thinking, Travis?" Her eyes shone up at him through the darkness.

"Good things."

"About?"

"You." He dipped his thumb under the lacy cup that covered her breast, tugging it down, freeing her softness to his waiting hand. "So beautiful." He lowered his head and captured her nipple, rolling it on his tongue, giving it a little nip with his teeth.

"Travis!" she gasped.

"Um?"

And she sighed. "Do that some more."

He pulled the sheet up and over their heads.

She laughed then, muffling the sound by pressing her face against his chest. "I feel like a naughty kid in a fort of blankets."

He kissed her hair, her cheek, the silky skin of her throat. "Works for me."

She stroked a hand, fingers spread, down his chest to his belly. And lower. He had to hold back a groan as she touched him through his boxer briefs. He was rock hard already, and they'd hardly begun.

"Let's take off the rest," she whispered in his ear.

"You're on." He let his fingers wander over the smooth flesh that covered her rib cage, all the way to her back and the clasp of her bra. A flick of his fingers and he had it unhooked.

She made a sweet, humming sound and did the rest, slipping the straps down her arms, pulling it off, lifting the blanket on her side just enough to drop it to the rug.

He slipped his fingers under the elastic of her panties. "Let me."

"Oh, yes!"

"Lift up." And she lifted. He took those panties off and away.

"Now these," she commanded, her cool, clever fingers on the waistband of his boxer briefs. He didn't argue. She eased the elastic over his erection. He took it from there, whipping them down and off, sticking his arm out from under the covers to toss them away.

And that was it. They were completely naked under the covers. Clasping the sleek curve of her shoulder, he pulled her into him. They lay on their sides, face-to-face.

She offered up her mouth, and he took it in one of those kisses that sent him straight to paradise. He dipped his tongue in and caressed all the wet, slick surfaces beyond her parted lips.

As he kissed her, he let his hands wander to the places he'd never dared to go before—the bare curve of her waist, the firm slope of her hip, the round, high globes of her gorgeous bottom, the strong, smooth length of her thigh.

No, he couldn't see her, not clearly. She was a sweet, soft shadow in this secret cave beneath the blankets with him. He wished he might feast his eyes on the sight of her.

But in the end, it didn't really matter.

He saw her in a deeper way. She was burned into his brain and branded on his heart.

And what he couldn't worship with his eyes right now, he would memorize forever by touching her everywhere. He cradled her breasts, kissing one and then the other. They fit his hands just right, her nipples tight and hard, pressing so perfectly into the center of his palm.

She whispered his name as he stuck out his tongue to taste the valley of sweet flesh between her breasts. He followed that valley down, rolling her to her back so he could rise over her and trail his hungry lips down into the hollow of her waist.

He dipped his tongue in her navel, nipped the softness just below it. She quivered beneath him, reaching for him, weaving her fingers into his hair, murmuring breathless encouragements as he kissed his way lower still.

Sliding a hand down the top of her thigh, dipping it under to hook the back of her knee, he eased her leg up so that he could slip under it, coming up in the place he most longed to be.

He kissed her, a rain of kisses, really. He scattered them across her belly and downward. She moaned when he nuzzled her, parting her, blowing out a slow breath on her wet, waiting core.

She smelled of flowers, of honey. She tasted so sweet, musky and womanly. He gave himself up to the taste and the feel of her, using his hungry mouth and his fingers, too, driving her higher, until she was whimpering, tugging at his shoulders, trying to pull him up into her arms.

Not yet…

He kept kissing her, caressing her, dipping one finger and then two into her wet heat, stroking her.

He knew the moment she couldn't hold out against him any longer. He felt her go over, and he smiled against her secret flesh as her climax rolled through her. She called out his name and he had to reach up, cover her mouth with his hand to help her hold back her breathless, excited cries.

Not until she finally went loose and boneless, the pulsing of her climax fading to a flutter, did he sweep up her body to press his lips to hers.

She grabbed for him, her fingers digging into his shoulders at first, a long sigh escaping her. And then she wrapped her arms so tight around him, kissing him back with sweet heat and hungry tenderness. Those eager hands of hers strayed down over his back, grabbing on tight and yanking him hard and close.

Now he was the one moaning, as her knowing fingers slipped between them and wrapped around the aching length of him, tight and demanding, just the way he liked it. She stroked him, long, strong strokes, running her thumb up over the flare, rubbing the head, until he was sure he would lose it right then and there.

But somehow, he held back, kept himself hovering just on the brink for an eternity of pleasure as she kissed him and played him with her sweet, clutching hand.

"You make me crazy." She breathed the words against his open mouth.

A laugh that was more like a groan escaped him. "*I* make *you* crazy? I might have a heart attack right here and now."

"It's not any more than what you just did to me."

"You're killing me." The whispered words came out of him sounding like a plea.

Her naughty hand moved up, over, down. "I want you to feel me, Trav. Every stroke, every kiss."

"I do, I swear to you. Bren, you know I do."

"I want you to remember this, remember *us*."

"I could never forget."

"I want…everything, Travis. For as long as this crazy ride lasts. I want all there is. With you."

"Yes." He really had no idea what he was agreeing to. Only that somehow, he had to make her understand that she was something special, that there was no one like her. "You have it. You…always did. You have to know that's true."

"Oh, Travis…" And she kissed him, another endless, seeking kiss as she continued to stroke him fast and hard and so, so good.

"I can't— We have to— Right now," he babbled low against her parted lips.

How she understood his meaning, he would never know. But she did. "The drawer!" she cried in a torn little whisper. She loosened her grip on him enough that he could lift up and reach out from under their tent of blankets.

He got hold of the drawer pull and gave it a tug. Then he dipped his hand in and took out a condom. He had no idea what kind it was. Ribbed, flavored, purple, bright green? He felt around the rim—no weird spikes or anything.

"Got it?" she panted, her whisper sweet and urgent.

"Yeah." He retreated back under the blankets again.

"Oh, please let me," she begged, eager and earnest and downright adorable. He gave her the pouch. "Roll over," she commanded, suddenly bossy.

Grinning, though he ached with the need to have her immediately, he stretched out on his back. A moment later, she held him steady as she rolled the condom down over him, snugging it in at the base with great care.

And then, before he could grab her and roll her under

him, she hitched a leg over him, taking him firmly in hand and guiding him to the brink of her sweet, waiting heat.

He groaned way too loud. How could he help it?

"Shh." She sat up tall on him, bending only enough to press a finger against his lips. "We're being quiet, remember?"

He answered with a tortured sound. It was the best he could do as she slowly took him into her.

Slowly, so very slowly, she came down on him. He reached for her, taking her hips between his two hands, steadying both of them as her body accepted him.

It was glorious. *She* was glorious, so wet and hot and tight—and so giving, too.

Always, he thought.

Always and forever. The words got stuck in his mind, echoing softly. He wasn't sure why. But they seemed like the right words.

Yeah, he'd been with way too many women. But there was only one Brenna. Her body felt just right to him, thrilling and perfect and also familiar. Like he'd been lost for the longest time and finally sighted the lights of home.

Found. He was found. Finally, with her.

She surrounded him, claiming him, until he couldn't take the wonderful agony of it. With a final sharp tug, he pulled her all the way down.

"Oh!" And then she let out a long sigh. "Oh, yes..." For a moment, neither of them moved a muscle. They absorbed the reality—that she held him within her.

All the way in.

And then, with a soft moan of surrender, she curved her body over him. Her sweet-scented hair fell along his shoulder, a big swatch of it slipping, like a whisper of silk, down the side of his neck.

Her tender breasts felt so good against the hard wall of his chest. He reached up and wrapped his hand around her nape, guiding her mouth down to meet his in a wet, open kiss.

And then they were moving, rocking together, urgent and hungry, then slow, deep and hard. But the kiss never broke. They kept their mouths fused together. She breathed in his yearning sighs, and he swallowed her moans.

He rolled so he had the top position and then rolled again. Now they lay on their sides.

She was all around him, scent and sweetness, spice and heat. He hadn't known, had never realized that sex could be like this. So true and simple, so deep and tender and right. She'd probably gone and ruined him for any other woman.

Well, so what?

He was finally ready and willing to be ruined. He could lie here with her, buried in blankets, rolling and rocking, straight through to the day after the end of forever.

Too bad this rough, hot magic couldn't last. He felt the end coming. There was no way to stop it.

He rolled again, striving to hold the last shreds of his control. She was under him, her mouth fused to his, her hands clutching his back, rocking him to paradise.

And then he felt her go over. He drank in her keening cry as her body pulsed around him.

That did it. His climax roared through him, mowing him down, dragging him under.

He let out a shout.

"Shh, Trav. Shh..." Her hand was there, covering his mouth. He chanted her name against her palm as the world turned inside out.

Chapter Eleven

Some idiot knocked on the suite's door at five the next morning.

Travis put his arm across his eyes and willed whoever it was to go away.

The knock came again.

He rolled to his side and kissed Brenna's bare shoulder. "Somebody's at the door."

"Mmm."

"I'll get it." He started to slide over the side of the bed.

But her hand shot out and closed on his wrist. "Get back here."

He put up zero resistance. She gave a tug and he rolled back to her, wrapping his other arm around her, drawing her close. She felt like paradise and she smelled of apples and sex. He wanted to spend the whole day in bed with her. But they had a million bucks to win.

Resignedly, he whispered, "It's Gerry. You know that, right?"

"Ugh." She tucked her head under his chin and wiggled a little, burrowing in.

He pressed a kiss into the wild tangle of her hair. "Gerry's not giving up."

She made more grumbly sounds and snuggled even closer.

The next knock was louder.

She bit his chest. Lightly. "Suddenly, I hate Gerry." With a sulky little moan, she pushed him away. "Go. Answer it."

He slid over to the edge of the bed again, sticking his head out from under the covers, spotting his jeans right there on the rug. Scooping them up, he dragged them under the sheet with him and pulled them on.

The knocking started up again.

"Hold on! I'm coming." He rose to his feet. "Stay there. I'll see if I can get rid of him."

"Ha. There is no getting rid of Gerry." She flipped the blankets over her head.

He laughed and shut the bedroom door behind him before answering the insistent knock. "Gerry. What a surprise." For once, the guy didn't have a camera crew with him. But there was a wrangler and a woman with a food trolley.

"Rise and shine." Gerry handed Travis a pile of clothes as the wrangler stepped forward and set both his boots and Brenna's inside the door. "We couldn't get the paint out of Brenna's shirt and jeans. Tell her she can trade them for something from her suitcase."

"Will do." Travis stepped aside so the woman could

wheel in the trolley bearing a coffee service and two covered plates.

Gerry glanced at his watch. "In forty-nine minutes you both need to be fed, dressed and ready to go."

"All right."

"Requests? Complaints?"

He almost smiled as he remembered the night before. "Not a one."

"Well, all right then. See you at six." With a wave, Gerry, the wrangler and the girl from hospitality services headed off down the hall.

The bedroom door opened and there was Brenna in a terry-cloth robe with High Lonesome embroidered above the tempting curve of her left breast. "I smell coffee."

"Come and get it."

But she didn't. She just stood there in that white robe, her red hair sleep tangled on her shoulders, her cheeks pink with beard burn and her eyes full of promises he aimed to make her keep.

"Trav..."

"C'mere."

She ran to him. He wrapped his arms around her. She pressed those soft lips to the side of his throat and whispered, "All those condoms in that drawer?"

"Yeah?"

"You need to figure out a way we can take them back to camp with us when we go."

Brenna spent the ride back to the canteen trying not to look at Travis. She knew if she met his eyes, she would lose it, just burst out laughing. Partly from happiness. Because last night was the best night of her life.

But also because every pocket they had between them was stuffed with condoms. As were their boots and their underwear.

Gerry stopped the van near the canteen. "Report to Roger inside," he said.

"Sure will," replied Travis as he pushed his door open. "Thanks, Gerry."

"My pleasure. Toodle-oo."

Brenna slid across and followed Travis out. Taking their sweet time about it, they started for the entrance to the canteen, switching course as soon as Gerry drove off.

Laughing, they took off running for the tent village, where the others were finishing up breakfast. Steve called out a greeting. Roberta, sitting with him beside the campfire, signaled them over.

"Be right there!" Brenna called and ducked into their tent behind Travis.

Chortling like a couple of complete fools, they emptied their pockets, undid their clothes and pulled off their boots to shake out the contents. Then they scrambled to put it all out of sight.

Brenna smoothed her hair and checked to see that she had everything buttoned. Then she followed Travis out of the tent. She got welcome-back hugs from Roberta and Steve, and then she and Travis raced back to the canteen to report in to Roger.

That day she got paired with Wally on another series of short challenges. It all went off reasonably well.

But the best part was that night. She and Trav zipped their sleeping bags together and made love until midnight. She got to fall asleep in his arms and wake up with him spooning her.

The next day, the judges named a winner and a loser of the four days of random challenges. Steve got his immunity bracelet. Fred Franklin went to the lodge.

And Brenna got another beautiful night in Trav's arms.

Sunday, they started a two-day challenge. They lost Wally on Monday. And then they were six.

Tuesday, the Fourth of July, they gathered at the canteen bright and early to learn there would be no challenges that day in honor of the holiday. "Instead," Jasper announced, "each of you remaining contestants will have a visitor from home." On cue, a white van drove up. Travis's cousin Eli Dalton stepped out. And then Fallon.

With a happy cry, Brenna ran to meet her sister.

Fallon's arms went around her. "It's so good to see you."

Brenna hugged her tight. "I can't believe you're here." Then she whispered a warning, "Anything you say could end up on the show."

Her sister laughed. "I kind of thought so when they put this microphone in my hair— Oh, and I couldn't help but notice there are cameramen everywhere." She waved a hand in the direction of the cameras trained on them.

Brenna gave a shrug. "Hey. Welcome to *The Great Roundup*. Come on. Let's get out of here."

Brenna led the way down to the creek. They sat on the bank. "How are Jamie and the babies?"

"Perfect." Fallon stared out over the rushing water. "Katie tried to eat a spider yesterday."

"Yikes. Toddlers. Into everything."

"And Jamie's still looking for..." Fallon's voice

trailed off. "Oops." She pointed at the microphone tucked into her red curls. She didn't need to finish. Brenna understood. No need to share the Stockton family history with the world.

It was a sad story. Jamie and his siblings had been separated after the death of their parents almost twelve years ago. He and his sister Bella had been taken in by their grandparents. But Jamie's other sisters had been adopted out of state. Their older brothers, both over 18 at the time, went off on their own and hadn't come back. Jamie and Bella had found one of their sisters, Dana, in December. They were still searching for Luke, Daniel, Bailey and Liza. Brenna couldn't imagine how awful that must be, to lose the ones you loved and not know where to find them. But Jamie, Bella and Dana were doing all they could to reunite their family.

"Tell Jamie I'm...rooting for him," Brenna said lamely.

"You know I will." Fallon wrapped her arms around her knees and gave Brenna a long, slow once-over. "So. You're looking really good. And very happy."

"Love will do that to a girl." It was so easy to say now, because it was one hundred percent true. And ironically, she *could* say it in front of the cameras even though she'd never said it when it was just her and Travis alone.

Fallon's blue eyes were full of questions. "Bren, I can't help worrying."

"Don't."

"But are you sure?" She whispered the words, as though that would keep her body mic from picking them up.

"Positive. Certain beyond the last shadow of a fading doubt."

"But we both know Travis. What if he—"

"Fallon." Brenna shook her head. Whatever happened, she had a goal for her future and a job to do to make that future real. She was sticking with her plan, and her plan was to deal with any emotional fallout after the show wrapped. "I promise you, I love Travis and he makes me very happy."

"And I see that. You've got that special glow, but I still—"

"Please, Fallon. Let it be."

Fallon respected her request and didn't ask again.

Travis had taken his cousin Eli on a quick tour of the High Lonesome stables, with a camera crew trailing along behind. Back outside, they sat on the horse pasture fence to talk.

"Gotta admit," Travis said, "I was surprised to see *you* here." The oldest of his aunt Rita's boys, Eli was as steady and stalwart as they came, not the kind of guy to spend a day on location with a reality show.

Eli shrugged his big shoulders. "One of those producers and that casting director woman came out to the ranch to talk to me. They said they liked my look, whatever that means, and they asked me if I wanted to spend a day representing the family, visiting my cousin on *The Great Roundup*."

"And you agreed?" Travis shook his head.

"Don't look so amused. I can stand a little adventure. It's only one day."

"Maybe you need to consider getting on a show yourself."

Eli grunted. "This here, today, is it for me. I've got stock to move and hay to cut."

Overhead a hawk soared. The sky was powder blue dotted with fluffy white clouds. Travis stared off toward the mountains, thinking of Brenna, wondering what she and Fallon were up to.

"You're looking good," said Eli. "Kind of easy. Relaxed. Not so wild and crazy as before. It's working, huh?"

"Working?"

"With you and Brenna."

Travis wrapped both hands around the fence rail and looked his cousin steady in the eyes. "She's the best thing that's ever happened to me. I'm a very lucky man."

"Yeah," said Eli, nodding. "That's real love for you. I keep hoping that someday it'll happen for me."

Real love.

The hawk was only a black spot far in the distance now. Trav watched it vanish into the blue.

Real love.

Whatever this thing was with him and Bren, he was in it and in it deep.

No, he'd never been a forever type of guy. But Bren, she was different than any woman he'd ever known. She was special to him in a thousand different ways.

And sometimes lately he couldn't help dreaming of what it might be like if this thing they shared never had to end.

After the holiday break in the action, Jasper laid out a new challenge—with a twist. He announced that the immunity bracelets were being retired. From then on, everyone would be vulnerable to elimination at every challenge.

Two days later, on Friday, Summer got eliminated. The rodeo star had been quiet, subdued even, since Brenna had fought her and won the week before. Brenna almost felt sorry to see her go. The following Tuesday, Rob Franklin was let go.

The cast was shrinking fast. Only she and Trav, and Roberta and Steve were left.

That evening, Steve brought out the last bottle of Jack Daniel's left from the night of the chili challenge. After toasting all their fallen contestants, they lingered by the fire until almost midnight, reminiscing about what they'd been through to get this far.

And later, in their tent in the dark, Travis made love to Brenna slowly.

She whispered, "Make it last forever."

As he rose up above her she watched his eyes through the shadows, memorizing every whisper, every touch, every lingering kiss, so that no matter how it all ended up, she would have every moment she'd shared with him to keep in her heart forever.

The following morning at the canteen, Jasper announced that the next two days would be challenge-free. Steve and Roberta got time to themselves at the campsite, while Travis and Brenna were taken, along with a camera crew, to the lodge.

The van let them off in front of the lobby, where more cameras were waiting, along with a brunette in a short skirt and cowboy boots who introduced herself as "Lori Luckly, the world's premier cowboy wedding planner."

Brenna grabbed Travis's hand and held on tight. All

of a sudden, her heart was beating way too fast. Her cheeks burned, and her stomach felt like she'd swallowed a vat of acid. No one had mentioned the marriage clause for weeks. Brenna had begun to let herself believe that the wedding wasn't going to happen.

But the appearance of Lori Luckly proved otherwise.

It *was* happening. They were getting married on the show, pulling the ultimate fake-out in a world where everything real between people seemed to happen in whispers in the dark, where the cameras couldn't see and thc microphones couldn't hear.

"This way, you two." Lori led them to a conference room inside the lodge.

Roger DelRay and a couple of the other production people were already there. As Brenna sat next to Travis, she didn't let go of his hand. No way. She clutched it like a lifeline.

The first order of business was whether or not to invite the families for the big day.

Lori said, "Of course, you'll both want your parents there. And your brothers and sisters."

Roger templed his fingers. "Definitely. We want that family feel, and that means we absolutely need the families there."

Brenna cleared her throat and croaked, "No."

Every head at that table swung her way.

She drew herself up. "Forget it. We don't want the families to come." Her mom and dad and Fallon and Fiona and her brothers did not need to be there to witness a marriage that was destined from the first "I do" to end in divorce. Neither did Trav's family, for that matter.

Roger had on his this-does-not-compute frown. "But

why not? Every woman wants Mom and Dad at her wedding."

Trav jumped to her rescue. "Roger, it's just not practical. We both have big families, and if you invite one family member, they're all going to want to come. That means a raft of confidentiality agreements from a bunch of people who have no skin in this game."

"Hmm," said Roger, rubbing his chin. "How many family members are we talking about, exactly?"

"Only counting parents, siblings and cousins?" Trav pretended to run numbers on his fingers. "Fifty, maybe? Sixty? Probably more."

"Hmm," Roger said again. Then he and the other producer put their heads together and conferred in whispers.

Trav kept after them. "Why don't we just bring back the rest of the cast for our big day? We're all like family now, anyway."

"Yeah!" Brenna piped up desperately. "That's what I want. I want Roberta for my maid of honor."

Trav chimed in with, "And Steve will be my best man."

The producers whispered to each other some more.

And finally, Roger nodded. "I like it. It'll be a family affair, after all. A family affair with your *Great Roundup* family."

Brenna almost felt like she could breathe again. She pasted on a giant smile. "Sounds perfect to me."

But it wasn't perfect.

Because it was actually happening. The only perfect thing about it was that at least her family *wouldn't* be there.

* * *

For the next three days, they had no challenges. *The Great Roundup* had gone wedding crazy. And Brenna and Travis were the stars of the show.

The professionals dressed them. They were filmed consulting with wardrobe people, trying on any number of possible wedding outfits, making their choices and then being fitted.

Brenna decided on a strapless marvel of satin and white lace—to be worn with her favorite purple boots. Trav chose a blue jacket and matching vest over a snowy-white shirt and a string tie. To keep it totally cowboy, he would wear jeans and boots. Roberta went for a short dress, chiffon and lace, in sunny yellow. Her boots were tan, tooled in white. And Steve got a vest and shirt like Trav's, but without the jacket. All the flowers would be daisies, yellow and white.

They scouted outdoor locations, riding around on horseback with a camera crew to film it all, checking out open fields and picturesque pastures.

In the end, they chose a spot not too far from the canteen, a wide, rolling field with the mountains in the distance. Jasper Ridge, it turned out, was an ordained minister. He would perform the ceremony.

The reception would be held outdoors, country-style, by the canteen. They would have barbecue for dinner, iced tea and champagne punch in mason jars—and a big white cake decked with frosting daisies.

After dinner, there would be dancing. Real Deal was bringing in a famous six-piece country band to provide music for the ceremony and the after-dinner dancing, too.

Bren and Trav worked with a choreographer on their

first dance, to "Wanted" by Hunter Hayes. Trav had picked the song, and Real Deal was trying to get permission to use the song on the show. If it didn't work out, she and Travis would have to redo the dance later to something Real Deal could get the rights to.

Brenna had tried to talk Trav into just dancing to something else. But he wouldn't budge.

"That song," he said, "reminds me of you." And that made her want to run away bawling. She was glad that he wanted her; she just wasn't ready to marry him.

Yet.

The whole process just felt so strange and disorienting. She prepared for her wedding in a daze. Somehow, through it all, she managed to keep her game face on.

They had to get a marriage license. Gerry and Lori Luckly took them to the county clerk's office. Nobody there seemed to recognize them, and they were in and out in no time. Still, to Brenna, getting that license was the worst.

All the rest of it—the dress, the dancing, the choice of location—just seemed like some weird, otherworldly fantasy. But the license brought it all home. Her fake engagement would culminate in a marriage that was all too real.

Through it all, Travis was wonderful. He stuck close to her, his hand wrapped around hers much of the time. She was so grateful for his strength and support, though she knew he wasn't any happier about it than she was. Yes, they were the bold ones in their families. But neither an O'Reilly nor a Dalton would ever get married unless they were deeply in love and planning on staying that way.

She tried to tell herself that what they were doing

wasn't *that* bad. Because she did love him, for real and true and probably forever. But her love couldn't really console her. They needed the time they weren't going to get, time for a real engagement, time to come to the choice of forever together.

Or not.

This wasn't about forever. This was about a million bucks, about winning the game.

And that made it cheap and wrong.

The night before the big event, in the privacy of their tent, Trav tried to get her to talk about it.

"Bren, come on. Look on the bright side."

"I'm trying. I am."

"We're so close. I'm betting that one of us will win the grand prize. Think about it. Look how far we've come."

"I know. Trav, you're right. We've done well."

"Damn straight. And you can't go checking out on me. We need to focus on making it all the way to the final challenge."

She reached up and pressed her palm to the side of his dear face. "I'm fine."

"You're lying."

She wrapped her arms around his neck and brought him down nose to nose with her. "I'm with you," she whispered. "You can count on me. I'm up for every challenge. Ready to give my all for the win."

"Bren." His warm breath brushed her lips. "It guts me to see you so freaked."

"I'm not freaked."

"You are. And beautiful, and so damn brave, trying so hard not to cave."

"Cave? Uh-uh. I'm not gonna cave, Trav."

"I know." His lips brushed hers. He tasted so good. Like everything precious and real and true. Like every great mystery she would never unravel.

She pulled him closer, needing him right then more than she ever had. Their lovemaking that night was so good, better than ever.

It didn't solve anything. But at least for a little while, she could forget everything but the feel of him within her, the strength in his arms around her. She focused on that, on the tender way he held her close to him. He swept her away to a place where there was only the two of them and she could pretend that what they had would never end.

Their wedding day dawned sunny and clear.

Brenna spent the morning at the lodge with Roberta. They were bathed, waxed and buffed within an inch of their lives, after which came the mani-pedis, and the professional hair and makeup, too.

While a pair of clever stylists did their hair side by side, Roberta suddenly reached out and clutched her arm. "I love him, Bren. I love Steve."

Brenna shifted a glance toward the ever-present camera crew. "Roberta," she warned softly.

Roberta threw up both hands. "So what? I love him, and I don't give a damn if the whole wide world knows it. I swear to God I never thought I would say that again. I swore I was through with love, that I would never in this lifetime trust my heart to another man. Wrong. Steve is it for me. The real thing. When the show's over, he's going back to his family's ranch in West Texas. He's sure I won't like it there. I don't know how to convince him to take me with him, that he's the one for me and I know it will work out for us."

Brenna leaned close to her friend. "Stop talking, start doing."

Roberta laughed. "What does that mean?"

"Follow him home."

"I don't— What if his family resents some woman more than ten years older than him moving in on him? What if *he* hates that I came?"

"What if *you* hate it? Either way, you need to find out, and the only way to find out is to go there."

"I know I won't hate it. I was raised on a ranch. If Steve's there, I'll be happy there."

"Well, then go there. It's all going to work out."

"You sound so sure."

"Roberta, I've seen you together. If that isn't love, I'll eat Jasper Ridge's ten-gallon black hat."

It was such a beautiful setting—the open field with a pretty, rustic fence off in the background and the thick evergreen forest beyond that, and the mountains, shrouded in wisps of clouds, looming off in the distance.

The wedding guests in their Sunday best filled a set of bleachers. The whole cast was there, including Leah and Seth Stone. Leah looked beautiful in a sea-blue dress and Seth was already getting around on one crutch.

Brenna, sitting with Roberta in one of the white vans as they waited for the Wedding March to start, could see the Stones clearly through her side window. Leah glowed with happiness. Seth had his arm around her. As Brenna watched, Seth whispered in his wife's ear. Leah tipped her head back and laughed.

"Look at Seth and Leah," Roberta marveled. "I've never seen them so happy."

Brenna's throat felt tight, and her eyes burned. No doubt about it. Leah had found what she'd been longing for.

Across from the bleachers, the six-piece band played country favorites. The judges sang along in harmony.

Travis, heartbreaker handsome in his blue jacket and vest, waited next to Steve and Jasper Ridge at the head of the dirt aisle between the bleachers and the band. Cameras were everywhere. Anthony and the crew moved around the periphery, assessing all the angles, getting all the best shots.

And then came the moment she dreaded. Anthony signaled the band and they switched to the Wedding March. Brenna's stomach lurched. This was it. It was really going to happen.

Lori Luckly, wearing a headset and a pencil skirt with her cowboy boots, flung back the door to the van. She held out her hand to Roberta.

Roberta took it, stepping down, bringing her small bouquet of yellow flowers up, holding them before her in both hands. And then she was doing the wedding walk, all slow and stately, toward Trav, Steve and Jasper at the end of the dirt aisle. The soft hem of her yellow skirt fluttered in the slight wind.

Lori shot Brenna a bright smile. Numbly, Brenna touched the crown of daisies she'd chosen instead of a veil. Lori spoke softly into her headset and then held out her hand to help Brenna down. Careful of her long skirt, Brenna stepped to the ground. "Slow." Lori mouthed the word, handing Brenna a big bouquet of daisies and shiny white ribbons. "It's your moment," she said very softly. "Make it last."

Brenna's feet felt disconnected from the rest of her body. But somehow, with great effort, she got them to move. Going slowly was no problem. Every step was a monumental effort of will.

She focused on Trav's dear face and made herself move toward him.

Too soon, she was there, standing beside him as the Wedding March ended. Roberta took her bouquet and Trav took her hand. By then, she couldn't look at him. She swallowed convulsively as they both turned to face Jasper.

The man in black opened the gold-tooled Bible in his hands and cleared his throat. "Dearly beloved..." Jasper's lips moved, and Brenna stared at them blankly, not really hearing the words he said.

And then the wind came up. It made a high, keening sound. Like someone lost and crying. Brenna's skirts belled out, and her hair whipped wildly around her face.

And she...

Well, she just *couldn't.*

"Trav."

He squeezed her hand. "Bren? What...?" He tried to pull her closer. She dug in her boot heels and held her ground.

Jasper stopped his droning and cleared his throat again. "We got a problem?"

Oh, you bet we do. "I can't, Trav." It came out a ragged whisper as she pulled her hand free of his hold. "I'm so sorry. I just...well, I can't."

And then she picked up her big white skirts and sprinted off across the pasture toward the fence and the forest and the faraway mountains.

People shouted at her, but she didn't listen. And she didn't look back. Her heart breaking to bits inside her chest and her eyes blurry with tears, she just kept on running as fast as she could.

Chapter Twelve

Brenna was over the fence before Anthony and Roger started shouting. Anthony began barking orders to get a camera crew to follow her.

Trav knew he had to stop them. "Let her go!" he shouted as Brenna vanished from sight into the trees. The director, producer and crew ignored him.

At first.

But then he bellowed, "Let her go or I'm outta here, too. I will run and keep running. You won't catch up with either of us."

Steve said, "Me, too!"

And Roberta chimed in, "And me!"

And then the bleachers erupted. "Let her go!" shouted Fred Franklin.

"Leave her be!" hollered Wally.

"Leave her alone!" cried Leah Stone.

Even Summer joined in. "Back off, you damned idiots!"

Director, producer, wedding planner and every last soul on the crew—they all froze and stared, openmouthed, at the bleachers, where the cast of *The Great Roundup* shouted and stomped their feet, every one of them scowling, looking downright dangerous, like an unruly mob.

Trav grabbed Steve's arm. "Keep them here."

"You got it, man."

Pausing only to rip off his body mic and toss it to the ground, Travis took off across the pasture after his runaway bride.

She didn't go all that far.

A quarter of a mile or so into the trees, he found her sitting on a fallen log, looking like a sad and slightly lost redheaded angel in her white dress, with her crown of flowers drooping down her brow.

She shoved the flowers off her forehead and then, with a frustrated cry, she grabbed them and yanked them off her head altogether, tossing them angrily over her shoulder. "Trav." She blew a hank of hair out of her eyes. "I'm so sorry. I'm really, really—"

He put a finger to his lips. Then he mouthed, "Your mic."

She only moaned and hung her head, but at least she wasn't going anywhere. He dared to get closer. She didn't even look up when he sat down next to her, didn't object when he plucked the microphone from the front of her poufy dress and pulled it free of the transmitter. Rising, he tossed the mic off into the trees.

"Now." He sat down beside her again and captured her hand. At least she didn't pull away. He took heart from that. With a finger, he guided a swatch of hair behind her ear. "I think it's time you maybe talked to me."

She took a shaky breath. "Yeah," she said in a tiny voice. "Yeah, I guess it's time."

"Come here." He put both arms around her.

She sagged against him, resting her head on his shoulder with a surrendering sigh. "I just couldn't do it. I couldn't marry you."

He smoothed her tangled hair. "It's okay. I get it."

"Do you?" She sounded so lost, so completely alone.

He took her chin and made her look at him. "I mean it. It's okay. I'm with you. It's wrong. I see that. It's wrong, and we're not going through with it."

She sagged against him again. "I really thought I could, you know? I told myself, *Just focus on the win, just do what you have to do*. But I…I love you so much, Trav. I think I always have, through all the years, forever and ever, since you came to my rescue the first time when I was six years old. I can't marry you—not when I love you, and know that I have to divorce you. I just can't do that. I'm sorry. *That* is just too wrong."

Does every man have a moment when it all comes together?

When all at once his whole life makes total sense?

Travis did.

And that moment?

It was now.

He tipped up her chin again. The tears that shone in her eyes started falling. They ran down her cheeks.

She sniffed and swiped a hand under her reddened nose. "Ugh. I'm a mess."

"I have never seen anyone as beautiful as you, Bren. Never in my whole life."

She blew out her cheeks with a hard breath. “Yeah, right.”

“It’s true. And you…” His voice got snagged up. But he tried again and managed to ask the question in a low, rough growl. “You love me, Brenna? You really do?”

Tears dripping off her chin, she nodded.

“Good,” he answered fervently. “Because, Bren, I love you, too.”

She gasped. “Oh, Trav.” She sniffed and then asked in a small voice, “You do? You really do?”

He brushed at her soft cheeks, wiping the wetness away. And suddenly the right words were there. He opened his mouth and let them out. “I love you, Brenna. Only you. I know I’ve fought it, my love for you. Fought it my whole life. At first you were too young for me. And then, well, somehow, I got stuck on a certain idea of myself, of being all about freedom, of not being the kind to settle down. But, Bren, if you love me, it all starts to make sense. Because why would I ever want to settle down with some other woman if you could be mine?”

She stared at him, her mouth a soft O. “Trav.”

“What? Bren. Dear God. Please believe me.”

She laughed. “Oh, Trav.” And then she framed his face between her hands. “You’d better kiss me. Do it now.”

He had absolutely no problem with that. Leaning in, he claimed her tearstained lips in a slow, ever-deepening kiss, a kiss that whispered of forever, a kiss that promised he would hold on tight to what they had. That he’d at last become the man she needed. The kind of man who would always be there to help her win every challenge she took on, to catch her if ever she needed a safe place to fall.

"Good," she said with a trembling smile when he finally lifted his head. "It's you and me, together."

"Together forever," he vowed.

And then she asked with a long sigh, "But what do we do now?"

"I know this much. I still want to marry you if you'll have me."

Her eyes gleamed so bright. "Oh, Trav. I will have you. I will never, ever let you go."

"Just not today. Because I want you to have the real thing in our little white church in Rust Creek Falls, with your sisters for your bridesmaids and our families filling every pew."

She widened those sea-blue eyes at him. "We are so gonna get sued. You know that, right?"

"I do—and yeah, it might get a little messy, breaking our contract."

She made a snorting sound. "A *little* messy?"

He kissed her red nose. "Think positive. Ryan Roarke is a hell of a lawyer, and he'll get us out of it somehow." She gazed up at him, her tear-filled eyes full of equal parts wonder and worry. He squeezed her shoulder. "So for today, we'll go back, face the others and tell them we are not saying our sacred vows on a reality show." He started to rise.

"Wait." She pulled him back down.

"What?"

"I just want to make this crystal clear. You are asking me to marry you—I mean, *really* marry you."

He took both her hands as he stood. And that time, she rose with him. "I am." He held her eyes. "Brenna

O'Reilly, I love you. Please say you'll marry me. Please tell me yes."

"Yes," she said, out loud and clear. "Yes, absolutely, I *will* marry you."

"That's what I wanted to hear." And he picked her up and whirled her around. She braced her hands on his shoulders and laughed, the sound echoing upward through the canopy of green over their heads. When he set her down, he grabbed her hand. "Come on now. Let's get it over with. We'll go tell Roger and the rest of them that we're not getting married on *The Great Roundup*."

But she held him back. "This is real, right? I mean, this is really happening?"

"Real as it gets. Let's go."

But still she wouldn't budge. "Wait, Trav."

He gave in and turned to face her fully again. "What now?"

"Well, I'm thinking that if it's real, if we're getting married and staying that way—"

"Brenna. It's real and it's true and I can't wait to marry you."

"Well, then. You don't have to wait. Because I would love nothing so much as to get married to you right now, today, on *The Great Roundup*, where we finally found each other."

He frowned. "You know, when you put it that way, it doesn't sound half bad."

"Well, then. Let's do it."

He felt honor bound to remind her, "We would still have months ahead of us pretending that we're *not* married. How are we going to hold up through that?"

"I'm thinking I'm renting the apartment over the

beauty shop right away. And I'm also thinking you're going to be visiting your fiancée just about every night. People will be whispering how that wild Travis Dalton can't keep away from Brenna O'Reilly."

"That sounds amazing."

She nodded. "Yeah. I think so, too."

"And then, next year, if we win—"

"Oh, Trav, there's no doubt in my mind now. We're gonna win."

"*When* we win."

"That's better." She made a low, throaty sound of approval.

"I want to build a house for us on Dalton land."

"Yes. And I want to buy Bee out."

"Absolutely." He clasped her shoulders. "Look at me."

"Oh, Trav. I am."

"Are you sure?"

She didn't waver. "I've never been so sure about anything in my whole life."

That did it. He grabbed her close and kissed her again.

And then again. Because he loved her. Because forever stretched out in front of them and it looked full of promise now, bright as a new day. But whatever the future brought them, they would own it together.

From this day on.

"We need to agree on how to handle them," he whispered finally. "This, you and me, just now, it belongs to us. Nobody else. But we need a good story for the show."

"I have it. We tell the truth, just not *all* the truth." And she pulled him down to whisper in his ear.

* * *

"I see them!" someone shouted as Travis and Brenna emerged from the shelter of the trees. "They're coming!"

Brenna felt wonderful. She had it all now. She had Travis at her side and his promisc to be there for the rest of their lives—a promise she believed in, a promise she returned.

He led her to the fence and helped her over it.

"You ready for this?" he asked as he set her down on solid ground.

"Oh, yes, I am."

Roger was furious, and Anthony seethed.

Brenna told them swcctly that she and Travis were ready now.

"Mic them up again!" Roger yelled. "Makeup! Wardrobe!"

A half an hour later, Brenna had a new body mic. Her makeup was flawless, and her hair was sleek and smooth, crowned with yellow daisies.

Roger called for OTFs. Brenna did hers sitting in a corner of the bleachers, her puffy skirts pulled up enough to show her purple boots, her wedding bouquet in her hand.

"I just got so emotional," she said with a long sigh. "I needed a minute to myself. You know, to deal with all the powerful, overwhelming feelings I was experiencing. And also, well, I did need a time-out with Travis, just the two of us."

"But you ran away," chided Roger. "How did you know he would follow you?"

"Of course, I couldn't be sure he would follow me

when I ran. But, oh, I did hope that he would. I needed to hear his words of love. I needed him to hold me in his strong arms."

"And how do you feel now, Brenna?"

"Now that I've gotten exactly what I needed, now that I've dealt with the enormity of this big step before me and spent a little time with my man, now I am definitely ready, willing and able to proudly and happily say 'I do.'"

By then, everyone was smiling, even Roger.

They all found their marks.

And Brenna O'Reilly married Travis Dalton in the middle of a pasture on *The Great Roundup.* They did it for real and forever—and for all the world to see.

Epilogue

That evening, after Brenna and Travis shared their first dance, Steve got down on his good knee and proposed to Roberta. Roberta burst into happy tears and cried out, "Yes!"

Three days later, Roberta was eliminated. Two days after that, Steve followed her.

The final challenge would pit Bren against Trav. They both loved that. No matter how it came out now, they'd won.

The next day, the bleachers went up again in the pasture where they'd said their wedding vows. The entire cast came out to watch.

The challenge: hay bale racing.

Trav knew he was beaten before the race began. Bren had taken more than one ribbon running barrels at the local rodeo. And she got that great little mare, Ladygirl, to ride.

But he got Applejack, a fine, fast gelding, his favorite of the mounts in the High Lonesome stables. And he gave the race his all, knowing Brenna would expect nothing less of him. He didn't mess up the cloverleaf pattern, and his time was damn good, too.

Hay bales or barrels, though, Bren still had what it took. She and Ladygirl looked like they were flying as they raced around those bales.

She beat his time by more than two seconds.

And that was how Brenna O'Reilly Dalton won a million dollars on *The Great Roundup.*

Or rather, that was how Brenna *and* Travis won. Together, they claimed both first and second prize and they would share their winnings equally, as they'd always agreed.

They had it all now and they both knew it. They had the money for a new start.

And most important, they had each other.

For the rest of their lives.

* * * * *

Look for the next installment of the new
Mills & Boon Cherish series
MONTANA MAVERICKS:
THE GREAT FAMILY ROUNDUP

Filthy rich cowboy Autry Jones has watched with amusement as two of his brothers have settled down and become family men, but he's convinced it won't happen to him. Until he meets pretty young widow Marissa Fuller and her three little girls and falls for all four of them...

Don't miss
MOMMY AND THE MAVERICK
by Meg Maxwell

On sale August 2017, wherever Mills & Boon books and ebooks are sold.